Applegreen

a novel

Lottie Jacks

Applegreen
By Lottie Jacks

Cover design: Hyliian Graphics, Elizabeth E. Little
www.hyliian.deviantart.com
Interior design: Ellen C. Maze, The Author's Mentor™
www.theauthorsmentor.com

ISBN-13: 978-1466461321

Also available in eBook publication

Dedication:

To my family and friends
who have faithfully supported me in my writing.

Jesus Christ the Apple Tree

The tree of life my soul has seen
Laden with fruit and always green:
The trees of nature fruitless be
Compared with Christ the apple tree.

His beauty doth all things excel:
By faith I know but ne'er can tell
The glory which I now can see
In Jesus Christ the apple tree.

For happiness I long have sought,
And pleasures dearly I have bought:
I missed of all; but now I see
Tis found in Christ the apple tree.

I'm weary with my former toil,
Here I will sit and rest awhile:
Under the shadow I will be,
Of Jesus Christ the apple tree.

This fruit doth make my soul to thrive,
It keeps my dying faith alive;
Which makes my soul in haste to be
With Jesus Christ the apple tree

~ Anonymous,
from the collection of Joshua Smith

Chapter One
Emily's Birth

Benjamin pulled his heavy flannel shirt up tighter around his neck and placed several small logs on the grate in the fireplace. He knew it would take more than a warm fire to comfort Lillie. Perhaps her unwillingness to accept this baby would ebb away before the child was old enough to sense it, but little did he know her resentment toward the baby would last for years.

"I must take Ella home," he said to his sister, Bettie Auntie, who was tidying up the room. "I believe it's stopped snowing, but the clouds still look threatening. I'll leave Lillie and the baby in your care." Bettie Auntie nodded, holding back any words that expressed her agitation with Lillie.

Except for the crackling fire, the room was quiet. Lillie was asleep, but little Emily began to fret. Soon her fret became a weak cry. Bettie Auntie tiptoed over to the bed, picked up the tiny infant and cradled her in her arms. Rocking her to and fro, she whispered, "I'll claim you, Emily …I'll claim you."

❧

Pine Belt, where Emily was born, was never the same grand plantation that it had been before the War Between the States. Before the war, it was a stately house of stone and cedar clapboard that rested at the end of a long lane in the small community of Stanton, Alabama. Proudly owned by Oliver Whitworth, it was framed on either side by tall, long needle pines, boasting large painted columns that had once gleamed in the sun as white as the cotton fields that surrounded it. The last day of its splendor was in the late spring of 1865. Twelve years later, Oliver Whitworth's son, Benjamin, with painful memories, viewed its peeling paint and charred upper story. Even though he was just a young boy when the Union Army invaded his home, Benjamin remembered vividly that fateful day. His father had pleaded with the soldiers not to set fire to the house. Recklessly they had pushed Master Whitworth aside, rushed up the stairs, torched the bedrooms and left as quickly as they had come. The fire all but destroyed the upstairs rooms of the house. The trauma was too much for Benjamin's mother, and she died shortly thereafter. Because of the destruction of the war, Benjamin's father could never restore the house to its original beauty and did well to keep the land. This misfortune and the loss of his cherished wife left him with bitterness and despair, and Oliver died before Benjamin was barely old enough to take responsibility of the house and land.

After his parents died, Benjamin's brothers and sisters married and moved away except his spinster sister, Bettie. In addition to Bettie, the only help Benjamin had were two of his father's Negro slaves, Cleopas and Hattie, who chose to remain with the family after the war.

He would never forget the first Christmas after his father's death when all his brothers' and sisters' families came to celebrate. One of his smallest nephews quickly took to Aunt Bettie, following her about and calling for his "Bettie Auntie" when she wasn't near. "Out of the mouth of babes…I like your new name, sister," Benjamin concluded. Everyone agreed, even Bettie Auntie.

The memory of that Christmas often comforted Benjamin. Though lonely and difficult, he spent years laboring to maintain Pine Belt; a memory could only do so much and the years had taken their toll. Benjamin longed for simple conversation, a gentle touch, even someone to argue with over next year's plantings, cotton or corn? He yearned for someone to work alongside him. In short, he needed a wife. To his sister, Benjamin confessed, "I don't even know how to talk to a woman anymore, Bettie Auntie. The only conversations I ever have are with Cleopas and sometimes with Sam down at the mercantile."

"So what are you saying? I don't count since I'm your sister? Is that right?" She asked with a sly twinkle in her eye.

"You know what I mean," he answered, unable to suppress a tiny grin.

"I noticed Miss Lillie Hamilton always lights up like a firefly when you talk with her at church. Ask her if you can stop by next Sunday after lunch. Remember, her father and our father were good friends before the war. I know our father would have approved if you found someone like Miss Hamilton to marry."

Benjamin took a deep breath. A feeling of hope began to build in his heart. He looked at his sister and smiled. "Well, enough of this, I must go and feed the animals."

After finishing his chores, Benjamin was restless. He sat down on a bale of hay and contemplated the conversation he had with his sister. He resolved to do exactly what his sister said. As he often did, he talked aloud to the animals. He had a long conversation about what he would say the next day when he saw Miss Hamilton at church.

Lillie Hamilton was the ideal picture of a southern lady. Her coiffed brown hair, perfectly fashioned dresses and delicate shoes showed every attention to detail. Nothing was out of place. She carried herself in such a way that caused Benjamin to recall the graciousness of the Old South; for him a gentler and simpler romantic time. He remembered how his mother dressed, especially when his father took her to the Grand Balls at Christmas. He always watched when she appeared at the top of the stairs in her very best velvet gown. She was very beautiful and epitomized dignity and graciousness - the kind of wife he wanted, yet he knew the glory of the Old South was gone.

Benjamin caught a glimpse of her as she stepped down from her father's buggy to go into the church. He took a deep breath and tried to remember exactly what words he would say to her after church. He was surprised when she smiled his way, and he turned to see if it was for his benefit or someone else's. Seeing only his horse Maggie, he decided to return the smile and began to walk towards her, but before he could get to her, she had already entered the small church and taken her usual seat.

Benjamin found it near to impossible to concentrate on the

preacher's sermon, something Jesus had said about forgiving others seventy times seven. He would never forgive the Yankees' terrible deed to his home. He tried to concentrate but was distracted by Bettie Auntie's stern looks, as he shifted his large frame in the pew over and over. When the last stanza of "Jesus Paid it All," was sung and the closing prayer was voiced, he hurried out of the church, stumbling through the crowd and hoping to catch Miss Lillie's attention. Bettie Auntie was amused as she watched her brother and covered her mouth with her Bible to stifle her laugh. She could tell by the triumphant grin on Benjamin's face when he approached their buggy, that all had gone well.

Each year Benjamin earnestly planned to restore the house to its former grandeur. Above all, he wanted to please his new wife Lillie. Her greatest desire was to recapture the pleasures and grandeur, she had known before the war of the Old South. Benjamin knew her dream could never be realized until he repaired the house and made the farm productive again. Lillie repeatedly complained, "Benjamin, how will we ever be able to entertain with the house in this condition?"

"I know, Lillie," he always answered, knowing there was no money. "Maybe, next year."

After eight years of marriage, six children, and another on the way, Lillie's dream began to fade. Benjamin remembered seeing that same demeanor in his father after the war. When Lillie realized she was expecting their seventh child and the house was still in disrepair, she lost all hope of ever having the social life that she had envisioned.

The morning sunlight was barely filtering through the windows when Benjamin came into the kitchen to light the fire in the large cast iron stove, his favorite room of the house - the place where he enjoyed being with his family and eating delicious meals that Lillie and Hattie took pride in preparing. The kitchen was the only part of the house that he had been able to restore. He had built it hoping to make cooking easier for Lillie. The original kitchen was apart from the main house where the cooking was done in a huge fireplace - most of which was done in a large cast-iron cooking pot that hung from an iron hook over a smoldering fire. The new kitchen boasted a large cast-iron stove, a metal sink with a small water pump and a long pine table where the family could all sit together for their daily meals. Hattie, still the faithful servant, kept the kitchen tidy. Miss Lillie insisted on cleanliness, and Hattie was often seen scrubbing the wide plank pine floors to meet these demands. Benjamin was proud of the work he had done to make their home more livable. Many people had lost their homes in addition to their loved ones during the Civil War, and he felt grateful that Pine Belt was still standing.

From habit, he took a handful of pine kindling and placed it on top of a piece of crumpled paper. Soon, a strong fragrance of pine filled the room. To finish his morning task, he took several small pieces of firewood from the large wooden box behind the stove and placed them on the burning kindling. He was warming his hands when Hattie came rushing into the kitchen. "Master Ben! Master Ben!" she called frantically. "Miz Lillie be needing the midwife; ain't gon be long neither!"

Benjamin turned in bewilderment and surprise. "Why, Hattie, you startled me. I knew the time was close, but I didn't think it would be today."

Hattie began rubbing her hands nervously. "Yassuh! It be now, all right." Benjamin had great respect for Hattie. She had been with the Whitworth family since he was a child. She and her husband Cleopas had been slaves on Benjamin's father's plantation and had remained with them after the war. He had always considered them part of his family. He knew that many plantation owners felt the same way.

"All right, Hattie, I'll hurry." He didn't want her to know that he especially dreaded the birth of this child – his seventh. He knew Lillie didn't want another child. Before the births of their other children, she had always told him the expected date of their arrival. How she knew, he had no idea, but she was usually right; but this time she wouldn't even discuss the baby with him.

కొన్ని

Quickly, he removed the round lid to the cook stove and placed more wood on the fire. Taking his heavy coat from the hook by the back door, he hurriedly put it on and rushed out of the house to the barn.

"Come on, Maggie," he urged his reluctant horse. "Come on; we've got to go." Taking her by the reins, he led her out of the barn and hitched her to the buggy. A cold wind chilled his hands and face. The ground was dusted with a light snow that sparkled like tiny jewels on a sea of white. The barns and hills were etched silhouettes against the horizon from the early morning light. For a moment he stood still, overcome by the beauty around him. Nothing was quite as peaceful as the dawn of a new day, especially in the quiet of winter. There was no time to enjoy it, for he must hurry and get Ella, the midwife.

When he approached her house, Benjamin was thankful to see a glow of light from her kitchen window and a spiral of smoke from her chimney. Perhaps she knew it was about time for the Whitworth baby to be born. He was comforted by the thought anyway. Ella was dressed when he arrived. "Benjamin Whitworth! Come in, come in. Let's go in the kitchen where it's warm. I'm not surprised to see you. I know it must be the baby's birth that brings you here so early." She took a sip of the black coffee from the heavy white cup she held with both hands as if to warm them. The steam from the hot coffee drifted in the air and gave a pleasant aroma to her small kitchen.

"That's right, Miss Ella. I'm sorry to disturb you without warning." Benjamin looked down and rubbed the back of his neck. "I'm afraid this birth might be a quick one. I hope you can come with me now."

"I'll get my coat and bonnet, and we'll be on our way." Benjamin looked at her with admiration and respect. She had delivered all of his children. He liked the way she expressed excitement with every delivery. Each newborn was special to her.

When they stepped outside, a light snow was falling. Benjamin put out his hand to help Ella into the buggy. He seated himself beside her and spread the heavy, woolen lap blanket over their knees. Taking the reins, he headed the buggy toward the Whitworth farm. Pulling the blanket more securely over her lap, Ella commented, "I know it isn't any of my business, Benjamin, but I gather that Miss Lillie isn't too happy about having another baby."

Benjamin was silent for a moment. Then he sighed and said, "Yes, I'm afraid you're right. The births are hard on her." Ella's observation reminded him of the day he had found Lillie sitting on a rock in the spring house. She was crying. "What's wrong, Lillie?" he had asked.

"You know that I'm going to have another baby and that's the last thing I want. I'll never get to go anywhere. Every time I get one baby big enough to leave with Hattie, I have another one. I wanted to go to that party at the Governor's Mansion. I wanted to meet the Governor. Your term in the legislature will be over soon, and now I'll never get to go." Her words cut straight to his heart, and he felt helpless. He had tried to put his arms around her, but she had resisted. Now, as then, there were no words to express his distress.

He pulled the reins tighter to make Maggie trot faster; the hot breath from her nostrils rose like a thick mist in the air. At times, the buggy wheels would spin in the snow, but Benjamin didn't slow down. When they arrived at the Whitworth farm, they hurried into the kitchen where Bettie Auntie had everything ready - clean linens and a large pot of boiling water on the stove.

Ella quickly removed her coat and went straight to the bedroom. Miss Lillie's labor pains were very close together and quite intense. Grimacing with pain, she looked up at Ella. "I'm really glad to see you, Ella. I believe this one's almost here."

"Well hold on, Miss Lillie, till I get everything ready. Put the linens on the table with the sterile water, Hattie, where I can reach them. Then Bettie Auntie can help me. Maybe you can keep the children occupied until we're finished."

"Yes'um," Hattie said. Carefully, she put the pan of steaming hot water down beside the snowy white cloths and returned to the kitchen to prepare breakfast.

Benjamin waited anxiously in the kitchen. When he heard the children getting out of bed, he called for them to come to breakfast. The smell of ham frying sharpened his appetite. He watched eagerly as Hattie put a full pan of biscuits in the oven. When the biscuits had turned a golden brown, she placed them in the center of the table along with a large ironstone platter of scrambled eggs and a

7

steaming bowl of buttery grits.

"You chillun, set right down and eat some breakfast with yo daddy," Hattie commanded. "We is gonna have us a new baby born in this house this mornin!"

"Hattie's right. We'll just have to stay in here and be quiet until the baby arrives," Benjamin added.

"Just try and bear down a few more times, Miss Lillie. I don't think it'll be long now," the midwife encouraged. Beads of perspiration collected on Lillie's forehead as the pains became more severe and finally ended with the birth of a tiny baby girl. Ella held the baby upside down and gave her a quick swat on the back. She was relieved to hear the baby's first cry. "She's small, about six pounds, I'd say, but her cry is strong. Put her birth time down in the journal, Bettie Auntie. It's 7:15 a.m., January 16, 1895."

Ella held the baby securely while she tied off the umbilical cord with a strong black thread. Gently, she wrapped a soft wide cotton band around the baby's abdomen to hold the navel down. "You can take her now, Bettie Auntie," she said. Lovingly, Bettie Auntie eagerly took the tiny baby and wiped her wrinkled red body with sweet-smelling oil. After putting a tiny cloth diaper and a soft white gown on the baby, she wrapped her in a cotton outing blanket and placed her at her mother's side. Lillie's rejection of the tiny newborn was evident. She would not look at the baby. Bettie Auntie stood beside the bed a moment, taking in the poignant scene. Reluctantly, she returned to the kitchen to announce the birth. "You have a baby girl, Benjamin … a little sister, children."

"When can we see her?" Louise asked.

"In a few minutes … Miss Ella will call you. Let your daddy go in first."

Ella collected the bloody linens, placed them in the wash basin and handed it to Hattie to be disposed of at the back of the house. After washing her hands, she bent down and gently wiped the perspiration from Miss Lillie's forehead. "This has been your easiest delivery yet, Miss Lillie. Shall we call Benjamin in now?" Lillie didn't respond.

Benjamin hesitantly walked into the room. A deep ache settled in his heart as he stood beside the bed and saw Lillie turned away from the baby. Nevertheless, he knelt down and kissed her. She was very beautiful to him. "I love you, Lillie," he whispered. Lillie closed her eyes and said nothing. He was hurt by Lillie's rejection of the baby and felt guilty that she was so unhappy. He stood up, reached down to pick up the tiny infant and turned toward Bettie Auntie who was closely observing. Holding the baby up, he looked at her pretty little face and asked, "What will we name this sweet little creature?" Then he answered his own question. "I like the name Emily Jane after the famous Bronte sister. I especially like the name Emily."

"Then you can name her," Lillie lamented.

Quickly, Bettie Auntie replied, "I like the name too."

Gently, Benjamin put the baby down on the bed and went to the bedroom door. "Come and see the new baby," he told the anxious children.

Louise, the oldest, loved her tiny baby sister at first sight. She and Eugenia, her younger sister, stood close beside the bed trying to get a good look at the baby. The four boys, Albert, Timothy, Jonathan, and Judson, stood at the foot of the bed afraid of getting too close. Lillie lay quiet and still, while Benjamin did all the talking. "Well, what do you think of your little sister?"

"She's so small I'd be afraid to hold her," Louise sighed.

"I like her little nose," Eugenia said, twisting and turning.

"What's her name?" Timothy asked coming closer.

"I think we'll name her Emily Jane," their father answered.

"Will we call her Emily?" Louise asked.

"Yes, I think so."

"Are you all right, Mama?" Louise asked.

"Yes, I'm all right. I just need a little rest."

"Then let's go out and let your mama get some rest. I need to put more wood on the fire; this room is getting cold." He pulled his heavy flannel shirt up tighter around his neck. "When I finish, I'll take Miss Ella home. I believe it's stopped snowing, but the clouds still look threatening."

Chapter Two

Emily's Secret

$\mathcal{B}$enjamin cherished the tender moments when he found Lillie in the bedroom nursing the baby. Perhaps the bonding of mother and child, over time, would erase some of her resentment. Sadly, it was only at nursing time when Lillie held the baby – the rest of the time she was cared for by Bettie Auntie and Louise. With mixed emotions, he was reminded that his sister saw Emily's first smile and watched her sit up for the first time. She and Louise coaxed Emily to take her first steps. Though he was happy they loved Emily, he was troubled that his wife took so little interest in their youngest child.

∂∽∾

"I think Emily's first words were 'my stomach hurts,'" Lillie complained to Benjamin when he came into the kitchen with a load of wood. "She continues to have an upset stomach. I guess I'm going to have to take her to see Doctor Duboise again."

"Maybe she'll grow out of it soon. Don't worry; Bettie Auntie never gets tired of tending to her. She's really fond of Emily. I often wonder if she regrets not marrying and having children of her own."

"Oh, I don't know," Lillie said. "I think she's perfectly happy here with us." She leaned forward and pulled her hands down over her face to relax her weariness.

"Well, I don't know what we would do without her. She's

really been a help with the children and especially with Emily."

Lillie rose from the table, turned her back to him and began to wash the vegetables she had picked from the small kitchen garden. She resented any praise of his sister. Does he even know all the things I do around here?

Benjamin bent down and placed the wood in the bin. Vigorously, he dusted his hands and waited a moment, wondering if he should continue their strained conversation, but Lillie continued to ignore him. "Well, I guess I need to get back outside. That cow in the barn is about to calve, and we need to finish chopping the cotton in the lower field." Lillie didn't answer.

✻

Emily's frail little legs barely hung off the porch swing. She was waiting for Louise to come and read to her. Reading had become a ritual for her and her sister - especially in the late afternoon when the summer heat had claimed all their energy.

"Are you ready?" Louise asked. She sat down close to Emily and patted her tiny arm.

Emily nodded, "uh-huh," with a broad grin on her face. She proudly held up a small stack of books.

"What shall we read today?" Louise asked. She saw that Emily had the reader at the top of the stack. Even at five years of age, she could read many words.

Holding up the reader, Emily said, "I like this one."

"Oh, *The McGuffey's Reader*. Tell you what, Emily. I'll read a page and then you read a page."

Emily's gray-blue eyes sparkled with excitement as she listened. Then she began to read. At first, she read slowly and haltingly, but each time she read, the words became clearer and her pronunciation improved. By summer's end, she was reading books that were difficult for a six-year-old. "Would you like to learn how to use the dictionary, Emily? Louise asked. "I'll teach you. Using the dictionary will help your reading ability."

"Do you think I can learn to do that, Louise?'

"Why, of course you can. Come on, I'll show you." Louise took Emily's hand and led her into the parlor. A large dictionary, bound in brown leather with gilded alphabetical tabs, sat on a table near the window. At first Emily had to stand on her tiptoes to reach it, but her search for the meaning of words soon became a lifetime pleasure. To learn a new word was fascinating, like seeing a new and different place.

❧◈❧

In the summer after her first year of school, Emily found several boxes of books stored in a small closet off the parlor where the old staircase once stood. When she took the books out of the boxes and examined each one carefully, she noticed a faint odor of smoke and mustiness. Often on a rainy afternoon her father found her completely engrossed leafing through the pages of her newfound treasure. "You know who's responsible for our not having a library, don't you, Emily?"

Emily looked up into her father's face. Even at her young age she knew the bitterness he still harbored for the Yankees and how he liked to talk about their acts of devastation. Keeping her head low, she backed out of the small space and sat on the floor leaning against the wall of the hallway. "Did you really have a whole library, Daddy?"

Benjamin sat down on the bench near Emily. "It was the room we now use as the parlor. Two of the walls had floor to ceiling cherry wood shelves full of books. My mother especially loved to read. There was a handsome staircase with a baluster as tall as you, right here where you're sitting. All the bedrooms were upstairs." Emily noticed again the look of sadness on her daddy's face. Even though she had heard the story many times, he continued to tell her how the Yankees had set fire to their home, "When the war was over, my father had to tear out the staircase, and we could no longer use the upstairs bedrooms. There was no money to repair the house to its original beauty. We lost the library but luckily saved the books. I hope one day we can rebuild the library and repair the upstairs. My father was never the same after the fire. He never got over the destruction done to our home and the death of my mother who was overcome by the smoke of the fire. He died not long after the war."

Emily stood up and put her arm around her father's shoulder. "I'm so glad you were able to save the books, Daddy. Someday, when I can read better, I want to read all of them."

འ∽ও

At the age of ten, Emily was small and frail compared to her robust siblings. Her father often called her his "Irish Beauty." Pale-ivory skin and soft, reddish-brown curls only intensified her grey-blue eyes that were uncommonly tinged with dark circles underneath. Emily had little energy because of relentless trouble with her stomach. It was a struggle eating and digesting food, so she never strayed too far from the house. Most of her days were spent reading while her siblings played out of doors. There were special nooks and corners in the house where she would sit on the floor and read. Her favorite place was behind a door in the dining room, off the kitchen. She liked the warmth that came from the cook stove and the sweet aromas from her mother's cooking. Sometimes, she stopped reading and listened to her mother and daddy talking when he came in from the fields. It was the acrimony in her mother's voice on this particular day that made her move closer to the door as they continued their conversation.

"I can't help but be resentful," Lillie said. "Just when I thought the children were big enough to leave for a short time and we could accept some of our invitations to the special events at the Capital, another baby was on the way. I didn't want any more children and certainly not one that is sick all the time, like Emily. We'll never get invited to any of those parties again."

"Lillie," Benjamin chided, "I think you're just feeling sorry for yourself. We have plenty of community parties to attend, and you know Bettie Auntie will look after the children. She's always here. Emily's a good child. I guess the seventh child isn't wanted in any family these days."

"Your sister is always here, all right, and always pampering Emily. She's been here since your parents died. I guess she'll always be here."

Benjamin winced. He detected, even in her resentment, a note of jealousy. He knew how attached Emily had grown to his sister, and he cherished her love for Emily. She had always done more than her share of the household chores. Thank goodness for the time she spent with Emily. He often noticed how she lovingly took Emily by the hand to give Lillie some relief. "Even if she wasn't here," he said, "Cleopas and Hattie are here to help take care of the children. You know how they love them. I've known them all of my life. Their daddy was my father's best friend in time of need."

"It doesn't matter now, Benjamin. It's too late now to change things. I just wish Emily could be well like our other children."

Emily sat frozen behind the door, hoping her mother wouldn't realize that she had overheard their conversation. Her mother's words were the cruel confirmation she feared. It's true, she thought. Mama doesn't love me. Judson said she didn't want me, that six children were enough. Powerless to deny any longer what she had hoped and prayed was not true, she pulled her skirt up and buried her face in it to catch her tears and to silence her weeping. Resting her head on her knees, exhausted, she soon fell asleep. When she awoke, she slipped out of doors to the well and drew some cool water to splash on her face. She was determined not to tell anyone what she had heard - not even Louise.

Chapter Three

Edwin

$\mathcal{L}$ ouise found Emily sitting alone by the fire in the parlor. No longer did she read behind the dining room door. Perhaps the floor was cold. Louise was perplexed. Something is troubling Emily. "Emily, you're awfully quiet lately. What's wrong? Aren't you feeling well?"

"Unh-unh," Emily muttered, pursing her lips tightly together, afraid some words would slip out or tears would well up in her eyes.

"I know something is bothering you. Tell me. You know I can keep a secret."

Emily turned away and looked at the fire not able to share her pain, not even with Louise. "There's nothing wrong, Louise. I just want to finish this book."

Louise stood quietly a moment pretending to warm herself by the fire. She missed the closeness that she and Emily had shared before Emily could read. Louise was seventeen now and would soon be going away to school. She wondered who would help Emily with her hair and who would defend when her brother, Judson, teased and badgered her. With all of her chores and with running the house, Mama has so little time, she thought.

"Okay, if you don't want to talk about it, I'll just leave you alone." Louise turned and walked slowly towards the door. She hesitated a moment, still hoping that Emily would reveal her secret, but her little sister remained quiet.

✿

Emily bent her frail body towards the breakfast table and moved her food around on her plate. "If you don't eat, Emily, you're going to dry up and blow away," her mother said.

"It makes my stomach hurt," Emily whined.

"Well it's almost time for school, so hurry and eat what you can."

After managing to swallow a few bites, Emily left the table. It was time to leave for the long walk to the small wood frame school house, almost a mile from the Whitworth farm.

"Hurry up, Emily," Jonathan called. "We'll be late."

"Just leave her," Judson scolded. "She can't always have someone around to watch out for her."

Jonathan ignored Judson and waited for Emily. "Are you all right, Emily?" he asked. He took her hand and noticed that it was very warm, though the February air was quite cold.

"Yes, I'm okay. I just can't walk fast."

✿

When they were returning home in the afternoon, Jonathan waited for Emily as she trudged along behind him and their brothers. Finally she caught up. Her cheeks were flushed and her eyes were weak and drooping.

"Mama! Emily is sick," Jonathan called as they came into the kitchen.

"Oh, my! Not again," Lillie said. She set down the bowl of hard green apples that she was peeling for a cobbler for supper and wiped her hands on her apron. "Help me get her into bed, Louise." Louise put her arm around Emily's shoulders and gently guided her to the bedroom.

"Where do you hurt, Emily? Is it your stomach again?" Louise asked, slipping the faded blue and white flannel gown over Emily's head.

Emily nodded, "Uh-huh," holding her stomach and frowning with pain.

"I'll make some tea to get her fever down," Lillie said. "I don't know why she has this trouble so often."

Emily pulled the covers up over her face, not wanting to look at her mother. She wished that she could disappear, so no one would have to care for her. She didn't want to be sick or have anyone, least of all her mother, to make over her.

Louise sat down on the side of the bed to help Emily sip the tea. She took a cool cloth and placed it on Emily's forehead. After drinking the tea, Emily closed her eyes and pretended to be asleep. Louise pulled the quilt up over her little sister's shoulders and left the room.

A week passed and Emily was no better. She was still in bed when Lillie sent for Doctor Duboise. Louise watched anxiously for the doctor and saw him as he stepped down from his one-horse buggy carrying his worn and rumpled black bag. Louise welcomed him to come inside to the bedroom.

"Oh, Doctor Duboise … I just don't know why she is always sick," Lillie said, standing at Emily's bed.

He stood for a moment and studied the very sick child. "Looks like we've got trouble, Miss Lillie." Picking up her wrist, he ran his hand along her frail, feverish arm. "How old is she now?"

"She just had her eighth birthday."

"Well, she's too small for an eight year old. She mustn't lose any more weight, or she'll be in serious trouble." After carefully examining Emily, he took a tall brown bottle from his worn black bag and handed it to Lillie. "I want you to give her this medicine twice a day." Then looking sternly at Emily, he said, "Try to eat, young lady; we want you to get well."

Louise was listening intently from the other side of the door. Tears began to run down her cheeks. "Is Emily going to die?" she whispered to herself.

"I'll be back day after tomorrow," she heard Doctor Duboise say as he was leaving.

❧

When Doctor Duboise returned, Emily was no better. Louise's hopes faded when she heard him tell her mother, "Emily has severe colitis. The medicines I've given her haven't helped. I'll have to contact another doctor in Birmingham and see if we can find some other treatment. Try to get her to eat. I'll be back as soon as I have something new. In the meantime, continue giving her the same medicine."

"Thank you for coming, Doctor Duboise." Lillie closed the door and walked back into the bedroom where Emily was sleeping. A feeling of guilt was working its way into her heart. She knew she hadn't been the loving mother she should have been to Emily, and now there was the chance that she might lose her. She sat down beside the bed and watched the shallow breathing of her very sick child. The tinged redness on her cheeks from fever and the dark shadows under her eyes pronounced her illness. Lillie breathed a sigh of despair as she bowed her head and put her hands over her face. "God, forgive me," she prayed. "Please help Emily get well."

☙❧

Louise found Bettie Auntie in the garden near the house. She and Cleopas were setting out cabbage plants. "Bettie Auntie," she called.

"What is it, dear?" her aunt said, getting up off her knees.

"You remember Uncle Goodwin in Oklahoma?"

"Yes, of course. He's a fine doctor there."

"Would you write and tell him about Emily? Maybe he could help her."

Bettie Auntie had felt the same anxiety about Emily as Louise. "It will certainly be worth a try. I'll come in as soon as we're finished planting and write to him. Maybe your daddy will be going into town tomorrow and will mail it at the Post Office."

When she returned to the house, Bettie Auntie washed her hands and sat down in the parlor to write. It grieved her that Emily was so ill. Her devotion to Emily was like that of a mother, yet she knew she couldn't take Lillie's place. *Could it be that Emily knew she was the extra child her mother didn't want? If Emily was conscious of this problem, could it be the reason for her illness?* Troubled by her thoughts, she returned to her letter and wrote down all the medicines that Doctor Duboise had given Emily and how none had helped. After she sealed the envelope, she went to find Louise and gave her the letter.

"I'll be going into town tomorrow," she heard Benjamin tell Louise. "I'll mail your letter the first thing."

Louise watched anxiously for the mail carrier every day. Emily was no better. She had even lost interest in reading. When the letter came, a packet of medicine was enclosed with practical instructions.

"Your Uncle Goodwin has sent this medicine, Emily. He says that we must carefully follow his instructions," Lillie said. She put the glass of medicine on the table beside the bed. "I do hope this will help you. Let me help you sit up to drink it."

Emily shifted her small frame and struggled to sit up with her mother's help. When Lillie bent down to fluff the pillow, she looked at Emily with great concern. Her guilt was overwhelming.

"It's bitter," Emily said, shuddering from its taste.

"But you must drink all of it," Lillie insisted.

The final gulp of the medicine caused Emily to make a terrible face. She gave a deep sigh and lay back on the pillow. Pulling the sheet up to her face, she wiped her mouth and turned away from her mother. "Let's hope this helps," her mother whispered.

&oc&

Emily's recovery was slow but steady. Doctor Duboise was delighted on his return visits. "I'd forgotten about this medicine that your cousin has prescribed," he said to Lillie. "She's responding well to it."

"Thank heavens; I was worried she might not respond to this prescription either. I knew we had turned a corner when she asked Louise for a book from the parlor," Lillie said.

During her time of convalescing, everyone did his or her best to cheer Emily. Cleopas built a small reading chair from whitewashed willow branches. Eugenia and Louise made cushions and pillows from the colored scraps of calico and batting left over from the last quilting. Emily spent many hours reading in the comfortable chair by the bedroom window as a way to escape her sorrow.

As the weeks passed, she began to notice a difference in her mother. Her mother brought her meals, helped her bathe and brushed her hair. One morning after the boys had left for school, Emily was surprised to see her mother, instead of Louise, with fresh linens for the bed.

"You know reading is an education in itself, Emily. Something good will come from this illness yet. You haven't suffered so much for nothing."

She was surprised and pleased at her mother's attention.

"What books do you enjoy most?" Lillie questioned smoothing the crisp sheets over the small feather mattress.

She smiled. "I like Mark Twain's *Huckleberry Finn* and I love *Treasure Island* and *David Copperfield.* I've read them twice and even know some of their pages from memory."

"Well, I think there are many more good books in those boxes," She paused a moment and looked intently at her daughter and laughed. "Don't you look just like a little monkey sitting there with your legs crossed? I think I'll nickname you Monkey."

∾∾

Summer came early. The tender green plants of the garden had already pushed out of the fresh-plowed earth before Emily was well enough to venture outside. From the porch she could see the blackberry blooms, a blanket of white along the fence and the maypops flowering along the road.

When she heard Jonathan talking with his brothers about going swimming, Emily asked if she could go and wade in the creek.

"No! She can't go," Judson smirked. "She's too little."

"Come on, Emily," Jonathan said. "I'll take you."

Judson and Timothy ran down the rolling hills of the pasture to the crystal clear creek that ran across the lower part of their land. Emily and Jonathan followed. The last heavy rain had shifted the sand in the creek bottom to make the water deep enough for a swimming hole. Her brothers wasted no time grabbing a branch of a small water oak hanging over the creek and jumped into the cool water. Emily took off her shoes, put them on the creek bank and began to wade in the shallow part of the creek just above the swimming hole. She held her dress tightly above her knees while the rushing water danced around her ankles and the round pebbles moved beneath her feet. When she grew tired, she sat on a large rock and watched her brothers frolic and swim in their cut off trousers. As she dangled her feet in the cool rushing water, she felt the loneliness of winter flow away, but the pain of rejection from her mother would take a lifetime to heal.

∾∾

"The berries are ripe," Benjamin said when he came in from the fields wiping his brow. "That hot July sun would ripen anything."

Emily reached for a shiny tin bucket that hung on the kitchen wall. "Let's go berry picking, Jonathan."

"You'd better wear long sleeves or your arms will get scratched," Benjamin cautioned.

"We want to go too," Timothy and Judson echoed, each grabbing a pail. As the children ran down the hill to the meadow where the blackberry bushes grew in thickets, they laughed and twirled their buckets in their hands. When they saw the plump berries glistening in the sun, they could hardly wait to begin picking. Emily eagerly picked the berries, dodging the sharp thorns which guarded them. It took only a short time to fill their buckets to brimming with the dark juicy berries. They hurried back to the house, hoping their mother would make them a berry pie sweetened with lots of sugar and topped with a buttery crust. Berry picking was summertime's best reward.

◸⩤

Everyone knew that the south end of the porch, where a slight breeze often blew, was Benjamin's favorite place to gather with his friends on Sunday afternoons. The men would fill their pipes with tobacco and enjoy a long and heated conversation, always debating the same topics. Would there be a better price for cotton this year, and how would they survive the hard times?

For the ladies, the gathering gave an opportunity to hear the latest news of their neighbors and acquaintances. Often, their husbands forgot to tell them important news, who had died or who had married.

It was on one of these afternoons that Emily first met Edwin. She had heard her father speak of the Anderson family and remembered they lived close to Mulberry Creek where her father had often taken them to swim. Even though her father had occasionally invited the Andersons to visit on Sunday, this was the first time they had accepted.

Emily stood next to her father when the Anderson family stepped down from their wagon. At thirteen, she had grown to her full height of five feet and six inches and was a picture of health.

Several years had passed since she had been sick. Her soft pink, cotton dress brought out the rosy color of her cheeks, and her eyes expressed her shyness, but she smiled as her father welcomed the Andersons.

"Welcome, folks," Benjamin said.

"Get off my dress, Edwin." Mrs. Anderson scolded. "You're stepping on my skirt. Can't you wait a minute?"

Edwin sat back down in the buggy. Emily saw him grit his teeth and frown.

"You've met my wife, Virginia, haven't you, Benjamin?" Mr. Anderson said.

"Oh, yes. How are you, Virginia?"

"I'll be fine if we can get these children down from the wagon."

Benjamin turned to Emily. "This is my daughter Emily."

"Miss Emily," Mr. Anderson nodded. "These are our sons Edwin, Chester, and Arthur and our daughter Alice." Emily's eyes met Edwin's. He smiled. She bit her lower lip and then released her smile as she looked down.

"Why don't you take them to meet the other children, Emily?" her father said. "I know they're anxious to play." He watched them follow Emily to the back yard and could see they were anxious to be away from their mother.

"This is Edwin, Arthur, Chester and Alice Anderson," Emily said to her brothers who were kneeling on the smooth, hard dirt shooting marbles.

"I'm Jonathan, and this is my brother Timothy and our other brother Judson. These are our friends," he said pointing to the smaller children who were playing tag.

"Come on, Emily. Play tag with us," they shouted.

"Come on," Edwin cajoled.

"Well, okay," she said.

Emily was breathless. The attention she was getting from the boys made her self-conscious. She was disturbed by her feelings when Edwin looked at her admiringly and grabbed her sash.

"Emily's got a fella. Emily's got a fella," her brothers teased.

Suddenly she was overwhelmed and embarrassed. She ran inside the house to her bedroom and shut the door. She lay down across the bed wondering why she was so attracted to Edwin and if he liked her. Her thoughts drifted to a book she had just read by Jane Austen called *Pride and Prejudice*. She imagined herself as the lovely Elizabeth and Edwin as the dashing Mr. Darcy as she drifted off to sleep.

When she awakened, the afternoon shadows darkened her room. She realized the Andersons must be gone by now. She lay back on the pillow, closed her eyes and dreamily thought of Edwin. An excitement came over her that she hadn't known before. "Maybe they'll come again soon," she sighed.

Chapter Four

Loves First Kiss

*D*esiring to find some relief from the summer heat, Emily went out onto the porch. She ran her hand through her damp hair and leaned over the wooden banister to catch more of the slight breeze that was stirring. Down the dusty road that led to the house, she saw a buggy approaching. She hoped it was Edwin, but she was not sure he would come since she had been disappointed so many times. At eighteen her beauty couldn't be hidden behind her shyness. Like her mother, her high cheekbones and deep-set eyes were well-defined by a very fair complexion. More than once her father had remarked how pretty she was, and he wondered if the young Anderson boy didn't agree, since he had come to call on Emily several times during the last two summers.

When the buggy drew closer, Emily knew it was Edwin. Anxiously, she watched until he stopped at the end of the lane. After stepping down quickly from the buggy, he tied the reins to the gatepost. *He's so handsome,* she thought, *and so sure of himself. I really like him. I like him very much. I wonder if this is how you feel when you're in love.* Trying to conceal her excitement, she turned and looked away as Edwin came up onto the porch. She put her hands up to her face and felt the warmth of her cheeks. Her knees were weak and her heart was pounding. Slowly, she turned around to see her father greeting Edwin. "Come on in, son. It's good to see you. How are your folks?"

Edwin smiled and reached out to shake Benjamin's outstretched hand. "My folks are well, but they think they're too busy to do any visiting." When he saw Emily at the other end of the porch, he gave a flirtatious grin. "Afternoon, Emily."

Before Edwin could move to where Emily was standing, Lillie came out to announce that dinner was ready. "Good afternoon, Edwin," she said. "Won't you join us for dinner?"

"Thank you, Mam. I believe I will."

"Hello, Edwin," Emily said smiling. Reluctant to go into the dining room with the rest of the family, Emily and Edwin lingered a moment in the parlor. Edwin reached out and took her hands in his, then pulled her close. She wondered if he could sense her trembling.

"Edwin, we mustn't," she whispered. "Mama might see us. She wouldn't approve."

"Why not? Doesn't she like me?" Pulling her closer he touched his lips to hers for a brief kiss. Emily blushed and pulled away.

"Come on," she said as she hurried into the dining room. Edwin followed. While her father said the blessing, Edwin took her hand in his. She liked the warmth of his hand and sitting close. When he released her hand, she took only a small portion of food when it was passed around the table. She wasn't hungry. All she wanted was to be alone with Edwin.

Edwin ate heartily and talked effusively. He seemed perfectly comfortable with her family. She listened, though the conversation was mostly men's talk about farming and business. "I don't like farming," Edwin said. "It's too uncertain. All that hard work to make the crops and you never know how the harvest will turn out."

"Oh, but there's something about being connected to the land," Benjamin said. "I guess I always hope for the best."

"My daddy feels the same, Sir."

After the meal everyone moved out onto the porch. "Let's sit here in the swing," Emily said.

"Wait, I need to tell your father one more thing." He rushed to join the conversation that had begun at the table, ignoring the disappointment on Emily's face.

After helping their mother and Annie in the kitchen, Eugenia and Louise joined their sister on the swing. "Well, Emily, did Edwin come to see you or Daddy?" Eugenia teased.

"Oh, he's just trying to make a good impression on Daddy,"

she said trying to conceal her unhappiness.

"Shhh, here he comes," Louise said. Emily's face brightened. "Would you like to sit here by Emily?"

"Oh no, this is fine." Restlessly, he sat in the old wooden rocker across from them. "They'll never be able to convince me to become a farmer," he said slapping his knee.

Eugenia stiffened. "Farming is part of who we are. Our father and his father have worked this land for generations. What would happen if everyone felt like you, Edwin?"

Emily blushed. The afternoon wasn't turning out as she had hoped. Louise frowned and poked Eugenia. "Let's go and see if we have any lemons for lemonade."

Finally, we can be together, Emily thought. But her hopes were dashed when Edwin said, "I can't stay much longer. I've got to get home with this buggy. Papa might need the horse." He took her hand in his and walked hurriedly to his buggy. Anxiously, he loosened the reins from the hitching post and paused for a moment.

Emily leaned on the hitching post and looked down, not wanting him to see the yearning in her eyes. She wanted him to kiss her but knew her mother was watching. As Edwin climbed into the buggy, their eyes met, and she knew he felt the same. She leaned on the hitching post and said, "Good-bye."

"I must go, I'll see you soon."

৵৽

Three weeks passed and Emily waited, but Edwin didn't come to call. Her brother Timothy told her he had heard that Edwin had left home. "It seems he had a row with his mother, and his father whipped him unmercifully. He left without telling anyone."

"What was the argument about?" Emily asked.

"Well, Edwin killed a snake in the yard and was slinging it around. It slipped out of his hand and somehow wrapped around his brother's neck. His brother ran screaming into the house, and his mother demanded that their father whip Edwin. They say, "'He's never gotten along with his mother,'" Timothy continued, "and you know it's unheard of to whip a young man Edwin's age. I'm sure Edwin must have been terribly hurt with his father."

Emily was stunned and could think of nothing to say for a

moment. She looked away to hide her tears. "Don't say anything about this to Mama," she whispered. *Will I ever see him again*, she wondered.

As fall approached, Lillie encouraged Emily to pursue a degree in teaching. "Why don't you attend the University in Tuscaloosa? You could stay with cousin Wilbert and his family. Maybe it would do you good to spend some time away from home. Louise is worried that you spend too much time alone reading."

Emily took her mother's advice. Her first year at the University gave her a sense of independence, yet she missed home. She especially missed her father. When she returned home for the summer, she noticed how tired he looked each time he came in from the fields. "I guess the boys aren't cut out to be farmers," she said to her mother. "Do they help Daddy at all?"

Lillie turned around from the hot stove where she was stirring a bubbling pot of peach preserves. She lifted her apron and wiped her brow. "Well, there's more to life than farming. Sometimes I really hate it. Always having to worry if the crops will fail or not, and then if they're good, whether the price for them will go up or down. With the possibility of war, I'm afraid your brothers will have to leave home soon. I can hardly bear the thought that they may not return home." *I wonder,* Emily thought, *if Mama ever worries about me. I wish I could feel that she loves me as she does the boys.*

❧•❧

After two years at the University, Emily received her teaching certificate. Her first teaching position was in a little one-room schoolhouse in walking distance from Pine Belt. With eight grades and fifteen children, the pandemonium of the classroom left her exhausted. She found relief at the end of the day when she sat down to supper with her family and listened for any news from her sisters. The house seemed empty since Louise had married and Eugenia had gone to Chicago to study music. She missed their times of confiding in quiet conversation and their walks along the creek-bank as they enjoyed being carefree in playful laughter. Every day she thought about Edwin. *Where was he? Why hadn't she heard from him? I thought he really cared for me.*

ॐ✑

"You were right, Mama, about Timothy and Jonathan being drafted. I guess Albert's and Judson's notices won't be far behind," Emily said. "I can't bear to think of Jonathan leaving and going off to war."

Lillie looked up from the breakfast table. She looked older. The lines around her eyes were deep, and her hair was more gray than brown. "I know," her mother said with a sigh. In just a month Timothy, Albert and Jonathan were off to the Army. Judson had failed the physical but decided to leave home and go to Washington, D.C. to find work.

Emily missed them terribly, especially Jonathan. She would read his letters several times trying to satisfy her loneliness. When he wrote that he had contracted tuberculosis and would have to remain in a sanitarium in Tennessee, she was devastated. Soon his letters were few and far between. Lillie knew he must be very ill. "I must go and see about him," she told Benjamin. "I haven't heard from him in three weeks." Emily desperately wanted to go, but her teaching responsibility prevented it. She felt a little more content when her mother returned and told them, "He's getting good care, but he still doesn't look good. He's so pale, and his cough is so consuming. I'm still worried about him. He misses you, Emily."

"And I miss him, terribly."

ॐ✑

Giving herself completely to her teaching, Emily began to love the children and find a great reward in their learning, but at the end of each day, she was exhausted. Her walk home was rejuvenating along with her anticipation to stop at the mailbox and examine each letter. Today was no different. Her longing to hear from Edwin hadn't waned. Carefully, she took each letter out of the old silver colored box. Trembling with excitement she saw the letter and knew it was from him. The name Seaman Edwin Anderson with some numbers for an address was in the left-hand corner. She laid her books down and tore open the envelope.

Dear Emily,   *September 10, 1916*
I guess you think I'm dead. I hope you'll understand. I had to leave home. I had a disagreement with my family and decided to leave and join the Navy. I'm on a ship now, and don't know when I'll come home. I miss you. I hope you miss me. Write to me. I will write when I can. I have seen some wonderful sights. I will tell you about them when I come home. Remember you're my girl. Don't let anyone else claim you.
   Love, Edwin

Emily read the short letter again, then tucked it in her dress pocket. She thumbed through the other letters and saw ones from Louise, Jonathan and Timothy. "When will this war be over?" she sighed.

↾⇛

A sense of defeat was noticeable on her father's face and even in his walk since her brothers had gone off to war. Emily knew he was worried about them and especially about Jonathan. It didn't surprise her when he announced, "Cousin Wilbert told me about a furniture store in Tuscaloosa that's for sale. He said I could buy it at a bargain price and make a darn sight better living than I'm making at farming. I'm going over there next week and take a look."

↾⇛

"Told you Master Ben gonna sell dis place. Now we's gonna haf to go live wif Master Hamilton," Cleopas told Hattie.

She looked up from the large enameled pan where she was shelling peas. "Don't matter to me, sep I's gonna miss Miss Lillie somtin terrible and Miss Bettie Annie. Don't look like there's nothin but heartache round here no mo. All dem boys gone and Miss Louise and Miss Eugenia. Miss Lillie don't do nothin but grieve over Master Jonathan, and Miss Emily seems so lonesome. I think she misses Miss Louise most of all."

"Ain't that," Cleopas said, leaning back in his chair. "It's that Mr. Edwin. He done gone off and joined the Navy and gone to war. I don't think she ever hears from him. I think he done broke her heart."

"What you know about that? You better help me finish shelling des peas and quit making up stories," Hattie said, frowning.

❧❧

After her daddy bought the furniture store, Emily knew that she was expected to move with her family. Her mother had given her little choice, saying emphatically, "It isn't proper for a single girl to live away from her family."

Lillie's father, Samuel Hamilton, was quite willing for Cleopas and Hattie to come and live on his farm. Lillie's mother's death had left him lonely these past few years. Lillie knew Cleopas could do very little work since he was almost as old as her father. Still, the two servants would be good company for him.

❧❧

When the last two items were packed on the two drays ready to be pulled by two strong mules to the railroad station, Emily found it impossible to hold back her tears. She saw that Bettie Auntie and her father were wiping tears from their eyes. Lillie kept her composure. She had hopes of city life being easier and more entertaining. She wasn't sad to be leaving the hard work and routine of farm life.

"We'll stay with Cousin Wilbert until our things arrive," Benjamin said. "The store has living quarters upstairs which are very nice. We'll be settled soon."

❧❧

By late October, the Andersons were settled and set for opening day of the furniture store. Benjamin tried to hide his exhaustion. To his surprise, some of the work was harder than farming. Getting the store stocked with the small items and where to place them had been more difficult than placing the larger pieces of furniture, but Emily found release in admiring the delicate vases and intricate figurines. It kept her from worrying about her brothers and yearning to hear from Edwin. She had received only five short letters in two years from him which made her question if he really had serious intentions about her. She feared Bettie Auntie didn't like him and hardly brought up his name while they worked together ... *if only I could talk to Louise,* she reflected.

ক্ষ

"The war is over! The Kaiser has surrendered!" Benjamin shouted when he came into the store. "Look at the news," he said, placing the newspaper before Emily and Bettie Auntie.

"Oh, that means that Timothy and Albert will be coming home!" Emily said. Suddenly the November sun seemed brighter, the smooth blue sky seemed more intense, and for the first time in months there was hope. "Maybe Edwin will come home too," she sighed.

"Where is Lillie?" Benjamin asked.

"She just went upstairs. She was tired and wanted to lie down a few minutes," Bettie Auntie said. She was also very tired at the end of each day. The furniture business required long days, and working with strangers was quite different from farm life. She missed that life.

"Well, I must go up and tell her the news." He hurried to the back of the store and rushed up the narrow flight of stairs. "Lillie, the war is over!" he shouted. When he came into the room, he saw she was lying down, her cheeks were flushed and she was confused. He touched her forehead and realized she had a very high fever. "Lillie, what's wrong?" When she didn't answer, he hurried down the stairs and declared, "I must find a doctor. Lillie is very ill." He rushed out the door of the store.

Emily bounded up the stairs. When she saw her mother lying motionless on the bed, she took a cool wet cloth and placed it on her mother's brow. Anxiously, she watched for her father to return. "She's up here," she heard her father say to the doctor. Emily greeted the doctor and walked over to the window when he began to examine her mother.

"She seems to have influenza," he said. "Hardly a family here in town doesn't have one case or more of it. There isn't much we can give to treat it. We have to let it run its course. I'll leave something for the fever. You must try to get her to drink plenty of liquids."

༄୰༄

In only a few days, Benjamin and Bettie Auntie came down with the illness. Emily was the only one to escape the ravages of fever, coughing and unbearable pain. She had to close the store and spend all her time nursing her mother, father and aunt with no time to think of Edwin or even her brothers. Her only hope was that they would recover. Even this hope faded when Bettie Auntie grew weaker and her cough more severe. The doctor had warned of pneumonia resulting from the infection, and now she feared Bettie Auntie had pneumonia. Nothing helped her. Another visit from the doctor confirmed her fears. Bettie Auntie had pneumonia. Emily listened carefully as the doctor gave instructions and medicine for Bettie Auntie, but her aunt grew worse each day. Lillie was barely out of bed when Bettie Auntie died. Benjamin hardly knew of her passing because his fever raged into delirium.

Emily got help from Cousin Wilbert with arrangements for the burial. When she sent word to Louise, she found that they were also stricken with the vicious disease and couldn't even come to the funeral. Emily knew God's hand of mercy must be on her, keeping her well to take care of the rest of the family.

It was the middle of January before Benjamin and Lillie were well enough to be up and out of danger. Emily was kept busy in the store with only occasional help from her father. Her sorrow of Bettie Auntie's death and Jonathan's illness, which had worsened, weighed heavily on her mind. Word of his death came suddenly one afternoon only a month after Bettie Auntie died. Emily accepted the telegram and handed it to her father. Benjamin's face turned ashen, and his large hands trembled reading the fateful news. He didn't say a word but handed the telegram back to Emily and went upstairs to tell Lillie. Emily sat down in the front of the store; her world seemed to be crumbling. Her grief for Bettie Auntie was still uppermost in her thoughts. Now Jonathan's death was almost more than she could bear. She could hear her mother's cries upstairs, yet she couldn't go to her. Tears welled up in her eyes and flowed down her cheeks. Scenes of happy times with Jonathan flooded her memory. She could see him now, running down to the fence row in the pasture to pick berries with her and always looking out for her when she was sick. She sat there motionless and grieving until darkness invaded the room. She knew she must begin to arrange for Jonathan's body to be brought home for burial. In two short months she had planned two funerals for two of the dearest people in her life. Afterwards, she hardly remembered how she survived.

In his weakness and grief, Benjamin lost all his enthusiasm for his furniture business. He realized more than ever how he missed the comfort of the land, the smell of fresh-plowed earth, the release of tension from toiling in the sun, but most of all, the joy of seeing the fields of cotton ready for picking. When a letter came from Lillie's father offering them his farm if they would come and live with him, Benjamin and even Lillie were ready to accept. "It'll be good to get back to the land," he declared, and Lillie had to agree. Perhaps their sickness had drawn them back to the familiar - to home. Emily had other thoughts, thoughts she wouldn't share with anyone. All she could think of was Edwin. She knew he would be coming home soon, and she wanted to be there to greet him.

The sorrow and misfortune of the past months seemed to pull Emily farther from her mother. Still feeling that she could never please her mother, she hesitated to confide in her or even to have a friendship. Deep in her heart was the ever present longing to be loved, to be held, to be wanted and needed.

ఇ≪

When Timothy and Albert returned home from Europe, Benjamin's grief seemed to subside, but their returning made Emily more aware of Jonathan's absence. Even her occasional visits to Selma to see Louise didn't fill the void left by Jonathan's death. He was the brother who had always looked out for her and who seemed to understand her. Somehow she didn't miss her brother Judson. He had written that he had married but couldn't find time to come home for a visit. Benjamin's plans for Albert and Timothy to help him with the farming were never realized. He soon learned that neither of them planned to stay on the farm. Patiently, he listened as Albert told him about the girl he planned to marry, and Timothy revealed his plans to attend the Baptist Seminary in Kentucky.

"Well, Lillie, our children are grown up now, and we might as well face it. I'll just have to hire some help for the farming. One thing for sure, old Cleopas isn't much help anymore. I know Hattie still tries to help you some. But on a brighter note, it looks like we're going to have us a preacher son. That makes me happy, and I know it makes you very happy. I'll have to credit you for that. You've been the one to teach them all these years to love the Lord and to study their Bible." He sat down by the warm stove and rubbed his hands.

"Timothy will make a very good minister. He's gentle and quite an orator," Lillie said. She leaned away from the table and stopped shelling the peas in her lap. "I wonder how long we'll be able to have Emily at home."

"Not long, I'm afraid. You know she's still pretty stuck on that Anderson boy, and he'll be returning home soon, I suppose."

"Yes, I fear he will," Lillie said. "I fear he will. I must go and check on Papa; I don't want him to go outside and get chilled."

Chapter Five
Promised Love

*L*ooking over the plowed fields, Benjamin felt a sense of relief and pride. He breathed in the musty sweet smell of the freshly turned earth while admiring the tiny plants that were pushing up through the dark, rich soil. All this and the blossoming peach trees gave him a feeling of hope for a good year. He was happy.

Though the war had ended in November, Edwin hadn't come home. Emily never lost hope that he would come. Lillie hoped he wouldn't come at all. Somehow, Emily had a feeling that he would come today. It was the first Sunday in months her mother and father had planned a gathering of family and friends. Miss Lillie and Annie had prepared a delicious dinner of barbecued goat, basted with vinegar and black pepper. To complement the barbeque, she took the last of the sweet potatoes from the root cellar and baked them with brown sugar and butter. Benjamin had picked and shelled plenty of early green peas from the garden. "Hattie," Lillie said, "will you go to the cellar and bring up two jars of apples? Everyone loves cooked apples."

Hattie shifted her feeble frame and moved slowly to the door, "Yes'um," she sighed. Last of all, the hot cornbread muffins and blackberry cobbler were taken from the oven and placed on the pine sideboard, filling the house with a bouquet of tantalizing aromas. "Dinner is served," Hattie announced.

☙❧

"I believe this is the best cobbler you've ever made, Miss Lillie," Cousin Wilbert exclaimed after wiping his mouth on the large white damask napkin.

"Why thank you, sir," Lillie said. "Your compliments are well taken."

"I think it's warm enough to sit on the porch this afternoon," Emily's father announced. He rose slowly from his chair and invited everyone to join him.

After Emily had helped her mother and Annie clear the table and wash the dishes, she went out onto the porch to join the others. Before she could sit down, she saw a buggy approaching on the narrow road to the house. Somehow she knew it was Edwin, though she didn't recognize the buggy. She felt a surge of excitement and leaned over the porch rail trying to discern if it was Edwin.

"Someone is coming," she said, pretending to sound indifferent.

"Is it the Anderson boy? I believe it is," her father said, turning to look at Emily.

Edwin slowed the buggy to a stop at the edge of the yard and hitched the reins to the post. His stride was quick and sure. Emily noticed that he had grown taller and more handsome, with coal black hair parted on the side and trimmed ever so neatly. Beneath his heavy, black eyebrows and eyelashes, his green eyes sparkled in the bright afternoon sun. He was dressed different, not like a country boy. Neatly pressed, his suit coat was buttoned up high, and underneath his coat was a white shirt sporting a round collar and a dark tie. *He's more handsome than I remembered,* Emily observed as she watched him come up onto the porch.

"Edwin! Come in, son. How are you? You've been gone a long time. It's really good to see you," Benjamin said.

"Good afternoon, Mr. Whitworth. It's good to see you." He reached out to shake Benjamin's hand and turned to greet Miss Lillie. "How are you, Miss Lillie?"

Lillie nodded amicably, "Edwin."

"I was sorry to hear of Jonathan's death and also your sister's death, Mr. Whitworth. My papa sends his regards." He leaned comfortably against the porch rail. "It's good to be home. I plan to help my papa with the crops this year." When he looked at Emily at the other end of the porch, he took note that she was even prettier than he had remembered.

When he walked over to where she was sitting, he noticed an apparent reluctance in her greeting. "I thought you weren't coming back. You've been gone so long."

He looked at her intently, taking in her delicate beauty. "Well I'm here now." He grinned and sat down beside her on the porch swing. "Now tell me what you've been doing since I've been gone, and I'll tell you where I've been." He moved closer and listened while she told him about moving to Tuscaloosa. When she began to talk about Bettie Auntie's and Jonathan's deaths, her eyes filled with tears. Calmly, she pulled a white embroidered handkerchief from her pocket and wiped her eyes.

"Emily," he said, ignoring her tears, "I'm going to ask your father if I can take you for a ride in my buggy." He jumped up and went to the other end of the porch where Benjamin was sitting.

Emily remained in the swing somewhat confused by his restlessness. She held onto her disappointments. He hadn't said why he waited so long to come home and why he had written so few letters.

"Mr. Whitworth, with your permission, I'd like to take Emily for a ride over to Mulberry creek and Kennon's Mill."

Benjamin smiled, "Just be home before dark."

When they sat down on the buggy seat, Edwin quickly maneuvered the buggy out onto the road. "Edwin, I thought you would be home by Christmas. Why didn't you come then?" Emily asked.

"Oh, I couldn't make up my mind whether to stay in the Navy for a career or not, but when I got to thinking about you, I decided I wanted to come home." He moved closer and pulled the reins to make the horse trot faster. "Let's go and see the old swimming hole. I've really missed these woods and creeks."

Emily settled herself more comfortably in the seat feeling better satisfied with his explanation. "I haven't been there in a long time myself," she said. Memories of her brother, Jonathan, filled her mind, and she felt a sudden chill, but Edwin didn't notice.

Edwin laughed. "Do you remember how your brothers and I would swim in our 'birthday suits,' and you and Louise would run and tell your father?"

Emily blushed and pulled her skirt down more securely over her knees. "Oh yes, I remember."

Edwin slowly pulled the buggy off the sandy road and down under a large water oak by the creek. The water, still muddy from a recent heavy rain, made a musical rhythm bouncing over the rocks and fallen limbs. Edwin jumped down and tied the reins to a tree whose branches were bent low by a recent rainstorm. He held out his hand to help Emily down from the buggy. When she stepped down, he took her in his arms and kissed her tenderly. Still holding her in his embrace, he said, "Emily, I love you, and I want you to marry me."

Emily felt a sudden warmth and happiness, feelings she had never experienced before. This was the moment she had dreamed about and longed for. She gave herself fully to his embrace, yet she couldn't give him an answer.

"Don't you love me?" he said, releasing her enough to look into her eyes.

"I … you've been gone so long, Edwin. I don't really know how I feel. I just know I want to be with you."

He held her close again and kissed her on the forehead. "I won't take no for an answer." Freeing her from his embrace, he took her hand and led her over to a large rock and sat down. Emily felt comfortable with his arm around her waist as they talked of the happy times they had spent in these special places of their childhood. This was the moment she had dreamed about while he was gone. Would this be how it would be, married to Edwin? Would they sit and talk and have tender moments just being together and embracing one another? She had hardly begun to consider his proposal when he slid down off the rock and held out his hand to help her down. "We had better go over to Kennon's Mill if I have to get you home before dark."

They passed the cemetery where Jonathan was buried, but Emily didn't mention him for fear of spoiling the perfect afternoon. When they came to the mill, they heard the familiar sound of water falling over the squeaking wheel. The smell of freshly ground corn still lingered from the day before, even though the mill was deserted and the millstone was silent.

Edwin thought of the many times that he had come here with his father to have their corn ground into meal. He remembered sitting and waiting while his father talked to the other farmers. He recalled with pain the time he had overheard his father telling his uncle how overbearing Edwin's mother had become and how demanding she was. He could almost hear again his father's harsh words, calling her insane. It seemed like yesterday when he had heard their conversation and pretended not to hear by skipping smooth stones across the water above the water wheel. He was lost in his thoughts when Emily interrupted him. "Edwin, we must go. It's getting late."

When they arrived at the Whitworth farm, the setting sun was blending with the clouds on the horizon in a beautiful pink color that flooded the sky. Emily was overcome by the beauty and romance of the day. Edwin held her by the hand as she stepped down from the buggy and kissed her softly on the lips. "I can't come in but I'll be back soon."

"Goodbye," Emily said, sorry he was leaving and wondering when he would return. From the porch she watched his buggy until it was out of sight; then quietly she went into the house, keeping all the wonderful secrets of the afternoon to herself. "Oh, Louise, how I wish you were here."

Spring ran into summer, a time of waiting for Emily. On his infrequent visits, Edwin explained, "There never seems to be an end to the work on his Papa's farm. We work from dawn to dusk since my brothers are gone, and Papa has gone and bought five cows that have to be milked. I don't think I could ever be a farmer. I think I would like to live in the city."

As they walked in a grove of trees down by the meadow on one of his visits, Emily asked, "What did your papa say about your leaving home so young?"

"Oh, he's never mentioned it. Mama wants to bring it up every now and then, but I just don't talk about it." He stopped and put his arms around her waist drawing her close. "When are you going to give me an answer, Emily?"

"I do love you and want to be with you … I."

"Then marry me," he insisted.

Emily's mind was racing. I'm happiest when I'm with him. Maybe when we marry, I can be with him like I want. Edwin pulled her close again and kissed her tenderly. When he released her, she found the words he wanted to hear, "I will. I will marry you, Edwin."

లదల

In the late summer Ebenezer Church had its annual picnic. It was a dry, hot day. Very little breeze stirred among the leaves on the trees that drooped from the summer heat. Edwin had sent word that he would meet Emily there, but he hadn't come. She had been disappointed so many times; she wondered if he would come today. She was sitting under a huge oak tree with several of her friends when she saw him coming across the churchyard. He looked handsome, but tired. Walter Johnson was sitting next to her. She had always been aware Walter liked her and she liked him as a friend or more like a brother.

"There's Edwin," she said jumping up and running to meet him. "I'm so glad you're here."

"It looks like you're having a good time without me," he remarked curtly.

"Oh, Edwin. You know I don't care for anyone but you." Surprised by her own words, she felt a flush of embarrassment. He took her hand and led her across the churchyard away from the crowd. They sat down under a large oak tree at the edge of the cemetery. The air was hot and dry, and all the foliage seemed to cry out for relief. Edwin complained again about how hard he had worked all summer and how he would be glad when the harvest was over.

"I plan to go to go to Birmingham to find work after my papa pays me. Then I'll come home, and we'll be married in the spring." He reached for her hand and enclosed it in his, leaving it on her lap. She felt a rush of emotion. She could hardly speak. For months she had waited for this moment, and now the words she wanted to say eluded her.

Finally, she said, "We can be married here at the church or maybe in Selma at Louise's."

"I'd rather be married at your sister's and only invite our families,"

"I like that idea too. Will you be able to come home any before the wedding?"

"Not too often. The train fare is expensive, and I won't have much time once I find a job."

Emily couldn't hide her disappointment. Would she ever get to be with him? She wondered if it would be the same after they were married. She wanted to be able to sit and talk with him the way her mother and father did, discussing their plans and going over their problems, even disagreeing sometimes. She leaned against the tree trunk and gazed out across the churchyard. "We haven't talked about children, Edwin."

"Oh, there's plenty of time to think about that. Come on," he said, jumping up and pulling her to her feet. "The picnic is over."

Emily looked across the churchyard and saw her mother watching them. She walked over to Edwin's carriage; she had mixed emotions. *Edwin says he loves me, but it seems that we can never be together. Does he really love me? I wonder what Mama is thinking.* When she was seated comfortably in the shay, Edwin guided the horse up onto the road. He still seemed out of sorts until they reached the narrow road that led to the Whitworth farm. "Ho, boy," he said to the old horse as he slowed the carriage down. He reached over and took Emily's hand in his. "How will it sound to you to be called Mrs. Edwin Anderson?"

Emily smiled, flirtatiously. He brought the horse to a stop, turned to her, took her in his arms and kissed her passionately, making her forget her doubts.

"I'll come and see you before I go to Birmingham."

"I'll miss you," she whispered. He took her hand and helped her down from the carriage and kissed her again. Climbing quickly back into the carriage, he turned the horse around and left her standing, looking and waving. *I must tell Mama our plans,* she thought as she walked to the house and waited in the parlor for her mother to return home.

Lillie was breathless when she came up the steps and into the house. When she saw Emily sitting in the parlor, she came in and sat down. "It's so hot, I feel faint." She took off her straw bonnet and fanned herself. "Has Edwin left so soon?" she said fluffing her hair.

Moving restlessly to the edge of the settee, Emily placed her hands on her knees. "Yes, ma'am, he was in a hurry to get back home with his father's carriage. He wants to marry me, Mama," she said abruptly.

"Is that what you want, Emily?" A look of disappointment was written on her face.

"Yes, ma'am, we want to marry in the spring, perhaps at

Louise's house."

"Well, I'm not surprised, but I had hoped you would marry someone like Walter Johnson. He comes from a much nicer family," her mother said disdainfully.

Emily felt like a child who had done something wrong. "Mama! I've never liked Walter that way. He's just a friend. Besides he's too short for me."

Lillie put her hand behind her neck and moved her head around. "Well, it looks as if you've made up your mind." She breathed a deep sigh. "I'm sure Louise will be glad for you to marry in her home. I'll try and find some time to help you make your wedding dress. Where will you live after you're married?"

Edwin's going to Birmingham soon to find work. We'll live there."

"Well, all right. Has he spoken to your daddy? That would be the polite thing to do, even though you are old enough to make your own decisions."

"I'll go and talk to Daddy now," Emily said. "I think he likes Edwin."

Chapter Six

Wedding Plans

Emily sat down at the tall secretary in the parlor to write Louise. She reached for the parchment stationary and began to tell her sister about her wedding plans. She was apprehensive about so many things; does Edwin truly love me? Will I be happy spending the rest of my life with him? I don't really know how he feels about having children. In her pensive state, she stared at a small picture of her mother at the back of the secretary. I wish Mama liked him. I think she would like him better if his family had a better social position; class is so important to her. Love is more important to me. I do love Edwin. She shook her head to rid herself of her deep troubling thoughts, then picked up her pen and continued to write.

It was difficult to put down on paper the kind of wedding she wanted. It doesn't have to be elaborate, but I would love a beautiful dress. Louise will know just where to start.

All her fears were quieted when she received a letter from Louise asking her to come to visit. *"We'll sit down together and make the necessary plans. There's a shop here that has beautiful lace and piece goods, perfect for a wedding dress. I am so happy for you and can't wait till you can come."*

After she read Louise's letter, Emily hurried to tell her mother the plans. "Louise has agreed to have the wedding at her house, Mama. I'll go to Selma next week to work out the details with her. We'll buy everything that is needed for my dress. I know it will take several weeks to make it after I come home. I can't wait to get started."

❦

The train ride lasted only an hour, long enough for Emily to complete a list of the materials she would need for her wedding dress. Louise's husband, John Freeman, was standing on the platform outside the ticket office. He wasn't handsome like Edwin, not nearly as tall, and he had put on some weight since he and Louise had married. Emily loved his sweet disposition. He exuded goodness. He was easy to love, and she knew Louise loved him dearly. When she stepped down off the train, John Freeman took her bag and set it down on the platform. "Look at you," he said and gave her a warm hug. "You'll really make a beautiful bride."

Emily smiled. John Freeman always made her feel like a lady. "Thank you for coming to meet me. I can't wait to see Louise."

Emily's excitement grew when she saw the large, white colonial house standing at the end of a pebble-covered lane lined with live oak trees. The gray moss hanging from the branches seemed to whisper, "Welcome." The house was surrounded by a large expanse of land reminiscent of a southern plantation. White columns joined by a low banister surrounded the gray porch floor which wrapped around the front and sides of the house. Late summer offered no relief from the hot, dry weather, and dust had settled on the bright colored cushions of the white wicker furniture.

Louise waited anxiously in the foyer, watching for the carriage to enter the long lane that led to the house. She looked in the mirror and smoothed her hair with both hands and went to the door just as John Freeman opened it.

"Here comes the bride!" John Freeman sang.

"Well, you certainly look like a bride, Emily," Louise echoed. She took her sister's hands in hers and gave her a tight hug.

"You and John Freeman surely know how to make me feel good. I feel like I'm more the nervous bride."

"Oh, you'll feel better after we've made all the plans," Louise assured her.

"I'll take your bag upstairs, Emily, and you two can talk," John Freeman offered.

"Oh, thank you, John Freeman." She ran her hand over the smooth oak wooden newel post. "This beautiful stairway reminds me of Daddy and his story about the staircase in our old home place. You remember?"

"How could I forget that story?" Louise laughed. "We've all heard it a hundred times. I wish Daddy could come here and enjoy this one." They both paused a moment looking at the flight of stairs. "How are Mama and Daddy? I miss them so much."

"They're fine, just getting older," Emily said.

"We don't get to see them as much as I would like," Louise said. "I can't wait till your wedding day when we'll all be together. Let's go into the parlor where we'll be more comfortable. I feel a slight breeze coming in the window."

Emily sat next to Louise on the pale green velvet sofa and looked around the lovely room. *Oh, to have a house like this,* she thought. *I wonder if Edwin and I will ever have anything like this.*

"Have you set the date yet?" Louise asked.

"Yes, March fifteenth, if that suits you."

"March fifteenth, almost spring. That'll be fine with me. You know, our brother Timothy is an ordained minister now. Why don't you ask him to do the ceremony?"

"I'd like that very much, and I believe Edwin would too. He's always liked Timothy." Emily looked down and picked up a small needle point pillow and began running her fingers over its delicate stitches. "Do you know what Mama said when I told her I was going to marry Edwin? She had hoped that I would marry someone like Walter Johnson because he comes from a nicer family."

"Oh, you know how Mama thinks social standing matters so much. The important thing is that you love each other."

"I do love him, Louise. It's that marriage is such a big decision, and I can't tell for sure if Edwin loves me. We don't spend much time together. He's always busy for one reason or another, but when I'm with him, I'm so happy. He says he loves me. He's very persistent that we marry soon."

"Oh, Emily, all brides are apprehensive. Don't you know that?" She reached over and patted her sister's hand. "Now tell me more about your dress. What kind of lace will you use?"

"Irish lace because it's so delicate."

"Then we'll go to town right after lunch. I guess you're hungry. Go upstairs and freshen up, and I'll see if Elizabeth has lunch ready."

After lunch, John Freeman brought the carriage around for the trip to town. When they entered the little sewing shop, Emily pushed her doubts aside and began admiring the beautiful merchandise. Carefully displayed were bolts of soft white batiste, silk and organdy, narrow and wide lace, Irish lace and crocheted lace. She and Louise picked up piece after piece examining and admiring them. "This is everything I need," Emily said, placing the fabric and lace on the counter for cutting exact yardage.

"Your wedding gown will be beautiful! I wish I could help you make it," Louise sighed.

When Emily took the train home, she was happier than she had ever remembered. She sat back in her seat and thought of the wedding. How wonderful to be a bride. Her doubts were normal, Louise had assured her. I hope Edwin will agree with the plans. Only if spring will come quickly.

The cotton was picked and baled, and the last leaves had fallen from the trees. Winter began with a heavy frost that appeared like a light snow on the fields and on the rooftops in the early morning. Emily was glad she had chosen not to teach this winter. Her mother had convinced her she needed to stay at home, make herself some clothes and to take plenty of time sewing her wedding dress. In truth, Jonathan's death had made her mother fearful of tuberculosis. Emily was still thin, and Lillie worried about her health. For years, Emily had been aware of her mother's over protectiveness and thought this was because of guilt remaining from Emily's childhood. Often she had wondered if anyone had told her mother she knew Lillie didn't want another child and the reason Emily doubted her love. Amicably, she thought, if she prefers I not teach this winter, I'm glad.

Thanksgiving Day was only two days away, and cooking had already begun. Freshly-baked pumpkin pie and soft yeast rolls from the oven filled the house with holiday aromas. Emily missed Jonathan the most during holidays. Special occasions weren't the same without her brothers and sisters.

Emily was standing at the dining room window watching her daddy and Cleopas trying to catch the largest turkey for the holiday meal. She heard her mother call to Hattie. "There'll be twelve at the table, Hattie."

"Yas'um," Hattie answered bringing the best linens into the dining room to set the table.

Emily watched as Hattie placed the white damask tablecloth and large napkins on the table. She knew the old servant had spent hours ironing them to perfection, and she noticed how carefully Hattie placed the napkins beside Miss Lillie's fine china and monogrammed silverware. Last of all the delicate crystal water glasses were set, casting colorful prisms of light across the table.

Lillie came into the dining room from the kitchen to give her approval of the table setting. "Put the glasses on the right at the tip of the knife, Hattie."

"I remember, Miz Lillie. I remember."

"All right. You know I want the table set perfectly." Taking a last look, she returned to the kitchen.

"Yas'um. I sho knows that," Hattie muttered under her breath. Emily laughed. She knew Hattie took pride in doing her best. Even in her dress, she was immaculate. She wore a blue chambray dress topped with a starched white apron, and her head was wrapped with a white bandanna tied neatly in a knot at the top of her head. Finished with her task, she put her hands on her hips and let her shoulders droop like a wilting flower. "Miz Lillie, she sho knows how to entertain."

"The table is beautiful, Hattie. You did set a place for Mr. Edwin? He'll be coming."

"Oh, yas'um, Miss Emily. I knows he's coming. I can tell by the glow on yo cheeks."

"Now, Hattie, don't imagine things." Emily hoped he wouldn't be late. "I'm so glad Louise and John Freeman will be here along with Timothy. You know he's engaged to be married, don't you? He met his fiancée at the Seminary in Kentucky. Albert's family can't come. They'll be missed. It sure would be nice if Eugenia and Judson could come home sometime."

Gobble! Gobble! Gobble! The noise drifted up from out in the yard. Emily turned and moved quickly to the window. "That turkey has made his last strut across the barnyard."

Annie moved over to the window to join Emily. "Sho has."

Benjamin was stationed at one corner of the barn, and Cleopas was at the opposite corner. Even though they had watched it grow from a small bird to a fine "Tom Turkey," their determination to catch him and place his head on the chopping block wasn't lessened. He didn't surrender easily, and the noise of his struggle was deafening to say the least. Emily moved away from the window. Once they had conquered the large unruly bird, she didn't want to witness his demise.

Edwin arrived shortly after the turkey was taken out of the oven and placed on a huge blue and white platter. Emily was relieved that he wasn't late. Everyone had already gathered around the dining room table. Emily had no opportunity to greet him alone. When they sat down, Edwin put his hand over his mouth to quiet his breathing while her father pronounced the blessing. Emily took a quick glance at Edwin while her head was bowed. He returned her glance and smiled. Emily felt her cheeks flush when Edwin reached over and squeezed her hand. After the blessing, he released her hand and took a helping of each special dish.

Benjamin stood to carve the huge golden-brown turkey complemented with Lillie's cornbread dressing. "The turkey is cooked to perfection," he said, smiling at Lillie. "This is my favorite time of the year; the harvest is in and our table is full. We're glad you could join us, Edwin. You all know Edwin and Emily will marry in the spring, don't you?"

"Thank you, sir." Edwin turned and smiled at Emily.

When the meal was over, Benjamin pushed his chair back from the table. "You outdid yourself this time, Lillie; everything was delicious."

"Certainly was, Miss Lillie," everyone agreed and moved their chairs back from the table. Emily listened to the relaxed conversation, which had become a family tradition after holiday meals. This was the family time she loved. Hearing Timothy and Louise was like a savory dessert. Most of the conversation was dominated by the men. Edwin talked frequently and seemed to be enjoying himself. Finally her father suggested they move into the parlor by the fire. Emily motioned for Edwin to sit down in the entrance hall on a small settee to be away from the others. There were so many things she wanted to ask him. Edwin had already told her family about his job selling insurance. Emily wanted to know more about where they would live and what living in the city was like.

"The city will be different from the country. Houses are closer together, and you have to use care making friends."

Emily moved uncomfortably in her chair. "Do you want to hear about the wedding plans?"

"Whatever you decide is fine with me," he said. "I'll be glad when we're married and settled." Their private conversation ended when Grandpa Hamilton began one of his long-winded tales. Because he was hard of hearing, he always talked loudly, and everyone was his captive audience.

As the afternoon wore on, the cadence of the conversation rose high and low, like the blazes of the fire in the grate. Although the furniture was old, the upholstery still retained its soft green color, lending an air of dignity to the room. The afternoon sun sifted through the lace curtains, a reminder that the day was almost over, and it was time for the guests to leave. "I must be going, too," Edwin said, rising from his chair. "I need to spend some time with my family."

Emily walked outside with him to his buggy. "We'll take a ride in the buggy tomorrow, if it's not too cold," he promised. Sliding his arm around her waist, he held her close for a moment and pressed his lips to hers to say good-bye. Emily shivered from the cold and hurried back into the house.

A strong blowing rain awakened Emily the next morning. When she heard the raindrops hitting against the window, she knew Edwin wouldn't come, but she didn't know it would be Christmas before she would see him again.

Chapter Seven

Last Christmas at Home

W e've plenty of pecans this year, Lillie," Benjamin reminded his wife as he entered the kitchen. "The ground is covered under the trees. I'll get busy and shell them so you can bake your fruitcakes."

Lillie smiled. She knew fruitcake was Benjamin's favorite. In early December, she always began making her baked goods for Christmas. Along with the pecans, she used dried fruit and rich dough flavored with cinnamon to make the delicious cakes. After Benjamin had shelled the pecans, he told Lillie, "Make plenty. We all love fruitcake!"

Later when she removed the fruitcakes from the oven, Benjamin was drawn to the kitchen by the delicious aroma. He savored the fragrance more when Lillie poured homemade blackberry wine over the warm cakes. Carefully, she wrapped them in a thin, porous cloth to stay moist until the holiday.

Other favorites were pound cake, egg custard and Lillie's flavorful blackberry jam. In the last week before Christmas, Hattie gathered eggs twice a day to make a large buttery cake and plenty of custard. No one in the community could make egg custard as delicious as Hattie's.

ॐ

"Over here!" Emily called to Cleopas from the fence-row at the edge of the woods. She had already found the perfect Christmas tree where the cedars grew in abundance. Cleopas moved slowly across the field. He was bent with age, but he wanted to come with Emily today since it was her last time to choose a Christmas tree for her family. Every year as long as she could remember, he had brought the same highly sharpened hatchet and cut the tree. Ceremoniously, he would place it on their little red wagon and pull it home. As she watched, Emily imagined that she could hear the happy voices of her brothers and sisters laughing and running over the rolling fields. "If they could only be here," she sighed.

"Which one did you pick?" Cleopas asked almost out of breath from hurrying across the field.

Pointing to a tall, well-shaped cedar, she said, "This one. I love the smell of cedars, don't you?"

"Oh, yes um," he said, smiling. He stooped down and chopped the trunk as close to the ground as possible, then struggled to put the tree on the wagon. Emily, realizing how feeble he was, grabbed the top of the tree to help the old black man.

"Let me pull the wagon this time Cleopas." She put her hand in the rusted handle and started up the hill.

"Let me help," Cleopas said, hardly able to keep up with her.

She sensed at his age, he didn't want to seem old and useless.

When they reached the house, the wind had become very brisk and cold, though the sun was still bright for the late afternoon. Cleopas took the tree and sawed the trunk to a smooth flat surface and nailed it onto two short crossed boards making a stand. "That's fine," Emily said. "I'll help you carry it into the parlor. We'll place it in the same corner where we've always had it."

Hattie was sitting next to the warm fire stringing popcorn for a garland. Lillie and Grandpa Hamilton looked up from the large bowl of cranberries they were stringing for another garland. "Where did you find the tree?" Lillie asked.

"Oh, down by the fence-row at the edge of the woods," Emily said.

When the tree was in place, Emily began to tie some small boughs of holly onto the limber branches. "I found the holly at the edge of the woods. I really like it tied with the red taffeta ribbon." After tying the holly, Emily set aside the star that she had made from cardboard covered with tinfoil. It was a family tradition for her father to place the star at the top of the tree as the last decoration.

"Now we have a very pretty tree," Lillie said when all the

decorations were complete. "I love the smell of freshly cut cedar."

"I'm glad you like it, Mama. The cedars are really plentiful this year." Emily put her hands on her hips and leaned back to examine the decorations, making sure they were perfect. As she took in the beauty, she was filled with emotion. This would be her last Christmas at home. Bending down, she placed the few small gifts that she had made under the tree. For her mother, there was a box she had covered with taffeta and lace from scraps of her wedding dress. For her father, a picture of *his* father that she had found among the books stored in the hall. *He will be surprised,* she thought. Her gift to Edwin was two beautiful linen handkerchiefs she had purchased at the dry goods store in Selma where she had bought the piece goods for her wedding dress. She thought of Edwin and wondered what their Christmases would be like. Just to be with him will be wonderful.

By Christmas Eve all the special sweets were prepared, the tree was decorated and the house was cleaned to perfection. The smell of cedar, cinnamon and citrus permeated each room. Edwin arrived in the early afternoon, his arms loaded down with a box of red Washington apples and a box of bright oranges from Florida. Emily was delighted with her mother's satisfaction when Edwin gave her the fruit. "This fruit is your Christmas gift," he said to her mother. Emily noticed that he had done several things of late to win her mother's approval.

"Why thank you. Come and sit at the table, and we'll have a cup of hot spiced cider. Benjamin can join us when he comes in from the barn."

After talking with her mother and father, Emily invited Edwin into the parlor. "Come see our Christmas tree," she said, all the while wanting to be alone with him.

Edwin walked over to the tree and looked at it attentively. "I like it. We haven't had one in a long time." He sat down beside her and took a small red velvet box from his pocket. "Now I've got something pretty to show you." Proudly, he opened the box and took out her wedding ring.

"It's beautiful," Emily sighed. Affectionately, she examined the lovely gold ring and gently moved her fingers over the tiny carved pink roses with pale green leaves bordering them. "May I try it on?"

Edwin smiled and slid it on her thin ring finger. It looked even more beautiful on her hand. "It looks like a perfect fit," he said, holding her hand. "I'll be glad when you wear it permanently." He moved his hand up to her face and tilted her head to his. His kiss was soft and passionate. Emily felt as if her heart would burst. Tears of happiness clouded her eyes, and her cheeks burned with emotion.

"I love you, Edwin," she sighed. Edwin pulled her close to kiss her again. "Wait, Edwin," she said, taking the ring from her finger. "It's bad luck to wear the ring before we're married. Besides, I want to tell you about the wedding plans. Louise and I have everything planned. I've even asked Timothy to do the ceremony."

"I didn't know Timothy could come. I thought he was in Kentucky."

"He is, but our wedding is important to him. He wants to be here."

"That'll be fine. I like Timothy." He leaned back and released her hand. "You know, I'm really enjoying being away from home, especially being away from Mama. I like my work, and I've met a lot of nice people, influential people."

Emily wanted to tell him many of the other details of the wedding, but he continued to talk about his work. She listened patiently until it was time for him to go. "I'll come for you the day after tomorrow and take you to visit my mama and papa. I have to spend Christmas Day with them."

Emily tried to hide her disappointment. Something always kept them apart, and his plans always seemed final. She knew he would be returning to Birmingham in a few days, but why couldn't he come tomorrow? Was he afraid of his mother? Did she have some kind of hold on him? Maybe I'll understand when I visit them, she rationalized. She walked with him to the door. Like a tight band, an uncertain feeling wrapped around her heart, but the fear was quickly erased when he bent to kiss her ardently on the lips. Then he was gone.

Christmas Day was celebrated in the usual fashion with feasting and visiting with relatives and friends. Everyone seemed in a festive mood and asked Emily repeatedly about her wedding plans. Talking about the wedding brought reality, yet the day seemed long and lonely without Edwin.

The day after Christmas, Edwin came early to take Emily to visit his family. She was very apprehensive. As they rode swiftly along, she said very little and found it difficult to listen to what he was saying. Since she hadn't been to his home before, she didn't know what to expect. She thought his father liked her. He had seemed friendly at the grist mill the few times she had been there with her father.

Edwin pulled the buggy up close to the front of the Anderson farmhouse. The plain wood frame house glistened from a fresh coat of white paint. The red tin roof reflected the morning sun with a blaze of color. Everything was neat and in its place, yet there was a sterile look about the outside and the inside of the house. There was no sign of a Christmas tree or any Christmas decorations. A large bowl of apples and oranges was on the kitchen table, and the smell of apple cider drifted to the other rooms of the house, giving a faint hint of the holiday season.

"Come over and sit by the fire," Edwin's father said. He stood up and stretched his hands toward the fire. Two wooden rockers were placed on either side of the fireplace, and a long wooden bench was on the other side facing the rockers. Emily sat down on the bench close to the fire. To her surprise, Edwin sat down in one of the rockers next to his father. "Virginia will bring us some hot apple cider. You'll have some, won't you, Emily?"

"That sounds good. It's very cold out." Looking over at him, she noticed that he looked considerably older than when she had last seen him. His hair was thinner, and the lines in his face were deep. He smiled with an expression of sadness, but exuded warmth that she hadn't yet seen in Edwin. Maybe I haven't been with Edwin enough to see all his good points, she thought. They say most men are like their father.

After Edwin's mother served the cider, she sat on the bench by Emily. Virginia Anderson was a big woman with an authoritative air. Emily thought her handsome more than pretty. "I don't know why Edwin had to move away to the city," Virginia said. "He could have been a lot of help here for his papa. The farm always has work." Edwin shifted in his chair and looked angrily at his mother.

"Oh, Virginia, let's not go over that again," Mr. Anderson said. "Edwin has his own life to live."

Ignoring her husband, Mrs. Anderson continued, "He'll never make it in the city. He's just a country boy."

Emily could see the conversation was making Edwin very angry. She wasn't surprised when he announced, "I must get Emily home. Her mother isn't feeling well. I guess she did too much cooking for the holidays."

Putting on her coat to leave, Emily thanked Mrs. Anderson for the cider and said, "Good bye."

When they were in the buggy, she asked, "Why did you say my mother was sick, Edwin?"

"I wanted to make Mama feel bad because she never cooks anything special for the holidays like your mama does."

"Shame on you," Emily said with a flirtatious smile. "I was disappointed not to be able to discuss any of our wedding plans with them."

"I doubt they'll come," he said with a note of resignation. "Mama never wants to leave the house, and Papa does what Mama says. I really don't care whether she comes or not, but I would like for Papa to come."

"Well, I hope they both come," Emily said.

As they approached the cemetery, Emily asked Edwin to stop. "I want to show you where Jonathan is buried." When they got down out of the buggy, they walked over to Jonathan's grave and stood there in silence for a few moments. The bitter cold, along with heavy clouds, hung over the graveyard and repressed the bright sunshine.

"I didn't realize that Jonathan was only twenty-four when he died," Edwin said, breaking the silence. Emily was turned with her back to him to hide her tears. When she turned around, he saw she had been crying. He took her in his arms and held her close for a moment and then kissed her on her forehead. His lips moved down her face to her waiting lips. He tilted her chin up and kissed her fully on the mouth. A flood of warmth surged through her body. "I'm glad it's not too long till our wedding day, Emily," he said.

She looked down in embarrassment, not wanting him to see her passion; still she clung to his embrace. Finally she pulled away and laid her hand on the head stone that bore the name of her brother. It was as if she were touching him on the shoulder. "Jonathan was much too young to die, and he was the best one of us. I hope we can have many children, maybe one like Jonathan."

Edwin made no comment and hurried her back to the buggy to go home.

The week passed quickly, and Edwin was gone, but Emily was consoled because their wedding day would soon be here.

Chapter Eight

The Wedding

A cold wind whipped around the small railway station as Emily boarded the passenger train to Selma. It was the day before her wedding. With one hand, she held her hat down on her head and with the other hand her skirt. "Whew!" she sighed. "That's how I feel right now, blown in all directions." She sat down, removed her hat and straightened her windblown hair. She weighed her thoughts which were like a debate. I should know Edwin better, but I think he loves me. I don't know whether he wants children, but I do, and I'll be the one to take care of them. Oh, Emily, don't be thinking like this, she told herself. She closed her eyes, rested her head on the back of the seat and quickly fell asleep. Suddenly, she was awakened by the loud announcement of the conductor, "Next stop is Selma."

John Freeman and Louise were waiting when she stepped down off the train. "Emily!" Louise called and waved her gloved hand. "Over here." Emily hurried to them in the small terminal. She hugged her sister and received a soft kiss on the forehead from her brother-in-law. "Well, are you ready for the big day?" Louise asked.

"I guess so," Emily said with a slight blush on her cheeks.

After claiming her baggage, they walked out to the front of the station. John Freeman reached to open the door of his shiny new Ford automobile. "John Freeman!" Emily said, "What a beautiful motor car. I have never ridden in one. This will be my first time."

"You'll like it," he said, pleased over her approval. "We've only had it a few days."

"How do you like it, Louise?" Emily asked.

"I'm not sure yet. This is John's new toy."

"Well I think it's a wonderful invention." Emily slid back in her seat ready to enjoy the ride to their house. As they approached the house, the branches of the live oak trees bowed and danced in the wind. Emily felt a sudden exhilaration. Her fears disappeared. She was happy.

"I can't wait to show you everything. I hope you'll like what I've done," Louise said. When they came inside the house, the fragrance of flowers filled every room.

"Oh, Louise!" Emily shook her head with amazement. "Oh, Louise, "I know it will be perfect."

After John Freeman helped Emily remove her coat, he took her things upstairs. Louise quietly watched as Emily took in all the special decorations. The first thing that caught her sister's eye was a large cut glass vase filled with snow-white gladiolus adorning the marble top table in the center of the parlor. Two lacy ferns drooped gracefully on stands placed on either side of the hallway opening into the parlor. "You and Edwin can stand here to say your vows."

"A perfect place," Emily said envisioning what tomorrow would be like with Edwin at her side. She took a deep breath, overcome by all Louise had done. Her happiness erased all her doubts.

When they entered the parlor, the soft blazing fire in the grate gave a glow to the rose-colored room. On one end of the mantle were two silver candlesticks supporting two creamy white candles, and on the other end a beautiful old mahogany clock ticked monotonously, reminding Emily the time she had waited for so long was almost here.

"Come see the dining room," Louise said. She took Emily by the hand and led her into the large room across from the parlor. An ecru lace cloth covered the long mahogany table and hung halfway to the floor. In the center was a large bouquet of yellow roses with two beautiful silver candelabra on each side. "These are the candle sticks Daddy hid from the Yankees when he was just a little boy. Remember?"

"Oh yes, I remember very well. They make the table look grand." She leaned over to smell the yellow roses and thought how perfect the table looked.

Tiny rainbows of colored light danced in the room as the afternoon sun shone through the prisms of the crystal chandelier. Four large silver trays, brightly-polished, were placed on the table waiting to be filled with finger sandwiches, roasted pecans, delicate mints, and *petit fours* covered with smooth white icing. A silver service on the sideboard was ready for hot tea and coffee. Tiny sugar cubes filled the sugar bowl, and heavy cream was chilling in the icebox to fill the creamer.

"I'm overwhelmed, Louise. Everything is so beautiful, really perfect. I hope our marriage will be this perfect," Emily said wistfully.

Louise laughed. "Emily! You know that'll never be. By the way, when will Edwin arrive?"

"He's already at his parents and will arrive about an hour before the ceremony. I'm not sure how many of his family will come, but I'm happy to have most our family here. I'm so glad Eugenia can come, and I'm really pleased that she will play the piano," Emily said. "She'll be coming with Mama and Daddy."

Louise walked over to a swinging door that led to the kitchen. Emily remained by the table still examining every detail of the room.

"Let's go in the kitchen. I want you to see the wedding cake. My neighbor Mrs. Bates made it."

The three-layered cake sat majestically on the table. Its smooth white icing was decorated with delicate yellow-tinted roses, bordered with pale green leaves. "I've never seen a more beautiful cake," Emily said. "How can I ever thank you?"

"I loved doing this, Emily, especially for you. Edwin is very lucky to be getting you for a wife. Besides, you've always been my favorite."

Emily smiled with a glimmer of tears in her eyes. "Mama will love all this."

❧

Emily awoke when the morning light erased the darkness from the room. It was a very chilly March morning. This was her wedding day! She pulled the bed covers up around her shoulders. Her mind was racing with thoughts of being married. I wonder where we'll live. I hope his friends will like me. Her thoughts were interrupted when Louise called her to come down to breakfast. She slid out of the warm feather bed and hurriedly washed her face and hands. How nice to have a bathroom with a tub and toilet inside, she thought. She tied her robe securely in front, slid her feet into her slippers and ran a brush through her hair.

She could feel the warmth of the cook stove and smell the aroma of bacon frying as she came down the stairs into the kitchen. The breakfast table was complete with bacon, eggs and hot biscuits. Hot coffee steamed from the cups in a spiraling aroma, but Emily had very little appetite.

"Are you nervous?" Louise asked.

"Just a little," Emily answered.

"Well, try to eat some breakfast and you'll feel better," Louise advised.

"You sound just like Mama." Emily laughed and sat down. She put a small portion of food on her plate. "I want to show you my dress after breakfast if you have time."

"Oh goodness yes! I can't wait to see it! I'll come up as soon as Elizabeth comes. She is bringing her daughter Mary to help you dress."

A warm, cozy fire blazed in the small grate of the guest bedroom fireplace when Emily and Louise came upstairs. The room was comfortably warm. "Oh, John has made a fire," Emily said. "He's so thoughtful."

"Yes he is," Louise said. "He's a good husband, but don't be fooled. Marriage isn't easy; there'll be some difficult times along with the good. I hope you and Edwin will be very happy." Emily sighed and felt the warmth of the fire. She couldn't tell Louise that she was worried on her wedding day.

"Now, let me see your dress," Louise said. Emily took the dress off the hook on the back of the door and carefully laid it on the bed. She was very pleased with the results of her labor. "Oh my, how beautiful!" Louise said. "Look at the tiny tucks and the lace insertions on the blouse. Are they all hand stitched?"

"With my own fingers." Louise examined closely the leg-of-mutton sleeves with continuous rows of tiny pleats and the full linen skirt that exhibited the same pattern of tucks and lace insertions. A wide white taffeta sash tied in the back flowed to the floor.

"I can't wait to see how it looks on you. How did you make such a beautiful creation?" Louise said and shook her head, running her hand down the soft batiste blouse of the dress.

"I did spend a lot of time, but I really enjoyed making it."

"I've got to get back downstairs," Louise said. "Take your time getting dressed. Maybe a warm soak in the tub will calm your nerves. I'll send Mary up when she gets here."

After Emily was dressed, she pulled her hair up into a loose bun on top of her head, leaving some thin wisps of curls around her face. She pinned the pink cameo pin Edwin had given her for Christmas to the high neck collar of her dress and asked Mary to tie her sash.

The young girl carefully tied the sash and stood back to admire the beautiful bride. "You sho does look nice, ma'am."

"Thank you, Mary. You have been a lot of help, and you've kept me from being so nervous. Now, let me see if everything is in place." Emily turned around several times and looked at herself in the tall mirror that stood in the corner of the room. As she smoothed the front of her skirt with her hands, she wondered if Edwin would think she looked pretty. The clock on the mantle chimed one o'clock, just an hour till the wedding. Wondering if Edwin had arrived, she looked through the narrow opening of the door and saw her family arriving.

Eugenia didn't stop to visit but hurried up the stairs to greet her. "Emily! Emily! Eugenia called. She stopped suddenly when she saw her sister. "Oh," she said, biting her lip. "You look so beautiful. Can I hug you without mussing your dress?"

"Of course you can." Emily put her arms around her sister. "I can't believe you're here. When did you arrive? We were afraid you wouldn't get to come, but you're going to play the piano for my wedding."

"I didn't get here until yesterday afternoon, but I was determined to come. I've missed you. I'm flattered that you think I play well enough. I guess I'd better get back downstairs. We'll talk later. It's nearly time to start," Eugenia said.

Emily watched Eugenia hurry down the stair. She saw her mother and father being seated and the Andersons arriving. She caught a glimpse of Edwin as John Freeman escorted him back to his study. Timothy was seated in a large leather chair. His Bible lay on John Freeman's desk. "Hello, Edwin. How are you?" Timothy asked.

"Oh, I'm fine," Edwin said confidently.

"I would like to go over the ceremony before we go to the parlor," Timothy said.

"All right," Edwin said. He reached inside the breast pocket of his coat, took out a piece of paper and handed it to Timothy. "Here's the license. We can't forget that."

"Oh, yes," Timothy said. "I will have both of you sign it after the ceremony."

Edwin bent down and took a cloth from his pocket and wiped his shoes. He was impeccably dressed in a navy blue suit, and his starched white shirt with a round collar held a blue and white-striped tie. "Thank you for coming to do the ceremony, Timothy," he said.

"I'm delighted. I always like an excuse to come home. Have a seat for a few minutes, and we'll go over the ceremony. I've already gone over it with Emily." Looking straight at Edwin, he said, "Emily's very special to us. I hope you'll be good to her."

"Oh, I will. I will," Edwin said, moving nervously in his chair.

Louise was relieved when all the guests had arrived and Edwin was on time. She hurried upstairs to check on Emily and opened the door barely enough to slip inside. "Turn around, Emily, and let me look at you. Your dress really becomes you. You look beautiful." Emily spun around gracefully. Her skirt billowed and fell just to the top of her white high-buttoned shoes that clung to her slender ankles.

"Here's your bouquet; I almost forgot it. I'm glad we decided on the small French bouquet with the yellow roses. It's perfect."

"Well, I guess I'm ready," Emily said and took a deep breath.

Eugenia sounded the first loud chord of the wedding march and silenced the conversation of the crowd. Edwin and Timothy came in and stood at the entrance of the parlor. All eyes were focused to the top of the stairs where Emily had begun to slowly descend.

When she came down the stairs, Edwin's smile was the first she saw. He's so handsome, she thought. I hope I look beautiful to him. Quickly, she surveyed the crowd and spotted her mother sitting poised and erect in her mauve moiré suit. She had a pleased expression on her face. Mama loves all this fancy goings-on, Emily thought, but I know she's not pleased over my marrying Edwin. Her father's smile was all she needed to erase her anxiety for the moment, and she smiled as she came to the bottom of the stairs to join Edwin.

Emily barely heard all that Timothy was saying. She was relieved when he said, "I now pronounce you man and wife. You may kiss the bride." Edwin held her face with both hands and kissed her lightly on the lips. The room was filled with soft laughter, and sighs of relief from the tension of the ceremony followed. Eugenia began playing the recessional music, and the wedding party moved into the dining room. Emily continued clinging to Edwin's arm.

Lillie stopped Louise as she hurried about making sure everything was in order. "You have really made everything beautiful for your sister, Louise."

"I enjoyed doing this, Mama. You know how I feel about Emily."

"I do hope they'll be happy," her mother said.

"So do I." The words had hardly left her lips when she spotted Emily's glowing face across the room. "Yes, so do I," she whispered to herself.

Edwin was taking some teasing from Emily's brothers as the guests began to leave. "Your troubles are just beginning," Albert joked. Since he had been married several years and had two children, Albert considered himself an authority on marriage. Emily blushed, not knowing what to say.

Benjamin interrupted their folly when he asked, "May I kiss the bride?" Lovingly, he leaned forward and kissed his daughter gently on the cheek. "I hope you'll be very happy, little monkey," he whispered in her ear.

Emily smiled and gave her father a hug. "Thank you, Daddy."

On leaving, Edwin's family congratulated the bride and groom again. Unnoticed, Edwin's father secretly slipped a twenty-dollar bill into Edwin's pocket. Edwin pretended not to notice.

"I must change into my traveling clothes," Emily said. "Our train leaves in less than an hour."

Chapter Nine

New Home

*E*vening shadows outlined the large terminal station in a giant silhouette when the noisy engine pulled into Birmingham. Emily had listened affably to Edwin's stories of his time in the Navy making the two-hour ride pass quickly. With great detail, he elaborated on the sights he had seen and the interesting people he had met. Only when he talked about his family, did she notice a change in his personality, even some hostility. "I'm glad we'll be living in Birmingham, Edwin. Maybe it'll be good for us to be away from our parents. I hope we'll soon have a family and a home of our own." The thought gave her a rush of happiness. She could hardly wait to see their apartment and be alone with him.

Soon the train slowed, and the metal wheels screeched to a jolting stop. When she stood up, Emily noticed that the faded green velvet seats were covered with tiny black cinders from the boiler of the engine. Cautiously, she brushed off her suit with her handkerchief. "It's a good thing my suit is dark blue. Maybe it won't show the spots from the soot. I guess we're ready to get off."

Edwin stood up and brushed off his coat sleeves. "Yes, I believe we're finally here." He took Emily by the hand and led her down the aisle of the passenger car to the outside door.

"Watch your step! Watch your step!" the porter called. Edwin stepped off and assisted Emily. Hurriedly, they walked over to the steps to the terminal waiting area. Edwin put his arm around his bride's waist to climb the stairs to the huge terminal. Emily stood in awe and looked at the huge room filled with beauty and grandeur.

An enormous crystal chandelier hung from a gold painted dome, casting streaks of light on the pink marble floor. The opulence reminded Emily of the magnificent buildings she had read about in Roman history. Carved wooden benches shaped like church pews gave the appearance of a grand cathedral.

She turned to comment on the chandelier, but Edwin was rushing across the room to an empty bench. "Come over here and sit while I get our suitcases," he called. "Then we'll get a taxi to our apartment."

Emily sat down slowly, still overcome by the enormous station and all the people. Where had they come from, and where were they going? She gazed over the crowd of so many different people. Her eyes followed a tall man wearing faded overalls over a white dress shirt with a red tie. He walked slowly across the busy waiting area. Behind him was a very fat woman with four unruly children. Obviously she didn't realize her dress had ridden up in back revealing her stockings rolled just below her knees and tied in knots to keep them in place. Emily felt a note of sadness for an old man whose nicotine-stained fingers held tight the very last of a strong-smelling cigarette. His head drooped and nodded as he almost fell asleep on the bench across from her. Looking down at her wedding ring, she wondered if anyone could tell that she was a new bride. Her cheeks reddened at the thought.

"This is the house. This one," Edwin said to the taxi driver. He pointed to a large colonial house with aged and peeling white paint. The houses on either side were nearly as large, allowing for little yard between them.

When they came inside, the entrance hall was dark and dingy with an ornate staircase made of dark oak. "Our apartment is upstairs," Edwin said. This was once a very grand old home, Emily thought. She hoped Edwin wouldn't see her feeling of disappointment. "I'll take the baggage up if you can manage the stairs."

"I'm fine," Emily said and took hold of the worn banister. Edwin took both suitcases up the stairs to the first door on the right. Emily followed. Nervously, he opened the door and turned on the light.

Happy to see that the sitting room was immaculately clean and adequately furnished, Emily said, "You've made everything awfully nice, Edwin. This is a nice sitting room. We should be very happy here."

"Come see the kitchen," he said. "We have a new gas stove. See, all you have to do is strike a match, and you have fire." Emily smiled at his obvious pride. She noticed that the high ceilings made every room seem larger, especially the kitchen, which was long and narrow. A small table and two chairs placed next to a window gave a clear view of the back yard. "You'll like having running water inside the house, even hot water. Here, put your hand under the faucet." He took her hand and held it beneath the faucet. The warm water felt wonderful to her cold hand.

She looked at him and laughed. "I believe you, Edwin." He took his handkerchief from his pocket and wiped her hand. His tender gesture gave her the feeling she had longed for, proving he really loved her and wanted to take care of her. Her love for him flowed with warmth through her body and a blush to her cheeks, but he didn't seem to notice and turned to show her the door that led to the back hallway.

"We'll have to share the bathroom with the people in the other apartment," he said. "Still that's better than going outside to a privy."

"That'll be fine," Emily said, somewhat embarrassed. Following him into the bedroom, she let her hand glide slowly over the furniture. To think, this is our home and I'm Edwin's wife. Even the dull, worn furniture looked good. She took off her hat and coat while Edwin brought in the luggage.

"Put your things here in the dresser, and I'll use the wardrobe," he said. After he put their suitcases on the bed, he began putting his things away. Emily quickly realized he was very disciplined, neat and orderly. She liked that.

"There's a nice little restaurant down the street where we can have supper, Emily. You can finish unpacking when we come back."

"I'd like to wash my face and hands before we go. Where's the bathroom?"

"Right out this door," he motioned. When she returned, he had removed his coat and tie. "Let's wait to go to dinner," he whispered and drew her close. Slowly he unbuttoned her blouse and kissed her neck. His passionate kiss on her parted lips filled her with a desire never experienced. It was her wedding night and she loved him. An hour later they started down the stair to the restaurant. Emily sighed with happiness from the intimacy of two people in love. Her doubts of Edwin's love were erased.

Chapter Ten

Mary's Birth

Emily turned the bacon in the skillet and felt a dull onset of nausea. Suddenly her stomach was like a simmering pot about to boil over. She ran from the kitchen just in time to get to the bathroom and hung her head over the toilet. Heaving and retching, she felt as if her insides would come out. Gradually the heaving stopped. Bending down over the small sink, she splashed her face with cold water. She felt better.

When she returned to the kitchen, Edwin was seated at the table. "You're expecting already," he accused. He leaned back in his chair and folded his arms across his chest. "You should have been more careful."

Emily sat down, put her elbows on the table and propped her head on her hands. Even now, her throat was tight with nausea, and her hands trembled with weakness. She waited for Edwin to console her, but he offered no sympathy, nor did he reach out to embrace her. Overcome with frustration, she said, "I don't really know what to do to keep from having a baby, but I do want one, and I hope you do." Wiping her tears on her apron, she got up and went over to the stove to finish his breakfast.

Edwin ignored her feelings and changed the subject. "Now, I don't want you being too friendly with the people in the building. I especially don't like that couple across the hall. Just don't say anything to them."

Emily didn't sit down. She stood at the sink and began to wash the dishes. With his last bite of breakfast, Edwin rose from his chair and left for work. When he was gone, she sat down. Her hands still trembled and her nausea lingered. She looked out onto the yard below. New life was blooming all around. It was spring. Moving her hand on her stomach, she felt excitement about the new life she was carrying. Maybe Edwin will change his mind once the baby's here, she thought. I know he must want children. He hasn't said.

After her morning sickness subsided, Emily ate a piece of dry toast and drank a cup of coffee. Feeling better, she went into the living room to write Louise. She sat down at a small table by the window and began to write.

Dear Louise, I hope it's not shameful to be expecting a baby so soon, but Edwin and I are expecting a baby at the end of the year. I'm very happy about it. I hope you will be. I don't know how Mama will feel. Write me. Love, Emily

Louise responded by sending a box of beautiful batiste and lace with a note of how happy she was for them. These lovely pieces must have come from the same shop we bought the material for my wedding dress, Emily thought. She picked up each piece of the soft, pastel material and visualized the pretty baby clothes she could make. Touching the soft fabric to her face, she was saddened by the thought that Louise and John Freeman had no children. She knew they wanted children, and they would make wonderful parents. Here I am just married and already expecting a baby. Some things in life we don't understand, she reasoned. Life isn't planned and packaged as neatly as this lovely material in this box.

It was a month later before she wrote to her mother about the baby, failing to mention that Edwin wasn't happy to become a father so soon and always changed the subject when she tried to discuss it.

☙❧

When Edwin left for work each day, Emily began sewing the baby clothes. On some of the tiny gowns, she embroidered tiny flowers down the front between the buttons, and on others she used delicate lace with some tucks to give the gowns fullness. She was happy when she finished the tiny garments and folded them carefully to be placed in the dresser drawer. Sewing was a way to overcome her loneliness, since Edwin worked long hours and insisted she be careful about being friends with her neighbors. She tried not to think of home, but at times her loneliness was overwhelming. A young woman in her building had talked to her in the hallway several times, but she remembered Edwin's repeated admonition. "Don't be friendly with the people in the apartment. We live too close." But after several conversations with Izora, they became the best of friends.

When Edwin objected to their friendship, she said, "Then why don't you introduce me to some people you know, the ones you told me about before we were married?"

"I'm too busy right now."

The few times she had gone to church, Edwin wouldn't go with her. Soon, she realized he didn't like to go to church, and she felt uncomfortable going alone, especially now that she was expecting their baby. Her thoughts turned to the small church at home. She imagined she could hear the congregation singing on a Sunday morning. Remembering the warm church fellowship made her homesick. Edwin doesn't understand how lonely I am. I can't give up my friendship with Izora, she determined.

స్త్రీ

"I guess we'll have to find you a doctor," Edwin said several weeks after learning of Emily's condition. "I know a Doctor Mitchell whose office is in the business district of Fairfield. You can walk to his office from here. I can't go with you because I can't take time off from work."

"I would like you to go with me the first time."

"I can't go with you, Emily."

Emily turned away from him to hide her disappointment. Suddenly she felt submerged in a chasm of loneliness. She had never been entirely on her own. Taking the corner of her apron, she wiped the tears before they overflowed down her cheeks. Turning around she said with resignation, "I'll find his office if you just give me the directions."

స్త్రీ

The red brick building was right in the center of the business district just as Edwin had said. A polished brass sign on the door read DR. JOE MITCHELL. Emily took a deep breath and went inside. She was greeted immediately by a nurse in a crisp white uniform. "Good morning. You must be Mrs. Anderson. We were expecting you."

Emily smiled, "Yes, I am."

"Please sign your name and have a seat. The doctor will be with you shortly."

Doctor Mitchell stepped from behind his desk and shook Emily's hand as his nurse introduced her. "Good morning, young lady. I know your husband, Edwin, and I'm pleased to meet you." Emily liked him immediately. His gentle, soft manner took away some of her anxiety. After some questions about her health history, Doctor Mitchell called to Nurse White to take Emily into the examination room. When the examination was completed, he turned to his nurse. "When Mrs. Anderson is dressed, she may wait in my office."

"You are expecting," he said to Emily when he came into his office. "I believe your due date will be the last of December. Now don't worry. When your labor pains start, I'll come to your house quickly. You shouldn't have any problems. I'll want you to come and see me once each month until you deliver."

"Thank you, Doctor," Emily said as she was leaving. His encouragement gave her a good feeling, as much as the medicine she needed. She mustn't fear the delivery. He made having a baby seem so natural and easy. Knowing he would be there when she needed him took away some of her anxiety. Later she would laugh at her fear of birthing a baby; rearing the baby was the thing to fear.

When her labor pains began in the early evening five days after Christmas, Emily was glad that her mother was with her. At first, the pains were nearly an hour apart. Slowly, they began to come at closer intervals. "When will Edwin be here?" Lillie asked. "We're going to need the doctor soon."

"He doesn't come home at any certain time," Emily said, grimacing as another pain took her breath. "I was hoping he would be home early today." No sooner than she had spoken, Edwin came into the house.

"Thank the Lord you're here, Edwin," Miss Lillie said. "I think the baby is coming. You need to call the doctor."

"Oh, my!" Edwin said. "I was afraid of this. I'll go next door to use their telephone."

Doctor Mitchell came immediately, just as he had said he would. He placed his black bag on the table near Emily's bed. "You've met my nurse, Mrs. White, haven't you Mrs. Anderson?"

"Yes, sir."

"I'm Emily's mother, Mrs. Whitworth. I guess you already know Edwin."

"Oh, yes, I've known Edwin for some time - met him at the Exchange Club. Quite a talker," Dr. Mitchell said smiling. "You'd best wait in the other room, Edwin. I've found that most husbands can't handle the birthing of babies."

Edwin gave a sheepish smile. "I believe I will."

"Now let's get busy and deliver this baby," Dr. Mitchell said. "I'm going to give you some medicine to lessen the pain, Mrs. Anderson, to make the delivery easier. Mrs. Whitworth, if you'll show Mrs. White where the kitchen is located, she will need some boiled water, a few clean towels, a receiving blanket and clothes for the baby."

In only a few minutes, Emily drifted off into a dreamy sleep, and her pain subsided. Nearly an hour passed before the pain returned. "The medicine is slowing your labor too much," Doctor Mitchell said. Emily looked up at him and frowned as the pain increased. Everyone seemed far away from her. Her hands felt cold, yet there was perspiration on her forehead. "Do you think you can endure the pain a little? If you can, it won't take as long to get this little one delivered, and you won't be so worn out."

"I'll try," Emily said.

Doctor Mitchell placed his hand on Emily's distended abdomen to monitor the baby's movement. "I think it won't be long now. Just take a few deep breaths." As the pain became more intense, Emily held tightly to Mrs. White's hand. "That's right. Just bear down with the pain," Dr. Mitchell instructed. With the last pain, Emily gave a convulsing cry. "Here we are," Dr. Mitchell said. Carefully, he laid the tiny baby on Emily's abdomen and tied off the umbilical cord. "Only a female could cry so loud. I'm not sure she's glad to be here. Maybe, she will calm down after you clean up, Mrs. White. Then her mother can hold her." After finishing the other tasks of the delivery, he patted Emily on the shoulder. "You did very well for a first baby, young lady. Let's call in the daddy and let him see the new daughter."

Edwin came in, hesitantly. Lillie followed. "You have a healthy seven pound baby girl, Edwin," Doctor Mitchell said. "I like to see one strong with a healthy color."

"What will we name her?" Edwin asked. But before Emily could answer, he said, "How about Mary? That was my grandmother's name, and I always liked it."

"I like it," Emily said. She was too weak to express she had wanted to name the baby after her beloved sister Louise.

Lillie came over to the side of the bed. Emily was holding the baby very close, not ready to be separated from the intimacy of the last nine months. "She's very pretty. I think Mary will suit her very well. How are you feeling, Emily?"

"Kind of tired, but I'm glad it's over."

Mrs. White collected the instruments and the small scales. Doctor Mitchell rubbed his eyes, and sighed, "We must be going. I'll leave a few pills here with some instructions, Mrs. Whitworth. The baby should have no problems, and I think Emily will be fine after a week or so of rest."

When Edwin escorted Doctor Mitchell to the door, it was shortly after midnight. "Well a new day is about to begin and also a new life," Dr. Mitchell said. "Congratulations, Edwin."

"Thank you, Doctor." Edwin said and closed the door.

৵৽৻

Since Dr. Mitchell left orders for Emily to stay in bed for ten days, she could only watch her mother take care of the baby. Lillie was careful to explain every detail of the baby's needs. When they talked of home, Emily felt closer to her mother than she had for years. Still, she didn't feel comfortable enough to tell her mother about her disappointments, especially how Edwin was gone so much and never took her anywhere. I guess I keep thinking he'll change, she thought.

Their long discussions of home had been like a soothing balm but left her with a deep yearning to see her daddy. The ten days passed quickly, and Lillie was anxious to go home. "Your daddy will be looking for me soon. I'm afraid he gets lonely since all you children are gone, especially since old Cleopas and Hattie have died. They always gave him a link to the past. He never tires of talking about the old home place, and they were good listeners." After folding the stack of diapers, Lillie put them on the small table by the baby's bed. "I'm going to pack my suitcase while the baby's sleeping."

"I know you must go, Mama, and I'll miss you. You don't know how much I appreciate you coming."

"Now don't be afraid of hurting the baby," Lillie said. "Babies aren't as fragile as they seem. I've written down some of the things to do for her each day." Suddenly Mary gave a strong cry. "Go change her, Emily. You might as well start now."

✺

Lillie put on her heavy coat and tight-fitting felt hat. She was ready to leave. Edwin took her brown tapestry bag out onto the porch. "Come on, Miss Lillie," he called. "I hear the taxi driver blowing his horn."

"I'm coming." Quickly, she gave Emily and the baby a last kiss. "Remember, don't get excited over a little crying from the baby and write to us."

"I will. Goodbye, Mama." Hurriedly she closed the door to a gust of cold wind.

✺

The baby was sleeping in her crib, and Emily was preparing supper when Edwin came in from work. She was glad Mary wasn't crying. Already she knew that Edwin didn't like to hear the baby cry. "Supper is almost ready," she said apologetically. She didn't want the baby to make him feel neglected, knowing he still wasn't happy having a baby so soon. If he would just pick little Mary up and hold her, he would feel more like her father, his own flesh and blood, and maybe he would love her. All I want, she thought, is for him to love the baby and me and to let us love him.

She looked up at him as she put some bread into the oven.

Hoping for an affectionate gesture from him, she moved closer to where he was standing. He picked up the afternoon paper and turned to go into the living room, but stopped suddenly and turned around. "You know having a baby will put a strain on our budget - let alone the way it's crowding us."

Emily couldn't find any quick words to reply until he had left the room.

๛๛

When they sat down to eat, Edwin never mentioned the baby or gave Emily a chance to mention her. She wanted to tell him how the baby had smiled for the first time and how, even though Mary was so tiny, she already showed a determined spirit. But he never gave her a chance to tell him. He talked about his work and the people in his office and complained about some who were trying to cheat him out of customers. Emily listened, wanting to know about his work and wanting to tell him her desire to meet the people he worked with. His success was important to her.

When she rose to clear the table, Emily realized she was still weak from the birth of the baby and the ten days in bed. Her legs felt as if they couldn't support her, and she was tired from lack of sleep. Did Edwin even notice? He had only to look at her to see the dark circles under her eyes and her paleness. She was startled later when he climbed into bed and pulled her to him to make love. She turned away, but he ignored her subtle resistance and continued to pull his body onto hers. Reluctantly, she let go of her fears and clung to a moment of passion to be reassured of his love.

๛๛

"I'm afraid your fears are founded, young lady," Doctor Mitchell said to Emily sitting in his office two months later. "I believe you are expecting again. I don't like to see babies this close together; it's not good for the mother. One good thing, you're strong and seem to be built right to have babies." He came from behind his desk and placed his hand on her shoulder. "Try to find some time to rest each day."

In her embarrassment, Emily could say little more than, "Thank you, Doctor Mitchell, I'll try."

"Come back to see me in a month; give my regards to Edwin."

Emily felt empty as she walked back to the apartment, even though there was another life growing within her. Another baby, what will Edwin say? He's not happy with the one we've got. I know he's already suspicious. I must tell him tonight. Will we have to move? Will I lose Izora, the only friend I've made? Suddenly the blustery, March wind whipped around her full skirt and lifted it up over her knees. "Oh, my," she cried as she hurried along the sidewalk to get home to Mary. Izora was pushing Mary in her buggy. "Are you all right?" Izora asked.

"I guess so. The doctor says I need more rest. Thanks for keeping Mary. I'd better take her inside and feed her." She would tell her friend later about expecting another baby.

ॐ∾∾

Edwin was late as usual. His supper had to be warmed. Emily's heart was racing. I've got to tell him I'm expecting again, she thought. I might as well get it over with. How she wished this moment could be tender instead of filled with tension. Why do I feel so guilty? Edwin wants to make love so often, and he has the only way to keep from having another baby.

ॐ∾∾

During supper Edwin voiced his usual complaints of how everyone was out to do him in. Before Emily could get around to telling him her secret, he retired to the sitting room hidden behind his newspaper. He looked unapproachable in his coat and tie, which he never removed until he went to bed. The dull brass floor lamp gave very little light, and the tall ceiling seemed to engulf that light like a sponge. How could she tell him? Yet she must. She sat down on the worn sofa and gave a sigh.

"What's bothering you?" Edwin asked, putting the paper down in his lap.

"Why do you think something is bothering me?"

"Well, you never sit down in here. You must have something to tell me."

"I do. I'm expecting another baby," she said.

Edwin threw the paper on the floor. "Another baby means

we'll have to find a larger place, and I don't know how we'll afford it."

"Well, the baby won't be here for seven months. Maybe we can find a place that won't cost too much more," Emily said, hoping to stay his anger. Edwin picked up the paper and began reading again as if to dismiss her. She sat there in silence for several minutes, too tired to know what else to say. Finally she said, "I'm going to bed and get some sleep before Mary wakes up." Edwin made no comment. Emily was almost asleep when he came to bed. Surely he won't reach for me tonight, she thought, but she was mistaken.

&~&

"I've found a house down the street; it's a duplex," Edwin said. He was home early. "It has two bedrooms with much more space, and it has a nice yard. Put Mary in her buggy and we'll walk down there and look at it."

The stroll was a delight to Mary and gave Emily a rare feeling that they were family. She was surprised to see Edwin's enthusiasm and also surprised he had picked a house that was much nicer than the one in which they were living. Each side had its own porch, one on the front of the house and one to the side which would give some privacy for sitting outside. A fresh coat of paint gave the house a new look, and a few purple irises bordered the grass beginning to green in the bright sunlight.

"We'll have a private bath," Edwin said. "I hate sharing the bathroom." Emily felt a rush of happiness as Edwin eagerly showed her through the small two-bedroom house. "I have a friend who owns a furniture store, and he said he would give me a good price on some furniture. I'll buy what we need and have him deliver it on the first of the month."

"Then you've decided to rent this place?"

He jerked his head around and said, "Don't you like it?"

"Oh, yes! And I'm excited about having our own furniture." She saw easily he didn't want her to question him about his decisions, but not wanting to spoil his good humor for the day, she said no more.

When they returned to the apartment, Emily left Mary in her buggy and hurried to kitchen to the warm her bottle of milk. She could hear Edwin talking to Mary as she began to cry. "Hush, Mary, hush that crying. It's not nice for little girls to make so much noise. Hush! I said."

"There's nothing slower than trying to heat a bottle," Emily said aloud to herself. When she came into the sitting room, Mary was crying even more, but Edwin had made no effort to quiet her. Emily quickly took her from the buggy to give her the bottle. Immediately, she stopped crying. With the last ounce of milk, Mary's big blue eyes closed, and one single tear rolled down her soft red cheek. She was fast asleep. Emily gave a sigh of relief and put Mary in her crib. She stood quietly for a moment admiring her beautiful child and thinking about the tiny baby growing within her body. I wonder if it'll be a boy... No matter. I know I'll love another baby as much as I love Mary. Oh, how I wish Edwin would love her as much as I do.

She was startled from her thoughts when Edwin called from the sitting room, "Are we going to have any supper tonight?"

"It won't be long," Emily said. "I'll fry some ham and make some biscuits." She knew Edwin liked fried ham with grits and red-eye gravy. Cooking his favorite wouldn't take long, and she hoped it would make him happy.

For the first time in months, Emily enjoyed eating. Finally, her morning sickness had subsided. "You're looking better today," Edwin said, as he finished the last biscuit with a little gravy.

"I'm feeling better." Encouraged, that he had noticed, she thought this would be a good time to talk about the expected baby. "I'll really be glad when we are moved and have a room for Mary. They're so many things we will need - another baby bed and clothes for Mary. She's out-growing all her clothes, but I can use them for the new baby." Emily had no knowledge of their finances. She worried that Edwin hated his work. Could he lose his job? With another baby coming, what would they do?

Suddenly his demeanor changed. He got up from the table, walked to the kitchen door and turned around. "I knew this would happen. I knew another baby would take all I could rake and scrape." He went into the sitting room, never giving her a chance to reply.

Bewildered, Emily began thinking about their conversations. They were not conversations at all, but rather just Edwin's opinions. Reminiscing, she thought how different Edwin was from

79

her daddy. Daddy always listened when I had something to say, especially on current issues. She smiled to herself remembering how he teased and called her "Patrick Henry" because of her speech making. Maybe the reason Edwin never gives me a chance to express my views is because he doesn't want to admit I'm intelligent. I miss Daddy.

Chapter Eleven

Margaret's Birth

Emily stood up, put her hands on her waist and stretched. "Two more boxes to be packed and that'll do it," she sighed. Her back ached, and her stomach felt heavy from the baby due in three months. She had mixed emotions as she folded the beautiful quilt that Bettie Auntie made before she died. She could see her dear aunt now, sitting in the parlor stitching the colorful fabric pieces together.

"This will be yours when you marry, Emily," she had said. She still missed Bettie Auntie and wished her children could have known her.

The white ironstone butter dish her mother had given her must be wrapped carefully. She was surprised when her mother gave it to her. Usually, a gift like that would go to Louise, but her mother had given it to her for a wedding gift. "Take good care of this, Emily," she had said. "It belonged to my mother."

In the last box, Emily packed the fine linens Louise had given her on her wedding day. She couldn't wait to use them. Closing the box, she looked around the dingy room. She wouldn't miss the apartment. Though it had been their first home, it hadn't been a "real" home. The only furniture they owned was the small baby bed which Mary would soon outgrow, but the new baby would need. Edwin had promised to buy Mary a bigger bed. She hoped he would remember.

❧⚘❧

"Thank goodness the sun is shining." Emily raised the window shades to let in the morning sun. This was moving day. She was excited. Izora had offered to keep Mary for the day. Surprisingly, Edwin hadn't complained about her friendship with Izora. I'll miss her, but now I need to feed Mary and cook our breakfast.

When she sat down to eat with Edwin, he quickly ran over his plans. "I'll take the boxes. Mr. Smith, the owner of the house, has offered his truck to move our things to the house. You can come down and unpack them."

Emily was beginning to see that Edwin was completely in control and expected her to do just as he said. "I'll walk down there as soon as I get Mary settled," she said.

When Emily arrived at the house, she was astonished to see that every room was freshly painted the same color. Even the cabinets in the kitchen were painted the same color. When Edwin brought the first boxes into the bedroom and put them on the floor, Emily remarked about the fresh paint. "Oh," he said, "I had a hard time convincing Mr. Smith to let me paint everything the same color. Don't you think it makes everything seem clean, like a freshly-polished apple? It's apple green, the color we had on board ship in the Navy."

"It does look nice and clean. I didn't realize you had painted the whole house. I like it," she said, stretching the truth and wondering if her opinion mattered. "I'll start unpacking in the kitchen."

There were seven boxes placed neatly on the floor in the kitchen. Not knowing what was in them, she bent down to open the first one, too heavy for her to lift. After removing the paper wrapping at the top of the box, she saw it contained dishes, very heavy white dishes, like the ones used in a restaurant. She laughed to herself when she saw the thin green stripe around the edge of the plates, cups, saucers and even soup bowls. "I don't believe you could ever break one," she said under her breath. The second box was filled with very heavy plain drinking glasses. Emily gave a sigh of despair, remembering Edwin's words, "Like we had in the Navy." Maybe, he wants our house to be run like a ship, she mused.

"Pull up to the porch," Edwin shouted to the men in the truck.

Emily went out onto the porch, anxious to see what he had bought. Two seedy looking men emerged from the cab of a white truck with "Spencer's Furniture" written in yellow on the side of the door. They removed a large canvas covering tied down over the furniture. The bedroom furniture was removed first. Looking closely, Emily saw that it had a dull veneer, the kind seen in every cheap furniture store window, unlike the fine furniture that she had become familiar with in her father's furniture store. Perspiration fell from the faces of the two men like soft pelting rain as they lifted a heavy green velvet sofa and matching chairs from the truck. "Oh my," Emily sighed.

Edwin moved about excitedly giving orders like a captain. "Be careful with the lamps. Oh," he said turning to Emily, "Mr. Spencer, the owner of the furniture store, gave us the lamps since I bought so much furniture."

Emily smiled, trying to hide her bewilderment and hurt because he hadn't asked her opinion on anything. Finally, they removed a table she approved - a dark oak, drop-leaf table. She watched for a few more minutes, anxious to see what else the two malodorous men would take off the truck. When they removed a shiny white table with four chairs, she directed them to the kitchen. The chairs are pretty, she thought - even feminine with spindled backs, held together at the top by a scalloped piece. "I like these," she said to herself. "The white will break the monotony of the green paint. Maybe some ruffled white curtains will shut out some of the afternoon sun."

She was relieved when she heard Edwin tell the men, "You'll be through when you get the baby bed."

After unpacking in the kitchen, Emily went into the bedroom. Edwin was bringing in the last box. She was aware he was proud of all his purchases. She sat down on the side of the bed, looked at the furniture and the freshly painted walls. For the first time since they married, she felt proud of their home. This was a tender moment for her, a new beginning. "Are you too tired to put your things away?" he asked.

"No, I was just taking time to look around the room. Everything is so clean and new. I'm so happy we have our own furniture."

"Well, we don't own it yet. I'll have to pay for it in monthly payments."

He leaned against the bed post a moment and looked at her rounded swollen stomach with disdain. "You can use the dresser and hang your dresses in the small closet."

Emily got up and went over to the dresser and began putting her things in the top drawer. "I like this place, Edwin. I hope we'll be happy here."

He didn't turn around to face her but continued putting his things away. "You should be happy with everything new."

Emily smoothed her things in the drawer and stood silent. His words erased the happy moment just experienced. She closed the dresser drawer and walked to the door. "I've got to go and get Mary." Edwin said nothing.

"Sit down a minute," Izora said. "You know the doctor told you to get some rest every day."

"Maybe I can sit for a few minutes." She was exhausted from the heat, all the lifting and reaching, but more from the disappointment that Edwin always held her at a distance. Would they ever be a family?

"I'll miss you and Mary. Ya'll are the only bright spot around here."

"You'll have to come down and see us. We're only three blocks away." Emily treasured Izora's friendship because she was the best friend she had in Fairfield. She was surprised Edwin liked her also. Oh, Doctor Mitchell was her friend and although Edwin's age, he seemed older. He was her doctor and friend. Emily pushed her tired, heavy body from the swing. "I must be getting back. We still have a lot to do. Thanks for keeping Mary."

"I'll put Mary in the buggy. Look at her. She's so pretty."

"Bye, Izora. I must go. Edwin will be waiting."

↾↽

October came too soon for Emily, and her labor pains began earlier than she had expected. Edwin began to prepare for the delivery before Doctor Mitchell arrived. Remembering that boiling water was needed, he put a large pot on the stove and placed plenty of clean linens beside the bed. "Looks like you have everything ready," Doctor Mitchell said when he arrived. "You might have to help me some, Edwin. Mrs. Anderson is ready to deliver now. Mrs. White will be along shortly. Don't be afraid of a little blood; it represents life itself."

The delivery was quick and the baby's cry was loud. Emily closed her eyes and breathed a sigh of relief. Doctor Mitchell took a soft cloth and wiped her brow. "You almost had this one too quickly, young lady, but she sounds like she's ready for the world with that cry."

Emily smiled and weakly remarked, "I'm glad you got here in time." She watched Edwin as he cleaned the baby up and wrapped her neatly in a soft receiving blanket. She thought she saw a glimmer of affection as he held her for a moment before placing the baby at her side.

"I've sent word to your mother. She should be here by this time tomorrow," Edwin said.

Doctor Mitchell's nurse will come and stay until your mother gets here."

Emily smiled. "Thank you for helping, Edwin." How she wished he would kiss her or make some gesture of affection. She could see that Doctor Mitchell was watching and wondering if Edwin would make this a tender moment, but he turned and walked to the door to usher Doctor Mitchell out.

"My nurse will be here shortly," Doctor Mitchell said. "By the way, Edwin, it wouldn't be a good idea to have another baby as close as these two."

Edwin appeared a little embarrassed. "I agree, Doctor. I agree."

ॐॐ

Lillie arrived early the next afternoon. She had hardly removed her coat before she busied herself with the needs of the baby and Mary. She refrained from making any comment on how pale and tired Emily looked knowing Emily was embarrassed for her to return so soon for another birth.

Edwin put her things down in the baby's room. He bought a twin bed for that room and was anxious for Miss Lillie's good opinion of their new place. Emily noticed her approval was very important to him. Perhaps, he was somewhat unsure of her favor. "Do you like our new place?"

"It's very nice, much more room than the other place."

"Oh, yes, and all the furniture belongs to us."

Lillie took another look around. Emily wondered what she

thought of the green paint throughout. She knew her mother would never voice an opinion about the monotony of it.

"Let me get a good look at the new baby," Lillie said, coming closer. "What did you name her?"

"Margaret Ann. I have always fancied the name Margaret, and Edwin liked it too."

"It is a pretty name, but I hoped you would name her after Louise."

"I'll name the next one after her." She never imagined she would have another baby in less than a year.

"Don't let that be too soon!" Edwin gave a nod of approval. Lillie could already see he wasn't interested in the new baby, and he was quick to scold little Mary.

≈≈

"Come sit down for a few minutes, Mama." Emily propped herself up in bed with pillows behind her. "Let's enjoy a moment's peace while both the babies are sleeping. Pull the rocker up close. I want to hear how Daddy's doing, and what do you hear from Louise? Are they expecting a baby yet? What do you think of Eugenia's fiancé? Will they marry soon? I guess I'm full of questions. I don't get enough news from home."

"Oh, your daddy's fine, but he's getting a little stiff with arthritis," Lillie said, settling comfortably in the wooden rocker. "He works too hard and has very little help. Louise and John Freeman are still hoping to have a baby. Maybe they'll have one soon. Louise tells me, they both want a baby."

Emily slid down a little farther in the bed, hanging onto every word of news. Anxiously she asked again, "And what of Eugenia?"

"I don't think we'll have a chance to meet Eugenia's fiancé anytime soon. They'll marry in Chicago."

Their conversation was like a delicious meal to Emily, warm and delightful, even reminiscent. "I miss Daddy and Louise," Emily said, heaving a deep sigh. Do you realize it's been over a year since I've seen them?"

Lillie studied Emily's comments, sensing Emily wanted to tell her something more and wondering how to continue their conversation. She smoothed her apron on her lap and fingered her wedding ring. "You are happy here with Edwin, aren't you?" she asked.

Emily hesitated. "Yes, ma'am," she said, not daring to tell her mother how Edwin shut her out of so much of his life, and how she sometimes felt she was just his bed partner.

"You mustn't have another baby anytime soon. There's something more to life than having babies. Speaking of babies ... I think I hear Mary now."

̂≻≺́

After her mother had gone, Emily found it doubly hard to regain her strength. There was a constant demand from the babies, and there was always that feeling that she never pleased Edwin. She always hoped their making love would draw them closer, yet so many times she was left with a feeling of being used. She fantasized about Edwin coming home and taking her in his arms in a warm embrace and then greeting the babies with a kiss. Her love for Mary and Margaret kept her from dwelling on her disappointment with Edwin. He was late coming home so much of the time, explaining that many of his sales had to be made at night. She never knew if his sales were good. He certainly worked long enough hours, they should be good.

If I could just talk to Timothy, maybe he would tell me how to approach Edwin about our finances. He wouldn't believe Edwin never gives me a penny or even lets me buy the groceries. I must talk to Edwin about some clothes for the babies. I can't put it off any longer. Suddenly she realized baby Margaret was crying. "And more diapers, I must have more diapers," she said reaching for the last clean diaper in the basket.

̂≻≺́

Emily chose an evening when Edwin seemed in a good mood to approach him about clothes for the babies. She waited purposely until after supper, and the babies were asleep. She sat down on the sofa and said, "Edwin, I must buy a few things for the children."

Slowly he put the newspaper down and looked up from his reading. "What do you need?"

"Some diapers. You know we have two in diapers now, and

87

Mary has outgrown almost all her clothes."

"Well, all right. You can go down to Ruffner's, a dry goods store. I'll tell Mr. Ruffner you're coming in, and I'll pay him later. But don't buy too much. Ruffner's is on this side of the street, about ten blocks west. You can't miss it."

❧❦

"I won't be gone long," Emily told Izora. She handed her the baby along with her diapers and bottles for feeding.

"Don't you want me to keep Mary, too?"

"Oh, no, I can push Mary in the buggy and then use the buggy to carry my packages. Mary will enjoy the ride."

The walk to Ruffner's was pleasant. The air was cool, and the smooth sidewalks made the buggy glide along like a sailboat on water. This was Emily's first time to be out of the house since Margaret was born, and the walk reminded her that she still wasn't as strong as she would like to be. The azure blue sky was a perfect background for a few brilliantly colored leaves that still clung to the trees. A feeling of liberation flooded her heart and filled her with exhilaration toward the Lord her Maker, a feeling she hadn't felt in months. It was difficult to find time to pray each day, but in this rare moment she thanked God for her precious daughters.

Slowing her walk, she read each sign on the windows of the stores. She had no trouble finding Ruffner's. The name was written in bold black letters edged with gold on both sides of the storefront windows.

The door of the store reminded her of the door to her mother and father's house - carved wood at the bottom and leaded glass at the top. Inside, she found a very friendly atmosphere. A very nice-looking gentleman quickly approached her.

"Good morning, ma'am. I'm Mr. Ruffner. May I help you?"

"Well, yes. I'm Mrs. Edwin Anderson. My husband said he would tell you that I was coming in to make some purchases."

"Oh, yes, he comes in often. In fact, he's one of our best customers."

Strange, Emily thought, I haven't seen anything he's bought. She looked away trying to hide her disbelief. "I need mainly clothes and diapers for our babies."

Mr. Ruffner led her to the back of the store. As she followed him, she saw a large counter filled with carefully stacked monogrammed linens, then another with the latest styles in women's shoes, and still another with silky under garments in the new shorter lengths. Ladies dresses were neatly arranged to catch the shopper's eye, and Emily took note of them all. The buggy made very little noise as she pushed it along on the wide, plank pine floors. A smell of "new" penetrated her nostrils, enticing her desires for nice things for herself and for the babies, but she remembered Edwin's last words to her, "Don't spend too much." She picked the cheapest clothes he had for Mary, not even looking at the more expensive ones. She added a dozen diapers to the order, wishing for two dozen. A soft pink baby blanket finished her purchases.

"Are you sure Mr. Anderson wouldn't want you to buy our better quality?" Mr. Ruffner asked. "He always buys the best."

Startled again, Emily assured him, "Oh, no, this will do fine. Children grow so fast, I'd rather buy the less expensive things."

"Very well," he said, packaging up her purchases.

Emily was puzzled as she left the store. What had Edwin bought? She looked down at her packages, things she so desperately needed for the babies, but not one thing was for herself. How she would have loved some new underwear and a stylish pair of shoes. "Isn't it a pretty day?" she cooed to Mary, who had awakened as they moved along the sidewalk. The exhilaration she had felt on the way to the store was now replaced with the knowledge of Edwin's deception.

She didn't mention to Edwin Mr. Ruffner's remarks about his frequent visits to the store or his purchasing the best quality of goods. Instead, she decided to look in his wardrobe the next morning after he had gone to work. She had never looked on the side of the wardrobe where he hung his suits, only on the drawer side where she always put his shirts after ironing and folding them. As she pulled the hangers forward, she counted one, two, three, four, five suits. Taking the first one out, she examined it carefully, then the second and on to the last. They were the finest money could buy. When she looked down at the bottom of the wardrobe, she saw three pairs of polished black shoes, almost like new. Heart sick and betrayed, she sat down on the side of the bed. Why she asked, why would he spend so much on himself and complain about the needs of the children? Putting her hands to her face, she bowed her head and prayed. "Lord, help me to understand Edwin, and let me be grateful for what I have. Please teach Edwin to share with me and the children." She stood up and closed the door of the wardrobe.

Chapter Twelve

Cruelty Revealed

Dark clouds concealed the morning sun and emptied in heavy showers. It wasn't the rain that awakened Emily, but the all too familiar twinge of labor-pains. She waited a few minutes before disturbing Edwin. The rain mimicked her labor pains, starting sporadically at first, then building to a heavy repeating rhythm. "Edwin, I think the baby is coming."

Edwin turned over and looked surprised. "What time is it?" He turned on the light and squinted at the small alarm clock. "It's five o'clock. I hate to call Doctor Mitchell so early."

"I believe you'd better call him now." She took a deep breath as her pain increased.

∂∽⳹

Soon after Doctor Mitchell arrived, a third baby girl was born. After the nurse had cleansed the baby with oil and wrapped her in a white receiving blanket, she tenderly gave her to her mother. Lovingly, Emily pulled the blanket back and counted the tiny toes and fingers of her newborn. As she ran her hand over the baby's legs and arms, she noticed she wasn't red like Mary or Margaret had been when they were first born. Her soft cap of hair held a slight tint of auburn, and her dark blue eyes were crowned with perfectly shaped eyebrows. "She's a beautiful baby," Emily said. "I think we'll name her Laura."

❧❦

The rain had stopped, Doctor Mitchell had gone, and the reality of having another baby in less than three years flooded Emily's thoughts. *How can I ask Mama to come? She's made it plain she doesn't approve of me having babies so close together. Somehow I feel I've done something wrong.* In her dilemma, she decided to take the advice of Doctor Mitchell and hire a woman he had recommended. Much to her surprise, Edwin agreed. "I'll talk to Doctor Mitchell and arrange for the nurse to come tomorrow. I'm surprised that her fee is so reasonable."

❧❦

A few weeks after the new baby's birth, Edwin complained to Emily, "You aren't careful. Look at your sister Louise. She's been married much longer than we have, and she has only one child."

Emily turned around from the sink where she was washing baby bottles. "She's wanted children for as long as I can remember. She'd like to have more, but it just hasn't happened."

"Humph!" Edwin murmured. He got up from the kitchen table and left the room. Emily took a deep breath and let go of her tears of frustration, tears hot as the dishwater on her hands. There was no need to argue with Edwin. If he didn't get the last word, he would just leave the room.

❧❦

On her next visit to Doctor Mitchell, Emily decided to ask him what she could do to avoid having another baby. Waiting in his office after her examination, she nervously twisted her handkerchief around her finger and shifted her feet back and forth.

"Now, young lady, do you have any questions?" Doctor Mitchell asked before he sat down behind his desk. "You really seem to be healthy for someone who's had three babies so close together."

"I ... I wanted to ask you what I can do to keep from having babies so often." She put her head down and moved nervously in her seat.

Doctor Mitchell rubbed his eyes with his fingers. "There's not much you can do, but Edwin knows what to do. Of course, abstinence at certain times of the month helps. That time is about two weeks after you have had your menstrual period." He paused a minute and looked directly at her. "Would you like for me to talk with Edwin about this? It is obvious he isn't abstaining."

Emily could hardly answer. She felt her face flush with redness. She looked down hoping he wouldn't see her embarrassment. "No, I'll tell him. I'll tell him what you've said."

As she got up to leave, Doctor Mitchell said, "You take care of yourself, and remember, no baby next year."

࿇

Even at three years of age, Mary showed signs of independence. She loved being out of doors, and Emily was glad for her to enjoy the warm April sunshine. The new baby, Laura, was only four weeks old, and Emily's help was gone. There were bottles to sterilize, diapers to wash, and Margaret was crying for attention. Emily didn't notice that Mary had climbed up, opened the gate and gone out of the yard. Suddenly, she heard Mary screaming. She ran to the door and was shocked to see Edwin had a long switch he had broken from a bush next to the house whipping Mary unmercifully.

"How many times have I told you not to go out of your yard, Mary?" His anger was evidenced by his repeated thrashing of Mary's legs. He dragged her, screaming, down the sidewalk.

When they came into the kitchen, Emily put her hand up over her mouth and gasped. Mary's legs were marked with bloody whelps. "She's too small for such a whipping, Edwin. She's only three." Mary's loud cries caused Margaret to put her arms around Emily's legs and cry; then the tiny baby joined in the pandemonium.

"I've told her over and over again not to go out of the yard, and she just won't mind." Roughly Edwin picked Mary up and pushed her into her highchair.

Emily felt like crying too, but she knew she mustn't. Instead, she took Mary into the bedroom with the other babies and tried to talk to her. Holding her and Margaret on her lap, she sat close to the baby bed and patted the tiny baby until she was asleep. Soon there was silence. Mary was asleep. Emily laid her gently on her bed,

93

then took Margaret into the kitchen and gave her some building blocks to play with on the floor. She took some vegetables over to the sink and began washing them for the evening meal. Only then did she release the tears she had held back for weeks and even months, tears from anger and frustration she felt towards Edwin. Why, she wondered, must I keep the children away from him. I'm so tired, and I think I hear Laura crying. I must change her diaper and feed her before I call Edwin to the supper table. After feeding Laura, Emily put Mary into her chair; then she took Margaret on her lap to feed her. She could hardly hold back her anger as she watched Mary hold her head down ignoring the food on her plate.

"Eat your food, Mary," Edwin scolded.

"I'm not hungry," she said defiantly.

"Well eat anyway." He wouldn't look at Emily. He ate quickly and left the kitchen. Emily couldn't eat either. The red marks on Mary's legs made her heartsick. The only thing I want, she thought, is sleep.

ð∽ô

Later she hardly recognized herself in the mirror as she pulled her long white gown over her head and ran the brush through her hair. The dark circles under her eyes, accentuated by redness, revealed her feelings. Edwin made no mention of how tired she looked when he came into the bedroom. She lay down feeling the comfort of the bed. Her body ached. When Edwin pulled her close, she knew he intended to make love.

She turned to face him. "I'm worried about us having a baby so soon, Edwin. Doctor Mitchell said, 'If we didn't make love so often, we might not have so many babies.'"

"Are you telling me you don't want my love? Doctors are for delivering babies, not for telling husbands when they can have sex with their wives." Angrily he turned his back to her and relented for the first time since they had married.

ð∽ô

With each passing winter and the blossoming of new growth of spring, a new baby was born each year to the Andersons. Eddie was the fourth child and then Jonathan.

After the birth of the sixth baby, Daniel, Edwin realized they needed a larger house. Emily liked the house he found - the neighbors were nice and a Baptist church was nearby, close enough for her and the children to walk to church. The new house had a large dining room where they could all sit down together for the evening meal. A bedroom for her and Edwin and two more large bedrooms for the children would be sufficient.

The routine of daily chores never ended for Emily. She was busy from early morning until all the children were asleep - still she found happiness with the children, watching each one as they learned to walk and to talk. She was fascinated to see them playing together, using their creativity with hardly any toys, but completely content. Still, she was saddened that she hadn't seen Edwin show much love for them. He was only quick to correct them and whip them for the smallest provocation. She wasn't sure now if he had any love for her. He showed no tenderness in their love-making. She would still welcome his kisses, but their intimacy only included his satisfying his passionate desires, and she wondered if he ever thought another baby would be the outcome.

જ્જ

It was in the early morning of April 10, 1929, when Henry was born. Frowning with concern, Dr. Mitchell said, "He's not as strong as the other children." This was Emily's seventh child in just eight years. All his advice to Edwin had fallen on deaf ears. He admired Emily's indomitable spirit. She had never complained to him about having so many children. Quite the contrary, he saw her strong love for them. "Take a little extra care of this one, Emily, and yourself," he said, leaving.

"I will, and thank you for everything." Emily smiled beneath the fatigue of the delivery.

જ્જ

On the evenings that Edwin came home early, the house took on a different atmosphere. The stock market crash caused him to worry about being able to buy enough food for their large family. The very presence of the children seemed to irritate him. Most of the time, his greeting to them was "Fade to the background." They knew what he meant and wasted no time scurrying out of sight.

"Don't you ever clean up this house?" Edwin nagged. Obviously he was more irritated than usual when he came into the kitchen where Emily was washing dishes. She didn't answer but dried her hands and walked to the living room. Looking around at the untidy room, she was too tired to care until now. Coats and sweaters littered the chairs. A few tattered storybooks were spread on the floor beside Laura's rag doll. The hearth was covered with ashes, and a few pieces of coal had spilled from the coal bucket. Looking at Edwin, she recalled he had recently been elected the best-dressed man in the Exchange Club. At this moment, to her he wasn't even handsome. He stood there in his blue surge suit with matching tie and white starched shirt in complete authority like the captain of a ship. She remembered the tedious time she spent ironing his shirts. Until now, she hadn't thought about how she looked in her housedress slightly wet in the front and in her well-worn shoes. Her eyes moved to the sofa where the children sat, afraid to move; each one was dressed in handed down clothes from their older sibling. Their shoes were scuffed and worn almost through on the soles. I guess they would be naked if it weren't for the clothes Louise sends them, she concluded.

Turning to Edwin she said, "Henry is sick, and I haven't had time to pick up." Slowly the children began to slip out from the room.

"Mary! Margaret! Laura! Get back in here - right this minute!" their daddy shouted. Margaret and Laura turned around and quickly came back into the room, terrified of what their father would do. They knew if they didn't hurry a whipping would follow. Mary came in slowly in obvious defiance. "I want this room cleaned, and I want it done right now," Edwin warned. Margaret and Laura began to pick up the coats and sweaters. Mary took the broom and started to sweep. "Sweep the hearth, too, Mary," Edwin commanded. When Mary reached down to pull the iron guard out that kept the ashes from spilling, Edwin began to curse. He pushed Mary aside, angrily took the small black shovel from beside the fireplace and filled the empty coal bucket with the ashes. Hurriedly, he took the bucket of ashes outside, emptied it and filled it with coal. His wrath erupted in a profusion of curse words when he realized that the coal pile had dwindled. Was it because of the continued cold weather, or had someone stolen some of it? he questioned. When he came into the house, the living room was neat and silent. Once the grate was filled with the shiny black coal, the fire began to blaze and quickly warmed the room. Satisfied, he sat down to read the evening paper.

৵৶

Later, Mary and Margaret began in silence to set the table for the evening meal. Emily pulled a stack of white damask napkins from the old oak buffet in the dining room. Hoping to divert their thoughts from Edwin's outburst, she said, "Let's use these napkins - the ones Aunt Eugenia sent us." She remembered Eugenia's note that came with her gift. *"Teach the children how to use a napkin. You know how important table manners are to Mama."*

Mary carried the heavy dinner plates into the dining room, and Margaret followed with the silverware. "Put the fork on the left of the plate and the knife and spoon on the right," Mary instructed. "No! Not like that. Put the knife next to the plate. Don't you remember how Grandma showed us?"

"You don't know everything Mary. I'm going to ask Mama," Margaret argued.

"Well get another glass while you're asking her. We need one more."

"Mama, does the knife go next to the plate?" Margaret asked.

"Yes, that's right."

Margaret frowned when she saw Mary laughing behind the dining room door. "We need one more glass, and I don't see another one, Mama," Margaret said.

"Oh, just use a jelly glass. Goodness knows, it doesn't matter. We break them so fast."

Frying the salmon patties was second nature to Emily. Often, they were the mainstay menu for the evening meal, along with boiled potatoes and corn bread. Edwin bought the groceries, and Emily cooked what he bought. Canned salmon was cheap, she had observed from the price on the can. Several times she had asked Edwin to let her buy groceries, but he always gave an excuse. With every decision, he wanted to be in complete control.

When they sat down to dinner, the three girls could sit comfortably in the chairs, but Eddie and Jonathan could hardly reach the table. "Can't you eat without getting your food all over you, Eddie?" his daddy asked. Eddie looked up with no answer. His eyes were wide with fear. "Wipe your brother's mouth, Laura!" Laura took the big white napkin and wiped her little brother's mouth, then pulled his chair closer to the table. "Look at you, Jonathan. You have more food on the table than on your plate. It'll take more than white napkins to teach these younguns any manners," Edwin said and shook his head in disgust.

Mary looked at her daddy with no expression. "Can we leave the table now? We're through eating."

"Yes, go on." Quickly the children went to their rooms. As Emily began to stack the dishes, Edwin announced, "I've found us another house with much lower rent. It's on the other side of town, not as populated as Fairfield, but a better place to raise this brood of yours. Emily knew that the Depression had its grip on everyone, but she hadn't expected this change. They had lived in this house for nearly two years, and she liked the location. It was close enough for the two older girls to walk to school and only a few blocks to church, where the children could go to Sunday School. She had longed to go to church but was either expecting a baby or taking care of a new born.

"I really like living here," she tried to say, but was interrupted by Edwin.

"Mr. Fuqua, the man who owns the house, will take us to see it tomorrow."

❧❦

Emily watched the black Model T Ford stop at the front of the house. A short, fat man bounded quickly out of the car. His dark suit fit snuggly over his round protruding belly, and his dark felt hat hid his baldness until a gust of wind blew it off his head. "Look, Mama, he's got a mustache," Mary said. "He must be Mr. Fuqua."

"Shush, Mary. Help me get the children together. We're going with Mr. Fuqua and your daddy to look at the house that I was telling you about."

After all the children were jam packed into the back seat of the car, Emily and Edwin crowded into the front seat with Mr. Fuqua. Emily held Henry on her lap. When the hot breath of the ten passengers began to fog the windows, Edwin took his handkerchief and wiped the windshield. "Your children are well-behaved," Mr. Fuqua said. The crowded automobile moved along, hitting bumps and potholes along the way, making the children snicker and giggle.

"Thank you," Emily said.

"I don't have any children," Mr. Fuqua said, wistfully. "You're really fortunate." Edwin continued wiping the windshield and didn't reply.

After what seemed to Emily a very long ride, Mr. Fuqua stopped the car in front of a small wood-frame bungalow that sat very close to the gravel road. The house wasn't very old looking, yet it begged for another coat of paint. A sparse patch of grass covered the very small front yard. Anxiously, the children jumped out of the car and ran up onto a wide porch extending across the front of the house. Emily noticed that there were only two houses close by. Seeing her disappointed look, Mr. Fuqua said, "There's a dairy over that hill to the west. A very nice family lives there with several children." Emily looked in that direction but could see nothing other than a rugged pasture.

Edwin walked ahead of Emily onto the porch. As she started up the steps carrying the baby, Mr. Fuqua took her by the arm. When he unlocked the door, the children rushed inside invading every room. "Where's the bathroom?" Mary asked.

"Oh, it's outside," her daddy said. "Like your mama and I had before we moved to town. You'll get used to it. You children will have to help your mama bring in water from the outside hydrant." Emily shivered from the cold wind blowing through the cracks around the windows in the poorly constructed house. Surely Edwin doesn't intend to move us into this house, she anguished.

Walking through the house, she saw that it wasn't very old, just shoddily built. The wallpaper in the sitting room had little design or color giving the appearance that someone had tried to cover up poor workmanship. There was no dining room, and the kitchen wasn't large enough for them to eat together. It would be hard to get used to a coal burning stove again, since she had been cooking on a gas stove. She gave a deep sigh when she saw the sink had no running water.

"We'll move in the first of December," she heard Edwin tell Mr. Fuqua. Emily slowly walked down the narrow hallway that led to the bedrooms. "How can we live here?" she sighed. For the first time, she thought of leaving Edwin, but where would we go? Who would take me in with seven children, or who would take care of them for me to teach school? No one in her family could do that. Henry began to fuss, and she put his head on her shoulder to quiet him.

"Mama!" Mary yelled, when she and the other children came in the back door. "The bathroom is a little house in the back yard like the one at Grandma's."

Edwin grabbed her by the arm and pointed her to the front door. "Get in the car now, Mary, and take the others with you. I told Mr. Fuqua we would take the house, Emily." Mr. Fuqua looked down and rolled his hat around in his hand. Neither of them looked at her.

She knew, arguing with Edwin would do no good. "Well, let's go. Henry is beginning to fuss."

The ride home was quiet. Only the hum of the motor could be heard. When the children saw the stern look on their daddy's face, they knew to be quiet. Soon Henry began to cry. Emily turned him over on her knees and patted him on the back. I guess he's hungry, she thought. I didn't know we would be gone from home this long. I didn't know the house would be this far from Fairfield. Finally, the car came to a stop in front of their house. Emily hurried inside to make Henry a bottle; the rest of the children followed behind. "Are we really going to move to that house, Mama?" Mary asked.

"That's what your daddy has decided," Emily answered with resignation.

"But …

"Not now, Mary. I've got to feed Henry."

When Henry was quiet and asleep, Emily went into the kitchen where the children were playing near the warm stove. "Y'all be quiet, and don't wake the baby."

"I don't see how I can manage with all these babies in a house with no running water," Emily told Edwin the next morning at the breakfast table.

"You'll have to," he said. "It's all we can afford."

"You know it's only a month until Christmas. Couldn't we wait until January to move?"

"No, I told Mr. Fuqua we would take the house next week." Without another word, he got up from the table and left for work.

❧

It was one of those rare sunny days in December, with the temperature already reaching seventy degrees, when the truck pulled up to the porch to move the Andersons. The sky was a cornflower blue and the air was still. I'll have to keep the children out of the way, Emily thought. When the two men got out of the truck, Edwin began giving them instructions about the furniture. "You girls bring out the boxes and set them on the porch," he shouted to Mary and Margaret.

After everything was loaded onto the truck, Emily walked out onto the porch and gave one last look down the street. Suddenly, she realized that she hadn't told any neighbors she was moving, not even Izora. Perhaps, she was ashamed to tell them where she was moving or too depressed to care. This house wasn't large, but it had been adequate. All the children had been born here, and they had been happy when Edwin wasn't there. She looked at him now, ordering the men around. Do I even know him? Maybe he's doing the best he can, but that's hard for me to believe.

Inside again, she took one last look at the kitchen and the gas stove that had been a lifesaver when she had so little time to cook. How can I go back to cooking on a coal-stove? she thought. As she walked out onto the small back porch followed by the children, she paused and let her eyes take in the peacefulness of the backyard. The old chinaberry tree, barren of its delicate leaves, stood like a faithful friend. "Goodness knows, you children have spent some time playing under that old tree."

"Why do we have to move, Mama?" Mary asked.

"Yeah, why do we, Mama? Why?" the other children asked.

"Because your daddy says we can't afford to live here any longer."

"Are ya'll ready to go?" Edwin shouted. "We can't stand around here all day."

Emily gave a deep sigh. "Come on, children. We must go."

Chapter Thirteen

Edwin's Illness

Emily had never lived in a house as small and primitive as this one. She found it impossible to keep any of the rooms other than the kitchen warm, and with no running water inside, there was no way to bathe the children every day. She never remembered life being this difficult when she was growing up. There was no sympathy for Edwin as he worked frantically trying to fit their furniture into the small rooms. How can he expect us to live in such a deplorable situation? I know we can afford better. Cooking meals on the coal stove was never ending and left her with barely enough time to take care of the children. To add to her frustration, Edwin expected the children to be quiet when he was at home. Often, she saw him punishing them with a whipping, when he told them to do something but never gave them time enough to do it.

❧❧

When they had been in the house only one week, Edwin surprised Emily by coming home early one afternoon. Without saying anything to her, he took off his coat and sat down in the sitting room. Emily wiped her hands on her apron and went into the living room. Edwin was sitting motionless in his chair with his head bent down on his chest. She was shocked to see that he was very ill. His face was flushed, and his breathing was labored. Hesitating a moment, she reached down and touched his hand. "Edwin, you are burning up with fever." Quickly, she withdrew her hand and clasped it to her chest. She was alarmed. Her memory flashed back to Bettie Auntie before she died with pneumonia. Edwin had the same symptoms. "Why didn't you tell me you were sick this morning?" Emily said.

"I didn't think you cared." He coughed uncontrollably and leaned his head onto his hands.

Emily shook her head in despair. "Is that how you feel? Do you think that I don't care if you're sick? Let me get the thermometer and take your temperature." Her thoughts were racing as she rushed into the bedroom. Surely, he doesn't think I don't care if he dies. I hardly have time to think, trying to live in this house with seven children and no running water. As she picked up the thermometer, she thought of Doctor Mitchell who had given it to her. What would I have done without his help all these years?

When she came back into the living room, Edwin was mumbling something about a cow and some chickens. He must be delirious, she thought. "Here, Edwin, let me put the thermometer in your mouth." Anxiously, she waited. One hundred four the column of mercury registered on the tiny glass instrument. "We must get you into bed and call Doctor Mitchell. I can go to our neighbor, Mrs. Henson's, and use her phone. She's offered her telephone if I should need to call anyone." Emily liked Mrs. Henson's openness and warm gentle manner from the moment she met her and felt that theirs was a friendship from the start. After getting Edwin into bed, she said, "I'll hurry there and call Doctor Mitchell."

"Mary," she called, "your daddy is very sick. Watch the baby and the other children, while I go over to our neighbor's house to call the doctor."

"Yes, Ma'am," Mary answered.

As she rushed out of the house, Emily slid her arms into her coat. Her heart was pounding. The thought occurred to her that Edwin might die. She knew her marriage was dying, but she couldn't think of Edwin dying. The cold wind made her face sting as if her skin was being pricked by hundreds of tiny needles. She breathed gaspingly through her mouth until her lungs began to burn, her lips cracked with dryness and her eyes watered from the fierce cold. It wasn't easy to walk on the gravel road - the rocks beneath her feet felt like marbles.

Breathless, she stepped up onto the Henson's porch and began knocking on the door. She could see Mrs. Henson through the small windowpanes of the door. "I need to use your telephone," Emily said abruptly when Mrs. Henson opened the door. "My husband is sick and I need to call the doctor."

"Come in. Come in. The telephone is over there on the table."

Even in her anxiousness, Emily took in the beauty of the room. Though the light was dim, she could see that the furniture was very fine, and the rosy tones of the sofa and chairs blended well with the floral rug. A mixture of delicious aromas coming from the kitchen permeated the room, and the blazing fire in the grate made the house seem homey and cheerful. "It must be very cold out," Mrs. Henson said.

"Oh, yes, It's very cold." She reached into her pocket and pulled out a crumpled piece of paper. Her hand trembled as she dialed the number for Doctor Mitchell. "Could I speak to Doctor Mitchell?" she asked.

Doctor Mitchell listened patiently as Emily told him of Edwin's sickness. "I'll come as soon as I see the three patients here in the office - in about an hour. Get him into bed, and be sure he's kept warm."

"Thank you, sir," Emily said.

Tears of relief clouded her eyes when the doctor said, "Don't worry - we'll take care of him."

"Is there anything I can do?" Mrs. Henson asked.

"No, I don't think so. But thank you for the use of your telephone. I must hurry home."

Walking as fast as she could, Emily took little notice of the cold air. As soon as she was inside the house, she went straight to the bedroom where Edwin lay. Seeing that he was in great pain and his breathing was even more difficult, she lifted his head higher on the pillows. "Doctor Mitchell will be here soon, Edwin." But he seemed not to hear her or even respond as she pulled the covers up around his shoulders. Fear and pity griped her heart as she looked at him - fear that he might not live, and pity that he had never enjoyed the children or shown them any love. It was hard to know just how she felt. At the moment, she knew she must do all she could to help him get well.

Suddenly, she experienced an abundance of energy. She picked up the children's toys from the living room floor, filled the small grate in the fireplace with coal and added more coal to the cook stove to prepare supper. As soon as she finished feeding the smaller children, the doctor and his nurse arrived.

"I'm so glad you've come. Edwin is here in the front bedroom."

Doctor Mitchell took one look at Edwin and pulled the covers back to listen to his breathing with his stethoscope. "Help me set him up, Nurse White." Holding Edwin up caused all the color to drain from his face. Emily put her hands up over her eyes. She couldn't look. Slowly, she moved her hands away. Doctor Mitchell turned to her and said, "Just as I feared when you called. He has pneumonia and in both lungs. I've brought some medicine. We'll give him the first dose now, and I'll leave instructions for tonight with Nurse White. He'll need a nurse until he improves. Now let's see if we can get his fever down."

Emily was relieved Nurse White was staying. Edwin was gravely ill, and to take care of the children was all she could do. As he was leaving, Doctor Mitchell placed his arm gently around her shoulders. "I'll come back in the morning to check on him and bring another nurse. Don't worry." Seeing the anxious expression in her eyes, he assured her, "Nurse White knows how to take care of the sick, and she'll call me if his condition worsens."

"Thank you, Doctor Mitchell. You are a blessing to our family."

After the doctor left, Emily pulled the small rocker from the living room to Edwin's bedside. "I hope you will be comfortable here, Mrs. White. I'll sleep in the room with the children. If you need anything, please call me."

"That'll be fine. Now don't you worry; I'll take good care of him."

Quietly, Emily left the room and went into the kitchen where Mary, Margaret and Laura were sitting at the table examining every page of the Sears Roebuck Catalog. Mary held the heavy book and turned the pages. When she came to the section on dolls, Laura said, "Oh, I wish I could have that doll."

"Wait, I'll show you what I want," Mary said, quickly turning the pages - "roller skates."

"Mama, make her turn back to the dolls," Margaret argued.

Mary held her hand tightly on the page. "Will Santa Claus come this year, Mama?"

"We'll see, Mary. I can't think about anything else now. Your daddy is very sick." When she saw the sad expressions on the children's faces, she realized Christmas was less than three weeks away, and she had no money. She had never been able to count on Edwin - sometimes he would buy a few toys, and other times he would buy nothing, not even fruit and candy. She felt overwhelmed and breathed a silent prayer, "Please, Lord, let Louise send a package."

"Eddie," Emily called, "you and Jonathan will have to sleep on the chesterfield tonight. Your daddy is sick, and I will have to sleep in your bed."

"Oh, boy, we get to sleep on the sofa, Jonathan," Eddie said.

"Well, I'm glad you're happy to give up your bed. It makes things easier for me. Now remember, you mustn't make a lot of noise. Come on, Jonathan, you can sleep on one end and Eddie on the other end."

When the children were in bed, Emily looked in on Edwin. "How is he?" she whispered.

"His fever has come down some but not to normal," Nurse White whispered. "He is resting now." Emily could see he was struggling to breathe, and his face was very red. "Try not to worry, and get some sleep. I'll call you if there is any change."

The night was long, and sleep came in bits and pieces. She could only think of how Bettie Auntie looked and how her breathing sounded before she died. Edwin had that same look and that same labored breathing. Would he die? What would they do? Even with his mean spirit, she didn't want him dead. But she realized her hope for being a normal family was dying, and her feelings for him were changing each day. There were no answers. Her only resource was prayer. If she prayed, relief would come. In silence, she called upon God, and a few hours of sleep descended like a shadow.

Before starting a fire in the stove, Emily went outside to fill the coal buckets. She felt sick at her stomach when she saw the coal pile. There's just enough coal for one day. Quickly, she scooped the last lumps into the bucket. What can we do? I must write to Louise for help.

Nurse White was washing her face and hands in a small basin of water from the kettle on the stove when Emily came into the kitchen. "Oh let me help you."

"Thanks, but I'm used to this chore. It's an all-day struggle," Emily said. She put the bucket down, rubbed her cold hands and took a deep breath. "How is Edwin this morning?"

"He's still very sick. I'll be glad when Doctor Mitchell gets here."

After adding some coal to the banked fire in the stove, Emily washed her hands and followed Nurse White into the bedroom.

Edwin lay still; his face was ashen, and his labored breathing was his only movement. Emily tiptoed closer to the bed. When she saw the concern on Nurse White's face, she knew he was in grave danger.

☙❧

It was a typical cold winter morning with a gray overcast sky that held back any rays of sunshine. Doctor Mitchell arrived early, with him a kind-looking, middle-aged woman dressed in a starched white uniform. "This is Mrs. Hoffman. She's one of the best nurses you'll find. How is our patient this morning?"

"Not much better, I'm afraid," Emily answered. "I'm so glad you're here."

"The bedroom is down this hallway, Mrs. Hoffman," Doctor Mitchell directed.

"I must get the children fed," Emily said, excusing herself. They were up and ready for breakfast, fighting for their mother's attention. Henry was crying with his diaper wet, Jonathan and Eddie were pillow fighting on the sofa, and Margaret was whining because she couldn't find her clothes. Fortunately, Emily had already cooked some oatmeal, still warm on the back of the stove. Quickly, she dished up the oatmeal for the older children and tended to Henry. When she returned to the bedroom, Doctor Mitchell was pouring a thick yellow medicine into a spoon for Edwin. The smell reminded Emily of the sulfa springs she had known as a child.

"This is what we call a miracle drug, Emily," he said. "He needs a miracle. He's not out of the woods yet. The sulfa should begin to take effect soon." After closing his bag, he walked over to the doorway where Emily was anxiously watching. "I have some things in my automobile Mrs. Mitchell has sent to you and the children. I think she has the Christmas Spirit early. Then turning to

107

Mrs. White he asked, "Will you help me bring in the gifts?"

Emily was standing in the kitchen holding Henry when they returned. Daniel held tight to his mother's skirt, and the other children's faces lit up with excitement as Doctor Mitchell and Mrs. White put four large sacks of groceries on the kitchen table. Emily smiled and wiped a quiet tear from her eye with the corner of her apron. The sweet smell of fresh apples drifted into the room, and the children could hardly contain their eagerness to open the bags. "How can I ever thank you?" Emily said, shaking her head in gratitude.

"You just take care of yourself," the doctor said noting her tiredness. "You have a lot of folks depending on you. We must be going, Mrs. White. I'll come back tomorrow."

Since Doctor Mitchell had brought some groceries, Emily's problems didn't seem to weigh as heavily now. The peppermint stick candy delighted the children, and the makings for a fruitcake delighted her. After the children were fed and dressed, she sat down to write Louise. Without sounding too desperate, she tried to describe her situation; with Edwin's sickness and Christmas a few weeks away, the difficulties seemed insurmountable. She took her last stamp and wet it with her tongue. After placing it on the envelope, she took it to the mailbox to be picked up in the day's mail. When she was returning to the house, she saw Mrs. Henson, wearing a soft blue coat and green scarf around her head, walking on the road. I wonder if she's coming here. I hate for her to the messy house. I haven't even had time to make the beds. When Mrs. Henson got to the edge of the yard, she called, "I wanted to see how your husband is today."

"I'm afraid he isn't much better. We have a nurse with him, and the doctor has already been here today. Won't you come in? It's so very cold."

"I'll come in for a few minutes."

Emily opened the door. "Let's sit here by the fire." She moved the chairs a little closer to the blazing fire.

"I wanted to see if I could help you in any way. I was wondering if you had enough coal. I know we've used a lot lately, but I bought some yesterday, and we have plenty to share. You can return it when your husband gets well."

God does provide, Emily thought, like Mama said so often.

"That would really help," Emily said. "We're almost out."

"I'll send some milk and butter from the dairy too," she said smiling. With the dairy, we always have plenty. One of our workers will bring the coal and the milk and butter. I hope your husband is better soon. I see you have your hands full." She smiled when the children came into the small sitting room.

"Yes," Emily said, laughing. "We have plenty of children."

As she was leaving, Mrs. Henson touched Emily on the shoulder. "I hope you have a Merry Christmas."

"Thank you. Thank you so much and Merry Christmas to you."

ॐॐ

"I wonder if we'll ever have a sunny day again," Emily said to Nurse White as they changed the sheets on Edwin's bed. Grey skies had lingered all week along with the bitter cold. Emily dreaded the thought of Mrs. White leaving at the end of the week. She had noticed that Edwin's temper had worsened as his strength and appetite returned. During the weeks of his illness, he had never asked how she was managing to buy food.

"Would you like a cup of coffee, Mr. Anderson? Maybe it would warm you up," Nurse White said. Carefully, she pulled a blanket around his shoulders. Emily had noticed she never lost patience with him, and he loved the attention she offered him.

"Yes, I would like a cup of coffee, but make it hot. I don't like lukewarm coffee."

"It is hot, Edwin," Emily said. "I just made it." She picked up the dirty sheets and left the room with Mrs. White following. "Well he's finally better," Emily said. "He's beginning to be ornery."

Mrs. White laughed. "Never seen a man yet who was a good patient. Maybe he can go back to work soon. A sick husband and a house full of children are more than anyone should bear." Emily wondered how much Mrs. White had noticed about her and Edwin's relationship. It was obvious to her that Edwin, even in his illness, cared only for himself, and she wondered if Mrs. White saw his selfishness.

ॐॐ

Four days until Christmas, Emily counted as she looked at the calendar hanging on the kitchen wall. Edwin was well enough now to sit in the rocker in the bedroom for a little while every day. The nurses were gone. How will we ever pay for all of this and what will we do about Christmas, she thought? No package had arrived from Louise. She always sent gifts for everyone. She walked into the living room to add coal to the fire. The Christmas tree the children had cut from the woods stood woefully in the corner of the room - a crooked pine with a few ornaments hanging on its sparse limbs. A garland of popcorn encircled the drooping branches like tattered lace on an old dress. Looking at the tree, Emily thought of the happy Christmases she had known as a child; the tree Cleopas had always cut and the wonderful cakes and pies her mother and Hattie had baked. Her thoughts were interrupted by a loud knock at the door. When she opened the door, the postman shouted, "Mrs. Anderson, I have a large package for you, and I need some help to carry it inside."

"Oh, my goodness," Emily said. Before she could call the children, they came running to the door from the kitchen. "The postman needs some help getting a heavy package inside. Mary, will you and Margaret go out and help him?"

"Come on, Come on, Margaret. Let's go see who it's from," Mary shouted.

Emily watched as they brought in the huge package. "Why, it's from Chicago. It's from Eugenia." All the children gathered around the package with excitement. For a moment Emily forgot all about Edwin and joined the children in their eagerness.

"Can we open it, Mama? Can we?" Mary asked, already tearing the outside paper.

"All right," Emily answered, savoring the happy moment. Inside were brightly wrapped presents for everyone. Each had a name tag attached and was tied with a pretty red and green bow. "Let's put them under the tree until Christmas Day, but we can open this one that doesn't have a name on it."

"Cookies!" The children shouted opening the box. Some of the cookies were shaped like stars, some like Christmas trees and wreaths, and all were decorated with red and green and white icing. Magically hidden beneath the cookies were three large sticks of red and white peppermint candy. Looking at all the cookies, Jonathan said, "I want a star."

"I want a tristmas tree," Daniel cried, reaching inside the box.

"All right, you may each have two cookies. I'll have one myself. Mmmm, they're really good. Eugenia always makes delicious cookies." She put the top back on the box and wrapped the paper around it. "Let's save some for Christmas Day. Now, I need to go and see about your daddy."

Edwin was sitting in the rocking chair with a blanket over his lap. His eyes still looked weak, and his face was as pale as his nightshirt. Emily could tell that he had lost considerable weight. "What's all the commotion about?" he asked.

"Eugenia sent us a Christmas package with gifts for everyone."

"Well, no wonder they're happy. They sure can't expect anything from me this year."

Emily walked around to the other side of the bed straightening the covers. She didn't want him to be aware of the disgust on her face. He had rarely bought them anything for Christmas, but this wasn't the time to mention his neglect.

❧❦

The next day another large package arrived with the mail. Emily helped the postman get the enormous box inside the house. This one was from Louise and included a letter with a five-dollar bill inside. Emily quickly pushed the package into her bedroom before the children saw it. "These are gifts from Louise," Emily told Edwin. "I'm keeping these from the children till Christmas Day."

Edwin looked up from the paper he was reading. His weakness was like a cloak. His hands trembled, and his coughing seemed to take all the strength he had. "Humph," he said and returned to his reading.

Emily made no comment and went into the living room and sat down to read the letter from Louise. Louise explained she had waited to send her package in order to include some fresh fruit and pecans. Reading the letter made Emily long to see her sisters and brothers. Christmas is a time for renewal of family ties, she thought. I wonder if Mama and Daddy will be alone this Christmas. If Edwin would do his part, our Christmases could be as happy as ours were when we were children or at least as happy as mine were. It isn't necessary to spend a lot of money; just a toy or two would make the children happy. But more than gifts, we need his love. I'm afraid his love will never be a reality. After reading the letter, she put the five-dollar bill back in the envelope, went back into the bedroom and laid it on the dresser.

"Would you like to come into the living room, Edwin?"

"I guess."

"Then, take hold of my arm." Edwin pushed himself up by the arms of the chair and took hold of Emily's arm. This is the first time since we married, I remember him needing me, she thought. She could tell he hated his weakness, his dependency on her.

When they came into the living room, the children were sitting around the Christmas tree, trying to guess what their package contained. "Don't bother mine," Jonathan cried.

"I'm not touching yours," Eddie argued and gave his little brother a push. Suddenly, he saw his daddy and shrank back in fear. No one said a word. They watched with uneasiness, as their mother helped Edwin into his chair by the fire. They hadn't seen him since his illness and looked at him in dismay.

"I'm not up to any of your loud arguing," Edwin said.

"Maybe you should go and play in the bedroom," Emily said. "Your daddy still isn't feeling well," Emily said.

Margaret hesitated a minute, "I'm glad you're feeling better, Daddy," she said shyly and ran to join her brothers and sisters.

Emily sat down in the chair across from Edwin and told him about the groceries Mrs. Mitchell had sent and how generous Mrs. Henson had been able to loan them some coal. "With the gifts from Louise and Eugenia, we will have a very nice Christmas," she said. She didn't tell him about the five dollars Louise had sent. She had plans to use the money for their Christmas dinner, and with the rest she would buy coal.

"I'm not thinking about Christmas this year," Edwin said. "I need to go back to work soon or we won't be able to eat. Right now I'd better go back to bed until supper." Emily reached out to help him, but he quickly said, "I can manage by myself."

Suddenly, she was overwhelmed with loneliness and rejection. Hadn't his illness taught him anything? Wasn't he grateful for all that had been given to them? Didn't he know how much she wanted them to be a family sharing and caring for each other? She left the room feeling completely disheartened.

⤞⤝

Even in her unhappiness, Emily felt some relief. There was enough coal until she could buy more, enough money for a hen and maybe something extra for their Christmas dinner. The vegetable truck would come tomorrow, and she would buy a hen. Then she would send word to Mr. Boyd at the coal yard to deliver a ton of coal. Now the house would be warm on Christmas Day. There were gifts for the children, and she would make the meal special. She hoped Edwin could return to work soon. He's really fortunate to have a job when many others don't, she deliberated.

"Mary," Emily called, "you and Margaret need to go out and get some water. Henry is crying, and Daniel is fussing because he's hungry. It was difficult for the girls to carry the heavy buckets of water, but she must prepare supper.

Finally, the children were fed and in bed, and Emily had time to make an egg custard. Mrs. Henson had sent more heavy cream and even some eggs as a Christmas gift. After taking the large white enamel bowl from the cabinet, Emily mixed the sugar and flour, beat the eggs and poured them into the heavy cream. To give flavor to the mixture, she added a little butter and vanilla like she had seen her mother do many times. When all the ingredients were blended, she cooked the custard, stirring to make a smooth consistency. As she stirred, she glanced over at the fruitcake on the shelf. A sense of contentment came over her. When the custard was cooked and cooled, she put it in the icebox. The small tin box on top of the icebox reminded her of the twenty-five cents for ice. That'll be enough to buy ice for several more weeks, she calculated. She felt very tired, but a good, tired feeling enveloped her.

When she came into the bedroom, Edwin was sleeping soundly. The light from the hall gave enough light to see the letter on the dresser. She tiptoed across the room and picked up the white envelope. She wanted to read it again before going to bed. The fire in the living room was dying but still gave enough warmth for her to sit a minute. When she opened the letter, disbelief gripped her heart - the five dollars was missing. Maybe she had dropped it. She rushed into the bedroom and stooped down to run her hand over the floor – the money wasn't there or on the dresser. She looked in the hall and on the living room floor.

Edwin has taken it, she thought. He's the only other person who's been in the bedroom. She felt anger and despair, then disgust that he would stoop so low. She sat down by the fire and stared at the dying coals. I will not let him get by with this, she determined. I must confront him, but I'll have to wait until morning. She could hardly bear to lie beside him. The bed offered no rest until exhaustion overtook her.

Emily awakened early on Christmas Eve to a cold house and the cold reality that she must confront Edwin about the five dollars. She wondered if he was pretending to be asleep. He must know I'm upset with my tossing and turning all night. In the kitchen, she hurried to start a fire in the cook stove. Henry will be awake and wanting to be fed any moment now, she thought, and I must warm his milk. When she finished feeding Henry, she wrapped him in his blanket, put him in his bed and went into the living room to start the fire. Soon the chill was gone from the house, but not the chill in her heart for Edwin's shameful act. There was no time to think about it now; the children must be dressed and fed. Their excitement over Christmas was contagious. She felt it herself even in all her difficulties.

"Will Santa Claus come tonight, Mama?" Eddie asked.

"If ya'll are good today, he'll come," Emily said.

"Will he really come?" the older children shouted.

Emily smiled, "Yes, but there's much to do and I'll need your help. Mary, you and Margaret make the beds. Eddie, you and Laura watch the smaller children while I clean the house. Now let me take your daddy some breakfast."

When Emily entered the bedroom, Edwin was dressed. "Would you rather eat in the kitchen?" she asked. She put the tray down on the small table by the bed.

"No, I'll eat in here," he said, quite out of breath.

Emily walked over to the dresser and picked up the letter from Louise. "Louise sent me five dollars in this letter, and now it's missing. Did you take it, Edwin?"

"Why do you think I took it?" He continued eating the eggs and biscuits without looking at her.

"Because, you and I are the only ones who've been in this

room, and you know it."

"I know I've got to go back to work next week, and I'll need that money." Unrepentant, he stirred the cream in his coffee and refused to look at her.

"I had planned to buy a hen for our dinner tomorrow with that money and a ton of coal next week." Her voice trembled as she tried to control her rage toward him. "Our neighbor, Mrs. Henson, loaned us some coal and I need to return it."

"Well, she'll just have to wait till I go back to work," he said, dismissing the subject as he usually did.

Emily's eyes clouded with tears. She didn't like the feeling of hatred filling her heart. She had never hated anyone, and she must not hate Edwin, the father of her children. Pulling her apron up to her face, she dried her eyes. I don't want the children see me crying.

"We'll get by," she sighed to herself. "Somehow, with God's help, we'll get by."

ॐ

You could set your clock by Mr. Wade's vegetable truck, and Christmas Eve was no exception. Emily looked at the small clock on the mantle. It was exactly nine o'clock. When she heard the chug of the old truck's engine and the loud continuous ringing of his cowbell, Emily knew he was coming up the road. She had hoped this would be a day she wouldn't have to let him pass by. Suddenly, she remembered the ice money on top of the icebox. Opening the tiny box, she began to count the change... five, ten, fifteen, twenty, twenty-five cents. She put the money in her apron pocket, quickly grabbed her sweater and ran out to wave down Mr. Wade.

The old, green truck came to a jolting stop, and Mr. Wade climbed slowly down out of the cab. As always, he chewed on the stub of his corn cob pipe. "Mornin', Ma'am," he said, smiling.

"Good morning, Mr. Wade." She stepped up inside the truck and began looking at the dressed hens hanging in a row by their feet. "How much are your dressed hens?"

"Seven cents a pound - would you like one? They were freshly dressed this morning."

Emily looked at each one, wondering if she had enough money, and if Mr. Wade sensed her dilemma. She pointed to one at the end of the row. "See how much this one weighs."

"Four pounds, exactly," he said. "That'll be twenty-eight cents." Emily opened her hand and looked at the twenty-five cents. "Twenty-five cents will do for today since it's Christmas," Mr. Wade said, smiling.

"Thank you, Mr. Wade." She was warmed by his kindness and generous spirit.

He tipped his hat. "Merry Christmas to you, Ma'am."

Emily smiled. "Merry Christmas to you, Mr. Wade."

ھۇ

A cold rain began falling in the afternoon after Emily finished cleaning the house. Since the children couldn't go outside, Emily decided to open the box of fruit and nuts Louise had sent. "You all can take some pecans and crack them on the hearth if you'll be careful not to make a mess …and throw the shells in the fire."

"I want a tangerine," Mary fingering the fruit..

"I want an orange," Laura shouted.

Jonathan eyes clouded with tears. Sensing his timidity, Emily reached down and put her arm around him. "Would you like to share an apple with Eddie?"

"Yes, mam, I like apples."

Happy to hear him talking made Emily happy. Even at four he didn't make many sentences. Of course, he has plenty of competition with Daniel, who never stops talking, she thought.

When she cut the big, red delicious apple, the aroma filled the warm kitchen with a sweet fragrance. Jonathan's eyes lit up when he took the piece of apple from his mother and savored its taste. "We must not forget to thank Aunt Louise for the fruit," Emily said.

While the children were busy eating the treats, Emily slipped into the bedroom to open the package from Louise. Edwin was sitting in the rocker and didn't look up from his reading. Emily stooped down, pulled the box from under the bed and opened it. There were three beautiful dresses for the girls, two sets of coveralls for Eddie and Jonathan, and two soft blue smocked rompers for Daniel and Henry. At the bottom of the box was a pretty blue print dress with a lace collar for her and a white dress shirt for Edwin. Louise is so kind, she thought. If only I could see her and John Freeman, I know I would feel better. "Louise has sent some very nice gifts," she said to Edwin and she pushed the box back under the bed.

"Good," Edwin said. "I hope they make you happy."

"Well, the gifts will certainly make our Christmas happier."

After supper Emily sat down in the living room with the children and began to tell them the Christmas story from the Bible. They listened anxiously as she told them about Joseph and Mary going to Bethlehem and about the birth of Jesus. They could hardly sit still long enough for Emily to finish the story. "What's a manger?" Laura asked.

"It was a box which held the hay for the animals to eat," Emily said.

"Why was he born in a stable, Mama?" Eddie asked.

"Don't you remember; the stable was the only place they could find with room for them." With every question, the children got louder, forgetting their daddy until he came into the living room and sat down, but he didn't scold them, and Emily was relieved. Soon, she must get them to bed. There was so much she had to do before going to bed. After the children were in bed and asleep, she went to her bedroom to get the packages from under her bed. Quietly she laid each gift from Louise on the sofa, along with the children's gifts from Eugenia. She put a stick of peppermint candy with each child's presents, filled a large bowl with fruit and nuts and placed it on a table by the sofa. Her body ached with tiredness, and she hurried to slip into her gown and get into bed. Thinking that Edwin was asleep, she turned on her side away from him and pushed her pillow comfortably under head. As soon as she closed her eyes, he startled her as he reached over to make love for the first time since he had been sick. She didn't respond, yet he continued his pursuit, fulfilling his desires and filling her with disgust. In only a few minutes, she heard him breathing in a deep sleep. It seemed hours before she could go to sleep. As always, she felt used and not loved, and as always she worried about having another baby. Morning came quickly. She was awakened by the children opening their gifts in joyous laughter.

Christmas Day was more peaceful than Emily had hoped for. Edwin was congenial and even talked with the children, not reprimanding them as usual. When she put the last bowl of food on the table, she stood for a moment admiring her creation with satisfaction. The hen was a golden brown accompanied with steaming gravy. She had managed to save the sweet potatoes that Mrs. Mitchell had given her. The butter and cream Mrs. Henson had sent added richness to the sweet potatoes and the egg custard. There was enough corn meal in the cupboard to make cornbread dressing like her mother always made, though it hardly measured up to her Lillie's recipe. Seeing Edwin and the children enjoying the meal brought a rare sense of fulfillment for all the work she had done to make this a special Christmas.

When she and the girls finished washing the dishes, they went into the living room by the fire. How could Eugenia have known the kinds of toys the children wanted? Maybe there is a Santa Claus, she thought. With a smile she watched the children playing. Laura clung to her doll with golden curls, and Daniel sat on the floor fascinated with his little metal train on a circle of tracks. Margaret's tiny tea set suited her perfectly, and Mary was able to play a semblance of "Silent Night" on her miniature piano. Eddie and Jonathan played endlessly with their little toy. Henry lay in his bed holding fast his soft, brown teddy bear as he slept. Christmas is a wonderful time. This is the most peaceful time we have had in months, Emily thought. She ran her hand over the skirt of her new dress and admired its beauty.

"Do you have a new dress, Mama?" Margaret asked.

"Yes, this is my gift from your Aunt Louise."

"You look very pretty."

"Thank you, Margaret. This has been a good Christmas. Louise and Eugenia have made us all happy."

Chapter Fourteen

A Christmas Baby

Emily looked out the window above the kitchen sink. January claimed a beauty unlike any of the other winter months. Heavy frost covered the fields, and a smoky mist veiled the trees in a distance, but the beauty of the morning couldn't erase her bitterness. To her relief, Edwin was returning to work, but with little food in the house and the coal pile dwindling, she wondered how they would make it through the day. I guess Edwin will leave for work, get some breakfast and go to a warm office, not carrying what we'll do, she thought. She called to him as she heard him leaving. "Edwin, you know we have no food. There's little or nothing here to eat and hardly any coal to heat the house."

"All right, I'll stop at the A&P this afternoon and get groceries, and I'll order some coal from Mr. Boyd this morning. You can manage until then, can't you?" She heard him close the door, not waiting for her answer.

"I guess we'll have to," she sighed. "But what will we do for today?" Maybe I can get some bread from the milkman and pay him next week. She pulled her sweater tighter around her shoulders, but she could still feel the cold wind that whipped through the cracks of the dreadful house. January had started off cold and had remained cold. The frigid air seeped in through every crack like flooding water. Mary and Margaret were back in school, but the other children were underfoot and always hungry.

Since Edwin had promised to get some coal, she decided to use all they had for the day. She buttoned her sweater and hurried outside to fill the scuttle, just enough to get the stove hot and to warm the kitchen. I was right, she thought, there's about two more buckets full. After adding the coal, the stove was warm enough to heat some milk for milk toast for the children. She would get more milk and bread later from the milkman. Finally the room was comfortable, and Henry had stopped crying long enough for her to wash out some diapers.

"Where has the morning gone?" Emily sighed. "There's the postman already." Laura looked up at her mother and continued playing with her new doll as she sat at the kitchen table. "I'll hurry out to the mailbox, Laura. Maybe there will be a letter from your grandmother." When she opened the mailbox, the letter lay against the cold metal like a gift from heaven. She quickly opened it. Miss Lillie never forgot the children's birthdays. Enclosed was Mary's birthday dollar and a five-dollar bill.

"Give Mary her birthday dollar. The five dollars is for you," her mother wrote. *"Lord knows you need it."* Emily ran back into the house and read the rest of the letter. Now I can stop the vegetable truck and have ice money too. "Thank you, Lord," she uttered. She felt warmer even before she filled the grate in the fireplace. Soon, the coal blazed brightly and quickly warmed the room. If Edwin doesn't order some coal, I will. I won't let him know about the money Mama has sent, or he'll find some excuse to take it. With the extra money, she was reassured that she could depend on her family to help her when Edwin wouldn't. God can always be trusted to care for us, Emily declared in her heart.

In the early spring, Emily saw something that she hadn't noticed before - an apple orchard in the field across the road from their house. The trees were in full bloom with soft white blossoms edged by a touch of pink. "Come see the pretty trees," Emily called to the children. "All those pretty flowers will make apples to eat." She reached down and picked Jonathan up to look out of the window.

"When can we have some?" he asked

Emily laughed. "It'll be a while before the blossoms are apples, just about the time when summer ends. That field must belong to Mr. Henson. Maybe he'll give you an apple when they're ripe."

"I'm going outside to look at them some more," Jonathan said. Emily walked to the door with him and stood several minutes, transported by the beauty and by the memory of the apple trees on her father's farm. Perhaps if we could get some running water in this house, living here wouldn't be impossible, she thought. Maybe after Edwin gets settled at work, he'll be more agreeable, and life will be better. Her hopes were dashed a few days later when she realized she was expecting another baby. She looked at the calendar on the kitchen wall and tried to figure when the baby would be born. If she counted right, the baby would be born on Christmas Day. Could this be a special baby? What will Edwin say? His approval no longer mattered. Her worry was where to put a baby in this tiny house. She gazed out the window at the beauty of the apple trees again, trying to understand why God was giving her so many children. Deep within her soul, she trusted that things would work out and life would eventually improve.

సౌ

When the soft blossoms fell from the apple trees and the spring rains drenched the soft plowed earth, everything seemed to turn green overnight. The warm days made it possible for the children to play out of doors. These could have been happy days with some relief for Emily, but Edwin had other plans. He hired a man to plow the vacant lot next to the house for a large garden and demanded that the children help plant it and weed it.

"Don't you think the children are too small for such hard work?" Emily asked. "Mary is only eight and the others even younger. Can't we get the Negro man who did the plowing to help?"

"Don't you see that I'm trying to make ends meet, woman? I worked in the garden when I wasn't much older than they are. It won't hurt them."

Emily breathed a sigh of despair. As always, Edwin seemed to win the argument. A few days later, as she watched him and the children in the garden, she couldn't believe her eyes. He was making them pull the small hand plow as he pushed it deep into the soil. If they complained, a whipping would follow. Day after day, she watched their fear of him grow, and her hope began to die. She saw no solutions, no way out of her situation, but still she couldn't bring herself to tell her family about his treatment of her and the children. How could any of them take her in, with seven children and another on the way?

❧❧

On her first visit to Doctor Mitchell, she wondered if he noticed that she was troubled. She wanted to tell him how she felt, but how could she? What could he do? "I guess I'm just tired," she said, when he asked if something was wrong.

"Well, I'm very concerned about you," he said. "Your blood pressure is up. I'm afraid you aren't taking very good care of yourself. I know it's very hard with so many children. Is there anything else you would like to tell me?"

Emily looked up at him. Tears didn't come as easily now. "The house we live in now is very small and has no running water inside. There's no time to rest."

He removed his small, round wire-rim glasses and began to clean them with his handkerchief and shook his head. "My nurse will give you some iron tablets, and then I want you to come back to see me in two weeks. I hope I'll see you looking better then."

Emily hurried out of his office. Edwin was waiting in the Model A Ford that he had recently purchased. "It took you long enough," he said frowning.

"The office was full of patients. He saw me as soon as he could. I hope Mary and Margaret were able to do all the chores while I was away."

"They better have the hoeing done I told them to do," he said.

Emily clasped her hands together tightly as they rode along. Having a car meant little to her. This was her first time to ride in it. There was no other way for her to go to the doctor. Edwin continued to talk as they rode, but Emily wasn't listening. The children were all that was on her mind. She was hardly on the porch when Margaret met her complaining. "Mama, I'm so hot, and Henry has been crying the whole time you've been gone."

"Oh, Margaret, I bet he's hungry." She went inside, picked Henry up and hurried to feed him. Soon he was quiet and asleep. When she came into the kitchen, she was relieved that Edwin didn't come inside. He must have gone on to work, she decided.

జ్ఞ

The vegetable garden yielded beans, squash, tomatoes and potatoes. Emily kept the cook stove hot most of the day in order to cook enough vegetables for lunch and supper. Since the older children worked tirelessly in the garden, they were always hungry. If only the house had running water inside, Emily anguished. With the baby coming, she could no longer lift the heavy buckets, and it was a constant chore for the children to bring the buckets of water inside. Edwin seldom brought any water inside, but he was quick to punish the children if he found the buckets empty. I'm going to tell him that we must have running water inside before the baby comes, but he'll probably remind me of the hard times we're in and how lucky we are to have a house. Just last night Edwin had reminded her again of the long bread and soup lines downtown because so many people had lost their jobs. Louise had written about the hardships of the Depression in Selma, *but "it hasn't affected our cattle business too bad,"* she wrote.

జ్ఞ

"There's not a breeze stirring," Emily said to Daniel, as she sat down in a kitchen chair and wiped her brow.

Daniel put his little cars aside. "I'll go and get a fan and fan you, Mama. Mary has a church fan."

Emily looked at him with deep affection. "That would be very nice, Daniel. I'll fix us a glass of ice water while you get the fan. Maybe that will cool us off." Daniel took the fan and began to move it up and down in front of his mother. "Let me do it, Daniel, while you drink your water."

"Okay," he said and handed the card board fan with a picture of Jesus on it.

"I wonder where Mary got this fan," Emily asked.

"I got it at the church tent meeting down the road," Mary said. She was outside the kitchen door and heard her mother.

"And when were you there, Mary?"

Mary smiled. "We slipped down there last night, while Daddy was reading the newspaper. We sat on the back row and watched the people get the Holy Ghost. You should have seen old Mrs.

Harding. She was running up and down the aisles and speaking in tongues.

"Mary," Emily said, pursing her lips, "don't talk about such things!"

⁂

The October sun formed brilliant patterns on the rippled clouds as it blended into the horizon. The days were shorter and blessedly cooler, but the little house seemed to grow smaller. "I don't know where we'll put a crib for new baby," Emily said. "There's no space in here or in any of the other rooms for a crib. You will have to get between the beds to change the sheets, Mary. It's too difficult for me."

⁂

"Mama, Mama!" Eddie shouted. "Mr. Henson gave me a basket of red apples."

Jonathan came running behind his brother. "Look, Mama! Look, big red apples. Can I have one?" he asked, trying to reach the basket on the table.

"Let me wash them, and we'll all have one," Emily said and took them over to the large basin used for a sink. After washing them she dried them with a clean dish towel. "Look," she said smiling. "They are as shinny as your sunburned nose, Jonathan."

Jonathan watched his mother expectantly. Holding out his hands, he was ready to savor the long-awaited fruit. Daniel didn't wait. He grabbed one of the apples that hadn't been washed. "Daniel," his mother scolded, "give me that apple. Take this one I've washed."

Daniel handed the apple to his mother and laughed. They all laughed as they enjoyed the apples in a rare moment of pleasure.

"Well, I can't sit here any longer. I must get up and cook supper. Your daddy will be home soon." Emily struggled to add coal to the stove and placed the last pots of the vegetables from the summer garden on the hot stove top. There were potatoes Edwin had stored under the house, but she knew she must use them sparingly. Potatoes can always be added to a stew or soup, and Eddie loves mashed potatoes, she thought. Needing some water to finish cooking the meal, she noticed as always the buckets were empty, and the children had gone out to play in the yard. "I'll just get the water myself," she said. "It'll be easier than getting them to do it."

"I thought I told you to make the children do that job," Edwin said. Emily turned around, surprised he had come home. "Give me the buckets! Mary! Margaret! Come here right this minute and get some water for your mama." He turned around and pointed his finger at Emily. "Don't you ever make the children do anything?"

"They fill the buckets over and over again, but they're empty every time I turn around. Do you have any idea how much water we use every day? We need to have running water inside before the baby comes." Edwin ignored her and gave the buckets to Mary and Margaret. The other children kept out of sight. Emily knew they were hoping their daddy wouldn't summon them and punish them for not getting the water. How could I have been so thoughtless? I should have known he would be home soon.

⸎⸎

As Christmas approached and the arrival time for the baby, Emily could barely get her housework done. Though they were in the depths of the Depression, Edwin had bought a few toys for the children and hidden them in the closet. A few days before, his boss had sent some presents for the children. Emily wondered how the people in his office knew about his family's situation. She had never met any of his co-workers or gone to any of his office social events. Was Edwin ashamed of her and the children, ashamed they had so many children? But now, none of this mattered. All she could think about was how much remained to be done and how tired she felt. Her immediate concern was a place for the new baby.

Once more a big Christmas package arrived from Eugenia, filled with presents for everyone and a big box of her wonderful cookies - "Aunt Eugenia cookies" the children called them. It wouldn't be Christmas without them, Emily thought, or without the gifts Louise sent every year. One of the best gifts this year was a letter from her mother saying, *"I'll be there five days before Christmas. Please have Edwin meet me at the train station. My arrival time is four-thirty in the afternoon on Saturday. Don't have the baby until I get there."*

"That's tomorrow," Emily said aloud. She got up from the chair in the living room and sighed as she looked around the shabby little room. Her back ached. The baby could come any time. I hope Edwin will be on his best behavior. He always tries to make a good impression on Mama. "Guess who's coming for Christmas?' she said to the children playing near the fireplace.

"Who, Mama?" they all shouted.

"Your Grandma. She's coming tomorrow."

"Will she tell us some stories?" Eddie asked.

"She will if she has time. She's coming to help when the new baby arrives. We mustn't ask her to do too much." Emily looked at their happy faces. She knew her mother represented security and respectability to them. She remembered her mother's past visits, how she had tried to teach them good manners, always rewarding them when they paid attention to her teaching.

☙❧

Miss Lillie wore the same old black moiré suit, her traveling clothes for the last three times she had come to help with the babies. Emily watched, expectantly, as Edwin helped her up the steps onto the porch. Her mother walked slower now and was slightly bent with age. She looks so tired and worn out, and Emily felt ashamed to have asked her help, until she heard the excitement of the children. "Come see our Christmas tree, Grandma!"

"Let your grandmama put her things down first," their daddy said.

Emily leaned on a chair and held to the back of it with her frail arms. Her stomach was fully distended under her dress and confirmed she was very pregnant. Very little color surfaced on her face. She looked like life had been drained from her. A few streaks of gray were beginning to appear in her hair. "Emily, Emily, if you don't stop having a baby every year, we're going to have to bury you," her mother reprimanded. A very faint blush colored Emily's cheeks. She felt her mother was scolding her as Edwin had done - as if getting pregnant was all her fault. "But let me give you a hug. I'm glad to see you."

Emily moved away from the chair and greeted her mother. "I'm so pleased you've come, Mama."

126

"Now, show me the Christmas tree." Miss Lillie moved over to the tree and gave warm hugs to Henry and Daniel. "Oh, it's very pretty. Maybe we can get some cranberries and string them to add to the decorations; they will add some color."

"What will Daddy do on Christmas without you?" Emily asked her mother.

"He'll have Albert's family. I haven't told you they moved in with us last month to help with the farming." Suddenly Emily felt sick to her stomach. She had thought moving in with her parents might be a solution for her problem; such a move now would be impossible. "It works out very well," her mother continued. "We've never had enough help with the farming, and your daddy isn't getting any younger. Farming gets harder for him every year."

"It seems an agreeable situation for you then," Emily said, trying to hide her disappointment. "I hope their children aren't too much for you."

"Oh, I just don't allow them in the kitchen while I'm cooking. Now, Margaret, if you'll show me where I'm to sleep, I'd like to change my clothes."

"Yes, ma'am." Margaret eagerly took her grandmother's hand. They need someone like Mama, Emily thought, someone to give them special attention. It seems like I never have the time to stop and take a moment with each one, even now and then.

ॐॐ

The baby didn't come on Christmas Day as Emily had thought. In a way, she was glad. She would have hated to disturb Doctor Mitchell's holiday. Her labor pains started early on the day after, and Edwin hurried to call Doctor Mitchell. Miss Lillie did what she could to prepare for the delivery, got the children out of bed and helped them get dressed. It would be a challenge, she thought, to keep them out of the way in this small house during the delivery.

The house was warm when Edwin returned, and Miss Lillie was cooking breakfast. "Mrs. Henson will come and get the older children and take them to her house for breakfast," Edwin said. "Mary, you and Margaret take Laura, Eddie, and Jonathan, and go over to Mrs. Henson's house for a while."

Mary was almost nine, and she had learned about delivering babies. This would be her mother's eighth baby – all delivered at home. "Let me stay and help, Grandma," she begged.

"No, Mary, you go on and help look after your brothers and sisters at Mrs. Henson's," her daddy scolded.

Margaret began to cry. "Why, what's the matter, Margaret?" her grandmother asked.

"Will Mama be all right?" Tears rolled down Margaret's cheeks.

"Your mama will be fine, and soon there'll be a new baby in the house." She put her arms around Margaret and wiped her tears with a handkerchief. "Now, go on with Mrs. Henson; she's waiting for you."

When Mrs. Henson saw that Margaret was upset, she took her by the hand and led her and the other children to her house. "Let's hurry," she said. "It's really cold. Look at the frost on the fields - so heavy it almost looks like snow. I think they call it hoarfrost." When they came into Mrs. Henson's house, the fragrance of fresh oranges, cinnamon and peppermint still lingered from Christmas Day. The house was quite different from their house - the rooms much larger and the furniture new and shiny. The children walked slowly behind Mrs. Henson, taking in the beauty of the living room and the tall Christmas tree with store-bought ornaments. Mary couldn't resist running her fingers over the highly polished mahogany dining room table. Her brothers and sisters stared, wide eyed, at the platters of cake and the bowls of fruit and candy on the buffet.

When they came into the kitchen, a breakfast feast awaited them. The Henson children were already seated and eating. "Lawzy, look at all dez chillun Miz Henson done found. Come on in here and set down," the cook beckoned to the children.

The two Henson girls, who were about the same age as Margaret and Laura, snickered holding the edge of the table cloth up over their mouths. Their little brother asked impolitely, "Why are they here, Mother?"

"Shush, Alex," his mother scolded. "I brought the Anderson children over here until the doctor delivers a new baby at their house. This is Mary," she said, putting her hand on Mary's shoulder. "She's the oldest." Then moving her hand to touch each of the others, she continued, "This is Margaret, Laura, Eddie and Jonathan, and they have two smaller brothers at home. Now, let's give them a seat, and I'll serve them some breakfast." Mary and Margaret sat down; then the others slowly followed, but they were all too timid to say what they wanted to eat. Sensing their reluctance, Mrs. Henson put plenty of scrambled eggs, a slice of crisp bacon and a hot-buttered biscuit on each plate. Then she poured each of them a glass of creamy white milk. Still they didn't touch their food.

"Grandma makes us say grace," Jonathan said, his voice hardly audible. The Henson children laughed.

"Oh, I'm sorry, son. In all my hurry, I forgot. Bow your heads, children, and I will offer a blessing." Mrs. Henson prayed, "For this we are about to receive, oh, Lord, make us humble and thankful. Amen."

After breakfast all the children went into the living room, and the Henson children began showing their new toys and sharing them. This was a new experience for the Anderson children who had made no friends since moving to the small house over the hill from the Hensons. Shortly after lunch, Edwin came for the children, bringing the news that they had a new baby sister. He was very polite and thanked Mrs. Henson effusively. Seeing their daddy, the children jumped up quickly from the floor where they were playing and were ready to go home.

৵৽৵

"Go in quietly," their grandmother said. All seven of the children filed into the bedroom to see the baby. She was wrapped tightly in a soft blanket and tucked lovingly by their mother's side.

"She's so little," Laura said.

"And look at her little nose," Margaret cooed.

"Can she open her eyes?" Eddie asked.

"What's her name?" Mary asked.

Before any of the questions were answered, Daniel and Jonathan pushed up closer to the bed to see. "Her name is Lucy Payne, after your great-grandmother," Emily said in a weak voice.

"All right, children, we must let your mama get some rest," Miss Lillie instructed. "Come in the kitchen. I've made some hot cocoa for you. Sit at the table, and I'll read you a Bible story." The kitchen was the warmest room in the house. There were wet diapers hanging on a wooden rack behind the stove, causing the windows to fog and shutting out the afternoon sunlight. Miss Lillie reached up to the electric light that hung from a single cord in the center of the room and turned the switch to brighten the room.

Daniel listened intently as his grandmother read about Daniel in the lion's den, his favorite Bible story. "I want to be strong like Daniel when I grow up. My name is Daniel too, and I'm gonna be strong."

"Remember," their grandma said, "Daniel was great because he loved God."

The day was too much for Jonathan. He was soon asleep, with his head barely resting on the table. When their grandmother finished reading, Mary picked Jonathan up and carried him to his bed. Lillie gave a sigh. It had been a long, hard day, but a good one.

❧

As Emily lay in the bed, listening, watching and enduring the prescribed bed rest from Doctor Mitchell, she was very aware of Edwin's efforts to win her mother's favor. He treated her mother totally different from the way he treated her. He was quick to bring in the water, keep the fires going and not scold the children harshly in her presence. If I told Mama, she would never believe how he treats the children and me, Emily thought. I might as well forget the idea of leaving him, she thought. Since he puts on such a good act, no one would believe my complaints. She looked at the tiny infant in the cradle beside her bed and her frustration subsided. I wish there was some way to show him how to love the children like I do. She closed her eyes, releasing the welled-up tears that ran down her cheeks and onto the pillow.

❧

When Emily finished giving the baby her bottle, Miss Lillie took the tiny baby and placed her in her crib. "Do you realize this is New Year's Eve?" Miss Lillie said. "I guess it'll be pretty uneventful around here tonight, no party or celebration. Oh, there wouldn't be a party if I were home. Still we have a New Year before us and cause enough to celebrate."

"Somehow, I never cared much for parties, but I know you have, Mama,"

"Yes, I enjoyed them when I was younger. I loved entertaining and going to parties, but I didn't go to many. It really doesn't matter anymore," she said with a certain resignation in her voice. Emily looked at her mother and thought her life has never been what she wanted. It's ironic that she seems to love children, but she didn't want a lot of children. Maybe we never know what we want out of life until we're old.

"The truth is, children are the most important thing," her mother said trying to heal the wounds of so many years past.

"They're everything to me," Emily said, stopping short of saying, all I've ever wanted is to be a loving wife and mother and be loved in return.

Miss Lillie got up from sitting on the side of the bed. "Well, I must go and get the children to bed. I hope they have enough cover. This house is getting cold."

When the children were asleep and the last dish washed, Miss Lillie hung a few diapers behind the stove on the wooden rack and readied herself for bed. "Children are for young folks," she sighed.

Chapter Fifteen

The Fire

It was the crying of the new baby that awakened Emily. As she reached from under the cover to turn on the small lamp by the bed, the coldness of the room reminded her that this was the first day of January - New Year's Day. "What time is it?" Edwin asked.

Emily looked at the ticking alarm clock on the bedside table. "It's five-thirty." Gently, she took the tiny infant from her cradle to nurse her.

"I'll build the fire in the kitchen stove and come back to bed until the house is warmer," Edwin shivered as he slipped on his pants and shirt. When he came into the kitchen, he didn't notice that Miss Lillie had pushed the wooden rack of diapers close to the stove to dry them. He lifted the round cover on the top of the stove, poked the ashes down and stuffed in newspaper with pine kindling. Quickly, he picked up the coal bucket and completely covered the paper and kindling with coal. After he lit the well-laid fire, he rushed back into the bedroom and climbed into bed.

The smell of burning cloth awakened Miss Lillie. Trying to decide where the smell was coming from, she immediately thought of the diapers behind the stove. She ran to the kitchen door. "Oh, my Lord! The kitchen is on fire!" She then ran towards Edwin and Emily's bedroom. "The kitchen's on fire! It must have started from the diapers."

Emily and Edwin sat straight up, filled with shock and fear. They quickly jumped out of bed. Emily grabbed the baby from her crib and screamed hysterically to Edwin, "Get the children out! Get the children out." Miss Lillie had already run to the back of the house to awaken the children. In the excitement, Emily rushed outside in her gown, not even stopping to put on her shoes. She stood shivering in the cold as the children came running out. I can't even think of their names, she thought as she counted them. "One is missing!" she screamed to Edwin when he came outside. "It's Margaret!" When he ran back inside, Emily prayed, "Oh, please, Lord, let him find her safe." She could see the kitchen windows had broken and red flames were leaping out. Heavy smoke began rising from the roof, and the children began coughing from the smoke and stifling smell. "Let's move back, children," Emily said. Suddenly, Edwin appeared on the porch carrying Margaret. Emily breathed a sigh of relief.

"She was still asleep," Edwin said. "I think she has a burn on her arm, but that's the only injury I see." He was barely out of the burning house when the heat began breaking the other windows, releasing a mass of smoke and scorching flames. Emily counted the children again. "They're all out. Thank you, Lord; they're all safe."

Down the hill from the burning house, the six o'clock freight train was approaching. When the engineer saw the smoke and flames, he blew the train whistle with one constant blast, waking the entire community to the dreadful disaster.

Edwin ran to the back of the house, hoping to save some of their belongings, but it was too late. The roof was already beginning to collapse. Hopelessly, he took a small hose hooked to the outside faucet and began spraying the roaring fire.

"It's no use, Edwin," Mr. Henson said. After being awakened by the train whistle and seeing the smoke from the fire, he had come quickly to help. "With only one faucet, you don't have a chance. The house is too far gone." Edwin looked at him as if he didn't understand what he was saying. He was defeated, and that wasn't easy for him. Mr. Henson reached down and turned off the water. He took Edwin by the arm and led him out to the road where the children and Miss Lillie were standing with Emily and the baby. The small wood-framed house was now a mass of flames and heavy smoke. "Don't look, children," Lillie said, tears streaming down her cheeks. Still the children looked on in silence, transfixed by the horrible scene.

A small crowd of neighbors watched helplessly until the house burned to the ground. Only the brick chimney was left standing amid a mound of glowing ashes. "I must get the baby inside, out of this cold," Emily said to her mother. When she turned to go, she realized that her feet were stuck to the frozen ground. Ignoring the pain, she forced her feet free and walked to the nearest neighbor's house - only a few yards away.

Mary Sullivan's house was the closest. It was a duplex next to a vacant lot. When she heard the continuous whistle of the train, Mrs. Sullivan had run to the window to see the terrible sight. Bright orange flames were leaping out of thick black smoke, windows were breaking and popping, and the Anderson family was standing completely helpless. When she saw Emily coming over to her house, still in her nightgown and carrying the tiny, crying baby, she grabbed her coat and ran outside. "Oh, Emily, what a terrible thing," she said. "Come in the house and let me help you. You must be freezing. I'll take the baby and you lie down."

When Emily lay down, she began to shake from the cold and the trauma. Finally, she was warm, but she felt completely numb and overwhelmed.

☜☞

"We must get these children and their grandmother out of this freezing weather," Mrs. Henson told Edwin and her husband. "I'll take them to our house and call Doctor Mitchell to come and check you and Emily. Where are Emily and the baby?"

"She's gone to the neighbor's house. Over there," Miss Lillie pointed.

Edwin pulled the front of his jacket up around his neck and turned to Mrs. Henson. "I believe I'll come with you and make some telephone calls. I have a brother who lives in Fairfield. Maybe we can stay with him for a few days."

Emily lay in the unfamiliar bed staring at the ceiling. A strange feeling came over her. It was if she had experienced this terrible event before. Could it be that she had dreamed of this disaster? Could she have brought it on by hating the little house so? What will we do? She anguished. Where will we go? As she held the baby closer, trying to control her racing thoughts, she heard Doctor Mitchell's voice. It was a welcome sound. When he came into the room, he pulled a chair up close to the side of the bed. "Well, Emily, looks like trouble is raining on you today." He gently took the baby from Emily. "Let me look at you, little one. We need to be sure you didn't get any smoke in your lungs."

"Is she all right?"

"Everything sounds all right. Her weight is in her favor, and she seems strong. Now let me listen to your heart and lungs. I'm so thankful that no one is badly burned. Oh, Edwin has a few minor burns, and Margaret has a burn on her arm, but it isn't too bad." He put his stethoscope back in his bag and looked directly into Emily's eyes. "I can examine your heart, Emily, but I know I can't hear all the hurt that is there. Sometimes we don't understand why so much trouble comes. But I know that you are a strong woman, and you will get through this. Spring will come." Emily listened, but she could find no words to say. Hot silent tears streamed down her gaunt face, but she didn't wipe them away. Everything seemed unreal, like a bad dream. "Edwin has told me that you all will be going to his brother's house in Fairfield. I want you to go by ambulance and continue your bed rest, if possible."

Doctor Mitchell's wife had been standing just inside the door and came over to the side of the bed. She handed Emily a small bag she had hastily filled. "This is for the baby; some things I've been saving, but I want you to have them. They'll be useful to you now." When she bent down, Emily could see her eyes were clouded with tears.

Emily looked down at the baby and then at Mrs. Mitchell. "Thank you, thank you for coming. There's no way to repay your kindness to me."

"When they learn of this tragedy, I'm sure the people of Fairfield will offer to help you and Edwin, especially the members of the Exchange Club," Doctor Mitchell added. He paused in the doorway. "I'll tell them where you're staying."

After Doctor Mitchell and his wife were gone, Lillie came in and sat down beside the bed. "Oh, Mama, you look so tired. Would you have ever thought such a terrible accident could happen?"

"I feel it is my fault because I put the diapers too close to the stove. But that doesn't matter now. How are you and the baby?"

"I don't really know. I'm so empty of feelings, but Doctor Mitchell assured me we were okay."

"Edwin is still standing out there gazing at the ashes as if in a stupor. One bright spot though, the automobile didn't burn," Lillie said.

Emily shook her head in agreement. "You always find something to be thankful for, Mama."

Lillie got up from the chair and walked to the bedroom door. "I'm going out to talk with Edwin about his plans. I'll be back in a few minutes."

Edwin looked up in surprise to see Miss Lillie. Since it was so cold, most of the neighbors had gone inside. "Miss Lillie, what are we going to do?" he asked, still in disbelief.

"The Lord will provide," she said, and he knew she believed it, but he wasn't sure.

Quickly, he changed the subject. "I called Louise. She and John Freeman are coming right away. They'll be here soon and take you and the boys to their house. I'll take Emily with the baby and the girls over to my brother's house in Fairfield. He and his wife have agreed to let us stay with them until we can find another place to live."

"For now, Edwin, we need to go inside to Mrs. Sullivan's. I think she has some hot coffee." Wearily, Lillie pulled her coat up close to her face and started over to the neighbors' house. Reluctantly, Edwin followed.

Mary Sullivan came to the door. "Come in, come in," she said. "I've just made a pot of coffee. Sit here in the kitchen where it's warm."

Edwin sat down. His face was red and dry from the flames and cold air, and his eyebrows badly singed. He had a few small burns on his hands and one on his neck. Though he didn't readily admit defeat, his past illness had made him more vulnerable, and now he felt overwhelmed and angry. He wanted to lash out at someone, but there was no one. He dare not reproach Miss Lillie about leaving the diapers too close to the stove. He had never spoken harshly to her. She was the kind of woman you didn't correct. He respected her resolve. After sipping the hot coffee, he felt warmer and his anger subsided. "We certainly haven't started this year off right. What a terrible time for this to happen, with the weather so cold."

"Tragedy always comes when you least expect it," Lillie said. "There's never a convenient time to face it. Somehow, you'll get through this tragedy. Now, don't you want to go to the bedroom and see Emily and the baby?"

The baby, he thought, another baby. If it hadn't been for the baby's diapers, there wouldn't have been a fire. When he came into the bedroom, Emily was asleep. Her face was ashen in color. Even as she slept, he could see the distress of the morning written on her face. Still he felt no pity for her. In his mind, she was at fault for having more children than they could feed or clothe, and now what would they do? Weary, he lay down beside her and fell asleep.

⁂∾⁃

The sun was well up above the treetops, and the embers from the fire had turned to ashes when Emily heard Miss Lillie call, "Louise is here and John Freeman, Emily." Mrs. Sullivan led them to the bedroom where Emily and Edwin were resting. Tears filled Emily's eyes when she saw her sister and John Freeman. She quickly sat up in bed, and Edwin got up to greet them.

Louise came and sat down on the side of the bed. She put her arms around Emily and whispered, "Don't be discouraged, Emily; we'll help you. We'll take the boys and keep them until you are well enough to be up."

Emily wiped her eyes. "Looks like you're always coming to my rescue. Did you meet our neighbors? I don't know what we would have done without their help."

"Yes, I met Mrs. Sullivan and her husband and thanked them. Now, let me see the new baby." Louise picked up the tiny baby and held her up to look at her face. "You always have pretty babies, Emily. She's a precious baby." As she got up off the bed, Louise turned to look at Edwin. "How are you, Edwin? You've been through so much." She hesitated to give him a hug. Somehow she had never felt comfortable showing him affection.

"I'm all right now that I've gotten over the shock of all this."

Louise rubbed her arms feeling the chill of the house. For a moment, she was overcome by the sad situation. "John Freeman has gone to the car to bring in some clothes for you and Emily, Edwin. I don't know how well they'll fit. I'll buy the little boys some things when we get home. On our way here, we went by to tell Daddy about the fire and got some clothes for you, Mama."

"I'm really glad to get them. I've been wearing Mrs. Sullivan's things all morning,"

John Freeman came in and greeted everyone warmly and set the box of clothes on the floor. "Mrs. Sullivan says an ambulance is here for Emily and the baby. We need to go out to let them come in for you and the baby, Emily." As he walked out of the room with Edwin, he took him by the arm. "Take this money," he said. "I know you'll need it. This is a terrible thing that has happened, and I want to help you."

Edwin looked at him, not knowing what to say. He had never had anyone give him money. He didn't understand such generosity. He took the money and put it in his pocket. "Thank you. This will help us get through these next hard days." Later when he pulled the roll of bills from his pocket, he counted two hundred dollars.

"Don't worry about the boys, Emily," Louise said. "We'll take care of them. When you've found a house, we'll bring them home."

"Good-bye, Emily," Lillie said. "I'll write you."

"Good-bye, Mama." No other words could come. She was weary beyond words.

అ⚭

Edwin's brother Arthur and his wife Jessie welcomed Edwin and Emily. A house full of children was difficult for them since they had no children, and the restlessness of the little girls soon wore their patience thin. After two weeks Emily worried they had worn out their welcome. Her fears were realized when she overheard Arthur ask Jessie, "How much longer are they staying? I don't think Edwin is trying to find a place. He isn't here enough to see how crowded we are. There are boxes of donated clothing everywhere, and the garage is so full of furniture that I can't get the car inside."

"Shush, they might hear you," Jessie whispered. "It won't be much longer. Anyway, I've enjoyed the little girls, and Emily is just now able to take care of the baby."

అ⚭

Dreading to divulge her in-laws feelings to Edwin, Emily waited another day to tell him. She was relieved when he came in the next day and announced, "I've found a house to rent - not too far from the one that burned. We'll be moving the first of next week." Though relieved, Emily was disappointed. She had hoped to move back to Fairfield where she had friends. "You'll like this house. It has an inside bathroom and running water in the kitchen, and the rent is only ten dollars a month."

Emily had thought many times over the past two weeks that if it hadn't been for losing all their belongings, she would have almost welcomed the fire. She hated the small house. There were no good memories attached to that place. Life there had been a constant struggle - bringing in water, bringing in coal to fight off the icy wind that chilled every room. She had never understood why Edwin had moved them there, but now all these problems were in the past. She would look forward to the new house. Later she said to Edwin, "I'll be glad to be settled and have the boys home. I miss them. I know Arthur and Jessie will be glad to see us go. They aren't used to children."

അക

When the last piece of furniture was on the truck and the children were in the car, Emily thanked Arthur and Jessie for their generosity and kindness. "I don't know what we would have done without your help." Holding the baby she got in the car. Edwin was still busying himself tying down the furniture on the truck and instructing the two men who were helping him. He left without a word of thanks to his brother.

"You take care of yourself," Jessie called as they drove away.

The road to the new house was bumpy and pocked with potholes. All Emily could do was hold the tiny baby and keep her from crying. Mary and her sisters giggled with delight as the car bounced up and down. Edwin seemed to enjoy the rough ride and even laughed at the enthusiasm of the girls. Emily could only wonder what the house would be like. It would have to be better than the last one, since it had running water inside. She thought about all the things the people of Fairfield had given them and once more longed to settle there. Could she make a new beginning in this house? Did she even have any love left for Edwin? She didn't know. Too much had happened in the last year - Edwin's sickness, another baby and then the terrible fire. She was tested beyond her limits. How could she know how she felt?

Edwin brought the noisy car to a sudden stop, and they all lunged forward. Emily braced herself to keep from hitting her head on the windshield. "Well, we're here," Edwin said.

Mary was the first out of the car. "Look, Mama, there's a church next door."

"I see, Mary." Emily stepped from the running board of the car to the dirt yard. "I like the big trees. They'll make a nice place for ya'll to play in the summer, but for now let's go inside out of the cold." It took only a glance for Emily to realize that the house was very small, but she was shocked when she saw that it had only two bedrooms. "Where will the children sleep?" She breathed a sigh of despair.

"We can put a bed in the dining room for Mary and Margaret. All the others can sleep in the bedroom. This is the best we can afford. It's not easy providing for all these children you're determined to have."

Emily gave a deep sigh. Maybe he's trying, she thought. Maybe it's all he can afford. I have no idea what we can afford. Edwin failed to mention the money John Freeman gave him. When he showed her the new stove in the kitchen, she wondered where he got the money to buy it. "It has a place on the side to heat water. Look," he said and pointed pridefully, pulling on a spiral handle to open it. "I'll build a fire here while the movers bring in the furniture."

To her surprise, the day after moving in, Emily felt that the small house wasn't as crowded as she had imagined. The wicker furniture in the living room was much prettier than the dark overstuffed chair and sofa that they had before. We have all the furniture we need, she thought, and to think it was all given to us. "God, you haven't forgotten us," she sighed. As she looked at the room with satisfaction, she saw the headlights of the car come into the yard. Edwin was home. "Do you like the house?" he asked, when he came inside.

"I do. I'm so glad to have our own place. The children are

asleep, and I'm very tired. I'm going to try out the tub. A warm bath is just what I need. Your supper is on the stove. I've kept the stove hot to have hot water."

Edwin picked up the evening paper and followed Emily into the kitchen. "I'll dip the water for you." He took the metal bucket and filled it with the steaming water. Emily looked at him in surprise. Was there a change in him? Maybe he was relieved, too. Life had been so very hard for them. She was pleased when she undressed that the house was warm. When she got into the tub, the warm water covered her body like a soothing balm - relaxing every muscle. Even her bones ached from the tension and worry of the past weeks. She slid down into the tub to wet her hair and lathered it with some perfumed shampoo Jessie had given her. From the bucket beside the tub, she dipped enough warm water to rinse her thinning tresses. Feeling relaxed and clean, she stepped out of the tub and dried her frail body. Would her stomach ever be flat again, she wondered? To her surprise, when she looked in the mirror, her hair was almost white. Before, she had only a few stands of gray intermingled with lighter brown. I guess the shock of the house burning must have turned my hair gray. Ironically, the light hair enhanced her beauty, making her gray-blue eyes more prominent and her complexion rosier.

When she came into the bedroom, Edwin took note of her beauty, but he didn't say anything about her hair. Drawing her close when she got into bed, he lifted his warm body onto hers and began to make love. Emily gave herself to him, hoping to experience the love she had sought since her wedding night and longing to hear him say he loved her. The words never came.

Chapter Sixteen

A Tragic Death

$\mathscr{E}$mily heard the loud knock and hurried to open the door. Edwin's father was standing on the porch, his shoulders slumped as he turned his rumpled, felt hat around and around by the brim. "Mr. Anderson! What a surprise! Come in. Come on in. Edwin isn't home yet. He should be here soon. How did you find us?"

"I saw John Freeman in Maplesville last week, and he told me about the fire and where you were living. I came to offer you some help." After he stepped inside, he put his hand down into the pocket of his worn brown suit and pulled out a crumpled bill. Gently, he took Emily's hand and pressed the money into it. Emily looked at the money. For a moment she was speechless.

"This is a lot of money, Mr. Anderson. Should I give it to Edwin when he comes home?"

"No, I want you to have it - for you and the children." Emily pulled at her apron string and began to twist it around her fingers. She looked at him, wondering if he could possibly know how Edwin ignored their needs and how cruelly he treated the children. How could he know? She didn't know what to say to this man who was almost a stranger, yet she could see that he understood her circumstances. Yes, she would keep the hundred dollars for herself and the children and not mention it to Edwin.

The tense moment was broken when some of the children timidly eased into the room. Emily smiled. "This is your Grandfather Anderson." Henry and Daniel looked at him with fear and distrust and clung to their mother's skirt. It was uncanny how much he looked like Edwin. Perhaps they associated him with their daddy. Seeing the intense sadness in his eyes, Emily reached down and tried to pull the children from behind her. "Don't be so shy. This is your grandfather."

"Well, I can't expect them to know me. They've rarely seen their grandmother or me. You and Edwin must bring them down to see us soon." Lovingly, he patted little Henry on the top of his head.

"Won't you come and sit down in the kitchen? I was about to start supper."

"I can't stay." Nervously, he adjusted his tie as if it were too tight. "I came to Birmingham to take care of some business, and I need to get back home. Tell Edwin I'll see him later."

Emily said good-bye and watched him walk slowly to his truck. "He looks as worn as that old truck," she told Henry who was still clinging to her skirt. "I wish we could see him more often. He seems so kind and thoughtful." A marathon of questions flooded her mind. I wonder why Edwin isn't more like him and if Virginia treats him like Edwin treats me. I wonder why he's so sad. She reached down and took Henry's hand. "It's cold, Henry. Let's put some more coal on the fire." She filled the small shovel and let Henry throw it onto the fire. "Now, I've got to start supper." Remembering the money in her pocket, she felt a new lease on life. Many of her worries were lifted.

Emily was eager to tell Edwin about his father's visit, but her enthusiasm was squelched when he came in the door scolding the children playing in the living room by the warm fire. "Fade to the background," he ordered them angrily before he sat down. Quickly they scurried out of the room. Later Emily told him of his daddy's visit, but she was careful not to mention the money. His only comment was, "he could have waited until I got home."

❧

"Someone has taken a dime from my pocket, and I'm going to find out who took it, right now," Edwin yelled, his face red with anger.

Emily looked up at him as she rolled out the biscuits for breakfast on the enameled apron of the kitchen cabinet. "Maybe you lost it." She went over to the sink, washed her hands and dried them with the dishtowel. "I don't think any of the children would do such a thing."

"You never think they do anything wrong," he said, growing angrier. "Eddie, come here and bring your brothers with you! Mary! Margaret! Laura! Get in here. I'm going to find out who took a dime from my trousers." Hesitantly, the children came into the kitchen, still in their nightgowns. Their eyes were wide with fear as he accusingly asked which one had taken the dime. All were silent.

"Well then, since no one will admit it, everyone will get a whipping." Slowly he removed his belt and wrapped it securely around his hand. Mary was the first to receive a severe lashing. Tears of anger filled her eyes, but she made no sound of pain. Fear gripped the other children, and soon the room was filled with wailing and sobbing. Emily felt sick to her stomach, but she knew she couldn't stop him. Not able to stand his cruelty, she went into the bedroom in complete distress and put her hands to her face and cried.

Shortly afterwards, Edwin came into the bedroom to get his coat. When he lifted his foot onto the chair to wipe off his shoe, the lost dime rolled conspicuously onto the floor from the cuff of his pants. Emily watched as the silver coin rolled to a stop in a moment of shining truth. She looked directly at him. "Are you going to apologize to the children?"

"No, I'm not! They've needed a good whipping for a long time now." The whipping had sadistically cleansed him of his anger. Emily looked at him in total disgust and walked out of the room.

❧

It was late August when word came of the tragic death of Edwin's father. Edwin told Emily as he was leaving for work. He seemed more agitated than grief-stricken.

"How did it happen?" she asked.

"I don't know the details. I only know that he went to the barn and hung himself from one of the rafters in the loft. This happened Monday, and he didn't die until yesterday.

"And this is Thursday." She could picture Mr. Anderson now, standing at her door, in his worn brown suit, with his eyes full of sadness. "When will the funeral be?"

"Saturday morning, at eleven, at the Ebenezer Baptist Church. He'll be buried in the cemetery up the hill behind the church," Edwin said, then picked up his hat and walked to the door.

"I'd like to go," she called, "and take the children."

Edwin turned around and stepped back inside. "Do you actually think we could all get in the car?"

"Well, I can't leave them, and I want to go."

"They can go if you think they can behave."

Emily dreaded telling the children about their grandfather's death and waited until Edwin was gone, before she went out to the backyard where they were playing. She sat down on a wooden crate they had been using for a table under the hackberry tree. When Mary saw her mother, she came running. "What's wrong, Mama?" Quickly the other children gathered around.

"Your Grandfather Anderson has died, and we'll be going to the funeral on Saturday."

"Is he the granddaddy that was here, Mama?" Little Henry asked.

"Yes, your daddy's father." For a moment, the children were quiet. Looking at their sad faces, Emily didn't know what else to say or how to explain his death. They hadn't known death before. She gave a sigh. "When we go we'll be crowded in the car, so you'll have to be on your best behavior and not provoke your daddy."

"How did he die, Mama?" Mary asked.

Emily put her hand up to her mouth and whispered, "I'll tell you later. I don't want to talk about it in front of the smaller children. Now, I've got to plan what we'll wear. We'll leave early, so you and Margaret will have to help me get the others ready."

ॐॐ

Emily had mixed emotions as she viewed the children's new shoes lined up on the bedroom floor, bought with the money Edwin's father had given her. How happy and grateful she had been on that day. Now she was sad. There were so many things she didn't know about Edwin's family, especially why Mr. Anderson would take his own life. After laying out the children's nicest clothes - the ones given to them after the fire - she felt a sense of pride. They would look nice, but she doubted Edwin would even notice how they looked. Her thoughts turned again to her father-in-law. "Well, he's in a better place," she whispered to herself, "and I know he's at peace now."

☙❧

It was a solemn day as the Anderson family, all ten of them, crowded into the old Ford automobile to go to the funeral. Even though there were a few more days left in August, there was a touch of autumn in the air. Mingled with the cool morning mist was a sweet smell of harvest.

The seven children twisted and turned until they were finally situated in the back seat of the car. Emily sat in the front seat holding baby Lucy, and soon they were on their way. "Thank goodness, it's only fifty miles to Maplesville," she said. "Maybe the cool air will hold until we get there."

The children couldn't hold back their excitement. They had no idea what a funeral was. They only knew they were going somewhere. With their faces pressed to the windows, they noticed every house along the way, even the small shacks that were ensconced among the trees or sitting in the middle of a cotton field. They counted the cows in the pastures and were fascinated to see black and white ones, red-faced ones and huge black ones. Edwin completely ignored them as long as they weren't too noisy.

"I found out why Daddy killed himself," Edwin suddenly blurted out. Emily gasped and turned to see if the children were listening. She was shocked that he would talk about his father's death in front of the children. Quickly, they grew quiet and were listening to every word their daddy was saying. He talked rapidly and looked straight ahead as he gave every gory detail. Emily had no opportunity to interrupt him.

"It seems that Arthur and Chester talked Daddy into buying some stock with his savings, and he lost all of it. Mama was furious with him. She nagged him about it for days. She's good at nagging," he said, with his teeth clenched. "So…he went to the barn, climbed to the hay loft and hung himself from one of the rafters. When he didn't come in for supper, Mama went looking for him and found him hanging in the barn. By the time she got help, he was nearly dead, but he lived another three days."

Emily looked over her shoulder at the children. They were sitting in silence as if listening to a scary story. Edwin's callousness shocked her. Finally, when she had a chance to say something, her only words were "I'm really sorry." But she doubted he heard her and wondered how she would explain this kind of death to the children. Death is hard enough for them to understand. She gave a deep sigh and held the baby up to her shoulder to quiet her, hoping her fretting wouldn't break into loud crying.

It was almost eleven when Edwin steered the old Ford into the churchyard. "Look at all the people!" Mary shouted.

"Hush, Mary," Edwin scolded. "Ya'll get out and behave yourselves."

When Emily stepped out of the car, she spotted Louise and John Freeman waiting in front of the church with her mother and father. She rushed over to greet them. "Daddy, you haven't seen our three youngest children. This is Lucy and Henry and Daniel." She held the baby up so he could see her pretty face, put her hand on Henry's head, then Daniel's.

"Well, look at these youngsters," their grandpa exclaimed. "And here are the rest of them. They're just like stair-steps, Emily." He shook his head and chuckled. "Well, hold out your hand and I'll give you something to buy some ice cream on your way home. He reached down into his pocket and handed each one of them a shiny new dime. Their eyes sparkled and a smile widened on their faces, as they looked at the treasure in their hand.

"Tell your grandpa thank you, then come over here and give your grandma a hug," Lillie said.

"Thank you, sir," they all said, then walked timidly over to their grandma, remembering how she had taught them how important it was to obey. Laura had a special love for Lillie and lingered quietly relishing her hug. The boys remembered their Aunt Louise and Uncle John Freeman from their visit after the fire. Still, they were timid with all the hugs. They had known little affection from anyone other than their mother, and that was scarce.

"Where's Edwin?" Lillie asked.

"Oh, he's here somewhere," Emily answered. "We'd better go and find him. It's nearly time to go into the church." As she looked over the crowd, she couldn't believe that so many people had come. I wonder if word has gotten out as to how he died, and many have come out of curiosity. Finally, she spotted Edwin talking with his family at the side of the church. "I see your daddy. We'd better go over there."

Ill at ease, she greeted her husband's family and told them the children's names. Her mother-in-law seemed preoccupied and hardly greeted the children, but they took little notice of her. They were completely fascinated by all the people staring at their daddy's family and whispering to one another.

"I don't know what they think they're looking at," Edwin's mother said angrily.

Emily was thankful when the preacher arrived and without further delay ushered the family into the church. He was a young man with a sympathetic air and a soft southern voice. His hair curled up above his collar and separated in wet strands from the August heat. His black suit, though wrinkled, looked as if it had been pressed too many times. As Mama says, "You could almost see yourself in it," Emily observed, holding back a quiet smile. Nervously, the preacher instructed the pallbearers to carry the casket into the church and led the family behind it. When they were seated, he opened the casket and let the long line of people view the body.

Emily was mortified as the curiosity seekers filed by and bent down to get a closer look at the rope burns on Mr. Anderson's neck. I hate this pagan custom of viewing the dead as some kind of side show, she thought. When it came time for the family to file past the body, she could hardly rise and usher the children past the casket. She was thankful they could only get a glimpse into the casket and walk quietly back to their seats. As she was returning to her seat, she saw that the small church was full, even with some standing in the back. Soon the whole church was a flutter of cardboard fans, since the late summer heat had moved in with the crowd.

What a pleasant surprise to see Miss Ida Harvey when she stood to sing. She still has a lovely voice, Emily thought. She listened, nostalgically, to the dear old hymn, "When They Ring Those Golden Bells for You and Me." There were a few tears from those who Emily thought must have been close neighbors and friends, but none from Edwin or his mother who sat stiff and unemotional. The preacher had many kind words to say about Mr. Anderson. Still, Emily couldn't see any sorrow on the faces of

Edwin's family, who moved restlessly in their seats. Unhindered by their restlessness, the preacher continued his long sermon ignoring the stifling heat. Finally, when the people began to whisper and several babies began to cry, he ended the service with prayer.

It was a relief to go out into the churchyard where the air was stirring and the children didn't have to remain still and quiet. As she stood and talked to folks she hadn't seen in years, happy memories of the days when she had attended the old Ebenezer church flooded over her. "Louise, isn't it sad that it takes a funeral to bring people together?" Slowly, they walked up the hill to the cemetery - the children trailing behind.

"But it's good to see them," Louise said. "I haven't seen some of these folks in years."

"Mama looks tired, and Daddy has really aged since I last saw him," Emily said. "I guess they think the same of me with this gray hair. Too many years have passed without my seeing Daddy. He was always my mainstay, along with you. I've missed you both."

After the crowd gathered at the cemetery, their conversations soon died to a whisper, then to dead silence. Only a few seats close to the open grave were provided for the family. Mrs. Anderson took the first seat; next to her were Edwin's sister, Alice, then Edwin, Chester and Arthur. Emily chose to stand away from the grave with the children. She heard very little of the Scripture that was read. Instead of listening, she was observing Edwin's family. She was puzzled at the lack of grief on their faces or any expression of sorrow for the one they had lost in such a tragedy. In deep contemplation the answer came; there's no love here. Edwin has never known love; he doesn't know how to give it or receive it. A sick realization was taking root in her heart. Edwin would never be able to love her and the children in the way she had hoped.

After the casket was lowered into the grave, Edwin said his short goodbyes to his family and rushed over to her and the children demanding to go. She hardly had time to say one last word to her family before she hurried with the children to the car. When they had traveled only a few miles out of Maplesville, Edwin pulled the car off to the side of the road. Emily had packed a meager lunch that morning, not knowing if they would be invited to the Anderson home for lunch. "We could have gone to the house to eat, but I didn't want to listen to Chester talk about getting the farm. I wouldn't mind having it myself. You and the children could move down here, and I could save a lot of money. I could come home on weekends."

"What about your mother? I'm not sure she'd welcome our children," Emily said, but Edwin pretended not to hear her. When they got back into the car, he continued complaining. He wasn't going to let his brothers take his share of the farm. I wonder, Emily thought, what they plan to do about their mother and sister. Surely, they won't take the farm from her. Emily had no desire to gain a house at her mother-in-law's expense.

"I want a drink of water. And I need to go to the bathroom. I do too," the children begged.

"All right," their daddy said. "We'll stop at the next farm house and get some water and maybe they'll let us use their outhouse."

The children were captivated by the old woman as she drew the bucket of water from the well and graciously offered them a drink from the metal dipper. "These is some mighty fine-looking children," she said and wiped the sweat from her brow with her apron. "We ain't got no children, but these are mighty fine looking."

Emily stood next to the well for a moment, cherishing the woman's words - words she rarely heard. She thought most people disapproved having so many children, like Edwin. She smiled and said, "Thank you for the water. We must be going. We want to get to Birmingham before dark."

For days after the funeral, Emily could think of nothing else. Why had Edwin's father taken his life? Was he that troubled over losing his money, or did Edwin's mother drive him to such a terrible fate? Had she become impossible to live with? She kept remembering the empty look on Edwin's face and his mother's angry expression. The harsh reality is Edwin will never have any love for me or the children. If I just had someone to talk to, she thought, someone to confide in, who could understand and answer my questions.

After she made the bed, Emily stopped a moment before the mirror and ran her fingers through her hair. "No wonder my hair is gray," she sighed. "There's no end to this housework and never money enough for our needs." She thought again about the money her father-in-law had given her just before he died. He would have been pleased that she was able to buy shoes for each of the children. It hadn't been easy to go downtown without Edwin knowing. She chose a time when Mary and Margaret could watch the smaller children, and even then she couldn't be gone very long. Emily was nervous since she had never ridden on the streetcar. She had planned carefully what she would buy, drawing on brown paper a tracing of each of the children's feet for their shoe size. With the hundred dollars and list tucked safely in her purse, she felt happy to be able to buy shoes and clothes they desperately needed.

෨෬

Like her neighbor had said, the large department store was on the corner where she got off the streetcar. Entering through the glass double doors, she anxiously looked for the children's department. When the clerk approached her, she told him the kind of shoes she wanted and gave him the drawings of her children's feet. "These drawings are very clever, ma'am. I haven't seen the use of these before. I'll see what sizes we have." Emily sat down and waited. She breathed in the smell of newness which had long been absent in her life. Most of the shoppers were women and very well-dressed. Conscious of her appearance, she smoothed her hand down over her modest dress and looked at her worn shoes. She was relieved when the clerk returned. "Here we are, madam. I had all the sizes," he said proudly.

"Thank you," Emily said, handing him her money. Now she must focus on buying underwear, socks and sweaters.

৵৽

It was like Christmas when Emily returned home. She opened the bags and carefully arranged the clothes and shoes for each child on her bed. "These are gifts from your Grandfather Anderson. He wanted us to keep his gift a secret." Looking at their faces, she knew they realized why they should not tell their daddy. In one visit her father-in-law had become her friend, only to die too soon. She wished she could have known him longer, but her lasting memory would be this gift of kindness. A quiet smile of contentment spread across her face as she remembered her children's joy and her father-in-law's generosity.

৵৽

Some days Emily thought she would smother in the small house by the church yard. Little relief came from the stifling heat of summer. When the hot days finally became cooler, she watched the last brittle, brown leaves fall from the large oak tree in the church yard. Since the girls were back in school, the house didn't seem so crowded. She wondered if Edwin ever noticed how crowded the house was. How could he? He always left early for work and returned home late. In a way his long working days were a blessing - the children were usually asleep when he came home which kept him from finding a reason to punish them.

৵৽

Winter came quickly, and slowly spring moved into summer as Emily's ninth baby grew within her. Calen was born on the Fourth of July with the temperature soaring into the nineties. When Mary and Margaret volunteered to help, Emily was pleased she wouldn't have to call on her mother. Somehow, she always felt a sense of shame about having another baby because she knew her mother didn't approve. More and more, there was no intimacy in their love making, only a sense of Edwin using her for his desires. There seemed to be no way for her to leave him and no way to avoid getting pregnant.

Mary took an unusual interest in the new baby. She bathed and dressed him, brushed his soft blond hair and fed him his bottle when her mother was busy. Emily was pleased that Mary gave her love so readily to Calen. She noticed a difference in Mary. Her anger and defiance towards her daddy lessened. When Calen was nearly two and not walking, Mary found a cardboard box and taught him how to push it up and down the porch until he could walk. In these small ways, Emily found happiness and gratification in the love her children had for one another.

⮞⬿

Seldom did Emily have a chance to enjoy sitting on the porch with the children. As she sat in the swing on a warm Sunday afternoon, she took notice of how pretty her girls had become. Even at the awkward age of thirteen, Mary's beauty couldn't be hidden under her dresses that didn't fit or her stockings that sagged. Her thick blond hair, bright blue eyes and smooth fair complexion gave promise to the beautiful girl she would become.

Margaret, frail and small for her age, was still very pretty. But her determined spirit often caused friction between her and her sisters. Emily noticed Edwin always favored Margaret, and many times their arguments resulted in Mary's getting a whipping.

Laura's beauty was in her eyes – eyes like Emily's, deep set, but more the shade of the ocean on a cloudy day. Her high cheek bones and soft brown hair made her stand out even now as a child. Little Lucy's black hair and green eyes gave evidence that she would be pretty like her sisters. They're so young and deserve so much more than this meager existence, but what can I do? Maybe, Emily thought, if we could move back to Fairfield they would have a chance of a better life, but it's no use. Every time I mention moving to Edwin, his answer is always the same. "I've told you we can't afford to live in Fairfield."

One evening, only a few weeks after her last plea to get Edwin to move the family, he came home and announced, "I've found another house for us. I plan to buy it. It only costs six hundred dollars."

"Where is it?" Emily asked, still hoping to move to Fairfield.

"It's only one block from where our house was that burned – on this side of the railroad tracks." It must be right beside the railroad tracks, Emily concluded. "There's only one house close by, and it's directly across the road at the front of the house. Several vacant lots are next to the house, where we can have a large garden and grow some corn. Maybe I'll get a cow. The boys are big enough now to do the milking."

"Eddie is only ten, Edwin. Jonathan is nine and Daniel eight. They are still very young children … I don't think …"

"Well, the girls will have to help too. I had to work the garden when I was small. A little work won't hurt them." As always, Edwin ended the discussion by opening the newspaper and beginning to read.

Emily bit her lip and looked down. She took a deep breath, trying to overcome her feelings of defeat and the insult of his dismissal. It frightened her to think there was no fight left within her. I must not give up, she thought. I can't. I have to think of the children. She rubbed her tired, red hands over her eyes and sat back in the chair. I wonder if we will have good neighbors. I guess the house won't be far from Mrs. Henson. The thought cheered her somewhat. Wanting to know more, she asked, "Who lives there now?"

Edwin put his paper down, surprised that she was still sitting there. "No one. A man and his wife lived there, but she died and he moved away. The house has been empty for a while. Their name was Holland. The neighbors told me, they fought like cats and dogs. They showed me a streak of coffee stain on the kitchen wall and said it was from where she threw a hot cup of coffee at him during one of their brawls."

As she listened, Emily noticed Edwin was enjoying repeating this bit of gossip. She wondered what kind of neighbor had told this tale, and she was surprised Edwin had listened.

"They said the old woman haunts the house. Maybe they are trying to scare me away." He gave a cynical laugh. "They don't know me. I guess they're afraid of us. The real estate man told them we had nine children and another on the way. That would scare anyone," he said with a smirk.

Emily didn't smile. "When will we move?"

"Not for at least a month. It will take me that long to get the house painted and cleaned. I'll take you over there when I get that done."

Emily had many more questions, but she was too tired to ask them. She didn't know whether to be relieved or not. Was the house larger? Did it have enough room for the children? Apparently she would have no say about painting the house or anything else concerning it. "Well, I hope we can get moved before the baby comes. Raising ten children in this house is impossible." When she looked up, Edwin had walked out of the room. Ten children, she thought, and in just fourteen years … I could never have imagined it. She could hardly remember not being pregnant, but she had no regrets about having the children – they were the only joy she knew and her love for them kept her going. Her only wish was that Edwin would love them also.

❧

It was late September when Emily got to see the new house - the day before they were to move. He said "no" when the girls asked to go. "You can see it tomorrow."

The house was a typical wood-framed bungalow, somewhat larger than their present house. Emily noticed immediately the fresh paint – a light gray that reminded her of ashes in the fireplace. Across the front porch was a concrete banister supported on each end with wide brick columns. Just as she had thought, the railroad tracks were down an embankment - only a few hundred feet from the house. She shuttered to think of the danger if the children got too near the tracks. When she stepped onto the porch, she could see that the front rooms were freshly painted too. Inside the house, she got another surprise from Edwin. "I painted all the rooms apple green, like the other house we had. Don't you like it?"

Emily tried not to show her bewilderment. "It looks very nice and clean."

"The outside is battleship gray."

Emily reflected. He wants the house to look like a ship, with him the captain. Even the pine floors are scrubbed to perfection, like a ship's deck. She turned away from him, fearing he would see her perplexity. She ran her hand over the dark oak woodwork. At least this dark color breaks the monotony of the green paint.

"I want to paint the wicker furniture green when we get moved. It needs painting. Oh, I forgot to tell you. I've put the house in your name – so no one can take it from me in a lawsuit. Lawsuits can happen in the insurance business."

Emily turned around in complete surprise. She didn't understand what he meant, but she felt a glimmer of hope. For the first time since they had been married, she owned something. He surprised her again when he said, "I plan to build two bedrooms and a bathroom onto the back of the house next summer for the boys. Then we'll have enough room."

The dining room was nearly as large as the living room. This arrangement pleased Emily. She wanted a space where all the family could sit down and eat together – like her family had done at home. A swinging door opened into the kitchen that housed a large wood cabinet and two tall, narrow cabinets.

"I bought these for the dishes," Edwin said. "I got them at a second hand store and painted them green to match the rest of the house. This larger cabinet came with the house. It has an icebox at the bottom."

"And this wide-enameled apron on the cabinet will be perfect for rolling out biscuits," Emily exclaimed. She thought of the two long pans that she filled with biscuits every morning for breakfast. The floor was covered with shiny new linoleum, patterned in a geometric design of tan and brown, bordered with green. Emily liked the clean look but not the green color everywhere.

Edwin moved about inspecting the walls and windows for any places he had missed with the apple green paint, or if he could see a speck of dirt. "We'll hook the stove up to the water heater and have plenty of hot water for washing clothes and bathing. I think our stove will fit in here."

Leaning against the large enamel sink, Emily said, "I like the house. Its nicer than any house that we've ever lived in. I'll be glad when we get moved."

Funny, she thought as she walked to the car, Edwin takes more interest in a house than in the children who make it a home. I really don't understand him. Maybe owning a house of our own will make him happier, and he won't be so hard on the children.

ॐॐ

Everyone was busy on moving day. Edwin gave strict orders to the children and assigned each of them a particular place of duty. "Mary! Margaret! Ya'll get in here and help your mama put away the dishes." Mary meandered into the kitchen from the dining room followed by Margaret. Suddenly, Edwin grabbed the girls by their arms and shoved them into the kitchen. "Now don't come out of here until every dish is put away. Where are Laura and Lucy?"

"I don't know," Mary said. "I think they're in the bedroom."

Edwin hurried to the bedroom. Laura and Lucy were putting sheets on the beds. They looked up in fear of their daddy but continued to make the bed. Edwin turned around and went outside to give instructions to the boys. "Take the last of the boxes off the truck and put them in the house!" he shouted. "Henry, you watch out for your baby brother and keep him out of the way."

Henry found a place to play under the shade of the elm tree. He was happy to be away from his daddy. Suddenly, a tremendous roar startled everyone. The house shook as a rushing freight train sped down the tracks, looking as if it would come straight through the house. Emily froze with fear, not knowing where the two small boys were playing. Calen began to scream, and Henry, who was only six, couldn't quiet him.

Edwin rushed over to his two small sons. "Calen! Calen! Stop that crying right now, or I'll give you something to cry about."

Emily ran to the front of the house just in time to see Edwin give each of the boys a powerful slap on the rear. "Now, go to the backyard, and don't let me hear anymore screaming."

Emily went into the yard and picked Calen up, holding him on her hip. She looked down at Henry. "That was a terribly loud train, Henry. You and Calen must never go on those tracks. Let's go in the kitchen and I'll get you some milk. Edwin looked at her with disgust but went back to unloading the truck.

Mary took Calen and sat down in the kitchen to quiet him. His big blue eyes with thick long lashes were wet with tears. Mary ran her fingers through his soft blond hair several times until he was settled. After he finished drinking his milk, he nodded and dropped off to sleep. Cuddled in her arms, Mary took him into the bedroom and laid him in his crib. With two double beds and the crib placed at the foot of one, there was hardly room to walk in the crowded bedroom. A large dresser was placed between two short windows, and its mirror shut out most of the air that was stirring outside. Margaret's cedar chest was pushed against the foot of the other bed - off limits to anyone. Inside the cedar chest were the piece goods her grandmother had sent her. Margaret had learned to sew her own clothes which led to a contention between her and Mary. Since Mary often slipped and wore her sister's clothes, an argument would ensue and Mary would get a whipping. She had learned to wear more than one skirt to bear the blows of her daddy's belt.

When Mary returned to the kitchen, the two Negro men who were helping with the move brought in the heavy, cast-iron stove. Edwin followed behind, anxious to get the stove connected to the chimney. Emily and the girls moved out of the way into the dining room. The large oak table in the center of the dining room was surrounded by ten sturdy, new ladder-back chairs that Louise had sent. She knew Emily's desire to seat all the children around the table for each meal. *"This is my contribution for the new house,"* she had written explaining her gift. Emily smiled as she thought hopefully they would last until the children were grown.

"I don't like this bed in the dining room, but it's the best we can do for now," Emily said. "You and Laura will have to sleep in here, Margaret, until your daddy builds the rooms onto the back of the house. Maybe it won't be too long." Laura looked at her sister and frowned, but she didn't complain for fear her daddy would hear her. Emily sat down in one of the new chairs and looked at her swollen feet. "Whew, too much standing today!" She felt as if the baby would come any minute, but it wasn't due for three more months.

Chapter Eighteen

Lillie's Illness

It was a perfect autumn day to hang the clean-washed clothes outside. Emily took a few deep breaths, enjoying the fresh air before she began fastening each piece to the sagging metal line. Bending down to the clothes basket was difficult, since she was in her sixth month of expecting her tenth child. She put some of the wooden clothespins in her mouth to avoid stooping. After the first line was full, she stopped a minute to take in the beauty around her. "What a glorious day!" The sky was the color of a deep blue lake, and the leaves on the trees were brushed with a burst of color. Some were the color of red clay - others as yellow as summer squash and as orange pumpkins waiting to be picked in the fields.

When she had time alone, Emily found pleasure in daydreaming - fantasizing of having a husband who would come home from work, take her in his arms and tell her how much he loved her. She pictured his greeting the children with playfulness and affection. To make her dream complete, they would live in a large comfortable house. She continued to fantasize until she had hung the last piece of laundry, filling each line to capacity. Turning from her chore, she felt relieved the clothes would dry quickly in the warm sunshine. Daily life was difficult but a little easier now that most of the children were in school.

"Calen, don't touch the sheets," Emily called. Playfully, her small son was running in and out among the clothes that were hanging like motionless banners on the windless day. "Come on," she added. "Let's go and see if the mailman has come."

Three letters lay in the bottom of the big metal mailbox - the electric bill, the water bill and a letter from her brother Albert. Her heart quickened when she saw the letter from her brother. He had never written her. Was something wrong with her mother or daddy? Her intuition was right. *Mama is very ill,* Emily read, after quickly opening his letter. *She has had a severe stroke, and we aren't sure she will live. Is there any way you could come?* Emily put her hand over her heart as it raced with fear. All the guilt that she had felt over the years about her mother was racing in her mind. She felt terrible remorse - remorse that she had never understood her mother's feelings for her and now the fear that she might lose her. As she walked to the house, she pulled her apron up and wiped the tears that flooded her eyes.

"Calen," she called again, "we must go in and see about Lucy. She'll wonder where we are." Calen continued to throw the handful of rocks he had picked up off the road. "Come on now."

"I'm hungry, Mama," Lucy said, when her mother came inside.

"All right, I'll see what we have to eat." She knew there was little food in the house, but she would find something. We have some homemade bread, milk, and some applesauce, she thought. Lucy loves milk, and Calen likes applesauce on bread. Maybe that will satisfy them. Emily wasn't hungry. All she could think of was her mother and whether she could go and see her.

When the older children came in from school, Emily found it painful to tell them about their grandmother. She was saddened to see their sorrow. Each time Lillie had come when Emily had a baby, she had read to them and told them stories about her childhood. They would sit for as long as she had time, listening and learning, but most of all enjoying the closeness of their grandmother. Emily knew her mother had given them something she hadn't had time to give. Life passes so quickly, she thought. Mama may never be able to come again. She caught her breath and asked Mary if she would look after her brothers and sisters for a few days in order for Emily to go and see about Lillie.

"I can take Calen with me."

"Sure, Mama... I will if Margaret will help. What about Daddy, will he take you?"

"I'll have to ask him when he gets home."

᷾ᚌ

Anxiously, Emily waited for Edwin to come home. It was late. The children were already in bed, perhaps not asleep, but quiet. When Edwin came into the kitchen, she took his supper from the oven that was still warm. "I'm tired," he said. He sat down, not even looking up at her.

After putting his supper on the table, Emily sat down across from him and waited a minute before saying anything. She dreaded telling him about her mother, not knowing what he would say about her going home and wondering if he would take her.

"I got a letter from Albert today," Emily said. "Mama is very sick. He said she might not live. She's had a stroke."

Edwin looked up from his plate, "Miss Lillie sick … that's hard to believe." Her mother was one of the few people Emily had ever seen him show any concern for. He had always been polite to her and always on his best behavior when she came to visit. He must care for her, Emily thought.

"I want to go and see her. Would you take me? I could take Calen. Mary will look after the others while I'm gone."

Edwin looked at her and frowned. "Looks like you've already got it planned. You mean you would actually leave the children? How long would you stay?"

"I don't know. I'll have to see how severe the stroke was." Her face revealed her complete despair. I can't leave the children too long … maybe a week at the most."

"Well, I guess since today is Friday, I can take you tomorrow and come home on Sunday." He continued to eat.

"We'll need some groceries for the children before we go," reminding him again there was hardly anything in the house to eat.

"They'll have to get by until I get back. They can find something,"

Emily got up and walked over to the sink. She couldn't look at him. She was seven months pregnant with her tenth child, her mother was dying, she had no money and no food in the house for her children. "Don't you care if the children have food, Edwin?" She turned around, but he had left the room.

ॐॐ

A strong wind was blowing when Emily got out of bed, and the sky was overcast. "Oh, I hope it doesn't rain," she said to herself. She moved slowly about the room to dress, careful not to awaken Edwin, always cherishing the few quiet moments she had to herself before anyone else was awake. It was one of the few times she had to think without interruptions. Was she really going to see her folks? How many years has it been? Too many to count, she thought. She slipped her plain, full house dress over her head and looked in the mirror to brush her hair. Somehow her hair looked grayer in color, and her stomach looked more distended. Reaching up to her face with both hands, she lightly traced her eyes as if trying to erase the dark circles under them. She sighed and walked over to a small chair to put on her thick, cotton stockings. Her thoughts turned to her mother, and she forgot about herself and how she looked. "Please, Lord," she prayed. "Please don't let Mama die now. What would Daddy do without her? What would we all do?"

In the kitchen she was surprised to find Mary and Margaret already up and dressed. "Well, are ya'll ready to take over?" she asked smiling. "Do you think you can manage while I'm gone? Your daddy says he'll take me."

"What are we supposed to eat while you're gone?" Mary asked. "I don't see much here."

Emily looked up from putting some coal into the stove. She felt her face flush with guilt. "I've asked your daddy to get some groceries, but he says you'll have to wait until he gets back home on Sunday."

Mary bit her lip, trying not to say the ugly things she was thinking. She turned her back to her mother and whispered, "I hate him. I hate Daddy."

Margaret saw the distress on her mother's face. "Don't worry, Mama. We'll be all right."

"I hope so." She lifted the round cover from the eye of the stove and poked the coals with the short poker. Taking a large pot from the cabinet, she filled it half full of water, added a teaspoon of salt, and waited for it to boil before adding three cups of oatmeal. She had done this maneuver so many times - she could have done it with her eyes closed. After she put a small percolator of coffee on the back eye of the stove, she went over to the icebox. When she bent down to look in, she saw a quart of milk, enough butter for the morning meal, a small piece of white salt pork and three eggs in a bowl. Moving each item, she couldn't see anything else. She took out the milk and butter and put it on the table. "Get some bowls out for the oatmeal, Mary, and go call the others to come and eat. Margaret, see if Laura has dressed Calen. We will need to leave soon."

"Yes, mam," Margaret said.

After the children were fed, Edwin came into the kitchen, fully dressed in his coat and tie. "I'll have some scrambled eggs," he said to Mary as she cleared the table.

"I have some oatmeal already cooked," Emily said. "I was saving the eggs for the children to have later."

"No, I think I'd rather have the eggs."

Mary turned and looked straight at him. "What are we supposed to eat while ya'll are gone?" she complained, angrily.

"You're eating now, aren't you? You'll have to get by till I come back." Mary looked at him hard and determined but held her tongue lest she push him too far. Emily continued to wash the dishes, not sure if Mary would provoke her daddy to a whipping. She couldn't turn around until Edwin left the room.

"Well, I've got to see if Laura has Calen dressed," Emily said. When she had washed the last dish, she turned around to Mary. "You can get some bread from the milkman, Mary. I hope I won't be gone but a few days. Remember to watch Henry and Daniel about the railroad tracks."

"Quit worrying, Mama. We'll be all right. At least we'll be rid of Daddy for a few days."

Emily looked at her and frowned. "Mary," she said, shaking her head.

When Edwin pulled the old Ford car out of the driveway, the children gave a shout of relief. "Yea! Yea! He's gone."

It wasn't until late afternoon that Mary saw the seriousness of the food problem. There wasn't enough, not even for one meal. "I have a plan," she told Margaret. "We can borrow some flour from the Lamberts, some sugar from the Wheelers and two eggs from the Holcomb's and we'll make a cake. We'll call it a sponge cake." They all began to laugh. Eddie and Jonathan leaned on the table with their elbows, their eyes wild with excitement. Daniel danced around the room. "Now, Laura, you go over to the Wheelers for two cups of flour. Eddie, you go and borrow two cups of sugar from the Holcombs, and you go and get two eggs from the Lamberts, Daniel. You can talk them into letting you have the eggs. It might be hard to get anything out of them."

"I still have my birthday dollar Grandma sent me," Daniel said. "I made sure Daddy didn't take it. I watched for the postman and took it out of the mailbox before Mama got the mail. I can buy something from the store with it."

"You'd spend your birthday dollar on us?" Mary asked.

"I don't care," Daniel said.

Mary thought a minute. "If that's what you want to do, you could buy some eggs, some peanut butter and a can of salmon." Funny, she thought, Grandma has always come to our rescue, even now when she's dying. She felt very sad and glad at the same time. Now they would have enough food to get by, but it made her sad that Daniel had to spend his precious birthday dollar on food for all of them. Their grandmother would be proud of Daniel for sharing. Mary could hear her now, "God will repay you for your good deeds."

While the others were gone, Mary added coal to the cook stove to heat the oven for the cake. She found some cocoa and baking powder and put them out on the cabinet. "We'll soon have a nice cake," she said to Lucy who was already missing her mama. When Daniel came in with the groceries, he also had turnip greens and sweet potatoes that Mrs. Lambert had given him. "You must have given Mrs. Lambert a good story, Daniel," Mary said. She took the food out of the sack and looked at everything before putting it away. She was relieved.

"I did. I almost had her crying," Daniel said grinning.

"What did you tell her?"

"I told her that daddy was sick and couldn't work, and we didn't have any food." He put his hands in his pockets, twisted and turned around the table, enjoying every minute of his tale.

"Daniel! Mama's gonna get you for telling a story, but I'm not going to tell her," Mary said, laughing.

When Laura and Eddie returned with the flour and sugar, Mary took care to mix up the best cake she could. She remembered her mother's recipe for a yellow cake. She took the second cup of sugar and mixed it with some cocoa and milk to make enough icing to cover the top of the cake. Suppertime was like a party; everyone had as much cake as they wanted, and Daniel had them all laughing with his story of Mrs. Lambert.

The feeling of celebration continued after supper. In the early evening, it was warm enough to sit on the front porch. The four girls sat in the swing, and the boys lined the banister with their legs hanging off like dangling ropes from a tree. This was the fun they had waited for - the thing their daddy had forbidden them to do. They wanted to watch the Wheelers who lived across the street and partied every Saturday night. Mr. Wheeler would carefully take his guitar out of its big black case and begin to play as the rest of the family sang along. The words of the songs floated easily across the road. "She'll be coming around the mountain, when she comes," sang the Wheelers. Soon the Anderson children were singing along. After Judd Wheeler had passed around a few beers, the singing became louder, and the Anderson children clapped with excitement. As the hours passed, the songs became more melancholy, till finally they were singing in perfect harmony some of the familiar old hymns of the church.

Though the Wheelers two daughters were in their late thirties, they were still living with their parents. Their courting had resulted in several husbands who came and went in a parade as colorful as one at Mardi Gras. Edwin had forbidden the Anderson children to set foot in the Wheelers' yard or even to sit on their own front porch and catch a glimpse of the real live drama taking place. But in his absence, the children sat spellbound by the Saturday night merrymaking.

"It's ten o'clock, ya'll," Margaret finally said, somewhat bored. "We'd better go inside and put Lucy and Henry to bed." The evening air had suddenly become quite chilly and she got little argument from them. Only Mary lingered. The Wheelers had always held a certain fascination to her. Perhaps it was because her daddy was so disapproving of them. But now as she watched and listened to her heart's content, she wasn't as fascinated as she thought she would be. Soon she went inside like the others and went to bed.

On Sunday morning, the house rang with freedom and

laughter. "I'm going to Sunday School and take Lucy and Henry," Margaret announced. "Does anyone else want to go?"

"I do!" Laura shouted from the bedroom where she was brushing her hair.

"I'm not going," Mary said. "I'm going to stay here and cook dinner."

Daniel, Jonathan and Eddie were outside playing marbles under the chinaberry tree. "Ya'll ought to be going with us," Margaret said, when she and Laura came out with Henry and Lucy.

"We don't want to go," Daniel said defiantly. Eddie and Jonathan never looked up from their game.

"Well, we don't care," Laura said. She took Henry and Lucy by the hand and began the long walk to the Baptist church, almost a mile from their house

৯৯৯

"Home, and too many years since I've been here," Emily sighed under her breath. Edwin paid little attention to her words as he drove the noisy automobile onto the dirt yard of the old house. She hadn't been here since she married - yet little had changed. The white paint was peeling like the bark on a sycamore tree, and the painted tin roof had faded to a dull gray-green. Emily was saddened to see the lack of care the house begged for. It reminded her that her mama and daddy were getting old, and now her mother was sick. She was reluctant to go inside. Slowly, she got out of the car and put her feet on the ground of the place she had once loved, but that seemed so long ago.

Albert and Louise rushed out onto the porch when they saw Edwin and Emily arrive. "Look at you, Emily." She put her arms around her sister and kissed her on the cheek. "And look at little Calen. He's growing like a weed." She picked him up and gave him a hug.

"Edwin," Albert said. "I don't think I've seen you since your wedding. Looks like you've been busy. How many children will this be? Ten?"

Edwin looked chagrined and put out his hand to Albert. "Oh, I've lost count," he said with a smirk. "Louise, it's good to see you."

"Hello, Edwin," Louise said askance.

"How is Mama?" Emily asked.

"The doctor thinks she's out of danger, but she's still very sick," Albert said. "There's some paralysis, but he doesn't think she has lost her speech."

There were more greetings when they came inside the house. Tears filled Emily's eyes as she hugged her daddy. He had aged more than she remembered. She watched as Edwin gave a cordial greeting to all and noticed how polite he was as he shook hands with her father and teased Sarah, Albert's wife, when she came out from the kitchen. He can be very charming if he wants to be, she thought. Little Calen held tight to his mother's skirt. "This is your grandpa, Calen," Emily said. "He's never seen you before."

"He's a fine little boy," Benjamin said. "Come sit on my lap, son." Calen timidly climbed up on his grandpa's lap. After a few minutes, he was smiling at the warm attention from his grandpa.

"May I go in and see Mama now?" Emily asked.

"Yes," her daddy said. "We've told her you were coming, and I think she understood."

Emily quietly opened the bedroom door and tiptoed to the side of her mother's bed. Suddenly she felt sick to her stomach, and the baby moved restlessly inside her. The nausea was like her early days of pregnancy. Maybe it's because I haven't eaten since breakfast, she thought. She rubbed her hands over her face and took a deep breath. A damp, dusty smell and a strong scent of medicine hung heavily over the room. The heavy drapes blocked out much of the light that was already held back by the cloudy day. Standing silently and looking at her mother saddened Emily. Her mother didn't open her eyes. She lay still and pale. Emily couldn't hear her breathing. "Mama … Mama, it's me … Emily. How are you?" Miss Lillie opened her eyes and gave Emily a glassy stare. "Don't try to talk, Mama. I'll just stand here beside the bed." When Miss Lillie closed her eyes, Emily stepped away from the bed and let her tears flow.

Mama will never be the same, she thought as she wiped her eyes. I wonder if it hasn't been too much for her with Albert's family here. She would never have survived all my brood. The years run by so quickly, and too soon life is just a time of surviving. I don't think Mama has ever realized her dreams. Most of her years have been spent in helping other folks, including me. Yet I never felt she truly loved me, and now I'll never know. Emily stepped back over to the bed, placed her hand on her mother's shoulder and patted her arm. "Rest now, Mama," she said and left the room.

Lunch was on the table when she came into the dining room, and her family had already gathered around the table. Sarah had prepared a banquet of golden fried chicken, creamy mashed potatoes, green beans and a hot apple cobbler. When she sat down next to Edwin and listened to her daddy say the blessing, memories of her courting days flooded her mind. Those were happy days. She had loved Edwin then. As she looked around the table at her family, those days were only a memory, but it was still good to be here with them. As she began to savor the wonderful meal, she thought of her children. What were they doing, and what were they eating? If only she had known their ability to survive. She felt her face flush with guilt when Louise asked, "How do you think the children will do without you, Emily?"

"I hope they'll be all right … I've never left them before."

"Oh, they'll be all right. They're big enough to get along without us," Edwin said. Emily wondered if her family could see that things were not right between her and Edwin, but she dared not tell them that they had left the children without enough food.

"What is the doctor saying about Mama?" Emily asked, deliberately changing the subject.

"He thinks she'll slowly get better but never fully recover from the stroke," Albert said. "How did you think she looked?"

"Very ill," Emily said looking down at her empty plate.

❧∞❧

As Edwin was leaving, just after lunch on Sunday, Emily said, "I can take the bus home on Friday afternoon, but I'll need some money for bus fare. Will you meet us at the bus depot when we arrive?"

"Yeah, I'll be there." He pulled just enough money for bus fare from his pants pocket, then turned to her daddy, who was standing on the porch. "Goodbye, Mr. Whitworth. Take good care of Miss Lillie."

After Edwin was gone, Emily and Louise sat for a long time in the parlor talking about their mother.

"What will happen if she can't walk or get out of bed?" Emily asked.

"I guess we'll just have to cross that bridge when we get to it," Louise said. "Now, tell me about your children."

Emily paused before answering. For a long time she had wanted to talk to Louise about Edwin's cruel treatment of the children, and now she found it difficult. But Louise would understand and she was relieved to tell her. "Edwin is very hard on them. He whips them too often and too severely either with his belt or his hand. Sometimes they don't even know why he's whipping them. I've thought about leaving him, but I don't know where I would go or how we would live." Emily looked down and picked at imaginary strings on her worn dress. "At one time I thought about asking Mama and Daddy to let us come and live with them, but that's when I learned that Albert and his family were already living here."

"Is there no way you can talk to him?"

"I've tried, and he says, he's their daddy and the only thing they understand is the belt."

"I wish I could help, but I'm lost for an answer."

"Oh, Louise, I don't know what I would have done without the help you've already given me. You have helped me so many times ... I don't know the answer to my problems either, especially since I'm about to have another baby. Surely this is my last one, but you know I love every one of them. I only wish Edwin would love them …I don't think he ever will." She pushed her heavy body up from the parlor sofa. "That's enough about my troubles. Let's go and see about Mama."

Early in the afternoon, Edwin pulled into the driveway. The house was clean and orderly. The boys were playing in the yard, and their sisters were sitting on the porch swing, except for Mary. She was in the living room reading the funny paper and was surprised to see her daddy come home so soon. When he came inside, she asked, "Is Grandma all right?"

"I think she'll be all right, but it'll take a long time for her to get completely well. Did ya'll behave yourselves while I was gone?"

"We made out okay, but we don't have anything to eat". She

put the paper down, stood up and folded her arms across her chest. "Are you going to buy some groceries?"

"I told you I'd buy some tomorrow before I go to work. Now put the paper back together like you found it. You know I don't like it separated before I read it."

"Yes, sir," Mary said. Folding the funny paper, she slipped it inside the other newspaper. "Here's your paper," she said, her hatred for him like the print on the newspaper was written plainly on her face. Quickly, she left the room and went out onto the porch.

❧

The first thing Mary did when she came in from school the next day was to make sure her daddy had bought groceries. A quick inventory revealed he had bought the barest amount of food, and she knew she would have to be very frugal to make it last until her mother came home. The house seemed empty and cold without her mother. Her absence made Mary more aware of her growing distrust of her father. *How can Mama love him knowing he doesn't even care if we have enough to eat?*

"Daniel, will you go and get Lucy from the Holcombs'? I know she's ready to come home, and don't linger," Mary said. The responsibility of caring for her siblings hadn't been easy, and she knew that if anything went wrong, her daddy would give her a whipping.

❧

On Thursday night when her daddy came home, Mary noticed he was in an especially good humor. Everyone was asleep except her. "I won't need any supper, Mary. I've already eaten."

"Okay," Mary replied. "Then I'm going to bed. I'm tired."

Mary slipped her long cotton gown over her head and started to get into bed when she heard her daddy call, "Mary!"

Mary didn't answer. She was hoping he would think she was asleep.

"Mary," he called again, "come in here." Mary went obediently into his room. Her daddy was sitting on the side of the bed in his underwear. "Why don't you sleep with me tonight?" he coaxed, grinning and patting the side of the bed. "I miss your mama, and I need someone to keep me company."

"Unh-unh," Mary answered abruptly and backed quickly towards the door. Her head was swimming with anger and fear. She didn't trust her father. He had never shone her any affection before. Why now? "I have to sleep with Lucy. She misses Mama, and she hasn't been sleeping well."

"All right, but if you change your mind, I'll be waiting."

Mary hurried into her bedroom and closed the door. She leaned against the door and put her hands over her mouth to stifle a cry. Hot tears of anger and frustration coursed down her cheeks. She pulled her gown up, wiped her face and took a deep breath, trying to calm down. When she got into bed, she turned away from Lucy and cried herself to sleep.

ঔৎ৺

By the end of the week, Lillie was out of danger, and Emily and Calen took the Friday afternoon bus home.

Early on Friday afternoon, long before the time for Emily to arrive, Edwin pulled into the driveway followed by an old green truck with a cow corralled in the truck bed. He hopped out of his car and loudly instructed the men to back down the driveway to unload the cow. Tugging and struggling, the two men held tight to the ropes around the neck of the frightened cow and pulled her down the ramp of the truck. "Take her behind the barn, there!" Edwin shouted. "She's mighty spirited."

"Mercy," one of the men said. "I believe that's the meanest cow I've ever seen."

The children crowded at the back door, watching. They had seen cows at the Hensons' dairy, but they had never seen a cow like this one. "Look at her horns," Eddie said. "She looks like she could butt you if you got close enough."

"Are we gonna have to milk her?" Jonathan asked - his eyes wide with fear.

"I guess so," Eddie replied, "if Daddy says so."

After the men left, Edwin came into the house and washed his hands at the kitchen sink. "What do you think of her, Eddie?" But before Eddie could answer, his daddy said, "She's a milk cow. I'll teach you how to milk her. I've named her Sulkey cause she's got such a bad temper." Eddie stood straight, almost rigid, and listened to his daddy, not knowing what to say. "Well, now I've got to go and meet your mama at the bus station. You better have everything clean when I get back," he ordered Mary and her sisters.

෨৵৵

In the morning, Emily learned all about the cow. She listened patiently as the younger children told her how the men got the cow out of the truck and how mean she was. She wondered how they would ever take care of a cow. Still, she thought it would be nice to have plenty of fresh milk.

"She's the meanest cow you ever saw, Mama," Jonathan said.

"Let's go and see how mean she is," Edwin said, coming into the kitchen. "Come on, Jonathan, you and Eddie are going to learn how to milk."

In the barn Sulky was eating the feed Edwin had put out for her. When she saw the boys, she began to raise and lower her head and kick her hind feet. "Whoa now," Edwin cautioned. He took the milking bucket and sat down on the low stool to milk. "You've got to win her confidence and don't let her know you're afraid of her. "See. Now, Eddie, sit here and try."

Eddie moved slowly to the side of the cow and took a seat on the small stool. When he placed his hands on the warm teats of the cow, his daddy showed him how to gently close his hand in a downward motion to make the milk flow into the bucket. After several minutes, Eddie began to relax and lose his fear of the cow. "That's it; now you can teach Jonathan," Edwin instructed.

෨৵৵

"Looks like you managed well while I was gone, Mary," Emily bragged when Mary came into the kitchen for breakfast. "I worried about you, but I shouldn't have. You did a good job." Mary smiled, taking in the praise. Praise was something she didn't hear often, and her mother's attention helped to lessen her anxiety about her father. But she wouldn't tell her mother about his asking her to sleep with him. She couldn't.

172

Chapter Nineteen
Death of a Child

The labor was short and the delivery routine. Doctor Mitchell placed the tiny, red and wrinkled baby boy on Emily's stomach while he tied off the umbilical cord. "Are you running out of names?" he said, teasing Emily.

"Oh, no," she answered with a weak smile. "We're going to name him Judson Whitworth after one of my brothers."

"That's a mighty distinguished name for this little feller. I believe he's your sixth boy?"

"That's right." Emily took the tiny infant from the nurse and closely examined his well-formed body. She could see a slight resemblance to her father. She smiled approvingly.

"Well, I hope your daughters will help with the baby. I bet they'll enjoy looking after him. I want you to take care of yourself. Stay in bed for at least a week, or better yet for ten days."

"I'll try." Emily said, knowing it would be near to impossible with so much to do. The girls would be in school most of the day and unable to take much responsibility until they returned home.

❧

January and February were difficult months for Emily – with very few days warm enough, or sunny enough, to hang the diapers and wash outside. She looked forward to the warmer weather of spring when the smaller children could play outside.

Before the March winds died down, Edwin had the vacant lots

on either side of the house plowed. The three on the left he planned to plant in corn and the one on the right, next to the house, would be a vegetable garden. He also engaged two men to build two rooms and a bath onto the back of the house. Emily quickly realized the large degree of work he expected from the children. Every morning he got them up early before school and had them planting, hoeing and carrying heavy lumber for the building of the rooms. Emily watched from the kitchen window. She could hear him shouting and demanding them to work faster. He took no consideration of their young ages or the fact that they were still in school.

Mary came running into the kitchen. "Mama, Daddy's making Laura and Margaret pull the garden plow and Margaret's crying."

"I see them, Mary. I'll go out and talk to your daddy." Emily wiped her hands on her apron and went out to the edge of the garden. "Edwin, don't you think pulling a plow is too hard for the girls?"

"You just get back in the house and mind your own business, woman! If they want to eat, they'll have to work."

Emily's face flushed with anger and humiliation. If only she had the courage to stand up to him, but confronting him would only make him angry, and he would take it out on the children. "There must be a way, Lord," she prayed quietly. "Help me; I don't know where to turn or what to do." She put her hands on her hips and called out. "It's almost time for school, time to stop!" She quickly went back into the house before Edwin could voice his objection. After packing their lunches for school, Emily looked out the window and was relieved to see the children racing to the house with hardly enough time to get to school. Hurt and anger masked Laura's face when she came into the kitchen. Her dress and shoes were streaked with dust, and the damp morning air had wilted her curls. Emily had seen her earlier that morning rolling her hair using paper-covered metal she had saved from the tops of the Eight o'clock coffee bags. She looked so pretty when she went out to the garden, and now it was time to leave for school with only time to wash her face and hands. "I'm sorry, Laura," Emily said, trying to console her daughter. Laura wiped the tears that coursed down her cheeks with her hand, and without a word, she picked up her small sack lunch and left for school.

჻

"March is coming in like a lion," Emily told the children as they ate breakfast on Saturday morning. "What does that mean, Mama?" Henry asked.

"Oh, I think it means God is doing his spring house cleaning with a very strong wind, like the roar of a lion, blowing away all the old leaves and getting ready for the new ones to sprout on the trees. Then everything will be new again."

"Can we make a kite?" Henry asked.

"I think so. While I finish washing the dishes, get your brothers to find some long, straight sticks. We'll use some old newspapers, and I can make some paste out of flour and water."

Eddie jumped up from the table and playfully thumped Henry on the head. "Come on, Henry, I'll help you find some sticks. A field down by the creek has lots of dried bull weeds - they'll make good kite sticks."

Emily watched happily as the excited boys left for their venture. She was thankful Eddie would take time for his little brother. She had noticed how inventive Eddie was, making toys out of almost anything. It hadn't escaped her notice how Eddie tried hard to please his daddy, but he was the one his daddy whipped the most. She wondered if Edwin would break his spirit, but she noticed punishment only made Eddie try harder.

Just as Emily finished washing the last breakfast dish, Henry came running into the kitchen shouting, "Mama! Mama!"

"What is it?" Emily said.

"The Wheelers have made a kite as big as our house and are trying to fly it."

"Well, let's go and see!" She followed Henry hurriedly out to the front porch where all the other children were watching. She stood in amazement as Judd Wheeler ran down the road holding the huge kite, almost the size of a bed. One of his daughters ran in front of him, holding the kite string and one followed behind, holding up the long tail made of strips of rags.

"I bet they'll never get it to fly," Daniel said, leaning over the banister.

"I bet they will," Mary argued. The wind whipped and gusted, the kite whirled and twirled, and the children laughed and jumped up and down in excitement as they ran to the edge of the yard - careful not to go any farther lest their daddy see them.

"See, I told you it wouldn't fly," Daniel boasted.

"Come on, Henry, let's take the sticks and make our kite. We'll show 'em how to make a kite that'll fly," Eddie bragged.

Unnoticed, Edwin had come around from the back of the house. "There won't be any kite making now. We've got planting to do." Eddie stepped back, startled to see his daddy. No one said a word. Emily and the girls went quickly into the house, followed by the smaller boys. "Come on, Eddie. Bring Jonathan and Daniel with you. Let's get going. Bring the garden tools by the garage door."

Emily saw Henry's disappointment when he came into the kitchen. "I wanted to make a kite."

"Mary," Emily called, "if you'll feed the baby, I'll help Henry make a kite."

"I'll feed him, Mama," Laura said eagerly.

Emily smiled and handed the baby and his bottle to Laura. She had already collected some newspaper, made the paste and cut the pattern for the kite. "You can tear the rags for the tail, Henry, and I'll cut the sticks. Mercy sakes, we don't have any string!"

"There's a ball of string in the tool shed Daddy uses to tie up the beans," Henry said. Emily looked at Henry. She knew Edwin had forbidden the children to touch anything in his toolbox.

"I guess we'll have to wait until we can buy some string. We mustn't bother your daddy's things. Stand the kite in the corner of the dining room until one of your brothers can go and buy some string."

It was near lunchtime when Emily heard Henry screaming as he ran into the house. His legs were bloody with switch marks. Daniel ran in behind Henry. "Daddy whipped him for getting string out of his tool box. He didn't have to whip him so hard," Daniel cried.

Emily took a damp cloth and wiped Henry's legs. Edwin knows no limits, she thought. She put her hands on Henry's shoulders and looked into his tear-stained face. "You must learn not to touch your daddy's things, Henry. We'll get some string. Now sit down to the table, and I'll give you some lunch."

෴

"I still have some of my birthday dollar," Eddie told Henry that night as they were getting ready for bed. "I'll buy some string on my way home from school Monday, and we'll fly that kite."

❧

When he returned home from school on Monday, Eddie took Henry with his homemade kite out to the open road. Eddie held the ball of string, releasing a small amount at a time. Henry ran holding the kite with its tail trailing on the ground. Soon the brisk March wind catapulted the diamond-shaped handiwork high into the pale blue sky. Henry screamed with delight. "Let me hold it, Eddie! Let me hold the string!"

"Okay, but don't let go," Eddie instructed.

Emily watched from the porch. "I'm not such a bad kite maker," she said, almost with a laugh, and for a moment her heart felt light.

❧

School ended the last day of May, and already the garden was showing rewards of the hard work of the children. There were rows and rows of fresh shoots of corn in the fields and in the garden the beginnings of beans, tomatoes, squash and onions. To make sure there were no weeds around the new plants, Edwin had the young boys hoeing from daylight to dark, and the work had to be done exactly as he instructed. If one of the boys hadn't done his part, they all got a whipping. Sometimes Emily would have to take the younger children down the road, away from the house, to keep them from hearing the cries of their brothers.

That same spring, Edwin bought a bushel sack of peanuts to plant and warned the children not to touch them. "I've tied this sack with a special knot and hung it on a nail in the back room where the men are working. If one of you unties it, I'll know it, and I'll wear you out with my belt."

❧

Two afternoons later, Lucy slipped into the back room and looked at the peanuts. "I can pull this ladder up and untie the sack, and Daddy will never know if I take only a few peanuts." Daniel was already eyeing the sack.

"No, Lucy, you better not. Daddy will know. You'll get a whipping." Lucy paid no mind to her brother, climbed the short ladder, untied the sack, got a handful of peanuts and put them in her pocket. Carefully, she retied the knot the way she thought her daddy had tied it and climbed down the ladder.

"Look, I tied it back just like he had it, and he won't know I've touched it. Sides I'm hungry," Lucy said. "Don't tell on me and I'll give you some." Daniel smiled and sat down on the floor with his sister as they relished every bite of the raw peanuts. When the forbidden treasure was gone, they ran off to play outside, believing they were scot-free.

❧

Before he went into the kitchen, Edwin went to the back of the house where the men were working and walked slowly around the rooms inspecting the work of the day. When he caught a glimpse of the peanut sack, he knew immediately that someone had opened it. His face turned red with rage. He reached up and closely examined the sack. "Someone's been in the peanuts."

"I think it was your little girl," one of the workmen said, not realizing the consequences of his statement.

Edwin untied the sack and retied it. He went quickly to the kitchen where Emily and Mary were preparing supper. "Where's Lucy?" he asked angrily.

"I think she's playing at her friend's house," Emily said. She looked questioningly at him, completely unaware of what Lucy might have done.

"Go and get her, Mary," he commanded.

"What's she done?" Mary asked, aware of his anger and sure he intended to punish Lucy.

"None of your business. Just go and get her, right now."

Daniel overheard his daddy and stopped Mary when she came out the door. "I'll go and get her," he said. Daniel ran as fast as he could and found Lucy playing with her friend in the backyard. "Lucy," he called excitedly, "Daddy wants you. He said for you to come home, right now. You're in trouble, Lucy. He knows you opened the peanuts."

Lucy's eyes widened with fear. "How does he know? Did you tell him?"

"No, I didn't tell him, but he knows."

Since Lucy was only five, she had never suffered a whipping like her brothers and sisters. Terrified, she walked hesitantly into the unfinished room where her daddy was waiting. He held one of the long narrow boards used to hold the plaster to the wall. It was covered with prickly splinters. "Come here, Lucy!" he shouted - his face red with anger as he tapped the board back and forth in his hand. "Didn't I tell you not to eat the peanuts?"

"Yes sir," Lucy murmured, her voice faint, as tears welled up in her eyes.

"Well, you're going to get a whipping." He grabbed her and threw her over his lap, beating her until her legs were a mass of bloody red whelps. Her cries cut to the heart of the older children standing and listening outside the room. When Edwin came out of the room, Mary ran in and found Lucy sitting on the floor, sobbing uncontrollably. She pulled Lucy up by her hands and put her arms around her little sister. Looking down, she saw the narrow board her daddy had used and grabbed it off the floor. She took Lucy into the kitchen where her daddy was warning the other children not to touch the peanuts. Opening the round lid of the stove, Mary pushed the piece of wood into the fire, hoping her daddy would see her hatred that blazed up like the piece of wood in the stove.

Emily offered no words of comfort. She felt completely numb and frightened of Mary's hatred for her father. Fear and hopelessness had become her daily companions. Hard as she tried there was nothing left to give, nothing left to offer hope. Edwin ignored Mary and left the kitchen with no regret for the pain he had inflicted on his very young daughter.

Emily had hardly laid her head on the pillow that night, when Edwin put his arm around her waist and pulled her body to him. She knew his intentions, but she pulled away, having lost all feeling for him, and he must have known it. Still he made his dispassionate advances, forcing himself upon her. In her disquieting dread, only a month later, she realized she was pregnant.

Ashamed to even let Doctor Mitchell know, she waited for months before going to his office. "How far along do you think you are?" he asked.

"I … I think about five months."

As he examined her, he observed her sad eyes and her rough red hands. Not knowing what to say, he gently helped her down from the table. When she came into his office, he said. "I think you are about five months along, but the baby is quite small. I want you to come back in two weeks. I need to watch you closely until the baby comes.

"Thank you, Doctor Mitchell, I'll do my best to get here." She hurried out to the car where Edwin was waiting.

෭ංෂ

Franklin was born in late February, early in the afternoon, just after Judson had begun to walk. He weighed less than six pounds, much smaller than any of her other babies. Before he was a month old, Emily realized something was wrong with him. "He just doesn't seem to digest his milk," she told Doctor Mitchell.

"Yes, I can see that he hasn't gained any weight. Let's try a different formula and add some sugar to make him more interested in eating." He looked at the tiny infant again, trying to conceal his concern from Emily. When she returned home, Emily gave the baby all the attention Doctor Mitchell had instructed; still the tiny baby grew weaker every day.

෭ංෂ

"I'm going to call the doctor and ask if he will come and check Franklin," Emily told Mary, before she left for school. "I can't get your daddy to take us to his office. He just keeps making excuses, and the baby isn't any better."

Mary looked at her mother and then down at the tiny baby lying in his crib. "Oh, Mama, is he going to die?" Tears filled her eyes.

"Only the Lord knows, Mary. Franklin is in God's hands now. Dr. Mitchell will do all he can, but healing doesn't always come in the way we want it."

When Doctor Mitchell arrived in the late afternoon, he carefully lifted the tiny, three-month-old baby from his crib, laid him on Emily's bed. After examining Franklin, he put his arm around her shoulders. "I'm sorry, Emily. He has a serious digestive malformation. There's nothing I can do for him. Try and keep him as comfortable with this medicine and continue to feed him, but his body will never be able to process the nourishment he needs to live. Let the girls help you with him. Call me when you feel I can help."

Emily looked at him in complete despair. No tears would come. "Was it something I did? Was it from not eating right? I couldn't bear it if it was my own doing, Dr. Mitchell."

"Some things are a mystery, Emily. We just don't know why and may never know in this lifetime."

A week later Franklin died. Emily was in a state of exhaustion. Even though she had ten other children, her heart was broken to lose this baby who had needed her love and care so completely.

When Doctor Mitchell came to write the death certificate, he told Edwin, "I'm so sorry. I wish I could have done more. Emily is not taking this well; she has been up night and day for a week caring for him. I hope you'll see she gets some rest. What will you do about burying the baby?"

"I'll go and make the arrangements." He put on his coat and hat, anxious to escape the scrutiny of Dr. Mitchell.

"I'll stay a little longer and talk to your children," Dr. Mitchell said. Mary and Margaret were sitting on the sofa; their eyes red and swollen. They were apprehensive, not knowing what to say. "Do you have a neighbor who can come and prepare the baby for burial?" Doctor Mitchell asked.

"I ... don't know," Margaret said.

"I'll go and ask Mrs. Holcomb and Mrs. Lambert," Mary said.

"Would you go and get them before I leave?"

"Yes, sir."

When Mary returned with Mrs. Holcomb and Mrs. Lambert, Doctor Mitchell introduced himself, thanked them for coming and took them into the bedroom to see Emily.

"We'll take care of everything," they told the doctor and Emily. "Don't you worry, Mrs. Anderson. Just get some rest."

After Doctor Mitchell left, Margaret showed the ladies the baby clothes Emily had set out for burial of the baby. "My aunt

Eugenia sent these." Gently, Margaret fingered the little garments. "Daddy has gone to buy a casket. He should be back soon."

"I believe we have everything we need right here, Margaret. Maybe you should go into the living room with the other children," Mrs. Holcomb said quietly.

"I'll go with her," Mrs. Lambert said. "I'd like to talk to the children."

When she sat down on the sofa with the smaller children, Mrs. Lambert could hardly hold back her tears. Their sad faces prompted her to say, "You know your little brother is already in heaven with Jesus, don't you?"

"How can he be in heaven with Jesus when he's still lying back there in the bedroom?" Daniel asked, his brows furrowed with confusion.

"I meant his spirit, not his body," Mrs. Lambert explained, seeing they didn't understand.

"I know," Jonathan said. "He's with Grandpa Anderson."

"That's right, son," she said, relieved that he understood.

Mrs. Holcomb went into the girls' bedroom and gently bathed and dressed the beloved baby. She sensed the deep sorrow that had invaded the house, yet she couldn't know all the sorrow and pain that was here day after day. After she finished her somber task, Edwin came in with the casket and laid the baby in it. He thanked the ladies and politely dismissed them. He walked into the bedroom where Emily was lying down. "I'm going to take the baby down to the Shiloh Cemetery tomorrow and bury him. There's no need for a funeral because you aren't able to go."

Emily quickly sat up in bed. "No!" she protested frantically. "Timothy has already agreed to come and have the funeral, and some of my family will come and meet us there. Timothy will come here and take some of the children in his car. I'll be all right."

Edwin looked at her scornfully. He gave no sympathy or comfort but turned and left the room. She was shocked that he gave her no argument.. Perhaps, she thought, he doesn't want to face embarrassment with my family. She slid back down in the bed, laid her head on the pillow and closed her eyes waiting for sleep that wouldn't come.

ॐॐ

Timothy arrived late that same afternoon and sat down beside her bed for a long time, trying to console her. She felt her sorrow lift with his kind words and fervent prayer. "Why don't we have just a graveside service?"

Emily hesitated a moment. "I guess that would be all right. Honestly, the children wouldn't be able to endure much more than a short service, but I do want someone to sing a hymn."

"I'll arrange that," Timothy said quietly, closing the door to the bedroom. "Now I have something I want to give you. He got up and went over to his suitcase and took out something small and silver. It was a gun. "Take this," he whispered as he came to her bedside. "There may come a day you might need it."

She looked at him, stunned, and wondered how much he knew about the way Edwin treated her and the children. Looking at the gun, she said, "I don't think I even know how to use it, but I can't pretend that I may not ever need it. Put it over there in the dresser, the third drawer, under my clothes. I hope I'll never need it."

⊱⊰

The children were quiet and sad as they rode down to Maplesville for the funeral. They remembered their grandfather's funeral. Even Edwin had very little to say. Emily was thinking of her baby. Though she had ten other children, it was difficult to let him go. Looking at the open fields beside the road just beginning to turn green, she was reminded of Christ's promise of life after death and she was comforted.

The graveside service was brief, but meaningful, especially after Mrs. Harvey sang "Safe in the Arms of Jesus." Tears rolled down Emily's cheeks, releasing her grief. Edwin showed no emotion but moved restlessly from one foot to the other until the last prayer was uttered. As Emily looked at her children's sad faces, she knew they were sad for reasons more than Franklin's death, and she resolved to do something about it.

Chapter Twenty
Runaway

In early spring, just after school, Margaret rushed into the kitchen where her mother was busy at the sink washing vegetables for supper. "Mama, the Debate Team is going to Fayette for the state finals. Mrs. Taylor said she'd come and ask your permission for me to go. I can go, can't I?" Breathlessly, she put her books down and reached for a flour muffin her mother had just taken from the oven.

Emily turned around and wiped her hands on her apron. It was good to see excitement and happiness on Margaret's face. She sat down in one of the small kitchen chairs by the table. "I don't see why you can't go, as long as your teachers are responsible for you, and will take you. I don't know what your daddy will say, but I hope he'll be as proud of you as I am and let you go." Surely, she thought, he won't object to something as honorable as this.

"The Debate Team ... the Debate Team, that's all you talk about," Mary complained. She put the last dish from the evening meal in the sink.

Margaret continued to wash them. "You're just jealous 'cause you can't go on the trip." Completely unaware their daddy was listening, they continued to argue.

"Margaret," her daddy called, "come in here." Margaret looked at her sister with fear and dread. She never antagonized her daddy, and she didn't know if he would punish her now for arguing. She walked hesitantly into the living room. "What's this about a trip?" he asked.

"I want to go to Fayette with the school Debate Team for the state finals. My teacher, Mrs. Taylor, will take us in her car," Margaret answered, her heart racing.

"You're not going anywhere, young lady. You should have asked me before making such big plans."

"I asked Mama, and she said I could go. It's just for one day and one night."

"Well, in the first place, your Mama isn't the boss around here, and I'm saying you can't go."

As he got up from his chair, Margaret backed away from him, "but they're counting ..."

"I said you're not going!" Edwin shouted with finality.

Margaret ran from the room sobbing. She found her mother in the bedroom getting the smaller children ready for bed. "Mama, Mama, you'll have to tell Daddy to let me go. I have to go. The team is depending on me," Margaret pleaded.

Emily finished diapering Judson and gave a deep sigh. "I was afraid of this. I'll go and talk to him, Margaret. I'm not sure I'll have any luck, but I'll try."

When Emily came into the living room, she stood behind a chair across from where Edwin was sitting. He had his usual pose, hidden behind the newspaper, still in his coat and tie and so unapproachable. He didn't fit in this house where she and the children dressed so modestly and lived so frugally. She would never understand him. "Edwin, I need to talk to you." She crossed her arms across her chest defensively. "Do you know how much this debate means to her?"

Edwin put the newspaper down in his lap and looked up. His face was flushed with anger. "I don't care what it means to her. She should've asked my permission before making her plans. I don't want to hear any more about it." He snapped the newspaper up to continue reading.

Emily stood there for a moment, wondering how to tell Margaret. She returned to the bedroom, knowing Margaret had heard the conversation. "I'm sorry, Margaret. I don't know what to do." Margaret looked at her despondently and burst into tears.

"I hate Daddy," she said and ran from the room.

❧⚬❧

After she finished washing the supper dishes, Emily hurried to get the smaller children into bed before the school principal came to call. She didn't tell Edwin Mr. Phelps was coming until after supper, and she wasn't surprised when he replied, "Well, he's wasting his time. I've said Margaret isn't going and I mean it."

The knock at the door was short and loud. Emily walked quickly over to the door and opened it. "Mrs. Anderson, I'm Mr. Phelps, the school principal." He was short, neatly dressed and had an air of self-confidence. Maybe he can change Edwin's mind, Emily thought.

"Come in. Margaret told us you were coming."

When they walked over to the center of the room, Edwin rose from his chair. "I'm Mr. Anderson," he said tersely.

"Mr. Anderson," Mr. Phelps acknowledged, extending his hand, "I don't believe we've met." Edwin gave a brief handshake and sat down without a word.

Pointing to the chair across from Edwin, Emily invited Mr. Phelps to have a seat. Emily sat down on the edge of the sofa and nervously smoothed her dress over her knees, trying to remain calm, not knowing what Edwin would do or say.

"You certainly have some well-behaved children, Mrs. Anderson, and they're all doing well in school," Mr. Phelps said amiably.

"Thank you, Sir. School work is easier for some of our children than others of them." She wondered how they could do so well with all the chores they had at home and never having adequate paper and pencils and other supplies they needed.

Mr. Phelps shifted easily in his chair and looked at Edwin. "I've come to talk to you about giving permission for your daughter Margaret to go with the Debate Team to the state finals, Mr. Anderson. Her participation is very important to her and the school. In fact, if she doesn't go, we'll be disqualified."

"Well, I'm sorry about that, but she won't be permitted to go. She broke the rules by not asking my permission before making her plans."

"Is there anything I can do to change your mind?" Mr. Phelps said, disbelieving Edwin's attitude.

"I'm afraid not." Edwin pursed his lips, sat back farther in his chair and looked down at his newspaper.

Mr. Phelps looked at Emily, hesitated a moment, then got up from his chair and looked directly at Edwin. "I'm very sorry you feel this way; I hope you will change your mind." Edwin nodded but didn't get up.

Emily walked to the door with Mr. Phelps. "I'm sorry," was all she could say.

Seeing the desperate look on her face, Mr. Phelps reached out and patted her on the hand and said, "Good night."

Emily closed the front door and went to the kitchen where she knew the girls had been listening. "I'm sorry, Margaret. There's nothing I can do." Margaret burst into tears but didn't say a word and ran from the room. Over the next few days, Margaret ate very little and stayed in her room when she wasn't in school.

☞☜

The conflict between the girls and their daddy was always greater than between him and the boys. Perhaps it was because the girls were older. The first time Edwin saw some young boys come calling on his daughters on a Sunday afternoon, he was livid. "I'll not have a bunch of sorry boys hanging around here!" he shouted. "If I catch them here, somebody will pay with a whipping.

' Mary said nothing, but defiance was written on her face. She wouldn't give up so easily, but her sisters feared their daddy more and decided courting wasn't worth the consequences. Nevertheless, with spring in the air, the girls continued their effort to look pretty, and their admirers couldn't be kept away.

The only place to keep cool on a very warm Sunday afternoon was on the front porch. Laura and Mary were sitting in the swing, and Margaret was perched on the banister. "Look who's coming!" Margaret shrieked.

"Oh, it's those boys from Central Park," Mary recognized. "I know their car."

"What'll we do?" Margaret considered, "...about daddy, I mean." Before they could make any decision, the four lively boys bounced out of their car and ran up onto the porch. Since their daddy wasn't at home, Mary didn't worry, but Margaret said, "Ya'll better leave before our daddy comes home. He won't let us have boyfriends yet."

"Aah, come on, Margaret, you know he doesn't care for us just sitting out here talking," one of the fellas said. Margaret was the one he admired, with her well-formed figure and her soft brown hair falling to her shoulders. Soon they were all laughing and easily forgot about their daddy. Emily listened from the living room, recalling happy memories of Sunday afternoons when she was a young girl.

No one noticed that hours had passed until they heard the hum of their daddy's car coming up the gravel road. Laura froze with fear. "Daddy's coming!" Quickly, the boys jumped over the porch banister like children playing leapfrog. They hurdled into their car and drove away but not soon enough to avoid being seen by Edwin. Quickly, the girls ran inside to their bedroom, hurrying to change their clothes.

"Put on two skirts," Mary said. "If he whips us, it won't hurt as bad."

As soon as Edwin came into the house, he called the girls to come into the living room. Mary marched boldly in. Margaret and Laura, looking terrified, stood just inside the room behind a chair. "I thought I made it clear that you were not to have boys coming here!" their daddy shouted, angrily.

"We didn't invite them. We didn't know they were coming. They just came over," Mary said, biting her fingernail.

"Well, you're going to get a whipping just like I promised. Now all of you go in the kitchen." He removed his belt and twisted it around his hand. Emily felt desperate. How could she stop him? She knew he had warned them, yet she knew if she said anything he would make the punishment more severe. She went into the yard where Lucy, Henry and Judson were playing and took them away from the house.

Before they could walk away, she heard loud sobbing and crying from the girls. "Why is Daddy whipping them?" Lucy asked.

"Because they didn't mind him, Lucy - like the time you didn't mind and ate the peanuts. You children must learn to mind your daddy." Heartsick, she walked out a little farther from the house. Edwin was entirely too strict on them, and she felt desperate to know how to stop him.

When they returned to the house, Emily left the children to play in the yard and entered by the back door. Mary was standing in the kitchen sobbing. The heavy, red marks on her legs gave confirmation to the beating. "You could have stopped him, Mama," she sobbed. Emily wanted to reach out to her, but Mary's expression of hatred and bitterness held her back.

Without telling anyone where she was going, Mary disappeared the next day. When she realized that Mary was gone, Emily sent Margaret over to the Holcombs and Laura to the Lamberts to find her, but she couldn't be found.

By late afternoon Emily was completely distraught, and Edwin could see that she seemed very ill. She was sitting on the side of the bed, holding her hand over her heart and having trouble breathing. "I'm going over to a neighbor's house and call Doctor Mitchell."

☙❧

"I'll come right away," Doctor Mitchell said.

Doctor Mitchell arrived shortly and went immediately into Emily's bedroom. He pulled a small straight chair up to the side of the bed. Edwin stood in the doorway, shifting back and forth from one foot to the other; and when Emily began to tell Doctor Mitchell about Mary's leaving, Edwin left the room. Suddenly Emily's breathing became more labored. Doctor Mitchell reached for his bag. "Don't talk anymore." Taking out his stethoscope, he listened intently to Emily's chest. Quickly he took a small syringe from his bag, filled it with medication and gave Emily an injection.

Slowly her breathing improved, and she opened her eyes. "What happened? Did I faint?"

"No, but you almost left us for good," Doctor Mitchell answered. "Now I want you to quit worrying about Mary. We're going to find her and bring her home. In the meantime, I want you to have complete bed rest. I'll leave some medication here for you to take every four hours for rest."

Emily closed her eyes. She couldn't hold back the flow of tears that streamed down her face. Doctor Mitchell reached down and offered her his handkerchief. Emily wiped her eyes. "I just can't rest until Mary is home."

"I'll go now and talk to Edwin and the children. I want them to know how important it is that you have quiet and rest. Don't worry. We'll find Mary."

Doctor Mitchell wasn't surprised to find Edwin sitting calm and unconcerned by himself in the living room. He wasn't fooled by Edwin's inordinate politeness, and now he knew what he had suspected for a long time - that Edwin was abusing his children. It was easy to discern that they were afraid of their daddy. Even though he didn't ask him to sit down, Doctor Mitchell took a seat across from Edwin and looked at him in all seriousness. "Emily is under entirely too much stress, Edwin. You nearly lost her just now. The situation with Mary is very serious. You must find her and bring her home."

Edwin moved uncomfortably in his chair. He tried to appear completely guiltless. He always wanted to make a good impression on Doctor Mitchell. With a smirk on his face, he maintained, "Mary is a headstrong girl, very difficult to control, but we'll find her … we'll find her."

"Maybe it would be a good idea to contact Emily's sister, Louise. Mary could be there," Doctor Mitchell said. He got up from his chair. "I've left some medicine for Emily that should help her rest. I'll be back to check on her tomorrow afternoon. Could I speak to the older children now? I want them to know their mother's condition."

"I'll get them." He quickly rose from his chair and went to the kitchen. All the children filed into the living room and stood like stair steps: Margaret, then Laura, then Eddie, Jonathan and Daniel, one just a little taller than the next. Last, were the three smaller children, Lucy, Calen and Judson.

"Hello," Doctor Mitchell said warmly. "I need your help. Your mother is very upset over Mary's leaving, and she needs your help. I'd like for you to do the chores for a few days and look after these smaller children. Will you do that for me?"

"Yes, sir," they replied. Doctor Mitchell looked at their sad faces and knew they were totally bewildered by their sister's disappearance. "We're going to find Mary. I'm sure she must be at one of your relatives." He reached over and patted each one on the head and smiled. "I must be going now. I'll come back tomorrow."

৵৵

Mary wasn't at Louise's, but Louise found her the next day and called Edwin at his office. "Mary's at your mother's house. The day she left home, she went downtown to your brother's office, and he gave her bus fare to your mother's. But she says she'll never come home."

Edwin was silent for a minute. "We'll see about that."

"She told me that she won't take anymore beatings," - the word "beatings" bursting from her mouth in a quick, painful rush.

Edwin tried to keep the anger out of his voice. He didn't want to discuss the discipline of his children with her or anyone. He was furious Mary had told Louise about his whipping her. "You don't know how difficult Mary is to handle. She's always defying my orders."

Louise hadn't seen this side of Edwin before, but she wasn't surprised. She remembered what Emily had told her when Miss Lillie was sick. Now she knew it was true. "Well," she said, "I think you need to let her come home and promise not to whip her anymore. She's a young lady now, too old for that kind of punishment. You have to think of how your treatment of the children is affecting Emily."

He could hardly listen to her reproving his behavior, but he gave in for the time being. "All right. All right."

"Then, we'll go and bring her home tomorrow," Louise said. "I'll tell her that you've promised not to whip her again." Edwin was silent. "Goodbye." Louise ended the conversation. Edwin hung up the phone.

৵৵

Late the next afternoon Louise and John Freeman arrived with Mary. Doctor Mitchell pulled into the driveway at the same time. He waited to go inside until he saw them get out of their car. "I'm so happy to see you," he said to Louise and John Freeman. Gently, he put his hand on Mary's shoulder. "I'm glad you've come home, Mary. Your mother was very worried. She's been extremely ill. After I check on her, I would like to talk to you, but for now let's go inside and see her. Your coming home will be better than any medicine I can give her."

191

"Yes, sir," Mary answered, her face coloring with embarrassment.

When they came into the bedroom, Mary waited until Louise and John Freeman greeted her mother. "There's someone else here to see you," Doctor Mitchell added and motioned for Mary to come to the side of the bed.

Hesitantly, Mary walked over to the bed. "Mary," Emily whispered.

"Hello, Mama," Mary said, void of any feeling.

Emily could see deep resentment etched on her face. "I'm glad you're home."

Doctor Mitchell watched intuitively. "Why don't you go see your brothers and sisters now, Mary? I know they're anxious to see you." Mary looked at him with a blank expression, closed her lips tightly, lowered her head in submission and left the room. After Doctor Mitchell had examined Emily, he went to find Mary.

"I'll go and see the children," John Freeman suggested, knowing Louise wanted to talk to Emily alone.

Louise pulled a chair close by the bed and laid her hand on Emily's shoulder. "I've talked to Edwin about Mary. I've told him he is too strict on her and the other girls. They're almost grown and eager for attention from boys - which is natural. He's agreed not to whip them anymore."

Emily looked up at her sister, lovingly. "I'm so glad you've brought Mary home. Doctor Mitchell volunteered to speak to Edwin about his unacceptable treatment of the girls. Maybe both of you can convince him, unless it's too late. Mary seems awfully bitter."

"I had no idea things were so out of control," Louise lamented. "I remember you told me, when Mama was sick, but I guess I just didn't want to believe how cruel he has been."

❧❧

"I'm looking for Mary," Doctor Mitchell told Edwin who was sitting alone in the living room.

"I think you'll find her in the kitchen with her sisters."

"My," Doctor Mitchell commented to Mary, Margaret and Laura when he came into the kitchen, "how pretty you all look today." Laura's and Margaret's cheeks colored with crimson. They had never received this kind of compliment before. Mary, he noticed, turned her head as if annoyed. "Mary, I'd like to talk to you alone if your sisters will leave us for a few minutes." Margaret got up from the table and moved shyly out of the room - Laura followed. Doctor Mitchell closed the door that opened to the dining room, pulled a chair close to Mary and sat down.

"Now, Mary, tell me why you ran away from home." Speaking hesitantly at first and twisting her hair around her finger, Mary shifted nervously in her chair. Suddenly, all the sorrow and grief her daddy had given her flowed out of her mouth like water over a dam. Forgetting her daddy was in the next room, she even told Dr. Mitchell about his asking her to sleep with him, something she had never told anyone. Doctor Mitchell listened with deep concern, and then lovingly reached over to put his hand over hers. "Mary, what I'm about to say, you probably will never understand until you have children. Some people think the only way to raise children is through strong discipline – this method has some value. But whipping never works unless it's balanced with love. Perhaps your daddy doesn't understand love." He paused a moment wondering if she understood anything he was saying. She looked at him through her beautiful, defiant, blue eyes. There were no tears coursing down her cheeks, only a set expression of a child filled with anger. He took his hand from hers and sat back in his chair. "One thing I want you to remember, you will always have the love of your mother and God's love."

Mary bowed her head, overcome by his kindness. When she raised her head, he saw her eyes were filled with tears. Doctor Mitchell rose from his chair, placed his hand on her shoulder and assured her he would talk to her daddy.

Late afternoon shadows darkened the living room where Edwin was still sitting. When Doctor Mitchell entered, Edwin started to get up from his chair. "Keep your seat," he said almost commandingly. "I'll sit here. I must give you some advice about Mary. She is in a very dangerous state of mind for a young girl. You must realize this and not punish her again with whippings. I'm afraid that kind of punishment will result in dangerous consequences to her and to the rest of your family."

Edwin's face reddened with anger. He got up and walked to the door. "I don't need your advice on how to raise my children, Doc. I just need your medical help."

Doctor Mitchell rose from his chair and picked up his bag. "I'm giving you this advice as a friend and hope you will take it that way, Edwin. My argument still stands." He extended his hand to Edwin, but Edwin continued to hold onto the door.

Chapter Twenty One

Confrontation

*W*ith the children growing older, Emily feared another tragedy could occur at any time. Edwin's sadistic cruelty to the children was growing more frequent. She never knew what would set him off into a rage. She wondered if he found pleasure in beating the children. She thought about the gun that Timothy had given her. *I don't even know how to use a gun, but using one would be a drastic solution.* She gazed out the kitchen window at the garden which reminded her of the hard work Edwin had demanded from the children. *I've got to find a better life for them, but there's no place to go with so many children.* How could we survive with no income? She dreaded Edwin's return home each day. No matter what they did, there was no pleasing him. Even though the children feared him, he had not broken their spirit. She was amazed at their resilience – at their laughter and happiness when he wasn't at home.

The first day of May began with a golden morning - bright sunshine and a clear blue sky, perfect weather for the May Day Celebration at their school. Sunlight streamed into the house, cleansing away the shadows of despair and fear. Emily listened as Jonathan and Daniel talked excitedly from their room behind the kitchen.

"I'm going to buy a hot dog," Daniel bragged.

"Aah, you don't have any money," Jonathan quipped. "How

are you going to buy anything?"

"I do have enough," Daniel retorted. "I've got enough to buy a hamburger, too, if I want to."

"Where'd you get any money?" He tied his shoes and turned around eager to hear his brother's answer.

"I collected some drink bottles and got the deposit on them," Daniel revealed twisting his shoulders proudly.

Emily smiled as she listened more closely. "That Daniel," she said to herself. "If there's a way he's going to find it."

"Will you buy me a hotdog?" Jonathan pleaded.

"Maybe."

When the boys came into the kitchen, Emily listened with amusement as they made their plans for the day.

"What's all the excitement about?" Edwin asked when he entered the kitchen and sat down for breakfast.

"It's the May Day Celebration today at school," Emily answered. She put a plate of biscuits on the table along with some scrambled eggs.

"Well, you boys know you've got hoeing to do. I want all the corn in the lower lot hoed. Today!"

Emily looked at him in dismay. She took a deep breath and let out a sigh. He can't let them have even one day of fun, she thought.

"Yes, sir," the boys responded - their excitement fading like the sun wrapped in a drifting cloud. Anxiously, they hurried out of the kitchen and left for the May Day Celebration.

Eddie and Jonathan came home early in the afternoon, went quickly to the cornfield and began hoeing between the long rows of corn. It wasn't long before Daniel and Henry joined their brothers. Emily could see the dust rising from the dry ground as the boys worked all afternoon among the rows of tender plants. Knowing they would be hungry, she placed a large pot of dry beans on the stove and made a skillet of cornbread. When they came into the house just after sunset, they devoured all that she had cooked and fell into bed.

After Calen and Judson were in bed, Emily sat down alone in the living room. Edwin had not come home, and the girls were still at the May Day Celebration waiting to see Lucy perform in a play. Emily leaned back in the wicker rocker and stretched her tired legs, but her moment of solitude ended quickly when she heard the hum of Edwin's blue Studebaker rounding the curve of the road and pulling into the driveway. When he came into the house, his face was fiery red. He clenched his fists, pounding his right hand into his left palm as he often did when he was angry. "Where are the boys?"

Sitting up straight, Emily put her hands on her knees as if to brace herself. "They're already in bed."

"They didn't hoe all the rows of corn like I told 'em. I stopped and checked just now. There are two complete rows that haven't been touched. Did they go to the May Day Celebration?"

Emily wondered how he could have inspected the field in the growing darkness. She shifted forward to the edge of her chair and looked straight at him. "Yes, they went to the school, but they came home early in the afternoon and worked in the field until after sundown. I thought they had gotten all the hoeing done. They were tired and went to bed right after eating their supper."

"Well, I'm just going to get 'em up and give 'em what's coming to 'em. They know that I told 'em to do all the rows." He unbuckled his belt, removed it from his pants and wrapped it around his hand. With the buckle dangling from the end, he went to the back bedroom where the older boys were sleeping.

Emily rushed into her bedroom to her dresser, opened the third drawer and reached beneath her tattered cotton underwear, searching the rough bottom of the drawer for the pistol she had hidden there – the gun her brother Timothy had given her when baby Franklin died. The memory of that day flashed clearly in her mind. "Take this," he had said, handing her the small gun. "You might need it."

She did not hesitate as she took the gun in her trembling hand and moved swiftly to the boys' bedroom. Before she entered the room, she could hear Edwin raving and cursing as he jerked the frightened boys from their bed. "Wait," she called loudly. "They did most of the work, Edwin. Besides they were supposed to go to school today, and you gave them much more hoeing than they had time to do."

"I don't need your observation, woman," he said, burning her ears with his cursing. "Get on out of here."

Emily stepped a little closer - pointing the gun directly at him. "I won't let you whip them this time." Quickly, he turned around, shocked that she would defy him. When he saw the gun, the blood drained from his face, and his eyes were wild with fear. His knees buckled, forcing him to sit down on the side of the bed.

Emily had never seen him frightened before, nor speechless. "Get back in the bed, Eddie, you, too, Jonathan. There won't be any whipping tonight," she said, hardly able to control her shaking voice. Eddie eased around to the other side of the bed and climbed in. Jonathan followed. In fear and disbelief, Daniel and Henry slid back into their bed and pulled the covers up over their heads. The two smaller boys, Calen and Judson, lay terrified in the other room, pretending to be asleep. Still pointing the gun at Edwin, Emily demanded, "Let's go into the living room."

Emily stepped aside as Edwin moved hesitantly in front of her, still not sure of what she might do. When they came into the living room, he reluctantly fixed himself in his chair, and Emily sat in the rocker across from him. She took several deep breaths to gain her composure, then released her tight grip from the gun and placed it on her lap.

Almost pensive, she looked around the room at the same old furniture that had been given to them after their house burned. The interweaving of the wicker was torn on the arms of the sofa and chairs, and the green paint was completely worn off in places. Countless times, Edwin had demanded the children scrub the pine floors and the apple green plaster walls. The floors were almost as dark as the stained woodwork, and the walls were badly faded.

A small white radio sat on a green wicker table in the corner of the room. Emily shook her head at the thought of the radio being the only thing in the room not painted apple green and the only thing that had ever given the children any pleasure. She imagined she could hear their laughter as they listened to "Fibber McGee and Molly" or "Amos and Andy."

Eleven children and twenty years of marriage, she thought, and he is a complete stranger to me. "Edwin, I won't stand by and tolerate your cruel treatment of my children anymore."

"I'm their daddy, and they'll do what I say. They can't understand anything but the belt."

"Well, you'll never whip them again," Emily warned, her voice shaking but positive and unhesitating.

"Where'd you get that gun?"

"That's not important - the important thing is I've finally

realized that you've never loved me or the children. You just want to own and control us. I've nearly gone crazy trying to rationalize your behavior. I can hardly believe my tolerance of your cruelty over all these years."

"You're crazy all right," Edwin said, ignoring the gun. "I'm their daddy, and they'll do what I say."

"You can't beat them into submission, Edwin. They're still young boys and can be expected to do only so much work."

"Work won't hurt them. I did my share when I was their age."

"And it has left you awfully bitter."

After an hour or more of trying to reason with him, Emily realized arguing with him was hopeless. Edwin looked over at her in a way that was all too familiar, a look of contempt. "May I go to bed?" he asked sarcastically.

Emily didn't answer. She stared at him as if she were looking through him. When she made no objection, he rose from his chair and left the room. Lost in her thoughts, she questioned. What will I do? How can I manage these children alone? She felt almost ethereal, like her daddy used to explain, "Walking in high cotton."

When she came out of her trance, she realized Edwin had gone to bed. She went to the bedroom door and heard his loud, even breathing. He was asleep. How can he sleep after such an episode? "He has no feelings," she sighed. She sat back down and was staring at the gun in her lap when she heard laughter through the open window. Mary, Margaret, Laura and Lucy were returning from the May Day Celebration and the spring play that was the finale of the day. Lucy, who was only ten, had the leading role in the play. Emily had wanted to go, but she would not leave the boys alone with their daddy – for fear of his whipping them. Pretending to read the newspaper, she laid it over the gun before the girls came into the house.

"Mama! Mama! You should've seen Lucy. She looked so pretty in the dress you made her, and she was really good, the best of the whole bunch," Margaret exclaimed.

"I really wanted to come, Lucy. I'm sorry. I'll explain later."

"You look so tired, Mama," Lucy said. She came over to her mother's chair and put her hand on her shoulder. "It's all right that you didn't come. Mary, Laura and Margaret were there on the front row, and the teacher said I did my lines perfectly."

"Is daddy home?" Mary asked, looking over at the door that led to his bedroom.

"Yes, he's in bed," Emily whispered.

"Let's go to bed," Laura said. "I'm tired." Quickly, Laura, Lucy and Margaret left the room, but Mary lingered.

"Is everything all right, Mama?" she asked.

"No, it isn't, Mary. I'll have to sleep in the room with you girls tonight. I'll explain tomorrow. Right now I'm too tired to talk. I just want to sit here and think for a while."

Mary hesitated a moment. She bit her lip trying to hold back harsh words about her daddy.

When Mary left her, Emily began to think back over her entire life. All the unhappy memories came flooding back like a powerful ocean wave; her mother's rejection, her brother's death, her first year of marriage to Edwin, their house burning, Franklin's death, and Mary's running away from home, and now, coming to grips with the reality that Edwin had never loved her. She bowed her head and prayed long and hard before she could go to bed. Somehow she would sleep. Somehow she would get through this.

Edwin left for work early the next morning, not eating any breakfast or saying anything to anyone. When he was gone, Emily sat down at the breakfast table and explained to the children why she had used the gun the night before. "I don't know what we'll do. I need to talk to your Aunt Louise and see what she thinks. We can't continue to live with your daddy's abuses."

"Why can't he just leave, Mama?" Mary said. "We did fine without him, when he took you to see Grandma, when she was sick."

Margaret and Laura looked at their mother expectantly for an answer.

"I don't know what we'll do, but we must do something. Don't worry; I know Louise will help us. Now you must go on to school."

After the children left, Emily sat down to write her sister. *I've decided to divorce Edwin,"* she wrote, and she knew Louise wouldn't be surprised. *There's no reasoning with him and no hope for the children to have any kind of normal relationship with him. I need your advice.* She sealed the letter and went out to put it in the mailbox, knowing Louise would reply quickly.

Chapter Twenty Two

Divorce

*E*mily waited anxiously to hear from Louise. Edwin said very little to her and ate no meals at home, but he continued to make harsh demands on the children, giving them strict orders to work in the garden, in the fields of corn and in the house. Emily questioned whether the boys were strong enough to endure such long hours of work, especially Henry since he had never been strong. Edwin's domineering conduct made her wonder how long they could continue under such irrational behavior. His aloofness towards her and continuous demands on the children were completely disheartening. Watching from the kitchen window, she could hear Edwin shouting his demands. I can see he's not going to make any effort towards reconciliation, she lamented.

⊱⊰

When the letter from Louise came, it was postmarked May tenth – reminding Emily she had forgotten Edwin's birthday. For the first time since she married, she didn't care and no longer had any love for him. For certain, she knew she couldn't live without love and respect any longer. She tucked the letter in her pocket and hurried back into the house to escape a sudden rain shower. Pulling her apron up, she wiped the raindrops from her face and sat down in the kitchen to read her letter. *John Freeman and I will come right away and try to talk to Edwin. We'll come to the Hilton Hotel. I'll call Edwin at his office and ask him to come and meet us there.*

Maybe we can talk some sense into him. Emily sighed and stared out the window. *Louise doesn't know how stubborn Edwin is, but she'll learn that reasoning with him is impossible.*

"Mama, we're hungry," Calen said, followed by his younger brother Judson into the kitchen. Emily looked at her two small sons, wondering what she would give them to eat. A deep dread came over her when she realized she would have to confront Edwin tonight about buying some groceries. It frightened her to think about what she would do for food in the future when he was gone.

࿐

Edwin walked confidently into the lobby of the hotel. "Look at him," Louise protested to John Freeman. They were seated comfortably in the handsome chairs of the lobby. "He always wears the very best clothes, and his children don't even have decent pairs of shoes. My, my," she uttered, dreading her confrontation with him.

Edwin approached them as if he didn't have a care in the world. He liked being seen with them. He knew they were well-off. "Hello! Hello!" Cordially, he clasped John Freeman's hand and patted Louise on the arm.

"Afternoon, Edwin," John Freeman greeted solemnly.

"Hello, Edwin," Louise spoke reservedly. "Why don't we go up to our room? We have a pleasant little sitting room, where we can talk in private."

Edwin walked briskly to the elevator as if he had been there before. When the elevator door opened and the attendant saw Edwin, he smiled. "Good afternoon, sir. Good to see you."

Edwin looked somewhat embarrassed as Louise and John Freeman moved away from the door. "I come here sometimes to call on my clients," Edwin explained quickly.

"We'll need the fourth floor," John Freeman told the old man, ignoring Edwin's pretext.

"Foth flo," the old man repeated and brought the noisy elevator to a jerking stop. John Freeman stepped off, holding Louise by the arm, and Edwin followed talking constantly as they proceeded down the narrow hallway.

After John Freeman unlocked the door, they stepped inside a

202

small foyer which opened to a very beautiful room. Louise watched as Edwin took in every detail from the satin brocade drapes to the dark mahogany furniture. "You know the Hilton is considered the best hotel in the city, don't you, John Freeman?"

"We like it because it's quiet and not in the middle of the business district."

"Let's sit over here," Louise said, pointing to the small sofa and chair by the window. She was anxious to get down to business. Thinking that diplomacy usually works, Louise began their conversation. "You have some wonderful children, Edwin. You and Emily are truly blessed. We want very much for you and Emily to continue to raise them together. We think they have the potential of becoming very responsible adults, but they need love and attention, not so much harsh discipline and punishment."

Edwin moved restlessly in his chair, his face flushed a deep red, and his eyes flashed with anger. "You don't understand how hard it is to control ten unruly children. The only way to discipline them is with the belt."

Louise looked away for a moment and clasped her hands together. She took a long hard look at Edwin. "Have you ever thought of giving them love as a way to make them mind? I find them very adoring children who mind very well."

Edwin's expression became even darker. His anger began to surface even more, but he held to the position that he had done nothing wrong and his way was the only way to raise his children. Finally he got up to leave. "You listen to me, Louise – I raise the flag of that ship. I'm the captain. I'll give the orders, and they'll follow them or I'll sink it!"

"I'm afraid, one day you'll be sorry," Louise retorted, completely disgusted with him. John Freeman remained silent. He stared at Edwin in disbelief as he watched him leave. When Louise shut the door, she gave a woeful sigh. "Well … I guess we'll have to go to see Emily and tell her Edwin has refused to compromise. We'll wait until tomorrow after he's gone to work. Now, we'll have to find her a lawyer."

"What in the world will she do with all those children and no husband?" John Freeman asked.

"I don't know … I don't know," Louise answered. "We'll just have to help her as much as we can."

ॐॐ

John Freeman pulled their pale blue Pontiac into the driveway just after Edwin had left for work. Emily was busy washing clothes. The old wringer washing machine hummed as it swished the clothes back and forth, infusing the house with the smell of Octagon soap. Out in the backyard, Emily hurried to hang out the first load of clothes. Judson and Calen were playing contentedly in the dirt with two small metal cars.

"We knew you must be out here when we came through the house and heard the washing machine running," Louise called to Emily.

Emily looked up with a broad smile, "Let me, hang up this last piece, and we can go inside." She took the wooden clothespin and fastened a pair of overalls to the sagging clothesline. "Look who is here," she said to Judson and Calen. They grinned and jumped up to greet their aunt and uncle, who greeted them with a warm hug. John Freeman took some candy from his pocket, handed it to the boys, then patted them on the head, laughing at their eagerness to open the candy and savor it.

John Freeman found a wooden crate to sit on. "I think I'll stay out here with the boys. Playing cars was always one of my favorites." Emily smiled and watched for a moment as he began talking to Calen and Judson about the toy cars he had as a child. She was reminded that she had never seen Edwin play with them. Enjoying the moment, she reluctantly picked up the laundry basket and followed Louise inside.

"It seems strange for the house to be so quiet," Louise observed.

"Yes, the rest of the children are in school. It's only a few more days before they are out for the summer. Let's sit here in the kitchen, and I'll fix some lemonade." She was relieved that Edwin had bought some groceries the day before.

"I don't think you'll be surprised to hear that our meeting with Edwin was futile." Louise pulled out a chair and sat down to the small kitchen table. "He won't bend, so if you still think divorce is the only solution, John Freeman and I will retain a lawyer for you."

"I didn't think you could persuade him, but I wanted you to see for yourselves how obstinate he is. Anyway, my mind is made up. I won't let him mistreat the children any longer. I haven't told you what happened last week." Emily sat down and handed her sister a glass of lemonade. "Edwin came in late one afternoon, and I knew he was angry the minute he walked in the door. He called Laura into the living room even before he sat down and accused her of having a boyfriend come to the house. When Laura denied it, he began slapping her unmercifully. Daniel saw his rage and ran to get my gun. I had no idea he knew where it was." Her voice became shaky and broken as she continued.

"When Daniel came into the dining room, Laura was running around the table trying to get away from her daddy. Daniel pointed the gun at his daddy and told him to stop hitting Laura. Edwin was not frightened and began chasing Daniel around the table. I was terrified and so were the other children. I was able to get the gun from Daniel and told him to run as fast as he could. Mary ran to a neighbor's house and called the police."

Louise sat back in her chair and gave a sigh, all the while listening with a heavy heart. "Did the police come?"

Emily took a sip of her lemonade to quench her dry mouth. "Yes, they came, really very quickly, and I explained to them what had happened. They told Edwin to come outside, and they talked to him a long time. Then they came inside and told me if I had any more trouble with him to call them. Edwin was furious and got in his car and left. So you see I must divorce him, or I'm afraid we'll have a real tragedy."

"Are you afraid of him?"

"No, not really, but I never dreamed we would come to such a violent conflict." She filled Louise's glass with ice and lemonade and began to fold the laundry in the basket. "One good thing - the house is in my name. Edwin put it in my name when he bought it, fearing he might lose it to some of his debtors. Now he can't change it without my signature."

Louise smiled. "Well, you know, Emily, the Bible says, 'All things work together for good for those that love God.' Now, John Freeman knows an attorney here in town, and he'll contact him to set up an appointment for you. Do you want us to go with you?"

"No, I'll be all right. I seem to have some added confidence now that I've made up my mind."

Louise got up and went over to Emily. "We must be going. I

wish we could stay longer and see the other children, but John Freeman is anxious to get home because he doesn't see well driving after dark."

৵৽

Emily dressed hurriedly. Her appointment was at eleven-thirty; she wanted to be on time and back home before Edwin returned. He had said very little to her in the last few weeks, yet she felt he had no intention of leaving. After brushing her hair, she turned around and looked at herself in the mirror; her dress was old but presentable. Her thick stockings showed very little under her dress that came almost to her ankles, and her shoes were worn - so worn, she thought and out of style. She heaved a sigh. "I must go, if I intend to catch the next streetcar."

When she boarded the streetcar, she remembered she hadn't been downtown in a long time. She sat back on the hard wooden seat, trying to relax, as the old yellow streetcar swayed and hummed moving along the tracks. For a short time she forgot her unhappy mission and became completely enchanted by the scenery on the thirty-minute ride. Some of the houses were awfully close to the streetcar tracks, and some sat farther back with pretty lawns and early blooming flowers. Mixed among the houses, businesses, churches and schools lined the streets along the way. At the edge of town, she was fascinated to see a farmers' market and many farmers bringing their early produce to sell. All the sights were ordinary, but Emily hadn't seen them for years.

After she stepped off the streetcar, Emily took the small map that John Freeman had given her from her purse and began to look for 2nd Avenue and 20th Street. "The attorney's office is located in the Frank Nelson Building," she whispered to herself. She looked up at the marker on the corner where she had gotten off the streetcar. 2nd Avenue and 19th Street, she read. "It must be up on the next block." She walked anxiously up the street to the corner of the block and found the building easily, the name inscribed on a brass plate on the corner of the building When she stepped off the elevator, she saw the name David P. Andrews, Attorney at Law. She hesitated a minute, almost losing her courage and tempted to turn around and go back home.

"May I help you?" a voice called from behind her.

Startled, she turned around quickly. "No, thank you. I believe this is the office I'm looking for."

"Let me get the door for you. I work here," the young man said.

After registering, the receptionist ushered Emily back to a very fine office with a huge mahogany desk. Mr. Andrews rose from his red leather chair and the receptionist introduced Emily. "This is Mrs. Edwin Anderson."

"Thank you, Mrs. Collins. Please hold my calls while Mrs. Anderson is here." He came around the desk and shook Emily's hand warmly. "I'm David Andrews. Please have a seat, Mrs. Anderson, and tell me what I can do for you." Emily sat down on the edge of the chair. "Make yourself comfortable," he encouraged, sensing her tenseness. Slowly she eased back into the chair and smoothed her dress, her hands trembled and she could feel her heart pounding.

She couldn't look at him as she began to tell him about Edwin's cruelty to their ten children, how he beat them with his belt at the slightest provocation. Then, looking straight at him, she continued, "Much of the time he doesn't provide us with enough to eat, and I know he has enough money." Mr. Andrews leaned forward in his chair and put his hands on his desk, listening intently. "There was a time recently when he missed a dime from his pocket and accused the children of taking it. I assured him that they wouldn't do that." Emily leaned forward and took a deep breath. "I knew they feared him too much to take anything of his, but he wouldn't listen to me; and when he couldn't get any of them to admit taking it, he lined them up and whipped them all unmercifully. Later, when he was dressing, the dime rolled out of the cuff of his pants. I asked him if he was going to tell the children he was sorry, and he said, 'No, they needed a good whipping anyway.'"

"Where does he work, Mrs. Anderson?"

"He sells insurance for Metropolitan Mutual. I really don't know how well he does. He never tells me and never gives me any money. He buys the groceries and pays the bills." She paused and shifted in her chair, amazed that she had been able for the first time to tell anyone her deepest grievances. Finally, she expressed her fear of a possible tragedy and told him of the recent episode of the gun. She couldn't hold back her tears telling him how Daniel could have killed Edwin.

"I hear what you're saying, Mrs. Anderson, although I'm not sure a judge wouldn't see this as a case of strong discipline, in which case no grounds for divorce."

Emily looked at him in shock and disbelief. She hadn't anticipated this response. She put her hand up to her chest to quiet her heart and fought back the tears stinging her eyes.

Seeing her frustration, he advised, "Let me talk to my associate and get his thoughts on this matter. I'll get back in touch with you. Your sister gave me a telephone number where you can be reached."

Emily rose slowly. She was bitterly disappointed. Mr. Andrews came from behind his desk and escorted her to the waiting area. "Don't be discouraged; we will explore every possibility." Emily nodded without speaking and walked to the elevator. She didn't remember the ride on the streetcar or even the walk home.

❧❦

Mary came out to meet her mother as she came onto the porch - anxious to hear what she had to say. She and Margaret, along with Laura, were the only ones of the children who knew where their mother had gone. The boys were busy with their hoeing in the garden, and the smaller children were playing in the yard.

"I don't know, Mary. I don't know what's going to happen," Emily lamented. She sat down in the living room exhausted. Laura and Margaret came and stood close to their mother's chair, not wanting to miss anything about the appointment with the lawyer.

"What did he say, Mama?" Mary asked anxiously.

"The lawyer says that the judge might consider the whippings by your daddy as just strong discipline. He did say he would talk to his partner and see what he thinks, and then he'll call me. Now, let me change my clothes. I've got to find something to cook for supper. Laura, would you and Margaret get the clothes off the line? I'm sure they're dry by now."

When Emily came into the kitchen, Mary was standing at the sink gazing out the window. She turned around and stared at her mother, hesitant to tell her secret. She bit her lip, trying to get enough courage to say what she must. "Mama … I'm going to tell you something I've never told anyone except Doctor Mitchell. When Grandma was sick and you went down to Stanton to see about her, Daddy tried to get me to sleep with him."

Emily was completely stunned. Her throat went completely dry, and her knees became weak. Mary took a deep breath and looked down at the floor. "I told Daddy, no, sir, that I needed to sleep with Lucy because she missed you so much. I was too frightened to tell anyone. That's the reason I ran away. When I came home, I talked to Doctor Mitchell, and he said he would speak to Daddy and this would never happen again." When she looked up, her mother's face was completely blank.

"Why didn't you tell us?" Margaret asked.

Mary turned around - surprised that Margaret had heard. "I didn't mean for you to hear me now," she said angrily. "I thought you were outside."

Emily put her hands on the table to pull herself up out of her chair and stood a minute leaning on the table. "Let's not talk about it right now. I'll have to decide whether to tell this to Mr. Andrews."

છૈ-જી

Three days later, Mr. Andrews called. Emily felt relief. She hurried over to Mrs. Holcomb's house to return his call. His voice was somber. "I'm afraid you don't have grounds for divorce, Mrs. Anderson. I've done some research, and the law will not support your case based on what you've told me."

Emily hesitated a moment, thinking of what Mary had told her. "I've something else to tell you," she breathed, her voice shaking, something my oldest daughter told me that I didn't know about when I came to your office. I don't want to tell you over the telephone."

"Can you come to the office on Friday morning? Let's say ten," he replied.

"Yes, I think I can manage that. Would it be all right to bring my daughter?"

"Yes, that would be good. I'll see you then. Good-bye."

"Good-bye." Emily called to Mrs. Holcomb who was in

another room and thanked her for the use of her telephone. "I must hurry home," she added.

❧❦

"Mary," she called as she came into the kitchen. Mary appeared in the doorway. "I'll have to go to the lawyer's office again on Friday. Will you go with me and tell him what you've told me? I don't know if this will make a difference, but he said the judge won't give me a divorce on the complaints I've given."

"I'll go … I'll go if you want me to, Mama."

"Well, I just don't know what else to do."

❧❦

Emily didn't want Edwin to know about the divorce plans until she had to tell him. He had hardly said anything to her in the last few weeks, leaving for work early and not returning until late in the evening. When she dwelt on her situation, she realized she really didn't know him. She only wanted him out of her sight. Some days she felt as if nothing were real, except the love of her children, which had kept her going and able to face the future.

❧❦

On Friday morning, Emily dressed hurriedly to get to the attorney's office. Edwin had lingered, and she had to wait until he was gone before dressing to go. She wondered if he was beginning to grow suspicious. "Margaret, you and Laura look after Lucy, Judson and Calen while I'm gone. Mary's going with me."

"Can we tell the boys where you're going, Mama? They've been asking."

Emily looked at her thoughtfully. "I guess so. They'll know sooner or later, but I would rather they not know about Mary's problem with her daddy. I don't want anyone but the lawyer to know. Where's Mary? We must be going."

❧❦

After they were seated in Mr. Andrew's office, Emily

introduced Mary. "This is my daughter, Mary."

Mr. Andrews came from behind his desk and took Mary's hand, "Hello, dear."

Mary gave a weak smile and sat back in her chair. "I want Mary to tell you what she has told me," Emily said anxiously.

Sensing Mary's anxiety, Mr. Andrews looked over at her. "Take your time, Mary, and don't be afraid. I'm here to listen."

Emily watched Mr. Andrew's expression as he listened. Mary stopped several times finding it very difficult to tell her experience to a complete stranger. "I understand how painful this is for you. Just take your time," the lawyer encouraged and continued to take notes. When Mary concluded, he leaned forward and looked at Emily. He could see her sorrow and deep hurt. "This situation changes the picture altogether. I'll talk to the judge, and I think we can proceed quickly from here. You're lucky that your husband put the house in your name. This will make the settlement easier. I'll do my best to get ample child support for you."

Mary moved over to the door, anxious to leave. Mr. Andrews placed his arm around her shoulder. "I'm sorry, Mary. You've had too much grief for such a young girl. I'll need you to come to the office one more time, Mrs. Anderson, for the settlement and signing of the divorce decree - that is, if the judge agrees after hearing Mary's testimony. I believe with this you have a legitimate claim for divorce."

On the street, the air was warm, and a gentle breeze gave relief to Emily and Mary as they hurried down the block to catch the next streetcar home. When they sat down in the streetcar, the windows were open and the fresh air felt good. With some hope in sight to resolve her problems, Emily's tension was eased. Life will go on, she recounted, just like the hum of the electric car, and we will get by somehow. Mary looked out the window and rode all the way in silence.

❧❧

Two weeks passed before Emily heard from Mr. Andrews. "The judge has agreed to the divorce," he reported in his telephone call to her, "but Edwin is being very difficult and doesn't want to give you any child support. He accuses you and the children of running him off. His lawyer claims Edwin is very angry."

Emily sighed. "That's his story. I'm not surprised he doesn't want to pay child support. He never wanted the children and barely provided for them. "

"Well, I'll try to get as much support as possible. Of course, it will take another three months before the divorce will be final. I'll be in touch."

"Good-bye," Emily said. Carefully, she put the telephone back on the receiver, hoping her neighbor hadn't heard her conversation. After thanking her neighbor for the use of her telephone, she hurried home.

When she returned home, Edwin was selling the cow to some men in a red pick-up truck. I guess he doesn't want to leave us anything, Emily thought, but it's just as well. That cow is nothing but trouble, forever getting loose, damaging someone's garden or frightening a neighbor's child. Its milk has never tasted good, often having flavor of wild onions that the cow had eaten. Before she went inside, Emily saw that Edwin had driven the boys back to hoeing the garden, even though they had finished his demands earlier. She stopped a minute, wanting to object, but she relented and went inside and found the girls scrubbing and cleaning. He'll never give up as long as he's here, she thought. "I see your daddy's home," she said to Mary.

Mary frowned. "Yes, he's here, Mama. Is he ever going to leave?"

"It'll be a while yet – probably not until September," Emily said, exasperated.

ം

Edwin was up early the day the divorce papers were to be signed. He came into the kitchen where Emily was cutting out biscuits on the enameled top table. Because the morning was warm, the heat from the stove made the room uncomfortably hot. Emily didn't see Edwin standing in the door until she placed the long black pan into the oven. "Well, you finally got your way, woman - you and Mary with your lies. You were set on having these children. Now you can have them all to yourself since you've turned them against me."

Emily looked directly at him. She had no fear of him. "If they've turned against you, it's your fault, not mine. He stepped back from the door, gave her a hard stare and walked swiftly out of the house.

⁂

Dressing hurriedly to reach Mr. Andrews's office on time, Emily forgot the new dress Louise had bought her, which she intended to wear. What does it matter how I look? She thought. Nobody cares. She felt sick at her stomach. Life is too complicated. Nothing makes sense anymore. All her hopes and dreams of having a happy marriage with love for her and the children had vanished. Feeling weak and dizzy, she sat down on the side of the bed to gain some strength.

Mary came into the bedroom. "Mama … are you going?" Emily raised her head. Mary could see the great distress on her mother's face. "Don't worry, Mama, we'll get by." She came over to the bed and put her arm around her mother's shoulder. Margaret and Laura joined her and sat on the side of the bed, and then the rest of the children gathered in.

Daniel had just had his thirteenth birthday and was growing into a tall, lanky young boy with a wonderful imagination and a keen sense of humor. He stationed himself in the center of the room where everyone could see him and declared, "Daddy thought he was the Captain of this ship. If he couldn't sail it his way, he would sink it. Well … we showed him. We threw him overboard!" Emily shook her head and laughed, and all the children laughed.

"All right, ya'll run on now and let me finish dressing. I won't be gone long. I'll be back as soon as possible."

⁂

Emily received very little justice in the divorce proceedings. She was appalled when the judge awarded her only twenty-five dollars a month for child support, pointing out she was getting the house and all the furnishings, except the furniture in Edwin's bedroom. She knew Edwin must have more income than he reported, and she left the hearing not knowing how they would live on such a small amount of money.

☙❧

When she returned home, Emily sat down with the children and tried to explain about the divorce and how Edwin would give them only twenty-five dollars a month. "But," she said, "we'll manage. We'll manage somehow."

Mary stood up and told her mother, "I can get a job as soon as I graduate, and I'll help buy the groceries."

Emily looked around the room at all of them. They've known nothing but fear and cruelty, she thought. Surely we'll be better off, even if we don't have enough money. "Don't worry, Mary - I believe your Aunt Louise will help us."

No sooner had Emily changed her clothes, that Edwin pulled into the driveway. He came recklessly into the house and to the bedroom where she was hanging up her dress. He looked at her with the same contempt he had shown every time she crossed him. "The judge ruled I could have this bedroom furniture, but I don't want it. I don't want anything that reminds me of this place. I'll get my other things and be out of your way." Emily showed no emotion as she turned and walked out of the room.

"Hooray!" the smaller children shouted when their daddy drove away. Emily gave a deep sigh and watched from the kitchen window. She felt nothing, not even a sense of relief - only emptiness.

☙❧

Emily welcomed the night and dressed for bed. She hadn't slept in this room for months and never without Edwin. She lay in the bed for hours, questioning her future. How will I get by? How will I even keep shoes on the children? Will Edwin ever want to see the children again? She knew she never wanted to see him again. He never really loved me, she anguished. She began to pray, long and pleadingly. Finally she drifted off to sleep, assured that her Heavenly Father loved her and would help her.

Chapter Twenty Three

A Brighter Day

Henry quickly looked up and down the rows of the dying vegetable garden for any edible vegetables. Emily watched him come inside with an empty basket. "I couldn't find one thing out there, Mama."

"Well, go out and look again, Henry. I know there are a few tomatoes out there and maybe some squash. Go and look again."

Before she could turn around, Henry was running back inside, swinging the market basket by the handle. "There ain't nothing out there but weeds."

"There isn't," his mother corrected. "Give me the basket. Let me see what I can find." Emily took the basket and went down the back steps and into the garden. The sweltering September sun beat down on her back, and sweat trickled down under her thin cotton dress. She wiped her brow and began scouring the entire garden. Soon her basket was full to brimming over with deep red tomatoes, bright yellow squash, a handful of green beans and a few red potatoes. "Look what I found," she said triumphantly.

Henry looked at the basket overflowing with vegetables. "God must have reached down and handed all these vegetables to you, Mama."

Emily stood speechless for a moment. Such perception for a ten-year-old, she thought. "Yes, I suppose He did. He's given us our daily bread for today, hasn't He? Now let's make some soup for supper."

ৰ∾ঌ

Edwin had been gone a week before Emily could find the right words to write to Louise or her mother. She had taken out her stationery twice but to no avail. Now she knew she must write and thank Louise for all that she had done to help.

Dear Louise,
We have peace now, something we haven't had in a long time. A burden has been lifted from the children. Mary has a part-time job with Postal Telegraph, which has hired lots of girls lately, since there's so much talk of war. If we go to war, Eddie wants to quit school and join the Marines, and Laura wants to quit school and get a job. It does my heart good to see their willingness to sacrifice, but I really don't want any of them to quit school.
Thank you and John Freeman for paying for the divorce. I couldn't have made it without you. I'd love to sit down and talk to you. I'll write to Mama soon. Love, Emily

Early the next morning after the children had gone to school, Emily put her letter in the mailbox.

A letter from Louise came at the end of the week and also a letter from her mother. Underneath their two letters was one from her brother Timothy. Emily took them from the mailbox and held them to her heart as if they were her only hope. The warmth of the October sun made it inviting to sit in the swing on the porch and read her letters.

When she opened the letter from Louise, a money order fluttered out with the breeze and fell to the floor. Reaching down to pick it up, she saw that it was for fifty dollars. After she examined it carefully, she put it in her apron pocket and read the letter.

Dearest Emily,
John Freeman and I want to send you fifty dollars a month until you can get adjusted. You know we consider your children as part ours. I believe things will be better for you all, in time. I wrote Timothy and Eugenia and told them about your circumstances. I know they will want to help you as they are able. I'm afraid Albert has all he can handle with his six children. We don't hear from

*Judson very often, so I didn't write him. Mama will probably write
him. Come and see us soon, and bring the four little ones. Love,
Louise.*

Emily moved out into the sunshine and sat on the low banister
to read the letter from her mother. It saddened her to see how
poorly her mother's handwriting had become. Mama is getting old
and feebler, she thought, as she began to read.

Dear Emily,
*I almost forgot Daniel's birthday dollar. I'm enclosing it with
five dollars for you. Louise has written us about your troubles with
Edwin. I'm sorry divorce was the only answer. You know how I feel
about divorce, but only you could make that decision. Your daddy
and I will try to send you a little money each month. Lord knows
you'll need it. Love, Mama.*

Timothy's letter was short but much more consoling.

Dear Emily,
*I have known for a long time that you couldn't live out your
life with Edwin. I think you've done the right thing. Now that he's
gone, I hope you can go to church and take the children. I know you
have been deprived of that blessing too long. I am sending you
money for streetcar fare so you can go to the Baptist church
downtown. I know that Edwin was the one who chose that church. I
think, he thought it was prestigious, but I think it is really a good
church for you all to attend. He never went, did he? Anyway, take
heart; we are always here for you. I can't imagine raising ten
children alone. Our three are growing just like yours – too fast.*
Love you, always, Timothy

After reading the letters, Emily felt encouraged. Looking up,
she saw Judson coming across the yard pulling his red wagon that
rattled with a deafening noise. "Mama, Mama, look what I've got."
Proudly, he pointed to the drink bottles that filled the little red
wagon. "Daniel said Mr. Wiggins at the A&P will give us two cents
apiece for these Coca-Cola bottles."
"Why, Judson, you have a wagon full. Where in the world did

you get them?"

"From the neighbors. I just asked them if they had any old Coca-Cola bottles, and they gave these to me. You can have the money, Mama. I want to help our family like the others."

Emily's eyes clouded with tears. Her young son's word filled her with emotion. "Judson, Judson," she sighed. "All right, when Daniel comes in from school, I'll ask him to take the bottles to the A&P for you."

"I want to go with him," Judson pleaded.

"We'll see. Come on in now. I've made some potato soup - your favorite."

⁊⊷⊰

Judson sat on the back steps waiting for Daniel. "Daniel! Daniel!" he called as soon as he saw his big brother come across the back yard. "Look what I've got."

Daniel looked at the wagon full of coke bottles. "Oh, boy, let's take them to the A&P and get the deposit for them, and then we can go to Mr. Whatley's store and get some moon pies."

"No …ooo. I'm going to give the money to Mama. I promised her," Judson protested.

Emily heard the boys talking and came outside. "I think I'll go with you. I need to buy some groceries, and you can bring them home in your wagon."

"What are you going to buy, Mama?" Daniel asked excitedly.

"Oh, some flour, sugar, lard, and maybe some bologna and some light bread," she answered fingering the list in her pocket. She had planned all afternoon how she would budget her money, knowing she must save for the electric and water bill due soon. She was reluctant to depend on the support Edwin was supposed to send. She wondered if he would send it at all.

⁊⊷⊰

The bottles in the wagon rattled noisily as Emily and the boys made the long walk to the grocery store. When they arrived, Judson pulled the wagon inside the store and up to the front counter. Emily began to explore the shelves, carefully noting the prices of every item she wanted. "We have some Coca-Cola bottles for deposit,"

Daniel told Mr. Wiggins who stood behind the counter.

"I see you have. Just put them on the counter, and I'll count them. Judson and Daniel counted as Mr. Wiggins placed each bottle in the crate on the floor. "I count thirty-five. That makes me owe you seventy cents." He opened the cash register and counted out the change to Daniel.

Judson watched intently. "Come on, Daniel. Let's go and find Mama." Emily was standing at the meat counter admiring the fresh cuts of meat and wondering what she could afford and what would satisfy her growing boys. "Here's the money, Mama." Judson opened his hand to show his mother the two twenty-five-cent pieces and two dimes.

Emily saw the change in her youngest son's hand. "You're a good boy, Judson." Reluctantly, she took the money. "Now, we can buy more meat."

"Can I cut some slices of bologna for you?" the butcher asked.

Emily stared at the long roll of bologna and then at the change in her hand. "How much is the whole piece?"

"The whole round? Why, that would be one dollar and fifty cents."

"I'll take it. Here, Judson, take this nickel and buy some candy for you and Daniel."

Daniel's eyes brightened as he grabbed his brother by the arm. "Come on, Judson. We can buy five BB bats."

Emily followed the boys to the front of the store and placed her groceries on the counter. She watched anxiously as Mr. Wiggins rang up her sale on the large cash register. "That will be seven dollars and twenty-nine cents."

"Will you cash this money order?" Emily said.

"I believe I can." He looked at her and then at her name on the money order. "Mrs. Anderson," he read aloud. "I haven't seen you in here before. Your husband usually does the shopping, doesn't he?"

"Yes, that's right," Emily answered not daring to make any explanations.

"Come again," he said cordially after he placed the last sack of groceries into the wagon.

"Thank you. I will."

Daniel pulled the wagon out of the store, and Judson pushed

from behind. Emily watched as the boys struggled along the graveled road. "I'll pull the wagon some."

Daniel continued to pull the wagon. "Aah, we can make it, Mama. We're almost home, and I'm ready to eat some of that bologna."

"Here's Mama," Jonathan called from the porch.

Eddie, Henry and Lucy came out, and each picked up a bag of groceries. "Looks like we have plenty of help now," Emily said. Daniel and Judson hurried in behind them.

"Can we have fried bologna for supper, Mama?" Daniel asked.

"We'll see. Now ya'll go outside and let Mary help me put the groceries away."

"I'll help fix supper," Mary offered. "I'm so glad to see something besides salmon."

Emily gave a hearty laugh at Mary's observation. She felt a new relationship beginning with her children, a warm friendship, even a partnership in which they would work together to make a happy family.

∂∽∽

As she sliced the bologna the next day to make sandwiches for the children's school lunches, Emily gave a disheartened sigh. Half the bologna was gone. There's no way to fill up these growing boys, she thought. Still, she felt happy as she lined up the six brown paper lunch bags, knowing they would have a good lunch today.

∂∽∽

November was unusually cold. The trees had lost all their leaves, and the grass was a dirty brown. A first heavy frost had come early taking away most of the color of fall. Emily was struggling to make ends meet and still no money had come from Edwin. After the tenth of the month rolled past, she decided to call Mr. Andrews, her attorney. "I'll take care of it for you," he said. "Don't worry." Sure enough, the check came three days later - the same day she noticed a leak on the living room ceiling.

≈≫⋖≈

Eddie was excited when he came in from school and announced, "I have a job at a filling station close to the school. I can work every afternoon, Mama." Emily turned around in surprise. She had just finished putting more coal in the kitchen stove. "Mr. Hudson owns the place, and he said maybe Jonathan could work too, pumping gas and wiping windshields."

"I don't know, Eddie. I don't want working to interfere with your studies. Still I know you need to have some money." She washed her hands at the sink and came over to the table to sit down.

"I can give you eight dollars a week," Eddie said proudly. He licked his lips as he ate a hot muffin and reached for another.

"I can give you some money too," Jonathan added, "if he gives me a job."

Emily thought of the leak on the roof and felt some relief. "Maybe with your help we can get a new roof." She was proud and sad at the same time. "All right, but you mustn't neglect your studies."

≈≫⋖≈

With the money that Timothy had sent, Emily bought two books of streetcar tickets. For the first time in years, she was able to go to church. She had never been to the church downtown. She had only heard about it from Edwin and the children.

≈≫⋖≈

The first Sunday in December was sunny, but the wind was cold and brisk. Emily dressed hurriedly and helped Henry and Lucy dress. "Hurry, Margaret, we can't miss the eight-fifteen streetcar." Margaret slowly put on her dress and shoes. She had waited until the last minute to get out of bed, but unlike Mary, she loved going to church.

"Let me stay here and cook the dinner, Mama," Mary said. "and I can watch out for Calen and Judson."

"Oh, all right. I guess we can start out with some of us going," Emily said. "If we try, maybe we can all go, soon. Then I'll be satisfied." She wondered if it would be possible to get them all up and ready at one time. Putting on her small felt hat and heavy woolen coat, she hurried out the door calling to the others, "Let's go."

The large, gray stone church stood on the downtown corner like a fortress. There was no steeple, but its beauty was revealed in the stained-glass windows that graced every side of the church. Each one radiated intense shades of blue, yellow, red and green, depicting scenes of Christ and other symbols of the Christian faith. Inside, the walls were stark white, bordered by heavy, dark, ornate woodwork and dark, oak pews. The carpets caught the eyes of Henry and Lucy. "Look, Mama, red carpets!"

"Shush, we must be very quiet."

The service began with beautiful music from the organ. Emily listened intently to the reading of the Bible, the beautiful prayer from the pastor and the encouraging words of his sermon. Sitting quietly in the pew, she felt a peace that she hadn't known in a long, long time.

‽‽

When they got off the streetcar to return home, they hurried to contend against the cold. "I liked that church," Henry told his mama. "I'd like to join and be baptized."

Emily turned to him and stopped. "That would be wonderful, Henry."

"Daddy wouldn't let me join when I went with him. He said I was too young."

"Oh, I think you're old enough to understand what it means to be baptized."

"I do know. I know that Jesus loves me and died on the cross for me. I want to be baptized 'cause I want everyone to know I'm a Christian."

Emily stopped again and put her arm around his shoulder. This is the most important decision you will ever make, Henry. We'll talk more about your decision this afternoon. I'm glad we're home. I'm freezing."

"I smell fried chicken," Laura said.

"Where did you get a chicken, Mary?" Emily asked.

"Daniel killed the largest fryer in the chicken yard."

"Well, I hope it isn't tough. It was a little past being a fryer." She relished the idea of sitting down to a meal she hadn't had to prepare and one in which Edwin wasn't constantly correcting the children. She could sense the children felt the same. "The chicken was delicious, Mary. You must have cooked it a long time."

"I steamed it, after I fried it … like I've seen you do."

"Well, if it had been any better," Emily shook her head and laughed, "I guess we would have eaten the plate." Everyone laughed. No one seemed ready to leave the table, and the conversation turned to plans for Christmas.

Margaret looked at her mother. "I hope we can have a good Christmas this year. It's just three weeks away."

"I've got enough money to buy everyone a present!" Daniel shouted.

"Daniel," his mother interrupted, "it isn't necessary to talk so loud."

"Maybe we can all give each other a gift," Margaret said. "It doesn't have to cost too much … just a small gift. I'm going to start working on Saturdays at Kresses and use my money for Christmas presents. I'll help Judson and Calen buy some presents."

"And I'll give Henry and Lucy some money," Mary added.

Emily stood up and began clearing the dishes from the table. "Since you cooked the meal, Mary, I'll do the dishes."

Not wanting to be left out, Lucy said, "I'll help."

Eddie and Jonathan went into the living room and turned on the small radio just in time to hear the announcer say, "We interrupt this program for a message from the President of the United States."

President Roosevelt's voice was strong and to the point. "This morning, the Japanese attacked Pearl Harbor. This is a day that will live in infamy. The United Stated has now declared war on Japan." Everyone moved quickly from the dining room to listen more closely. No one spoke for a moment. Emily felt an unfriendly chill flow over her body. What would this mean for her family that had just gotten over the crisis of their daddy's departure? Little did she know that they would face four long years of war.

ॐॐ

Colored blazes spewed from the coal in the fireplace, and the cedar Christmas tree sparkled in the corner of the living room. Daniel and Henry bragged they had found "the perfect tree."

Emily sat down in the green wicker rocker. She was tired. "It does have a nice shape. I remember when I was a child we went to the woods and cut a tree for our family. We had an old Negro man who worked for us, and he always went with us to cut the tree. We would haul it on a little red wagon to the house." Judson and Calen listened intently as Emily told every detail of decorating the tree. "Our ornaments were quite different from these. We strung cranberries for a garland and also popcorn. I would also make small bunches of holly tied with red ribbon and put them on the tree. Your grandpa always placed a star, made of cardboard and covered with tinfoil, at the top of the tree. This was a very happy time for our family."

The shiny red and green balls hung from the limber branches, and silver tinsel was draped over the entire tree like frozen icicles. This was the first time they had store-bought ornaments. Mary had bought them wanting to make this a special Christmas. Each ornament adorned the fragile branches like bright trimmings on a new dress, and the Silver Star on top of the tree twinkled from the string of colored lights draped randomly over the branches. If only I had some money to buy gifts for the children. Oh, there will be the packages from Eugenia and Louise, I'm pretty sure, but that's not the same as a gift from me. If Edwin would send his check, maybe I could buy something, but he's late again, and I don't know when he'll send it. I'll just have to be content with cooking a good Christmas dinner and there's the fruitcake. Although, it'll be a wonder if any is left by Christmas Day - the way Daniel and Mary keep eating it. The fire blazed in the grate, and the fragrance of the cedar tree permeated the room. A feeling of warmth and peacefulness was no longer a stranger. The apple green paint was the only reminder of Edwin.

ॐ•ॐ

Eugenia's package arrived four days before Christmas with her traditional cookies packed and wrapped carefully so as not to be crushed. After opening the big box, Emily placed the gifts under the tree and gave each of the children some cookies before putting them away for Christmas Day. "I guess I had better make a chocolate cake," she told Mary. "I think the fruitcake is almost gone." Mary looked sheepishly guilty but didn't admit to her misbehavior.

When the huge package came from Louise, the excitement of the smaller children could hardly be contained. After opening the package, Emily let each of them place their gift under the tree, savoring the happy scene and thinking how grateful she was for the love of her sisters.

∂∙∂

Daniel watched anxiously as his mother spread the rich chocolate icing on the yellow cake. "Can we lick the bowl, Mama?" He leaned on the table to get closer to the cake.

"Let me finish." Sparingly, she spread the last bit of the cooked icing on the sides of the cake and stood back to admire her creation. "Now we'll have a cake for Christmas Day. Here's the bowl, Daniel. Get another spoon for Henry. Daniel! Don't eat it all."

∂∙∂

"Don't pick it off the top, Henry. Pick it off the sides, so Mama won't notice," Daniel instructed. They had waited until their mother was busy in the kitchen, slipped into the dining room, lifted the cover off the cake and were picking the icing off and eating it. When Jonathan and Eddie saw what they had done, they decided to take their share by de-icing the top of the cake. Soon all the icing was gone, and the cake remained naked as a shorn sheep.

Emily noticed when she went into the dining room to set the table for supper that the cake cover wasn't straight on the cake plate. She lifted the cover and saw a cake just tinged with chocolate. No icing remained. She breathed a sigh of despair. "I believe they will eat the furniture next," she sighed. "Well, I'll just ice it again."

When everyone was seated at the supper table, she declared, "I don't believe I've ever seen a cake lose its icing before. Have you, Daniel?"

Laura and Lucy laughed as their brothers' faces colored with guilt. Emily looked at them in condemnation. "I've iced the cake again, so remember, it's for Christmas Day."

ॐ⋞

The room was warm from the blazing fire in the fireplace, and the smell of oranges and peppermint hung on the laughter of the children as they opened their gifts on Christmas morning. "I thought you were giving us a pocket knife, Henry, and it's only a tiny tube of toothpaste," Daniel chided.

"Don't make fun of my gift. These socks you gave are marked irregular." He punched his brother on the shoulder and laughed.

Emily sat by the fire and opened her gifts from her sisters – a dress from Louise and much-needed underwear from Eugenia. . She watched with complete surprise to see Lucy opening her gift from Mary; a beautiful doll with eyes that opened and closed, and life-like golden hair that fell to its shoulders in a bevy of soft curls. Suddenly the terrible scene of Edwin's throwing Lucy's only doll into the fire flashed in her memory because Lucy hadn't put it away correctly. She was saddened to think that Mary had never had a beautiful doll like this one. She thought of all their past Christmases with Edwin, but she didn't miss him.

ॐ⋞

All the chicken and dressing was eaten, along with the candied sweet potatoes, canned English peas and the Waldorf salad. Emily began to clear the table for dessert. "I guess all of Aunt Eugenia's cookies are gone, but we still have the chocolate cake and some ambrosia I made from the oranges Louise sent. Bring the small bowls from the china cabinet, Lucy, and I'll get the cake." When she took the cover off the cake, her happy expression changed to one of vexation. The cake was completely stripped of its icing.

Everyone looked at Daniel, scornfully. "Don't look at me. I didn't do it."

"Well, we'll just eat it without any icing," Emily said shaking her head in despair. "Except for this poor naked cake, this has been a happy Christmas." Everyone laughed, but no one admitted eating the icing, and no one mentioned Edwin.

Chapter Twenty Four

A Brighter Day

*C*old rain and heavy frost marked the first days of January. On some days the cold air remained throughout the daytime hours. Emily had little choice but to keep the fires going all day in the fireplace and in the kitchen stove. Eddie brought up a scuttle of coal from the basement and put it behind the stove. "The coal pile is really getting low, Mama. If you'd sign for me to join the Marines, then I could send you an allotment check, and you wouldn't have to worry about running out of coal."

She looked at her son, only seventeen years old, and ignored his desire to join the Marines. She couldn't bear to think of his going to war. Already she had heard of the fierce fighting in the Pacific. "Well, at least I don't have to worry about anyone stealing the coal. I'm really glad we have the coal bin in the basement." Eddie lingered a moment. He saw this was not the time to plead with his mother about the Marines. He put some coal in the stove and left the room.

Problems, Emily thought. She peeled the last potato and added it to the stew. I never have enough food for the children, and the younger ones are growing so fast I can't keep them in shoes. The leak in the roof must be repaired, and now Eddie wants to join the Marines. She heard the cold wind whip around the house and thought about the small amount of coal in the basement. After putting the stew on the stove, she warmed her hands. The colorful calendar on the wall reminded her that Edwin had been gone four months. She pondered the happiness that she had seen in the children since he had left. Pushing her troubles aside, she counted her blessings.

❧❧

Emily looked at the pile of dirty clothes on the floor beside the old Maytag ringer-washer. "I can't wait another day to wash, but I doubt if the clothes will dry in this freezing weather." Before going out to hang up the wash, she warmed her hands and slipped on a heavy sweater. The bitter cold stung her face as she went down the five steps to the back yard. Without delay, she pinned the wet clothes to the metal clothesline, her hands becoming red and stiff as she shivered from the biting wind. Before she could finish, the clothes began to freeze. Later in the day, she brought the cold stiff clothes inside and hung them behind the stove on a rack, careful not to let them touch the stove, remembering the terrible fire after Lucy was born.

❧❧

When Eddie came home from his after-school job, he sat down at the kitchen table and began to plead again with his mother to let him join the Marines. "It looks as if I'm going to have to give my permission, Eddie. You're so determined."

Eddie smiled and handed his mother the paper to sign. "I'll be sending you an allotment check every month. I know you need the money, and I really want to be a Marine."

"I know, Eddie, and I'm thankful that you want to help me." Reluctantly, she signed the paper, the pen heavy in her hand, and her fear for him heavy in her heart. "I'm really proud that you want to defend your country." She moved over to the sink to wash her hands, then turned and looked intently at Eddie as he rolled the paper up in his hand. "It's just that you're so young to leave home and go to war, and I don't like the idea of you quitting school."

"I can finish school when the war's over. Maybe it won't last long."

❧❧

Eddie had been gone only a month when Jonathan began to beg his mother to let him join the Navy. Emily heaved a deep sigh. "I don't want you to quit school, Jonathan. I don't think you have any idea of the danger you're getting into, but I see there is no stopping you." She wiped her hands on the dishtowel and sat down at the small table. "Let me see the paper." She took the pen, hesitated a moment, and then she signed her name.

"I'll be leaving in three days," Jonathan said, brimming over with excitement. "I've got to go tell Daniel." Emily contemplated all that was happening for a few moments, her mind in a whirl. I guess there's some consolation that Mary and Margaret have graduated. Maybe Margaret can finish college. She really wants to go. It'll be hard for her, working her way through. And the others? I'll do my best to keep them in school till they finish. It won't be long before they're all grown. A painful emptiness gripped her at the thought. What will I do when I'm all alone? Later, when she lay down in bed, her every muscle tired to the bone and weariness her bed partner, she drifted off to sleep.

ॐॐ

Everyday Emily watched for the mailman, hoping for a letter from Eddie and Jonathan. In the two months since Eddie had been gone, she had received only three letters from him and two from Jonathan. She missed them.

ॐॐ

The first check from Eddie came on the day when Emily wondered how she could possibly prepare another meal with so little food in the house. She looked at the check with a feeling of relief and breathed a prayer of thanksgiving to God. A tug at her heart seized her when she thought of Eddie and the sacrifice he was making for his family and his country. She tried not to think of the danger he would be facing, knowing he would soon be going to the South Pacific. She must trust God to protect him. Looking at the check again, she planned how she would go to the grocery store after Henry got home from school. He could take his wagon to bring the groceries home, and later, she would think about a new roof for the house.

ॐॐ

"Have you noticed the peach tree blooming in the back yard, Henry?" Emily asked. "It makes me itch to make a garden. I love the springtime and the smell of freshly-turned earth. Would you and Daniel help me plant a garden?"

Henry's mouth spread across his face in a wide grin. "Yes, ma'am, I can help. I know how to plant. I know how to make a garden." To get Daniel to help was another matter, she thought. He spent many of his afternoons looking for scrap iron, which was easy to sell with the war going full blast, but his money was quickly spent at the movies. He discovered the movie theater was only a mile down the railroad tracks. Once he passed the small private airport, he had only a few more blocks to go. On Saturdays, he would see the feature twice.

"Why do you like to see the movie twice?" Emily asked when Daniel came into the house late on Saturday afternoon.

"I want to be sure I don't miss any of it. You should go sometimes, Mama. You'd like it."

Emily smiled. She reasoned this was the first time in his life he had found some enjoyment. "Well, if you can find time next Saturday, Henry and I need your help to plant a garden." But she knew full well that she couldn't keep him from the movies.

❧❦

Saturday was a perfect day for planting. The early morning sunshine permeated the freshly-plowed garden plot. A soft mist rose from the warm furrowed earth and carried a sweet fragrance heavenward. Emily had taken an old Negro man's offer to plow the garden just days before. "That's the best two dollars, I've ever spent," she measured, after she had paid the old man.

As soon as Emily and Henry finished breakfast of hot biscuits, syrup and a few slices of thick, fried bacon, they were ready to start the planting. "Wait, Henry. I want to tell Lucy to clean the house while we're gardening."

"Yes, ma'am, I'll clean, if Judson and Calen will play outside till I'm finished."

"I'll tell them to come outside with us. Maybe they can help Henry and me." Emily had noticed that Lucy liked the house clean and orderly, definitely characteristic of her daddy. Thank goodness she has taken on his good qualities and not his bad ones.

❧❧

"Your grandpa sent us seeds for everything we want to plant, Henry. You can look at them, and I'll get the garden tools." Henry took the seeds from the sack and examined each packet as if they were sacred. His grandpa had labeled them in big letters, BEANS, SQUASH, CORN, TOMATOES, and PEAS, even CUCUMBERS and EGGPLANT. He pictured the garden full grown and could hardly wait to get started. "Henry," his mother called from the garage, "where are all the tools? I know we have more than these."

"The Wheelers have been borrowing them and have never brought them back." He ran over to the garage and came inside.

Emily stood for a moment contemplating what to do. "I'll just go over there and get them." Although she knew the Wheelers, she had never been across the street to their house, but now she was determined to get the garden tools. She walked boldly across the street to the edge of their yard. She stopped and almost turned around to go back home. "No, the tools are ours, and I'm going to ask for them." Quickly, she climbed the steps to the porch and knocked on the door. When Mr. Wheeler opened the door, she felt her courage leave.

"Good morning, Mr. Wheeler. My son Henry and I are planting a garden today, and I wondered if you have borrowed any of our garden tools. I can't seem to find them."

"Oh, no, I don't think so. We have our own tools. Would you like to borrow some of them?"

Emily hesitated a moment. This was her first time to see Mr. Wheeler close up. His fingers were yellow with tobacco stain, and he reeked of the smell of cigarettes. He was taller than she had thought, but not a big man. His thinning, brown hair was streaked with gray, and his face was red and ruddy. What kind of man was he, she wondered? Feeling defeated, she stepped back from the open door. "I don't know what happened to our tools. I guess I'll have to borrow a good hoe if you can spare it."

"Come out back to the shed, and I'll get it for you." Emily followed him around to the back of the small, modest house. At the edge of the yard was a tar papered shed with a very low ceiling. When she stepped inside, she saw a hoe, a hoe fork and a spading fork with familiar apple green paint dabbed on each handle. She knew only Edwin would have put that color of paint on the tools.

"On second thought, I believe I could use the spading fork and the hoe fork, along with the hoe. Some of that ground isn't broken up very well."

Mr. Wheeler's face reddened with guilt as he handed her the tools. "Thank you. I believe these are just what I need." Mr. Wheeler stood speechless as he watched Emily cross the road to her house. *Now I want to see him try to borrow them again.*

"How did you get these tools, Mama?" Henry asked. "These are ours."

"I know, and we'll be careful not to loan them again."

By midafternoon, the garden was planted. Before going into the house, Emily stopped to look at the planted rows. Placing her hands on her hips, she stretched her tired body to relax her back. Henry stood beside her like a proud soldier surveying the neat rows of freshly-planted earth.

"How would you like to raise some chickens?" Emily asked, as they walked to the garage to put away the tools.

"I'd like that. I'd take good care of them and clean the brooder."

Such enthusiasm, Emily observed, seeing his eagerness. "Your uncle Timothy is sending us fifty baby chicks in the mail. I got a notice they'll be here next Saturday. They're black and white speckled and are called Plymouth Rocks."

Henry's eyes sparkled. "I'm going to tell Daniel."

"Yes, I see that he's home from the movies, conveniently after we've planted the garden. Daniel will always be Daniel."

Though she was only ten years old, Lucy had cleaned the entire house to perfection. Each piece of furniture was polished and the floors freshly mopped. Emily found her on the porch swing with her two small brothers. "The house really looks nice, Lucy." Lucy smiled at her mother's approval. Turning to go inside, Emily told the children, "I'll rest a minute before I start supper. The girls will be home soon. I must start a fire to cook supper." She faced no dilemma finding something to cook. Eddie's check had made it possible to buy enough food and to keep enough coal for heating and cooking. Every night she thanked God and prayed for Eddie's and Jonathan's safety. In Jonathan's last letter, he wrote that he would be sending an allotment, and he wanted her to buy a new gas stove. That would be a luxury, she thought. No more having to heat up the kitchen in summer or waiting for the stove to get hot. She smiled at the thought of such convenience.

☙❧

Emily came out onto the porch to get a breath of fresh air. "What's all the excitement about?"

"It's the chickens!" Henry shouted. "The mailman just delivered them. Can we bring them inside to look at them, Mama?"

"Oh, I guess so. We mustn't let any of them get away. Don't take the top off the box until we get inside."

"Oh! Look! Look! Ohooooooooooo." Fascinated the children shrieked and watched the fuzzy, yellow creatures move about in the box, chirping and scratching.

Judson moved closer. "They're like little balls of yellow fur. Can I hold one, Mama?"

"Let him hold one, Henry. Just don't squeeze it, Judson. They're very delicate."

Judson held the fuzzy little chick up to his face and rubbed its soft feathers across his cheeks. Emily saw the perfect delight in his eyes. "Oh, the wonder in small and simple things," she breathed. "All right, let's take them out back and put them in the brooder. We mustn't handle them too much, and we'll need to keep a light in the brooder to keep them warm until they are larger. Daniel, help Henry carry the box to the chicken house. Count them, one by one, as you put them in the brooder, and be gentle with them."

"Fifty-one, fifty-two," Henry counted, as Daniel placed the last tiny chick in the make-shift incubator.

"Mama said to be sure to hook the door, so nothing can get to them," Daniel told Henry.

"Okay." Henry knelt down and carefully hooked the small door. Still kneeling, he continued to admire his new treasure.

"Come on, Henry. You don't have to stay out here with them," Daniel chided.

☙❧

Emily didn't have to remind Henry to take care of the young chicks. He was up early every morning, feeding them and putting fresh water in a quart jar he filled and turned upside down on the watering tray. Each Saturday, he removed all the chicks from the brooder, put them in a cardboard box and cleaned the small wood and wire structure with a stream of water from the garden hose. With great pride, he would count them as he put them back into the brooder.

One morning, after the chickens were six weeks old, Henry told his mother, "We've only lost two."

"Good. It won't be long until we can have some fried chicken."

❧

Emily had just cut the last biscuit and placed it on the pan to go into the oven, when Henry came running into the house, hysterical. Tears streamed down his cheeks. "Mama! Mama!"

"What is it, Henry? What is it?"

"Something … something has killed every one of the chickens," he sobbed. "They're all laying on the ground in the chicken yard."

Emily put her hand over her mouth in disbelief. Holding back her tears, she ran with Henry to the back yard. When she saw the terrible sight, she felt sick to her stomach. There lay fifty young chickens, each with a touch of blood on their necks. "A weasel, a weasel did this. Let's not let Calen or Judson see this terrible sight. I'll get Daniel to come and help you pick them up and throw them in the garbage." She put her arm around Henry's shoulder to console him.

No one spoke at the breakfast table, not even Daniel. Finally Emily broke the silence. "We must not let this get us down. We'll just buy some more chickens and start again. We can fix the chicken yard so no other animals can get in." Henry rubbed his swollen red eyes and tried to smile, but Emily knew his heart was broken.

"Henry, I've got enough money to pay your way to the movies. Do you want to go with me this afternoon?" Daniel asked with his special grin.

"Can I go, Mama?" Henry's eyes brightened and a faint smile came on his face.

"I think that would be good. Do you think you can walk that

far?"

"I can. I know I can," Henry said

"And Daniel, will you promise to watch out for him?"

"I'll stay right with him, Mama. I won't walk too fast."

అsix

On Sunday morning, Emily rose early to attend church. Remembering the disappointments of the past week, she admonished herself not to become bitter. She knew she would feel better after going to church, regrettable for the many years she couldn't go. For a brief moment she thought of Edwin and all the anguish he caused her. She wondered if he ever had any regrets.

A few heavy clouds quickly obscured the morning sunlight, darkening the room. Emily turned on the overhead light, went to the small closest to take out her best dress and finished dressing. After she ran the brush through her short-cropped hair, she put on her hat and pinned the pretty broach Eugenia had given her to the lapel of her dress.

Lucy came into the bedroom, ready to go. "You look nice, Mama."

"This is the blue crepe dress Louise gave me for Christmas. I really like it. I'll be ready to go in a few minutes. Are you and I the only ones going to Sunday School?"

"I guess so. Margaret is still asleep. Maybe she'll come to church."

"Well, let's go. It kind of looks like rain." She picked up her purse and Bible. "Maybe we can get to the streetcar line before it starts."

అsix

"I don't think we're going to get there before the rain, Lucy. I just felt a drop or two. Let's hurry." Suddenly the rain came down in a heavy shower. "I see the streetcar coming," Emily said. "I guess we can dry ourselves off once we get on. I have a handkerchief in my purse."

Emily and Lucy stepped quickly into the streetcar. "Looks like you ladies got caught in the rain," the conductor said.

Emily brushed the raindrops from her dress. "I'm afraid so." After they were seated, she took a small handkerchief from her purse and wiped her face and arms. "I don't think my hat is ruined since it's straw." Lucy took her headscarf and dried her face and arms as best she could, and they both settled back on the hard wooden seats for the thirty-minute ride.

"It's really warm in here," Lucy said, "but it's raining too hard to open the window."

"Maybe it will help our clothes to dry."

Just before their final stop, Lucy looked over at her mother and began to giggle. "Mama, look at your dress. It's drawn up over your knees, and it's pulling apart at the buttons down the front."

Emily looked down at her dress. "Oh, my stars and grief! My dress has shrunk three sizes. I can't go to church like this. We'll have to stay on the streetcar when it turns around and go back home. Give the tickets to the conductor. If you walk in front of me when we get off, maybe no one will notice."

❧❧

As they hurried home, Emily began to laugh. "I have to laugh, or I would cry." There was another good laugh when they got home, and the other children saw her dress and heard her tale of woe. After she went into the bedroom to change her clothes, Emily couldn't help but feel let down. When she laid her damp dress on the chair, she realized it was ruined. Pulling her drab housedress over her head, she felt as if she had pulled a cloak of loneliness over herself. Suddenly, she yearned to see her sister Louise. Wouldn't it be wonderful to see Eugenia and her brothers? How she cherished the bond of brother and sister - one that could never be broken.

❧❧

"I'm going to write to your Aunt Louise after we finish eating lunch and ask if we can come to visit. I'll take Lucy and Calen and Henry and Judson with me," Emily announced. "Louise asked me some time ago to pay her a visit."

"How will we get there?" Henry asked.

"We can take the Greyhound bus. I won't have to buy a ticket for Judson since he isn't six yet. Daniel, you'll have to look after the garden while we're gone."

"But who'll look after Daniel?" Mary asked, laughing.

"I'll be okay, and I'll look after the garden when I'm not at the movies."

Mary looked at her brother and shook her head. "We'll be all right. I'll do the cooking. You need to go, Mama, and I'll even look after Daniel … if that's possible."

῾∞῾

Louise wrote that she would be delighted for Emily and the children to come. *Come as soon as you can. John Freeman will meet you at the bus station. Maybe we can drive down to see Mama and Daddy while you're here.*

Emily was ecstatic when the day of the trip arrived. After she packed the only two suitcases they owned, she dressed hurriedly and prompted the children to hurry. Taking one final look in the mirror, she sighed. Her dress was old and slightly faded, and her thick, light-colored stockings drooped around her ankles, but she had an inner beauty that was visible on her face and in her eyes.

"How will we ever get there on time? Let me fix your hair, Lucy. It isn't parted straight. Hand me the comb. Tie your shoes, Calen. Help him with his shoes, Henry. We must be on our way."

῾∞῾

Henry and Lucy tugged at the heavy suitcases as they walked across the crowded waiting room of the bus station. Emily walked in front of them, holding Calen and Judson by the hand. "Sit here," she pointed to an empty bench. "I'll buy the tickets at the office window, right over there. Ya'll sit right here until I get back."

The four shy children sat in wonderment as they watched the people move about. A group of sailors in the ticket line reminded Emily of Jonathan. *I bet he looks just as handsome, in his uniform, as they do.* When she reached the ticket window, she took the only money she had from her purse, a ten-dollar bill. "I'd like one adult and three children's round-trip tickets to Selma." She handed her money to the clerk and was relieved to read a sign on the wall, "All children under six years of age, ride free."

"That was eight dollars and forty cents," the clerk said handing her the change and the tickets. Emily crumpled the money in her hand and hurried over to the children. When she sat down, she opened her hand and counted her change.

"Why, he gave me too much change. He must have thought I gave him a twenty instead of a ten. I'll hurry and return it. Our bus leaves shortly."

Henry and Lucy looked up at their mother with excitement. "Why don't you keep it, Mama? We need it," Henry suggested.

"Why don't you, Mama?" Lucy added.

She stood up to look at the money in her mother's hand. "Why Lucy, I'm surprised at you and Henry. You know this isn't my money. I must return it."

As she hurried over to the ticket window, she heard the clerk call, "Bus now loading for Selma and Montgomery." Quickly, she explained to the clerk that he had given her too much change and handed the money to him. "Thank you, thank you very much," he replied.

She returned to the children and led them to the loading area to board the big silver and blue bus. After boarding, she and the children walked down the narrow aisle to find seats. Quite out of breath and excited, too, she managed to get two seats across from each other. "Henry, you and Calen will have to take turns sitting by the window. Judson and Lucy can sit by the window with me." She straightened her dress and leaned back on the seat to relax. With a terrible roar, the huge bus pulled out of the station. Farther down the road, the driver stopped to pick up more passengers. Finally the bus was filled to capacity. Enchanted by the scenery, the children pressed their faces to the window and questioned their mother as they viewed small shanties, herds of cows and farmers on their tractors.

It seemed foreign to Emily to be going anywhere on her own with no restrictions. She felt a sudden nostalgia as she listened to the bus driver call the names of the small towns she had known as a child. The thought of seeing her sister made her feel like a child again, and her heart pounded with excitement when the bus driver called, "Next stop, Selma."

John Freeman was waiting when they stepped off the bus. "My how these children have grown, even since I last saw them." He led them to the car parked in front of the small bus station. Before getting in, he turned to Henry, Calen, and Judson. "You boys will like the big swing we have in the backyard, and you too, Lucy." The boys' eyes brightened with excitement, and broad smiles showed their approval and respect for their uncle.

⇛⇝

Louise was waiting, eagerly, on the porch when they arrived, and bounded down the steps to greet the children with warm hugs and her sister with a kiss. "I'm so glad you've come. Come on in."

When they came inside, Emily looked at the beautiful staircase. She thought back to the day she had married and was reminded how much she had loved Edwin, but she now knew he had never loved her, and her thoughts of him only brought sadness. She wondered if Louise could read her thoughts or if she were thinking the same thing.

"Let's take your bags upstairs, boys, and then we'll come back down for some lemonade," John Freeman directed, breaking the silence. "I think your Aunt Louise has some cookies, too."

"And let's go in the kitchen, Lucy. I'll let you help me pour the lemonade." Louise put her arm around Lucy's shoulder and walked to the kitchen.

"Elizabeth, these are Miss Emily's children. Elizabeth is our cook and a fine one too." Lucy and the boys gave timid smiles.

The large black woman turned around from the kitchen sink and smiled. "My, my, dey sho is some fine chillun, Miz Emily."

"Why thank you, Elizabeth."

"Lucy, you and the boys sit down over here at the table and have some cookies." Emily watched as the children enjoyed the cold, refreshing drink and tasty sugar cookies - a delight they had known only at Christmas. She felt happy for the first time in years.

Calen pulled at his mother's skirt. "What is it, Calen?"

"The swing, Mama. I want to go and see the swing."

"Well, come on, son," John Freeman said laughing. "I told him about the swing on our way from the bus station, and he hasn't forgotten it. Let's all go out and let your mama and Aunt Louise catch up on their visiting.

"Let's you and me go into the living room, Emily. I want to hear all about the other children."

A light breeze fanned the sheer white curtains, making the room more comfortable from the early summer heat. Emily sat down in one of the wing chairs by the fireplace noting the beauty of the room. There were new pictures on the walls and new slipcovers on the chairs and sofa. Louise has always had a knack for decorating. "This room is really pretty, Louise. I especially like the slipcovers."

"You know how I've always loved pink and green. I found this floral in just the shades I like." Proudly, she ran her hand over the arm of the chair. "I talked to Mama and Daddy on the telephone yesterday, and they want us to come and visit for a few days. I thought we would go day after tomorrow - if that suits you."

Emily's face brightened. "I can hardly wait to see them." Looking down demurely, she continued. "In a way, I dread seeing Mama. You know she doesn't approve of my divorce."

"Knowing Mama, I don't think she'll mention it. I think it's probably best not to discuss it with her. I know she'll be eager to see the children and to hear about the others. What do you hear from Eddie and Jonathan?"

"I don't hear from Eddie very often. I think he's in the thick of fighting in the South Pacific. I worry about him." As she listened, Louise noticed the strained lines etched on Emily's face. "Jonathan will be going to the Pacific soon - I think. You know he's in the Navy, but on a brighter note, Mary and Laura have steady beaus and want to marry soon. Both the boys are in the military, and we won't have time for fancy weddings for either of them."

"What about Margaret?"

"Oh, she's working at Western Union where Mary works and going to college, too. She doesn't have much time for dating. I think she wants to be a doctor. She can probably reach that goal. She was valedictorian of her graduating class, and she's very determined."

"Margaret has always seemed very smart to me. What about that mischievous, Daniel? What's he up to?"

"He wants to join the Merchant Marines as soon as he's old enough. I don't know if I can talk him out of it. I think he can join at sixteen without my consent. I just hope when the war is over the boys will come home and finish school," Emily said wistfully.

"I agree. I know how you feel about their getting an education, but at this point, with the war and lack of money, it's difficult to keep them in school. You'll just have to concentrate on the younger children. I want to take them downtown tomorrow and buy them some clothes."

Emily bent forward in her chair and smiled. "Oh you've already done enough for us, Louise. I'll never be able to repay you."

"Oh, Emily! I know if our roles were reversed, you'd do the same for me. Anyway this is John Freeman's idea."

ò∼ó

"It's warm already," Louise said, when she and Emily and the children came out of the house to go to visit their mother and father. Henry stood close to the side of the blue and white Dodge and ran his hand along the side of the shiny car, admiringly.

"Help me put the suitcases in the trunk of the car, Henry," his uncle called.

"Yes, sir."

"Can you all get in the back seat?"

"Yes, ma'am," Lucy said. She jumped in and pulled her new dress over her knees. Calen and Judson could hardly contain their excitement as they crowded onto the seat between Henry and Lucy. This was their first time to visit their grandparents. Emily shared their excitement as she seated herself in the front seat.

After saying goodbye to John Freeman, Louise took the driver's seat. "I think we'll have to roll the windows down. I'm afraid it's going to be a hot day."

After only a few miles, the scenery changed from buildings to farmland with large herds of cows grazing in green pastures along the road. When Louise heard the children talking about the different kinds of cows, she told them the names of each kind. "Those white-faced cows are Herefords. They're beef cattle like the ones we have at the stockyards."

Henry reached out the window and pointed to a group of reddish tan cows grazing near the road. "I know what kind those are; they're Guernsey cows like our Sulkey."

"That's right," Emily said. "Henry likes anything to do with farming. Maybe he'll be a farmer someday."

Finally the farmlands gave way to the flatlands, and the soil changed in color from dark brown to sandy clay. Among the oaks and the other hardwoods, tall pines grew in groves. Along the side of the road, the bushy growth took on a tropical appearance. Louise wiped her brow with her handkerchief. "Whew, you can tell we're getting farther south, by the humidity. Thank goodness we're nearly there."

Emily felt a sudden sadness as they pulled into the driveway. It was hard to picture her parents living anywhere but Pine Belt. This is Albert's home, she thought, not Mama and Daddy's. They don't have a home of their own anymore. Albert and Sarah are good to care for them in their old age. The children bounded out of the car into the sandy yard with only a few patches of grass. A large palm tree with ragged and brown branches stood at the side of the house. "Are we in Florida?" Lucy asked.

"No, but it's only a few miles down the road to the state line," her aunt said. This little town is known as Lockhart. I'll take you down that way tomorrow, so you can say you've been to Florida."

Albert and his children rushed out to the car to greet them. "Hello! Hello! Where's John Freeman?"

"Oh, he thought he was too busy to get away, and the car will hold just so many," Louise said. "Let me give you a hug."

"Emily!" Albert said with delight. He hugged her tightly. "Let me look at your children. These are your cousins from Birmingham. We'll have to take them on a picnic to the lake tomorrow. We have a nice big lake close by. Now, let's get these suitcases inside." It didn't escape Emily's eye that her children were quickly becoming friends with their newfound cousins.

Aging hadn't been kind to her mama and daddy. Emily was quick to observe that neither got up from his or her chair when they all entered the living room. Her daddy was leaning on a cane in front of his chair, and her mother seemed somewhat distracted. Still, it was wonderful to see them. She greeted them warmly and was happy to see them welcome her children so lovingly. Sarah came out of the kitchen to greet everyone. "Well, look who's here. I wish all the children could have come, Emily. How I'd like to see them! And, Louise, how are you?"

"Oh, I'm fine… just a little hot."

"I've got some sweet tea to cool you off. Let's sit on the porch.

I think we might get a breeze there. The children can help bring the glasses out."

After Benjamin and Lillie were seated on the porch, Emily and Louise found comfortable rockers, and the children seated themselves on the wide steps that were shaded by a large oak tree. Albert and Sarah served the iced tea along with some sugared cookies. This was the time Emily had dreamed about - time with her family.

かめ

Louise spread the blue and white checked cloth over the picnic table and smoothed out all the wrinkles. As she stooped down to take the food from the large basket, she realized that it was the old cotton basket that had belonged to her daddy. "Is this the basket you saved from Grandpa's plantation, Daddy?"

"Yes," her daddy said, beaming. "It's really old but still good."

Emily remembered how he always loved to talk about his daddy and their old home place ...so many stories ... so many memories.

The delicious aroma of baked ham drifted across the table. Sarah had prepared potato salad and deviled eggs to go with the ham Louise had brought. Emily opened a can of pork and beans and poured them in a heavy earthenware bowl. Louise held up a large loaf of homemade bread. "Here's Daddy's favorite, and I know this pound cake is what you like, Mama."

Albert filled the washtub to ice the soft drinks. "I'll put the drinks here on this table." All the preparations made a perfect picture underneath the huge, live-oak tree where Benjamin and Lillie were sitting. A feeling of tranquility hung in the air like the gray moss that decorated the old tree. For the first time in years, all the sorrow and grief that Emily had endured faded away with the quiet conversation now with her family. Neither Edwin nor her divorce was mentioned. It was a time of happiness as warm as the lake water where the children were swimming.

かめ

Louise watched Albert change the flat tire beside the road. "I don't know what I would have done had you not come with us."

Albert examined the tire closely. "That's what the war will do for you. Look at that tire. It's supposed to be a new one but obviously it's a retread." Perspiration flowed off his face as he tightened the tire on the car.

Louise wiped her brow as she watched her brother. "I thought about taking the children down to the beach to see the ocean. It's only an hour's drive, but now I'm afraid to risk driving farther on these tires. I'm glad I didn't mention it to them."

"Well, you had good intentions. I'm glad I came along with you. The state line is just over that rise. I'll walk with them down there. Maybe that will satisfy them."

"Just wait till I tell Daniel that we went to Florida. He'll be jealous," Henry said.

"Roll the windows down and keep your hands inside," Albert instructed. "I'm afraid that's all of Florida we'll get to see today."

∾∿

The visit with her family was the encouragement Emily needed, and the children were given a pleasant memory to last a lifetime. Emily sat back in her seat and closed her eyes as the loud Greyhound bus traveled to Birmingham.

Chapter Twenty Five

Changes

*E*mily was doubtful. There was something about the little old man. Did he really know how to roof a house? "Just two hundred dollars, ma'am," he said. Emily looked skeptically at him. His suit was worn and frayed on the edges, and his shirt was a dingy white. His broad smile revealed a missing tooth, as he repeated himself. "Yes, ma'am, I was just driving by and saw how bad you needed a new roof, and I said to myself, them people need a roof, and I'm just the one to help 'em."

Emily studied him, again. "I don't know."

He walked farther out from the house looking up at the roof. "Anyone else would charge you more," the little man bargained.

"What kind of guarantee would you give me?"

"Oh, I give a five-year guarantee against leaks, and I can arrange for you to pay for it monthly - if you like."

"Well, all right. I know we certainly need a new roof. I'll sign. I'm the one who will make the payments. I don't have a husband." The words stung her lips. "But I can manage it."

⊱⊰

The house was roofed in only five days, and Emily was pleased at the way it looked, but the proof will come with the first rain, she thought.

The first heavy rain came in September. Water poured off the roof in torrents. The force of the wind made the trees bow to its command. It didn't take long for the dampness to appear on the same spot of the living room ceiling. Emily was sick at heart as the moisture slowly formed into heavy droplets that fell to the floor. "Bring me that bucket from the kitchen, Henry!" Henry placed the bucket under the dripping ceiling and watched as each drop hit the bucket with a monotonous rhythm. "What was the man's name who put on the roof on the house, Henry?"

"Mr. Simpson, that's his name."

"That's right. I remember now. I have his telephone number." Emily opened the top narrow drawer of the buffet in the dining room. "I'm so glad Mary got us a telephone. Now I don't have to go to the neighbors."

Emily's hand trembled as she dialed the number. She had barely released her finger from the last digit when the operator answered, "I'm sorry; that number has been disconnected." Emily held the receiver a moment. Completely perplexed, she placed it gently back in its cradle. She took a deep breath and examined the leak again. Anger and hurt, along with despair, overwhelmed her.

"What'll we do, Mama?" Henry asked.

"I guess I can call the bank where I make the payments. Maybe they'll know how to contact him."

"No, ma'am," the lady at the bank said. "We have no record of Mr. Simpson's whereabouts. He sold us the note and didn't leave an address. "I'm sorry."

"I see," Emily said and hung up the telephone.

"Don't worry, Mama," Henry said. "I can fix it. I can get some roofing tar and fix it. I'll go to the feed store. They have roofing tar."

"How much is roofing tar?"

"It's about a dollar, I think."

Emily went to the bedroom and took out the only money she had in her purse. Fifteen dollars, she counted. This has to last until the first of the month, unless Edwin sends his check. He's two months behind, now. She didn't even like to think about him, or the humiliation of calling the Juvenile Court to force him to send his child support check. Taking a five-dollar bill from her purse, she returned to the living room and gave it to Henry. "Take this and get the tar, Henry. It's finally quit raining. Be careful not to lose the change. It's almost all the money we have."

"Don't worry. I'll be careful." Henry took the money and put it in his overall pocket.

Two days later when the roof had dried, he climbed up on the top of the house as his mother held the ladder. Meticulously, he daubed the tar on the leak. He could see that the old man had been stingy with his shingles and nails, but he decided not to mention it to his mother. "I think I've got it fixed now." He came down the ladder and took the bucket of tar to the garage.

"Well, I guess I've learned not to trust just anyone who comes along. Thank you, Henry. Oh, I see the postman coming. I'll go and get the mail."

"Good morning, Mrs. Anderson," the postman said cheerfully. He reached into his mailbag. "You have two letters."

"Good morning." She reached out to take the letters and quickly examined them. Both were long awaited; one was a check from Edwin and the other a letter from Eddie.

Eddie's letter was short, and she read it twice before she went into the house.

Dear Mama,

I'm getting a sun tan. It's very hot here. We don't get much sleep, and the food is just rations. Don't worry about me. I'm fine. Miss you all and I miss home. I don't have much time to write. Love, Eddie

She could only guess where he might be and the danger he was in. She tried not to worry about him and Jonathan. When she opened the envelope from Edwin, the check enclosed was for fifty dollars. It was time for the third month's payment, but he had only sent for two months. I guess I'll have to be satisfied that he's sent this, she rationalized.

❧❧

Jonathan didn't let his mother know he was coming home. This would be his last furlough before shipping out to the Pacific. The bus ride was long from Virginia, but his tiredness couldn't overcome his excitement of surprising his mother. After arriving in Birmingham, he claimed his heavy duffel bag and took a taxi home.

"Have a good visit," the taxi driver said when Jonathan paid his fare. Putting his bag on the ground, he stood for a moment and looked at the house. It was home - home where the elm tree grew larger every year and where the porch swing held many happy memories of his youth. Quietly, he slipped into the house and found his mother, as always, at the kitchen sink.

"Mama!"

Emily turned around. "Jonathan!" She put both her hands up to her face. "We didn't know you were coming." Quickly, she dried her hands on her apron and gave him a warm hug; then she stepped away from him. "Let me look at you!" In his uniform, there was a haunting resemblance to his daddy. She still remembered how handsome Edwin looked in the pictures in his Navy uniform. I guess I can't forget him completely, she thought.

"I wanted to surprise you, Mama."

"And what a surprise! Let's sit down to the table. I was just washing the lunch dishes."

Jonathan could feel the heat that still radiated from the cook stove, making the room uncomfortably warm. He noticed how everything looked smaller and more worn. "I just have a three-day leave, but while I'm here, I want to buy you a gas stove. I can connect it. I learned how to do that kind of work in my training."

"Do you have enough money? You already send me an allotment."

"Yes, ma'am," Jonathan said, proudly. "I've been saving for a stove ever since I've been gone."

How is it that the boys are so different from their daddy? She questioned. Since they're grown, both Eddie and Jonathan want to make my life easier. Trying to hide her emotions, she got up and went over to the cabinet for some glasses. "Would you like a glass of ice water? It's still so hot, and it's nearly October."

"It's sure hot in here. Let me chip the ice. He bent down and opened the small door to the metal-lined ice box. "The next thing I'm going to get you is a refrigerator. Maybe I'll just send you some money, and you can buy it."

"Oh, this icebox is all right, but I know I'll enjoy the new stove."

❧

There was a lively reunion with Jonathan when his younger brothers and sister came in from school. Lucy couldn't keep her eyes off his handsome uniform, and Daniel wanted to hear about all his adventures. "I have some souvenirs for ya'll." Calen and Judson moved closer to their brother to collect their gift - a small replica of a ship, for both. Lucy's gift was a white naval middy. She was ecstatic, and it fit perfectly. For Daniel and Henry, Jonathan had brought each a pocketknife. Emily watched the happy reunion with pleasure.

☜☞

Along with the new gas stove, Jonathan bought a water heater. "I decided to get the water heater, too. The stove isn't new, but it's a nice one. That left me enough money to get the water heater. This one is so old. Now, you'll have all the hot water you need."

As Jonathan, Daniel and Henry carried the old cast-iron stove outside, a flood of memories filled Emily's soul - all the meals she had cooked – how many biscuits had been placed in the oven, and no telling how much coal it had burned.

"Can I sell it for scrap iron, Mama?" Daniel asked.

"Oh, I don't know, Daniel. We'll have to see how much they will give us for it."

☜☞

It's hard to believe that Edwin has been gone a year. With all the children in school and the older girls working, Emily had more time to think and more time alone. Many of her thoughts were of Eddie and Jonathan and their safety. She wouldn't let herself think of her failures. Divorce was something she never thought she would experience, and she certainly knew she would never marry again. She had lost her desire for romantic love, but not her longing to know love. Chores always seemed to help push her feelings aside. She looked at the two large baskets of wet clothes beside the washing machine. With the threat of rain, she deliberated whether to hang them outside but knew she must take that chance. Her thoughts turned to Mary and Laura as she hung each piece on the line. Both wanted to marry before their fiancées were sent overseas. The only kind of wedding possible would be a small one in the chapel of the church. There was no money for fancy weddings. The war had put a different perspective on everything. When the last sock was hung on the line, a touch of blue sky parted the clouds and released a ray of sunshine. "Glory be!" Emily sighed. "Maybe they'll dry after all."

☙❧

"Mama! Mama!" Daniel called as he ran inside. "I saw an advertisement coming home from school. I can join the Merchant Marines when I turn sixteen. That's next week."

"Yes, I know, Daniel. That's all you've talked about since Jonathan left. You know there's even danger in the Merchant Marines."

"I know, but I want to be a part of helping win the war like Eddie and Jonathan." He picked up a hot muffin that his mother had just taken from the oven and stuffed it in his mouth.

"You're so young, Daniel. I think you're looking for adventure more than anything." Daniel gave a broad grin. His mother knew him well. "It looks like I'm losing my children as fast as I got them."

☙❧

Daniel left home one week after his sixteenth birthday, and with him went much of the laughter and folly that had helped his family through the bad times of the last year. Emily was right about the danger he would face. Six months after he had gone, she got word that his ship had been torpedoed. He wasn't injured, and he would be home for two weeks as soon as he could get a seat on a train from New York. Well, Emily thought, I was more worried about Eddie, and Daniel is the one who could have been killed.

"Since Daniel is coming home, let's use some extra ration stamps and try to get some meat," Emily said. "You know how he loves to eat."

"Yes, ma'am," Lucy said. "I can ride over to Mr. Evan's Meat Market on the bicycle in the morning. If I go early, I might get something special." Lucy had eagerly taken over the chore of buying the groceries now that she was older. She never seemed to mind the long walk or tire from carrying the heavy bags. Since she had Jonathan's bicycle, she was always ready to go.

❧

Before anyone was awake, Lucy dressed, went to the garage and rolled the bicycle out onto the driveway. Jonathan had bought the bicycle, painted it to look like new and bought new tires. Each time Lucy rode it, she admired the name Western Flyer, written boldly in the gold letters on the cross bar. She lifted herself onto the seat, pretending the bicycle belonged to her, and rode proudly down the road to the market. The early morning air felt fresh on her face, but she knew it wouldn't be long before the heavy July heat would take over. She wanted to get back home as soon as possible. The familiar smell of freshly-butchered meat mixed with the scent of sawdust, greeted her as she propped her bicycle against the store wall and waited for Mr. Evans to open the market. By the time he opened the door, there was a large crowd of anxious women waiting. Like Lucy, they had come early hoping to buy a piece of meat, since it was so scarce. She moved quickly to the counter and looked at the small amount of meat behind the glass case. Her hopes of getting anything special began to fade.

"What will it be for you, young lady?" Mr. Evans asked. "Aren't you one of the Anderson children?" Lucy looked up timidly and shook her head up and down. She was surprised that he knew her. All the anxious women, pushing and shoving to get up to the counter, had left her speechless. "How about this half of a ham? It's just two dollars."

"Yes, sir, I'll take that." Unfolding her sweating hand that tightly held her money, she handed it to the butcher along with the ration stamps. Some of the envious women loudly complained to Mr. Evans. Totally unconcerned, he wrapped the ham in the brown butcher paper and handed it to Lucy. Happily, she rushed out of the market and jumped on her bicycle to hurry home. She could hardly wait to show her mother the ham and tell her about the women in the market. "Mama, Mama," she called when she came into the house. "Look what I bought." Emily listened with amusement as Lucy told about the women wanting the ham. "But Mr. Evans sold it to me, and he knew who I was," she said, her face glowing with regalement.

Emily opened the package and admired the ham. "This is just what we need for Daniel's homecoming. Mr. Evans is a nice man. Did you use all the ration stamps?"

"All but ten," Lucy said, still beaming over her success.

ತಿಂ

Daniel's visit brought laughter into the house again. Henry wanted to hear how his ship was torpedoed and how long he was in the lifeboat before being picked up by another ship. "Tell it again," Henry said. Daniel was happy to tell it the second time, even adding a little imagination to the story. Emily had noticed that Daniel had a talent for embroidering a tale.

When Lucy heard that he had received some extra money because his ship was torpedoed, she persuaded him to buy a new rug for the living room. "Well, okay. I like the way you keep the house so clean, Lucy, and I know how hard it is to stretch the lace curtains. I've watched Mama many times starch them and stretch them, her fingers bleeding from all those tiny nails that hold the curtains on the frame. We'll go to town and buy a rug tomorrow. It'll make this room look better."

Each night after supper, Daniel entertained with another of his anecdotes. Emily looked forward to this time along with the children, and she could see that Daniel was certainly enjoying himself. "Do you remember Mr. Whatley's little store down on the main road?" Daniel began. "One afternoon, after school I went by there to see if he would give me a moon pie. I didn't have any money. I leaned on the front of the glass counter and looked longingly at the candy and the moon pies." Emily watched his expression. He was like an actor with a captive audience. He shifted in his chair as he continued. "You remember old man Whatley. He was tall and skinny with thinning gray hair, and he had lots of teeth missing. However, the thing I noticed most about him was a very long fingernail on his right little finger. When he got up from his chair and asked me what I wanted, I stepped back from the counter almost afraid to say anything. "I don't have any money," I said, trying to look sad.

Then he asked me, "Does your mama have any chickens, son?"
"Yes, sir," I said.

He leaned farther over the counter. "If you'll bring me a few fresh eggs, I'll trade you a moon pie for them."

"I ran out of the store as fast as I could. When I came into the house, I made sure Daddy wasn't at home. Then I sneaked out to the chicken house and got two warm eggs out from under the setting hen."

Judson and Calen pulled their chairs up closer to the table, to support their elbows resting their heads on their hands. Emily lifted her eyebrows in disbelief. "You won't do, Daniel."

"Finish the story, Daniel!" Henry begged.

Daniel put the last bite of ham in his mouth and continued. "I carefully put the eggs in my overall pockets and walked slowly back to the store. When I came inside the store, I took the two eggs from my pockets and handed them to Mr. Whatley."

"Okay … Okay!" he said. When he reached out his hand and took the eggs, I jumped back from the counter and stared at his long fingernail. Suddenly, he began to laugh. He couldn't stop laughing."

"Well, I'll be darn, son. I asked for an egg and you gave me a chicken." He held out his hand and in it was a fuzzy yellow, baby chicken. "That ought to be worth five moon pies." Still laughing, he handed me a sack filled with the pies. I grabbed the sack and ran out of the store and didn't stop until I was nearly home. I sat down beside the road and ate every one of the pies. I guess it was the first time I was ever full in my life."

"I never heard you tell this story before, Daniel," Emily said. "Are you sure you are not making it up?"

"Wait, I didn't finish. I thought I was home free and no one would know my secret, until Eddie and Jonathan discovered the little store, and Mr. Whatley told 'em all about me bringing him the eggs. The chicken turned out to be a rooster. He named it Prince Albert and kept it right there in the store. Eddie and Jonathan threatened to tell you, but they were afraid you'd tell Daddy, and they knew he would give me a whipping. So they never told anyone."

"What a tale, Daniel. There's never a dull moment with you around," Emily said smiling.

৵৽

Emily got the telephone call of Albert's death the day after Daniel left. Louise gave her the sad news of their brother's death. "Sarah said, 'he died suddenly.' He just lay down across the bed and was gone."

Emily was silent a moment as quick tears rolled down her cheeks. "Where ... where will he be buried?"

"They'll bring his body here to Selma. He'll be buried in the Live Oak Cemetery, in the lot where Mama and Daddy will be buried, and Sarah, if she chooses. I guess now I'll need to bring Mama and Daddy to live here with us."

Emily sighed. "How can you do that? John Freeman isn't well enough for you to take on that responsibility."

"I don't have any choice. It wouldn't be right for Sarah to continue to care for them. She still has very young children at home. I can do it."

"I'll come down tomorrow. Margaret can look after the children and I'll just come alone. We can talk when I get there." When she hung up the telephone, Emily sat down in the wicker rocker. Things change, she thought, and death can come so quickly. Albert was a good man. I know Sarah will miss him, though she does have the memory of a happy marriage. I wonder if divorce isn't worse than death. "I must go and tell the children," she whispered. "Albert was so good to them when we visited him and his family. I'm so glad we have those good memories."

Chapter Twenty Six

A Room for Benjamin and Lillie

Each time she saw them, Emily realized how old and frail her parents had become. Her daddy was bent with age and walked with a cane, and her mother could hardly walk, even with a cane. There were no more long conversations with her mother; too much of the time she sat in her chair in silence. With John Freeman so debilitated from a stroke, Emily wondered how Louise could possibly take care of them. Before she could come to any resolution, the telephone rang. It was Louise saying that John Freeman had suffered another stroke and was gravely ill. John Freeman's generosity and goodness flashed through her mind like a chronicle of the past twenty years. Was there a better man? He had certainly helped her and the children when they needed it most. Now, the best thing for her to do was to bring her mother and father to Birmingham and care for them. She knew they wouldn't want to come. Her daddy had never liked Birmingham, and her mama still enjoyed the well-to-do lifestyle that Louise and John Freeman could afford. But knowing there was no other solution, she told Louise, "You'll have to let Mama and Daddy come live with me, at least until John Freeman gets better. But I don't know how happy they'll be about living here. Maybe Daddy will enjoy talking to my boys."

Louise gave a deep sigh. Emily could hear the distress in her voice and feel her anguish. "Life never gets easy, does it? Maybe Daddy will come if he knows he can help you financially. And I'll send you some extra money, too. I'll talk to them about it and call you later."

కింత

Emily found it difficult to tell the children that her parents were coming to live with them. It would mean the bedrooms would have to be rearranged, and their whole way of life would change. Lucy and Margaret would have to give up their room for their grandparents and move their twin beds into the other bedrooms. When Emily told Lucy and Margaret, Lucy put her hand up to her mouth and looked down to hide her disappointment. For the first time since Mary and Laura had married, she and Margaret had a room to themselves, and she had made the room attractive with new curtains and bedspreads that Margaret had bought. "I'm sorry, Lucy. Aunt Louise can't take care of your grandma and grandpa now that your uncle is so ill. We'll want to make them feel welcome. They're old and feeble and need our help. We'll move all the furniture out of your room because they'll be bringing their own furniture. Making room for them won't be an easy task."

Judson came to the door of Lucy's bedroom. "We'll help them, Mama. I like to hear Grandpa tell his stories about the Civil War." Emily looked at Judson, her youngest. She could see in him the sincere benevolence her brother Jonathan always had. God is good, she thought, to give us reminders of those we have lost and loved so dearly.

"Well, your grandpa has lots of stories to tell and will sure enjoy telling them. Now, let's see if we can get this room ready for them."

Lucy was quiet as she moved hers and Margaret's things into her mother's room. Emily knew that cleanliness and orderliness were important to Lucy, but there were no other solutions. They would all have to sacrifice. "One of the twin beds will have to go into the back room and one in my bedroom for Margaret. You'll have to sleep with me, Lucy."

"It's okay, Mama. I don't mind."

"Maybe sleeping with me will help you get over your fear of the dark. Margaret is hardly ever here - only to sleep. I don't think the change will matter to her."

Finally the room was empty and clean. A slight autumn breeze billowed beneath the starched white curtains and gave a fresh scent of the outdoors to the room. Maybe Mama and Daddy will be happy here, Emily thought. She stood in the doorway and took a final look at the room. The apple green paint on the walls was always a reminder of Edwin. Will we ever be rid of that color? She mused. I guess apple green will always remind me of him.

❦

Early in the afternoon on the next day, Benjamin and Lillie arrived. Louise's son brought them. A truck filled with their belongings followed. Emily was nervous, but the children were excited and waited on the porch to welcome them. Since it was a warm day, Emily suggested that her mother and daddy sit on the porch until their furniture was placed in their room - the room that was to be theirs until they died.

❦

The house will be full again. Since the War had ended in August, Eddie would be coming home soon, and he planned to go back to school, then on to college. Jonathan had written, he would return in December. Her allotment checks from the boys would come to an end. With the extra money from her parents and Louise, she would get by. The boys have their own lives now, she thought. I can't depend on them for help any longer. She was proud that Jonathan had plans to learn electronics at a trade school. Electronics always appealed to him, and he will be good in that field. Everything always works out no matter how I worry.

❦

Mr. and Mrs. Whitworth settled in happily with an abundance of attention from Henry and Judson. Emily was surprised at the special care the boys gave their grandpa. As Lucy assumed more of the cleaning chores, Emily proceeded to give the much-needed care that her mother required. Strange, Emily pondered, all the years I've longed to spend time with Mama and Daddy, and now that I have my chance, they need me more than I need them.

❦

Judson and Calen sat in the wooden swing, and Henry sat on the banister of the front porch. Their grandpa had his own special chair, a heavy oak captain's chair worn smooth on the arms from continuous use. He was still a very big man and required everything of his to be oversized.

Emily came out onto the porch with a large pitcher of lemonade. "I can't believe you haven't told the boys about old Alf, Daddy."

Mr. Whitworth smiled. "I haven't told you about the time the Yankees came and took my daddy."

"No, Grandpa. You haven't told us that story." Henry pulled his knees up, wrapped his arms around them and leaned back on the brick column of the banister.

Mr. Whitworth took a sip of lemonade and leaned forward with both hands resting on his heavy walking stick. "Well, the Yankees had gotten as far down South as our home, but they wanted to get to Selma because the arsenal was located there - the place where they stored all the guns and ammunition. They had no idea of how to get there. They were tired and ragged by this time." Taking his handkerchief, as he often did, he wiped his mouth and continued his story. "When the Yankees got to our house, they made my daddy go with them to lead the way to Selma. It was about a twenty-mile march. My sister ran to the barn to tell Alf, and he got an axe and went to rescue daddy."

"Who was Alf, Grandpa?" Judson asked.

"He was a slave. He had been with our family from the time I was born on our plantation. He loved my daddy and stayed with us until he died. Luckily, the Yankees didn't harm my daddy. They just wanted him as a guide, and he was on his way back home before old Alf got to Selma. My daddy often wondered what he would have done with that axe." Benjamin laughed.

Emily listened through the open window as her young sons asked question after question, and her daddy told every detail of his stories of the past.

❧❦

Days ran swiftly into weeks, weeks into months, and soon those days were ended for Lillie. Quietly, in her sleep, she died.

❧❧

As she stood by her mama's grave in the old Live Oak Cemetery and listened to the comforting words of the preacher, Emily felt sorrow mixed with relief. Her mother's health had deteriorated so much in the last few months. She had no quality of life and no days free from pain. Emily's great sorrow was that she had never come to a good relationship with her mother. All the disappointments of her youth clouded her mind, and now she would never experience the love she had hoped for from her mother. "Let not your heart be troubled, ye believe in God, believe also in me," the preacher continued. The fourteenth chapter of John's Gospel - that was Mama's favorite Scripture. Your heart will never be troubled again, Mama, Emily thought as she bowed her head for the closing prayer.

When the graveside service was over, she said goodbyes to friends and family and walked slowly with Louise to the car. "How is Daddy taking Mama's death?"

"He seems to have accepted it very well. Doctor Mitchell said when he came to the house to confirm her death, that many times when a mate of an older person dies, the other one doesn't live very long thereafter. He was very satisfied to stay with Judson and Henry since he really wasn't able to come to the funeral."

"I'm glad the older children got to come. They always loved Mama," Louise said.

"Yes, they did," Emily agreed. "She gave them security when they needed it most. Edwin always behaved himself when she came to visit, so it was always a more pleasant time when she came. Now, tell me what the doctor is saying about John Freeman."

Louise leaned on the side of the car to catch her breath. The air was still and quite warm for a spring day. Emily saw in her expression more than sorrow for their mother's death. "He says it's just a matter of weeks. What will I do without him, Emily? He's always been the love of my life."

Emily was silent for a moment; her thoughts were deeper than Louise could have imagined. What would it be like to love as they have loved and to share each other's dreams and successes - even to accept each other's failures? She lifted her head and looked out past Louise to the crowd. "John Freeman is a dear man, Louise. You'll always be comforted by those memories."

Louise reached over and gave her beloved sister a hug. It was as if she knew Emily's thoughts. "We must be going," Emily said. Mary's and Laura's husbands are anxious to go home."

❧❦

Henry and Lucy were the first in line for the graduation exercises. Emily was proud because they graduated with honors. Yet, she was sad, knowing that they both would soon leave home. Lucy would be spending the summer with Margaret in Minnesota, and Henry, like his brothers, planned to join the Navy.

With the ceremony ended, Emily and the children walked the nearly mile and a half home from the school. The thought occurred to her, Henry and Lucy had walked this long way for twelve, long years, whatever the weather. I guess walking hasn't hurt them. They're hardly ever sick. Lucy walked closer to her mother and took her hand. She would soon be leaving to go to Minnesota, and she dreaded leaving her mother. "I hate to leave you, Mama. There's so much housework to do, and Grandpa requires so much attention."

"But I want you to go, Lucy. You've never had a chance to go anywhere. I'm really glad you'll get to visit your Aunt Eugenia, and I know Margaret misses you or she wouldn't have bought you an airline ticket."

"I know, but I still hate to leave you."

"I'll be all right. Judson and Calen will be here to help me. Besides, Daddy isn't sick - he's just old. Did you know that he'll be ninety-five in June? Sometimes I think he's afraid to die. Doctor Mitchell says that's why he wants him to come and see him so often. I bet he's the only doctor in town who pampers an old man like your grandpa, and he's not young himself."

As they came to the last turn in the road, Emily breathed a sigh of relief. She was anxious about her daddy. This was the first time she had left him.

❧❦

Lucy could tell by her sister's face that something was wrong when she answered the phone. Her aunt Eugenia was calling to say

260

that their grandpa had died and their uncle John Freeman had died the day before. Lucy wasn't surprised. Still, she and Margaret were saddened. Though they didn't have a father's love, the love from their grandfather and their dear uncle eased the lack of fraternal love of those terrible years. It wouldn't be the same without them. "I know Mama will miss Grandpa. I can almost hear the pounding of his walking stick on the floor, calling for Mama in the night. And what will Aunt Louise do? I know she loved Uncle John Freeman so.

Emily's letter came at the end of the week.

You remember how Grandpa seemed to fear death. Well, his last days were completely different. He became calm and almost reconciled, making me remember what Mama said about death. "When it comes time, God will give us grace to die, just as He gives us grace to live." That sure was true for your grandpa. I've attended two funerals in one week of two of the dearest people in my life. I will truly miss them. Our house is growing empty again. I miss you both.
Love, Mama

Chapter Twenty Seven

Happy Wedding

The oppressive August heat failed to yield to any breeze as Emily sat in the porch swing trying to cool off. I'll sit here until the mailman comes, she decided. Maybe there'll be a letter from Margaret and Lucy. Her thoughts didn't betray her. The letter was from Margaret.

Dear Mama,
Lucy is coming home next week, on Friday, and I'm coming with her. I'm in love. His name is Phillip Gilbert. I met him at a retreat. He wants to be a foreign missionary, like I want to be. We want to marry next June. Lucy has helped me plan a beautiful wedding. I'm saving my money for it. I guess I'll give up the idea of going to Medical School. Phillip will have to attend Seminary, and then we hope to go to Thailand as missionaries. I'll tell you more when we come home.
With love, Margaret and Lucy

Suddenly a strong breeze stirred and Emily felt relief. "I'll be so happy to see the girls. I've missed them," she whispered to herself.

෯෧

Margaret's wedding day was one of those happenings in time that you never want to end - a time where happiness and love join together to make a perfect day. Emily took her seat at the front of the beautiful old church made fresh by large bouquets of white flowers and green smilax draped on the choir rail and candelabra. As the organ gave the reverberating chords of the Wedding March, Mary's and Laura's two small daughters came haltingly down the aisle strewing rose petals in wake of the bride. Margaret had never been more radiant and beautiful as she glided down the aisle, her arm clasped in the arm of her brother Eddie. Her white wedding gown of satin and lace fit perfectly, and her soft brown hair was crowned with a wreath of miniature white roses. Emily was pleased that Margaret had made her dress. It brought back memories of the time she had spent making her own wedding dress.

When the entire wedding party stood at the altar of the church, Emily gave a sigh of approval. Laura and Lucy were regal in their white organdy dresses. Their bouquets of red carnations were complimented by the deep red carpet of the sanctuary. We haven't had many special days like this one, Emily reflected. I wish all the girls could have had a wedding like this. Again, she thought of her wedding as the preacher read the vows to Margaret and Phillip. I guess I will always regret that I had to break my vows. I wonder if Edwin took them seriously even from the beginning. Her thoughts shifted to the loud refrain of the organ recessional played and the handsome bride and groom as they left the altar.

ক্ষ

A sense of family was already emerging for Emily with her new son-in-law. She especially liked his father and mother who had come all the way from Minnesota for the wedding. Emily stood by the reception table in the church parlor enjoying the wedding cake and all the other delicacies. "I hope you and Margaret will be very happy, Phillip. And to think, you plan to be missionaries. I don't know very much about Thailand, but I do know it is half way around the world."

"You'll have to come and see us there, someday."

"Oh, I'm afraid that would never be possible for me, but I have always dreamed of taking a voyage on a steamer," Emily said with a wistful look in her eyes.

"Well, hold on to that dream," Phillip said. "You never know what can happen."

Emily smiled, hoping that someday her dream might be a reality.

❧❦

The house was empty. All the children were gone. Calen and Judson were the last to go – both joining the Air Force as soon as they graduated from high school. Emily knew they were thinking of it as an adventure, not realizing the seriousness of the Korean War. I hardly know why we are fighting that war, she thought, and now my boys will be risking their lives over in that far-off place.

Now that Lucy, Henry and Eddie had married, Emily found herself alone in the house that had always been so crowded. She looked around the living room as she sat warming herself by the fire. There were no signs of apple green paint to remind her of Edwin, but she couldn't help but think of all he had missed with the children. When she heard that he had married again, the news didn't bother her. Now she must face the reality of loneliness and living on the small income she got from substitute teaching. She sighed as she thought of how quickly the children had grown up and left home … almost as fast as they had been born. Rubbing her arms, she moved closer to the fire but still felt the cold of the empty house. There's still the invitation to go and live with Louise, she pondered. Her invitation is always open, she has said. If I'm honest with myself, I need her.

Hesitantly, she made the call to her sister, dialing the operator and asking for Trenton 22452. "I've decided to come and live with you, Louise, if the invitation still stands."

"I'm so happy, Emily. I think we'll be very happy living together. Maybe we can even take some trips."

"I've thought about your offer a lot, and my living with you seems the best solution for both of us. I'll come as soon as I can figure out what to do about my house. Maybe Jonathan and his wife will live here for a while. I don't think Daniel will ever marry, but I don't think he'll come back here to live either. You know he's in the Army now, in Germany."

"Well, you shouldn't feel responsible for him anymore. He's a grown man. What about Eddie since he's graduated and married?"

"Oh, he and his wife have moved to Georgia. Lucy and her husband have just bought a new house - Henry and his wife, too. They all have their own lives, so I think coming to live with you is a good decision. I'll call you in a few days to let you know when I'm coming."

❧◆❧

Emily heaved a sigh as she packed the last piece of her personal belongings. She didn't know exactly how she felt about leaving. Her years in this house had been so difficult that she felt no remorse in leaving, but she regretted that she would be moving away from her children and grandchildren. "I won't be taking any of the furniture," she told Jonathan as he placed her things in the back of his truck for the hundred-mile journey.

"I hope this is the best thing for you, Mama. It won't seem right without you here in this house. We'll miss you, but it's not so far that we can't visit."

Emily settled back in the seat and looked at the house as Jonathan backed out of the driveway. Her emotions were mixed. She had never loved this house with its years of apple green paint and never-ending work. The years spent with her children after their daddy was gone were the best memories in that house, and now they were gone to live their own lives. Louise was waiting, and she was determined to start a new life and be happy.

❧◆❧

Life with Louise was completely different. Emily had long hours to spend alone, to read or sew or anything else she wanted to do. At first, she felt guilty about not helping with the housework, but the servants took care of all the household chores. Her days would have been lonely without their company, since Louise was gone most of the day attending to her cattle business. She really loves her work, Emily thought. I guess it takes the place of not having a lot of children.

❧◆❧

When Emily and Louise sat down to Sunday dinner, Emily announced, "The preacher asked me if I would teach a Sunday School class. It's been a long time since I've done any Bible teaching. What do you think?"

"Why, you know you can do it." She spread her napkin on her lap and began to serve her plate. "Don't you remember how Daddy used to call you Patrick Henry for your persuasive speech making? If you felt strongly about something, there was no end to your debate."

Emily wiped her mouth with her napkin, blushing from her sister's praise. Still, it felt good to have someone show confidence in her. "Well, I think I'll give it a try."

❧❦

"I have another grandchild," Emily said. Judson called today. It's a boy. That makes twenty-seven grandchildren."

Louise put the newspaper down in her lap and looked up. "Mercy me, how will you ever keep track of all of them?"

Emily smiled. The news made her more conscious of how fast time was passing. "I'd really like to see more of them, but they're all so busy. They'll grow up not even knowing their grandmother." Carefully, she folded the letter and put it in her pocket. As she settled back into her comfortable chair, she picked up the novel she had been reading, but the story didn't hold her interest. She was remembering that tomorrow was Mother's Day. "I haven't heard from any of the children. It's not like them to forget Mother's Day."

Louise laid her paper down again. She saw the distress on her sister's face. It was hard for her not to give away the secret that all of Emily's family were coming down tomorrow to surprise her. "Oh, don't you think they'll call? I'm sure you'll hear something from them."

❧❦

Louise stepped out onto the sidewalk and looked for the caravan of cars from Birmingham, but they were not in sight. She had promised to not let Emily go into the church before they arrived at eleven. With no one in sight, she and Emily went inside and took their usual seats. The surprise of the day was when the preacher announced that Emily was "Mother of the Year" because she had

266

the most children of anyone there. Emily stood up with pride to receive a beautiful bouquet of roses from her pastor.

No sooner was she seated, and an usher came and told her to come outside. For a moment Emily was confused and embarrassed at so much attention. Following the usher, she walked quickly up the aisle and out into the brilliant spring sunshine. Standing on the sidewalk were most of her children and grandchildren. Her eyes flooded with tears. It was almost as if they had known how much she had missed them. "Where did ya'll come from?" she asked, shaking her head in disbelief.

"We meant to get here earlier but just couldn't make it," Mary told her mother. With hugs and kisses from everyone, Emily's loneliness vanished. "We've brought a picnic lunch and thought we could go down to the park by the river."

Still overcome by the excitement, Emily walked over to the usher and asked him to tell her sister where she would be. "Maybe she'll come down after church," she told the children, not knowing that Louise already knew all the plans.

When Louise arrived, she was overjoyed to tell the family that the preacher had announced from the pulpit about their visit. "He thought it was wonderful that all of you came down on Mother's Day, and I know your mother thinks it's wonderful."

The day was perfect for a picnic. Only a few white wispy clouds drifted by to obscure the warm rays of the sun. There was a fragile freshness on the leaves as they rippled in the breeze in a symphony of rhythmic sounds. Each tree was a different shade of green. The grandchildren played happily on the sandy banks of the river, while Lucy and her sisters spread two long cloths on the wooden picnic tables. "Lucy, are these the same blue and white checked cloths that I gave your mama years ago?" Louise asked.

"Yes, ma'am, they are. We've used them over and over again."

Louise took her hand and smoothed out the wrinkles in a gentle gesture. "They have really lasted well."

The aroma of southern fried chicken, potato salad and baked beans drew the children from their play and the grown-ups from their conversation. Lucy sliced piece after piece of her delicious chocolate cake. Mary poured glass after glass of sweet tea and opened too many Coca-Colas to count. It still takes a lot of food to fill this crowd, Emily thought.

ॐ∽

After the food was cleared away, all the Mother's Day gifts were placed on the table before Emily. Lucy looked lovingly at her aunt. "These gifts are for you, Aunt Louise."

Emily felt proud that they would remember their aunt who had given so much to them. Louise looked at the gifts. "Well, thank you! I've always claimed you as my children, too."

Henry placed the folding chairs in a circle and instructed everyone to move over into a shaded area.

"When did you get home, Daniel?" his mother asked.

"I got here Friday. I'm staying with Lucy. I'd like to spend a few days down here with you and Aunt Louise if that's all right."

"We'd love a visit with you, Daniel," Louise invited. "I hope you have some stories to tell us about your time in Germany."

As the afternoon passed, the conversation turned to reminiscence and laughter. "Aunt Louise, do you remember when Wilma and I married, and you brought a smoked turkey for us to have for lunch on the day of the wedding?" Eddie asked. "The night before the wedding, Calen and Judson came in late from working at the movies and ate the whole thing."

"Oh, yes, I remember, and your mama didn't even get upset. She just went in and fried some chicken. I guess at that point, it wasn't much of a crisis for her."

Daniel told stories of how he attended the funerals of their neighbors, so he could go to the wakes afterwards and enjoy all the good food.

It was an afternoon of savoring memories long to be remembered.

Chapter Twenty Eight
Thailand

Emily stopped her sewing and went to the window to look out at blowing rain and heavy, gray skies. It was a dismal morning, chilly even for April. The dreary day added to her loneliness. She walked back to the kitchen to speak to Elizabeth, the cook. "Mornin, Miz Emily. Was you looking for the mail? Deh postman jes brought it. I brought it in cause the rain is blowing so hard I was afraid it would get wet."

Emily's demeanor brightened. "Thank you, Elizabeth. Maybe there'll be a letter from one of my children." She picked up the small stack of letters lying on the kitchen table. Right on the top was a letter from Margaret. The rest was for Louise. "I think I'll go up to the living room and read my letter. The light is better in there. It's such a dark day."

"Yes'um. Sho is," Elizabeth sighed.

Emily turned the lamp on by her chair and settled back to read. "I can hardly believe it," she said in a whisper. "Wonders never cease." She read the letter again.

Dear Mama,   *May 1, 1969*
I'm coming home in just two weeks. I'll be attending Emory University in Atlanta for six weeks. It will be a special course in amoebic dysentery. I need this study for my work at the hospital. I will be in Atlanta all week and then spend the weekends with Lucy. I'll come down and spend one weekend with you and Aunt Louise. When I return to Thailand, I want you to come with me. Phillip has

bought your ticket. He really wants you to come. He used some of the money he inherited from his father to buy your ticket. We want you to stay at least three months. We miss you.
Love, Margaret

What will Louise think if I'm gone that long? she wondered. I don't even have a passport, and I don't know if I have enough clothes. She looked at the clock on the mantel. It was hours before Louise would be home. I can't wait to tell her. One thing I know for sure, I really want to go.

ۀۀ

Emily was putting the dishes on the table for the evening meal, when Louise came into the house. "My, it's nasty out there. I think it's rained all day."

"You know what they say, 'April showers bring May flowers.'"

"I think these are more than showers today. I've got to get out of these wet clothes."

Emily waited anxiously for Louise to come and sit down. "I had a letter from Margaret today. I want you to read it."

Louise sat down and slowly unfolded the familiar blue airmail letter - one like she had seen Emily receive many times. She was puzzled that Emily wanted her to read this one.

Emily watched anxiously as Louise read. "I'll have to get a passport. I'm glad I finally got my birth certificate. Do you think you would be all right if I'm gone that long?"

Louise laid the letter down and looked at her sister lovingly. "Oh, Emily, you're always thinking about others. Of course, I'll be all right. I want you to go. It's a trip of a lifetime. John Jr. will come if I need him, and the servants will be here. It's not like I'll be alone."

"I can hardly believe this," Emily said. She took the letter, folded it carefully and took a deep sigh. "Phillip told me on their wedding day that he wanted me to come to Thailand someday, and now I'm going."

ۀۀ

Margaret felt the warmth of the past as she looked out the window of the Greyhound bus. She knew she was nearing Selma when she saw the kudzu vine covering the trees. Some, she thought, looked like giant topiaries along the sides of the road. Selma had been a place of refuge for her and her siblings when they were young children - always a place of happiness with her aunt Louise and uncle John Freeman. Her heart skipped a beat when she saw her mother and aunt waiting in the bus station. She couldn't wait to give them a hug. "I'm so glad to see you," enfolding her mother in her arms. Turning to her aunt with a hug, she whispered, "Aunt Louise, how are you? I've missed you both so very much."

"We could hardly wait for you to get here."

"That's right," Louise added. "We've counted the days. Now let me get the porter to bring your bags to the car. Elizabeth is waiting lunch for us."

Saturday lunch was the same as Margaret had remembered. The table was always set with the best china and the silver goblets that frosted on the outside like windowpanes on a cold winter day. There was always the same menu of fried chicken, mashed potatoes with gravy, and bowls of fresh vegetables. The ritual which Margaret had known as a child was followed verbatim as Elizabeth cleared the table and brought in ice cream and cake for dessert.

"This really brings back wonderful memories for me, Aunt Louise. You gave us some very happy days when we were children."

"Those were happy times for me and especially for John Freeman. He loved all of you and always enjoyed your visits. I still miss him, though it's been almost fourteen years since he died. A sad expression revealed her aunt's sorrow when she mentioned John Freeman.

"He was very special to us." She wiped her mouth on her napkin and looked at her mother. "Mama, I have another surprise for you. We've booked you on a steamship for your return home. It's The President's Line - a great ship."

"Well … Glory be! I guess if we wait long enough, we soon realize our dreams. I never thought a trip to Thailand would be possible, and to think about that voyage on an ocean liner." She shook her head and smiled a broad smile. "I'll take these next weeks and make myself a few things to wear."

271

"Remember, the weather is never cold over there, and the summer is very hot and humid."

చావ

Emily went to Birmingham two days before she and Margaret were to leave. Lucy met her mother at the bus station. "I've never seen you so excited, Mama."

"I've never been around the world before – not even out of the country."

"I hope I have everything I need. I certainly have enough advice on what to do and what not to do."

Lucy laughed. "Oh, Mama, you still have your sense of humor. Daniel said he will come and take you and Margaret to the airport. He'll be here early. I think your plane leaves at eleven."

చావ

Daniel bid a fond goodbye and watched from the huge window of the terminal until his mother and Margaret boarded the plane. The giant airplane taxied out to the runway, turned on its jet engines and quickly lifted up out of sight. Emily relaxed her shoulders and gave a deep sigh. Her eyes were still wide with excitement. "I just can't believe I'm really going."

Margaret smiled and patted her mother's hand. "We'll stop over in Tokyo and spend the night there. The next stop will be Hong Kong. We'll have a day and night there. It's a very fascinating place. I have some friends there who will take us to dinner."

Emily loosened her seat belt and leaned her head back on the seat. "I think I'll try to calm down a little. I know it's a very long flight."

"Yes, it is. I hope you don't get too tired." Margaret remembered that her mother was now seventy-five years old.

చావ

Thailand was a different world. Emily had an uneasy feeling to think that she was so far from home. That feeling didn't last long as Phillip and the children welcomed her with open arms. "I can hardly wait to write to Lucy and tell her about our trip here," Emily told Phillip on her second day there. "There's so much to write."

"Why don't you sit here at my desk to write? The morning light comes easily through this window. I'll clear my things away."

Before beginning to write, Emily gazed out the window where the children were playing. Tall bamboo plants bordered the yard for privacy and other lush, green plants flourished in the warm humid air. An overhead fan gave a comfortable breeze to the room as Emily began to write.

Dear Lucy,   *June 11, 1969*

We had a very trouble-free flight, long but I was able to sleep some of the time. We left Seattle at 7:30 P.M. on Wednesday and then had Thursday without any night. It mixes up your sleeping. When we got to Tokyo, we only had time to sleep and didn't get to see any of the sights. We were in Hong Kong twenty-four hours and managed to see a good bit there. One of Margaret's missionary friends took us to a Chinese restaurant for dinner, and I experienced eating Chinese food that is quite different from what we have in our country. Bangkok is a strange place – so many people. We went on a boat ride on one of the canals. The scenery was so primitive, I felt as if I had gone back in time. You would have to see it to believe it. I think Margaret has plans for me to see all the sights here. She will have time since she has two servants who do all the housework. They even turn out the lights at night for us. Hope everyone is well there.

Love, Mama

ॐ

"Mama, I want to take you to a special Chinese Baptist Church," Margaret said, after they finished a breakfast of ham and eggs, warm sweet rolls and hot coffee. "This church is one hundred and fifty years old. The preacher will preach in Chinese, but you'll enjoy meeting the people."

ॐ

In the evening when she sat down to dinner, Emily felt a sense of family. She enjoyed talking with the children about their visit to the small Chinese church. "I was fascinated by the way the people and the animals wondered in and out of the little church. Did you see the small boy who came in completely naked?"

"Oh, the people think nothing of that," Margaret said smiling. Phillip and the children laughed. "Tomorrow, I want to take you to see the Marble Temple with about fifty Buddha statues lined up in a corridor. They are quite ornate."

༚

Emily looked forward to the afternoons with Margaret when they sat down to a cup of tea and talked about family and plans for the next day. Margaret poured the hot tea into the tiny cups with no handles. "I was thrilled that you got to see the Queen today. She was at the temple for a memorial service."

"She was dressed beautifully," Emily said. "I can't get over all the Buddhas and the magnificence of the temple. I love the colorful silks that the Thai wear. I wish Louise could see some of the sights here, but I'm afraid she wouldn't be able to stand the crowds and the dirty streets. I must write her soon."

༚

Writing home became almost a ritual for Emily. There was so much to tell, and writing the details made her memory of them more real. Each place she visited was a new experience, and she wanted to remember as much as possible. Letters from her other children reminded her of how far away she was, and they eased her homesickness

"Daniel writes that it's been 100 degrees in Birmingham for the last several days. I know it must be hotter in Selma. I want to write him about our trip to Laos and to the floating market. He likes to hear about interesting places since he's traveled so much."

༚

Margaret joined her mother as she sat in the sitting room late one afternoon. "I got a letter from Mary last week. She's busy getting ready for Elaine's wedding. She writes that the wedding will be quite elaborate. "I'm sorry I'll miss it, especially since it's my first grandchild's wedding."

Margaret looked up from the book she had opened to read. "I know ... I'd like to be there, too. There are so many things at home I've missed, but I knew when I chose to come here with Phillip to work, I would have a different life, and I've never regretted coming."

"Well, I've certainly enjoyed being here. I wouldn't take anything for coming."

Margaret smiled and looked at her mother with deep satisfaction. "And I'm so happy you're here. By the way, what do you hear from Aunt Louise? Is she unhappy that you're staying longer than you had planned?"

"She hasn't complained in her letters, although she does write that she misses me terribly. She plans to go to Birmingham for Elaine's wedding. Later in the week, Lucy is giving a party to celebrate Louise's birthday. She loves all that attention, but she deserves it. She has certainly done a lot for others in her day." Feeling restless, Emily walked over to the window and watched the children playing. "I believe the children have grown since I've been here. You're fortunate to have such good help to care for them."

"Yes, I know. Puntah is very fond of them, and they love her."

❧⚬᷍

Emily rose early the next morning to write her letter to Mary. The house was quiet. There was only the hum of the overhead fan as it stirred the heavy, humid air. She sat down at Phillip's desk, a place that had become familiar and comfortable with a pleasant view from the window. Taking out her regular blue airmail stationery, she took up her pen to write. There was so much to describe - the Chinese feast they had attended, the trip down to the Gulf of Siam and her latest shopping trips with Margaret, plus the English classes she was teaching at the Christian Center. She rubbed the back of her neck then returned to her writing about all the places where she had gone and all the things she had done. *The other night I dreamed that Margaret insisted I fly home to Elaine's wedding and then fly back to Thailand. I'm sorry I'm missing the wedding. I'm afraid I won't be home until Christmas."*

ॐ∼ॐ

"I have arranged for you and me to go to Burma on October the forth, to renew your visa, Mama," Phillip said. "We'll be gone four days. I want to take some supplies to a missionary there. Everything is in short supply in Burma."

"I declare you all talk about going from one country to another as if it was no more than going downtown. But I really can't wait to go. I've read so much of Kipling's writings. He wrote of Burma, 'It's a greener, fairer land.'"

"And that it is! You'll enjoy the scenery. I hope the trip won't be too tiring. For now, I think I'll have a second cup of coffee and go into the sitting room to read the morning paper."

ॐ∼ॐ

"I want to sort out all my souvenirs and gifts before I pack to go home," Emily said. "I wonder if I can wrap them as Christmas gifts." She looked over the various assortments spread out on the bed.

"Oh, I don't think that would work with customs," Margaret said. "Besides, you might want to buy a few more things when we go up to Chuang Mai later this month. The tribal people make some very pretty things they sell to tourist. I especially like their Christmas table cloths and napkins. They also make some small, colorful dolls."

"Well, all right. I guess I have a little more room in this suitcase. I didn't tell you about my letter from Louise. She really enjoyed going to Birmingham for the wedding. She was impressed with all 'the pomp and circumstance.' She said the ceremony lasted an hour and fifteen minutes. You know Elaine married a Catholic, and their ceremonies are always long. Oh, I almost forgot, Louise has a great grandchild now. It's a girl."

Margaret sat down on the edge of the bed and examined several of the small gifts. "I know Aunt Louise is thrilled to have another grandchild, and especially a girl. I know she misses you."

"Yes, I think she does. I'm going to sit down and write her as soon as I finish here."

When she sat down to write, Emily could hear the heavy rain as it pelted the roof. The air was cooler. It reminded her of home.

૭∾ઉ

"You look tired, Mama," Phillip said. "Why don't you take a little rest?"

"I will, as soon as I write to Eddie. You know he lives in South Carolina now and doesn't hear from his brothers and sisters too often. I guess he gets homesick sometimes." Emily liked the way that Phillip always made her feel comfortable. He had special warmth that she hadn't known since her daddy died. She liked the way he called her Mama so readily. He was just like another son to her.

When she opened her box of stationery, Emily realized she had only two air-mail letters left. Maybe that's all I'll need, she thought. After finishing a letter to Eddie, she wrote to Jonathan, eagerly enumerating all the wonderful sights she had seen. She ended with, *"I'll be coming home on a ship. It will be reminiscent of your time on the Pacific. I'm really looking forward to it. I'll get to Birmingham at midnight on December twenty-second. I hope you'll be able to meet me. Margaret will come as far as Hong Kong with me. See you soon."*

Love, Mama

Chapter Twenty-nine

Homecoming

A late morning fog was lifting when Margaret and her mother got out of the taxi on the pier in Hong Kong. A few rays of sunlight broke through the misty haze making it possible for Emily to read the name written on the side of the huge ship - *The President Cleveland.* "Would you like me to take your luggage onto the ship?" the taxi driver asked.

"No, someone from the ship will come and take these to her room. Thank you," Margaret said and handed the driver a tip. There were people rushing in all directions - some boarding, others saying good-bye and some leaving.

Emily uttered a sigh. "I'm so glad you came with me to Hong Kong, Margaret. This is a very busy place. I'm excited about going home but sad to be leaving you and your family. I've had a wonderful time."

"Oh, I would never have let you come to board the ship alone, Mama," looking around, apprehensively. "I'm not too happy about you going from here alone, but I know this is what you want to do."

"I'll be fine. Don't worry. I plan to relax and enjoy every minute. I've looked forward to this too long to fear it."

Margaret smiled. "I do hope you enjoy it. Two weeks on the water is quite a long trip. Maybe you should go on up. I think most of the passengers have already boarded. This is as far as I can go with you." She put her hand protectively on her mother's arm. "The steward will take your bags and show you to your cabin."

Emily hesitated a moment. There was so much she wanted to say, but didn't know how to say it. "How can I ever thank you and Phillip? There aren't enough words."

Margaret reached out, put her arms around her mother and kissed her on the cheek. Tears filled her eyes. "Goodbye, Mama."

When she reached the deck of the ship, Emily walked over to the railing where many of the passengers were standing and waving. She looked down on the pier to see her daughter, one last time. She was overcome with emotion when she spotted Margaret standing alone and waving. Her mind flooded with wonderful memories of the past six months. I'll miss her. She waved and caught Margaret's attention. "Goodbye," she whispered.

"Goodbye, Mama," Margaret mouthed to her. With a loud blast of the ship's horn, the gangplank was removed, and the ship maneuvered slowly into the harbor and out to sea.

Emily found her small cabin adequate, but she was amused that it was so small. "I bet you couldn't cuss a cat in here," she said under her breath. "Well, it doesn't matter. I plan to spend most of my time out of the room anyway." As soon as she had unpacked her bags, changed her clothes and settled into her tiny room, the steward came to escort her to the dining room for dinner. She was grateful, since she didn't know her way around the ship at all.

The dining room was spacious and beautiful. After the steward introduced her to the people at her table, she took her seat. "Madam, you may order from the menu or go to the buffet."

Remembering what Phillip had told her about the delicious buffet, Emily answered, "I believe I'll go to the buffet tonight, thank you."

The long buffet table was a picture of opulence just as Phillip had described. Emily could hardly believe her eyes. She had never seen such a beautiful display of food - almost anything you would want to eat. Sliced roast beef and ham were piled high on silver platters. Tiered trays held all kinds of fresh fruit and cheeses. All kinds of warm breads enticed her appetite … and the scrumptious desserts - some Emily had never seen before. As she stood a moment taking in the grandeur, the ship suddenly gave a quick list, and the food took on a different look. I'm not really very hungry, she thought, but I'll try to eat something.

"Are you feeling all right?" A young Japanese girl asked, when

Emily returned to her table.

"Yes, I think so." After she sat down, Emily placed her napkin on her lap and looked at her plate of food. "I hope I'm not getting seasick," she whispered to the young girl seated next to her.

҉

The ship's promenade was Emily's favorite place. On sunny days, she could view the vast ocean and watch the passengers make their way around the sun deck. She was fascinated with so many different people speaking in foreign languages and dressed in very different apparel. Some appeared lavishly dressed and others in their native attire. All greeted Emily as they walked the promenade. Some days, it was warm enough to sit in a deck chair and have interesting conversations with other passengers. Many were fascinated when she told them where she had been and where she was from. Her voyage was all she had dreamed it would be. Sitting on the sun deck, in the cool air, helped avoid seasickness, and she discovered eating only a meager amount of food also helped. Isn't it a pity, she thought, I've never been offered such wonderful food in my life, and now I don't want it. She pulled the wool blanket on the chair over her lap and looked far out to sea. There was no end to the vast ocean. It reminded her of how far she had come in life. Strange how she had gone from near poverty to such abundance.

She sat back in the deck chair and closed her eyes remembering the difficult days – days of meagerness, wanting, lacking, needing and missing. Why had she tolerated Edwin's neglect and abuse of the children for so long? Could she ever forgive herself? She knew there were times when Mary thought she could have done differently. She remembered her dilemma and even now, she had no answers. The air had become cold and she decided to go to her cabin. After removing the blanket, she walked over to the rail of the ship and looked out as far as she could see. There was no distinct line between the water and the sky. Life is like the ever-moving sea, she thought. Even though the horizon is there, we can't see it, and we must make decisions without knowledge of the future. The only thing we can be sure of is that God will be with us.

৵৽

The first port of call was Honolulu, but Emily didn't feel like going ashore - though the Captain had said there would be a three-hour delay. When the ship was safely docked, Emily walked over to the rail. On the pier a band was playing, and the passengers were given colorful leis of orchids as they departed the ship. Everyone was in a festive mood. She felt better as warm sunshine wrapped around her shoulders and her queasiness subsided. Maybe she would be able to enjoy dinner tonight.

৵৽

All the talk at dinner was about San Francisco - their final destination. Many of her new friends had never been there and were excited about going. The little Japanese girl expressed her desire to see the famous San Francisco Bridge.

"I'll just be glad to put my feet on dry land," Emily commented. "Maybe I'll be hungry again, and I'll really be glad to see my children. I've been gone for six months."

৵৽

As the huge passenger ship approached the San Francisco Bay, a dense fog obscured the view of the majestic bridge. Slowly, the huge ship navigated between the wide steel supports of the bridge and into the harbor. "We're sorry," the Captain said to the disappointed passengers. "It's not unusual for the bay to be fogged in this time of year. Please be careful as you leave the ship."

Emily said goodbye to her new friends, as they all stood on the promenade waiting for the ship to dock. She continued to watch the longshoremen secure the mooring lines that held the ship to the pier. Finally, she was able to go down the gangplank and leave the ship. She smiled as her feet touched the ground, and her seasickness left her. There was no reason to be anxious about getting to the airport. Phillip had arranged everything for her safety. A young man dressed in a black suit, waiting on the pier, held up a large sign to identify himself as her driver. He cheerfully greeted her and carried her luggage to a limousine. When they arrived at the airport, only an hour remained before her flight, the last part of her journey home.

༺ঌৡঌ༻

Emily moved restlessly in her seat as the jet airliner roared to its final destination. She hadn't slept on the long flight. She was anxious. It would be midnight when she arrived. She regretted the late hour, but Jonathan had written her not to worry. He would be there when she arrived. Suddenly the pilot's voice came over the speaker. "A light snow is falling in Birmingham, folks, but it shouldn't present any problems. Maybe we'll have a white Christmas. Fasten your seat belts. We are about to land … and Merry Christmas!"

Emily fastened her seat belt across her lap, leaned back and closed her eyes. "It's good to be home," she whispered.

The tires on the jet made a loud squeak as the pilot brought the plane to a smooth landing. Emily removed her seat belt, stood up to put on her coat and gathered her belongings. A steep set of steps had been rolled up to the door of the airplane. When she stepped out into the night air, she felt the cold wind and falling snow flakes on her face. It was midnight.

The windows of the terminal were clouded by condensation, making it impossible to see inside. As she entered the waiting area, Emily was surprised to see so many people … and little children. Suddenly, her heart melted like the snowflakes on her coat. These were her children and grandchildren. All of them had come to meet her. "Mama! Mom! Grandmother!" they called, showering her with hugs and kisses. Her journey was over. Her dreams and hopes fulfilled. She was loved.

About the Author

Following her retirement as a registered medical laboratory technician, Lottie Jacks began her second career as writer, taking numerous Creative Writing courses, attending writer's conferences, and Christian Boot Camp writing seminars with Denise George and Carolyn Tomlin. Former president of Samford Auxiliary, Lottie is presently a contributing editor for the Legacy League of Samford and the Samford Auxiliary Newsletter.

Lottie has lived in Birmingham, Alabama, her entire life where she and her husband raised their three daughters and one son and now enjoy their eight grandchildren. Foremost in her life has been her love of family and her church where she has taught Bible for all of her adult years.

Made in the USA
Columbia, SC
07 September 2025

61937233R00174